Alan Furst

Born in New York, Alan Furst has lived for long periods in France, especially in Paris, and has travelled as a journalist in eastern Europe and Russia. He has written extensively for *Esquire* and the *International Herald Tribune*. Now a full-time novelist, he lives on Long Island, New York.

It was a journalistic assignment to Moscow that inspired him to write *Night Soldiers*, the first of his highly original, atmospheric novels about espionage in eastern and western Europe before and during World War II. Since then he has published *Dark Star*, *The Polish Officer* and *The World at Night*, all of which have received outstanding critical praise.

Alan Furst's most recent novel is *Red Gold*, the highly acclaimed sequel to *The World at Night*.

'Nothing can be like watching *Casablanca* for the first time, but Furst comes closer than anyone has in years.'

WALTER SHAPIRO, *Time*

THE WORLD AT NIGHT

'This subtle, grown-up wartime thriller/love story set in occupied France works rather wonderfully as a *billet doux* to Paris and atmospheric evocation, with Furst more taken by casual entrapment over a leisurely lunch than high-speed chase. He produces unmanufactured suspense from making his characters walk the thinnest of lines between loyalty and betrayal. Eric Ambler, the story's obvious godfather, is matched for achievement.'

CHRIS PETIT, *Guardian*

'A tense thriller of espionage and black intrigue isn't easy to come by these days . . . In this fine novel . . . the plot coils tighter and tighter until the heart-thumping, dry-throat climax. Inevitably, Furst is compared to John le Carré, and they should both be flattered . . . superb.' RAYMOND SEITZ, *Sunday Express*

'Alan Furst is a master . . . he has cornered the market in the world of the espionage thriller. There is unlikely to be a more engrossing read this year; it's a perfect companion to that lengthy railway journey . . . and he knows bourgeois Paris like the back of his hand. Just wonderful.' BRIAN CASE, *Time Out*

THE POLISH OFFICER

'One of the best novels of the year . . . brilliant.'

ROBERT HARRIS, *Daily Mail*

'Brilliant . . . you can almost hear the chained wheels of the Gestapo car on the snow, the whack of bullets in the moonlit Polish forests, the quietness of occupied Paris by night. A page-turner, yes, but also one of the most evocative works of history I have come across.'

JOHN SWEENEY, *Observer*

'Surely among the most convincing war books of our time.'

NICHOLAS BAGNALL, *Sunday Telegraph*

DARK STAR

'Imagine discovering an unscreened espionage thriller from the late 1930s, a classic black-and-white movie that captures the murky allegiances and moral ambiguity of Europe on the brink of war . . . Nothing can be like watching *Casablanca* for the first time, but Furst comes closer than anyone has in years.'

WALTER SHAPIRO, *Time Magazine*

'A classic spy story . . . Alan Furst brings to life better than most historians the world of fear in which so many human beings felt trapped.'

ALAN BULLOCK, author of *Hitler and Stalin*

'A jewel – a gripping thriller which is also a fascinating history lesson.'

SHAUN USHER, *Daily Mail*

NIGHT SOLDIERS

'Furst's intelligent, ambitious, absorbing novel charges along from the rise of Fascism in Bulgaria, to Spain during the Civil War, to France and back to eastern Europe as World War II draws to an end. The history is deftly incorporated; the viewpoint civilized; the characters and the settings picturesque; the adventures exciting; the writing pungent.'

WALTER GOODMAN, *New York Times*

'*Night Soldiers* has everything the best thrillers offer – excitement, intrigue, romance – plus grown-up writing, characters that matter, and a crisp, carefully researched portrait of the period in which our own postwar world was shaped.'

GEOFFREY C. WARD, *USA Today*

BY ALAN FURST

Night Soldiers
Dark Star
The Polish Officer
The World at Night
Red Gold

ALAN FURST

THE WORLD
AT NIGHT

HarperCollins*Publishers*

HarperCollins*Publishers*
77–85 Fulham Palace Road,
Hammersmith, London W6 8JB

www.**fire**and**water**.com

This paperback edition 1998
5 7 9 8 6

First published in Great Britain by
HarperCollins*Publishers* 1997

First published in the USA by
Random House 1996

ISBN 0 00 651097 3

Set in Meridien

Printed and bound in Great Britain by
Omnia Books Ltd, Glasgow

Avec remerciements à Ann Godoff, pour son
support et ses encouragements

The boat left the Quai de la Joliette in Marseilles harbour about midnight. It was new moon and the stars were bright and their light hard. The coast with its long garlands of gas lamps faded slowly away. The lighthouses emerging from the black water, with their green and red eyes, were the last outpost of France, sleeping under the stars in her enormous, dishonoured nakedness, humiliated, wretched and beloved.

– Arthur Koestler, 1940

THE 16TH
ARRONDISSEMENT

10 May, 1940

Long before dawn, Wehrmacht commando units came out of the forest on the Belgian border, overran the frontier posts, and killed the customs officers. Glider troops set the forts ablaze, black smoke rolling over the canals and the spring fields. On some roads the bridges were down, but German combat engineers brought up pontoon spans, and by first light the tanks and armoured cars were moving again. Heading southwest, to force the River Meuse, to conquer France.

In Paris, the film producer Jean Casson was asleep. His assistant, Gabriella Vico, tried to wake him up by touching his cheek. They'd shared a bottle of champagne, made love all night, then fallen dead asleep just before dawn. 'Are you awake?' she whispered.

'No,' he said.

'The radio.' She put a hand on his arm in a way that meant there was something wrong.

What? The radio broken? Would she wake him up for that? It had been left on all night, now it buzzed, overheated. He could just barely hear the voice of the announcer. No, not an announcer. Perhaps an engineer – somebody who happened to be at the station when news came in was reading it as best he could:

'The attack . . . from the Ardennes forest . . .'

A long silence.

'Into the Netherlands. And Belgium. By columns that reached back a hundred miles into Germany.'

More silence. Casson could hear the teletype clattering

3

away in the studio. He leaned close to the radio. The man reading the news tried to clear his throat discreetly. A paper rattled.

'Ah . . . the Foreign Ministry states the following . . .'

The teleprinter stopped. A moment of dead air. Then it started up again.

'It is the position of the government that this aggression is an intolerable violation of Belgian neutrality.'

Gabriella and Casson stared at each other. They were hardly more than strangers. This was an office romance, something that had simmered and simmered, *and then, one night*. But the coming of war turned out to be, somehow, intimate, like Christmas, and that was a surprise to both of them. Casson could see how pale she was. Would she cry? He really didn't know very much about her. Young, and slim, and Italian – well, Milanese. Long hair, long legs. What was she – twenty-six? Twenty-seven? He'd always thought that she fitted into her life like a cat, never off balance. Now she'd been caught out – here it was *war*, and she was smelly and sticky, still half-drunk, with breath like a dragon.

'Okay?' He used *le slang Américain*.

She nodded that she was.

He put a hand on her cheek. 'You're like ice,' he said.

'I'm scared.'

He went looking for a cigarette, probing an empty packet of Gitanes on the night table. 'I have some,' she said, glad for something to do. She rolled off the bed and went into the living room. *Merde*, Casson said to himself. War was the last thing he needed. Hitler had taken Austria, Czechoslovakia, then Poland. France had declared war, but it meant nothing. Germany and France couldn't fight again, they'd just done that – ten million dead, not much else accomplished. It was simply not, everybody agreed, *logique*.

Gabriella returned, lit a cigarette and handed it to him. 'May I take a bath?' she asked.

4

'Of course. There are towels –'

'I know.'

Casson found his watch on the night table. 5:22. Water splashed into the bathtub. The tenant on the floor below was a baroness – she didn't like noise. Well, too bad. She already hated him anyhow.

He got out of bed, walked to the glass door that opened on the little balcony. He pushed the drape aside; you could see the Eiffel Tower across the river. The rue Chardin was quiet – the 16th Arrondissement was always quiet, and Passy, its heart and soul, quieter still. One or two lights on, people didn't know yet. So beautiful, his street. Trees in clouds of white blossom, dawn shadow playing on the stone buildings, a lovely gloom. He'd shot a scene from *No Way Out* here. The hero knows the cops are onto him, but he leaves his hideout anyhow, to see his rich girlfriend one last time.

The telephone rang; two brief whirring jingles. Paused a few seconds. Rang again. *Jesus, the baroness.* Gingerly, Casson picked up the receiver.

'Yes?'

'Have you heard?'

It was his wife. They had been separated for years, living their own lives in their own apartments. But they remained married, and shared a set of old friends.

'Yes,' he said.

'I'm not disturbing you, am I?'

'No, Marie-Claire. I was up.'

'Well, what shall we do?'

Fight, he thought. Support the troops, hold rallies, you had to –

'About tonight, I mean.'

Now he understood. They were giving a dinner party at her apartment. 'Well, I don't see how, I mean, it's war.'

'Bruno says we must go on. We must not give in to Hitler.'

5

Bruno was Marie-Claire's boyfriend. He owned an agency that sold British motorcars, had his hair cut twice a week, and spent a fortune on silk dressing gowns.

'He's not wrong,' Casson said.

'And the cake has been ordered.' The twentieth wedding anniversary of the Langlades – a cake from Ponthieu.

'All right. Let's go ahead. Really, what else is there to do?'

'Are you going to the office?'

'Of course.'

'Can you telephone later on?'

'I will.'

He hung up. The door to the bathroom was half-open, the water had stopped. Casson paused at the threshold.

'You can come in,' Gabriella said.

Her skin was flushed from the heat of the bath, wet strands of hair curled at the back of her neck, her breasts and shoulders were shiny with soapsuds. 'They are going to arrest me,' she said, as though it were hard for her to believe.

'Why would they do that?'

She shrugged. 'I am Italian. An Italian citizen.'

Enemy alien. It was absurd, he wanted to laugh, but then he didn't. Mussolini was Hitler's ally, a treaty had been signed in 1939. The Pact of Steel, no less. But it was only ridiculous until police came to the door. Gabriella looked up at him, biting her lip. 'Now look,' he said. 'It's too early for tears. This is *Paris* – there's always somebody you can talk to, always special arrangements. Nothing's final here.'

Gabriella nodded gratefully, she wanted to believe he was right.

Casson caught a glimpse of himself in the steamy mirror. Dark – like a suntan that never really went away – naked, lean, with a line of hair up the centre and shoulders a little heavier than his suits suggested. Not so bad – for forty-two.

6

Still, if he were going to be authoritative, he'd better get dressed.

He stood in front of his closet, gazed pensively at a row of suits. In the distance, a two-note siren, high/low. Police or ambulance, and coming nearer. Casson went to the balcony and looked out. An ambulance, rolling to a stop just up the block. Two women ran into the street, one clutching a robe against her chest, the other in the black dress of a concierge. Frantically, they urged the men from the ambulance into the building.

Casson went back to the closet. On the radio, the premier of France, Paul Reynaud, was reading a statement: 'The French army has drawn its sword; France is gathering herself.'

A little after ten, Casson left for the office. In the streets of Passy, the war had not yet been acknowledged – life went on as always; *très snob*, the women in gloves, the men's chins held at a certain angle. Casson wore a dark suit, sober and strong, and a red-and-blue tie with a white shirt – the colours of France. But the blue was teal, the red faded, and the shirt a colour the clerk had called 'linen'. He stopped at a newspaper kiosk for *Le Temps*, but it was not to be. A huge crowd was clamouring for papers, he would have to wait.

The day was fine, cool and sunny, and he liked to walk to his office, just off the Champs-Elysées on the rue Marbeuf. Like it or not, his usual cabdriver was not at his customary spot on the place Iéna so it was walk or take the Métro, and this was no morning to be underground. Somewhere along the way, he would stop for a coffee.

He was, to all appearances, a typical Parisian male on his way to the office. Dark hair, dark eyes – France a Latin country after all – some concealed softness in the face, but then, before you could think about that, a small scar beneath one eye, the proud battle trophy of soccer played with working-class kids when he was young, in fact the most violent moment he'd ever experienced.

In real life, anyhow. *Last Train to Athens* had a murder in an alley in the Balkans, pretty nasty by the time they'd got it cut. Emil Cravec! What a ferocious mug on him – where the hell was he, anyhow? *No Way Out* was tame by comparison, except for the ending. Michel Faynberg had directed for him, and Michel had never really left the Sorbonne. He'd had the hero clubbed to death at the base of a statue of Blind Justice – what a load of horseshit! *No Way to Make Money* the exhibitor Benouchian called it. Yet, in all fairness, that hadn't really turned out to be true. The students went.

He liked *Night Run* best of all, he loved that movie. It was better than *The Devil's Bridge*, which had got him the little house in Deauville. He'd almost directed *Night Run*, stood with old Marchand all day long, watched rushes with him every night. Marchand was a legend in the industry, and the great thing about stature, Casson had discovered, was that egoism was no longer the issue – now and then, anyhow. Even a producer, despised moneyman, might have an idea that was worth something. Marchand had been in his seventies by then, was never going to get the acclaim he deserved. White hair, white beard, eyes like a falcon. '*Tiens*, Casson,' he'd said. 'You really want it right.'

It was, too. The smoke that billowed from the locomotive, the little cello figure, the village scenes they shot around Auxerre – every frame was right. A small story: beginning, middle, end. And Marchand had found him Citrine. She'd had other names then, what she'd come north with, from Marseilles. But that was eleven years ago, 1929, and she'd been eighteen. Or so she said.

Casson strode along, through the open-air market on the place Rochambeau. The fish stall had a neat pile of fresh-caught *rouget* on chipped ice. Grey and red, with the eye still clear. A goat was tied to the back of a wagon and

8

a young girl was milking it into a customer's pail. The market café had tables and chairs out on the pavement, the smell of coffee drawing Casson to the zinc bar. He stood between a secretary and a man with red hands and a white apron. Unwrapped the sugar cube and set it on the spoon and watched the walls crystallize and tumble slowly down as the coffee rose up through it. He brought the cup to his lips: hot, black, strong, burnt. Casson allowed himself a very private little sigh of gratitude. To be alive was enough.

Ah, a band.

Casson stopped to watch. A unit of mounted Gardes Républicains in hussars' uniforms, chin straps tight beneath the lower lip. On command they rode into formation, three lines of ten, horses' hooves clopping on the cobbled street. Then played, with cornets and drums, a spirited march. In the crowd, a veteran of the 1914 war, the tiny band of the Croix de Guerre in his lapel, stood at rigid attention, white hair blowing in the breeze from the river, left sleeve pinned to the shoulder of his jacket.

Now the band played the 'Marseillaise,' and Casson held his hand over his heart. War with Germany, he thought, it doesn't stop. They'd lost in 1870, won – barely – in 1918, and now they had to do it again. A nightmare: an enemy attacks, you beat him, still he attacks. You surrender, still he attacks. Casson's stomach twisted, he wanted to cry, or to fight, it was the same feeling.

28, rue Marbeuf

Turn-of-the-century building, slate grey, its entry flanked by a wholesale butcher's shop and a men's haberdashery. Marbeuf was an ancient street, crowded and commercial, and it was perfect for Casson. While the big production studios were out at Joinville and Billancourt, the offices

of the film industry were sprinkled through the neighbourhood in just such buildings. Not *on* the Champs-Elysées,
but not far from it either. Honking trucks and taxis, men
carrying bloody beef haunches on their shoulders, fashion
models in pillbox hats.

To get to Casson's office you went to the second courtyard and took the east entry. Then climbed a marble staircase or rode a groaning cage elevator an inch at a time to
the fourth floor. At the end of a long hall of black-and-
white tile: a sugar importer, a press agent, and a pebbled
glass door that said Productions Casson.

He was also PJC, CasFilm, and assorted others his dia-
bolical lawyers thought up on occasions when they felt the
need to send him a bill. Nonetheless, the world believed, at
least some of the time. Witness: when he opened the door,
eight heads turned on swivels. It brought to mind the
favourite saying of an old friend: 'One is what one has the
nerve to pretend to be.'

As he went from appointment to appointment that
morning, he began to get an idea of what the war might
mean to him personally. For one thing, everybody wanted
to be paid. Now. Not that he blamed them, but by 11:30 he
had to duck out to Crédit Lyonnais to restock the current
account from reserves.

When he returned, the scenic designer Harry Fleischer
sat across the desk and bit his nails while Gabriella prepared
a cheque: 20,000 francs he was owed, and 20,000 more
he was borrowing. 'I can't believe this is happening,' he
said gloomily. 'My wife is home, selling the furniture.'

'I wish I knew what to say.'

Fleischer made a gesture with his hand that meant *just
because I am this person*. He was heavy, face all jowls and
cheeks, with a hook nose, and grey hair spreading back in
waves from a receding hairline. 'I ran from Berlin in 1933,
but I thought: so, I have to live in Paris, the whole world
should be tortured like this.'

10

'Where are you going?'

'Hollywood.' Fleischer shook his head in disbelief at what life did. 'Of course I could say "*Hollywood*!" I know plenty of people who'd see it that way. But I'm fifty-six years old, and what I'll be is one more refugee. Arthur Brenner has been trying to get me to come to MGM for years. Well, now he'll get. I don't want to leave, we made a life here. But if these *momsers* do here what they did in Poland . . .'

There was a big, dirty window behind Casson's chair, open a few inches. Outside was the sound of life in the Paris streets. Casson and Fleischer looked at each other – that couldn't end, could it?

'What about you?' Fleischer said.

'I don't know. Like last time – the thing will settle into a deadlock, the Americans will show up.' He shrugged.

Gabriella knocked twice, then brought in Fleischer's cheque. Casson signed it. 'I appreciate the loan,' Fleischer said. 'It's just to get settled in California. What is it in dollars, four thousand?'

'About that.' Casson blew on the ink. 'I don't want you to think about it. I'm not in a hurry. The best would be: we give Adolf a boot in the backside, you come back here, and we'll call this the first payment on a new project.'

Casson handed the cheque to Fleischer, who looked at it, then put it in the inside pocket of his jacket. He stood and extended a hand. 'Jean-Claude,' he said. That was Casson's affectionate nickname, in fact his first and middle names.

'Send a postcard.'

Fleischer was suddenly close to tears – didn't trust himself to speak. He nodded, tight-lipped, and left the office.

'Good luck, Harry,' Casson said.

Gabriella stuck her head around the doorway. 'James Templeton is calling from London.'

Casson grabbed the phone with one hand while the

11

other dug through a pile of dossiers on his desk, eventually coming up with one tied in red ribbon. *Mysterious Island* was printed across the cover. The movie wouldn't be called that – somebody else had the rights to the Jules Verne novel – but that was the idea. *When their yacht sinks in a tropical storm, three men and two women find themselves. . .* In one corner of the folder, Casson had written *Jean Gabin*?

'Hello?' Casson said.

'Casson, good morning, James Templeton.' Templeton was a merchant banker. He pronounced Casson's name English-style; accent on the first syllable, the final '*n*' loud and clear.

'How's the weather in London?'

'Pouring rain.'

'Sorry. Here the weather is good, at least.'

'Yes, and damn it all to hell anyhow.'

'That's what we think.'

'Look, Casson, I want to be straight with you.'

'All right.'

'The committee met this morning, in emergency session. Sir Charles is, well, you've met him. Hard as nails and fears no man. But we're going to wait a bit on *Mysterious Island*. It's not that we don't like the idea. Especially if Jean Gabin comes on board, we feel it may be exactly right for us. But now is not the moment.'

'I understand perfectly, and, I am afraid you are right. We are at a time when it doesn't hurt to, uh, not continue.'

'We were hoping you'd see it that way.'

'Without confidence, one cannot move ahead, Monsieur Templeton.'

'Do you hear anything, on the situation?'

'Not really. The radio. Reynaud is strong, and we know the Belgians will fight like hell once they organize themselves.'

'Well, over here Chamberlain has resigned, and Churchill has taken over.'

12

'It's for the best?'

'Certainly in this office, that's the feeling.'

Casson sighed. 'Well, thumbs-up.'

'That's the spirit.'

'*Mysterious Island* will wait.'

'This doesn't leave you – I mean . . .'

'No, no! Not at all. Don't think it.'

'Good, then. I'll tell Sir Charles. In a year we'll all be at the screening, drinking champagne.'

'The best!'

'Our treat!'

'Just you try it!'

'Good-bye, Casson. We'll send along a letter.'

'Yes. Good-bye.'

Merde. Double *merde*.

Gabriella knocked and opened the door. 'Your wife on the line,' she said.

He always had a mental picture of Marie-Claire when he talked to her on the phone. She had tiny eyes and a hard little mouth, which made her seem spiteful and mean. Not a fair portrait, in fact, because there were moments when she wasn't that way at all.

Of course – *Parisienne* to the depths of her soul – she made herself beautiful. She smelled delicious, and touched you accidentally. Had you in bed before you knew it, had life her way after that. Knowing Marie-Claire as he did, Casson had always assumed that Bruno, a pompous ass at the dinner table, was a maestro in the bedroom.

'The Pichards cannot come,' Marie-Claire said. 'Yet Bruno insists we have this dinner. Françoise called and said that Philippe's younger brother, an officer, had been wounded, near the town of Namur. A sergeant had actually telephoned, from somewhere in Belgium. It must have been, I don't know, dreadful. Poor Françoise was in tears, not brave at all. I thought well, that's that. Cancel the cake,

13

call the domestic agency. But Bruno *insisted* we go on.'

Casson made a certain Gallic sound – it meant refined horror at a world gone wrong. Again.

Marie-Claire continued, 'So, I rationalize. You know me, Jean-Claude. There's an elephant in the hall closet, I think, oh some circus performer's been here and forgotten his elephant. Now Yvette Langlade calls, Françoise has just called her – to explain why she and Philippe won't be there. And Yvette says we *are* going to cancel, aren't we? And I say no, life must go on, and she's horrified, I can tell, but of course she won't come out and say it.'

Casson stared out the window. He really didn't know what to do. Marie-Claire had a problem with her lover and her circle of friends – it didn't have much to do with him. 'The important thing is to get through today,' he said, then paused for a moment. The telephone line hissed gently. 'Whatever you decide to do, Marie-Claire, I will go along with that.'

'All right.' She took a breath, then sighed. 'Will you call me in an hour, Jean-Claude? Please?'

He said yes, they hung up, he held his head in his hands.

He thought about cancelling his lunch – with the agent Perlemère – and asked Gabriella to telephone, cautiously, *to see if Monsieur Perlemère is able to keep his lunch appointment.*

Oh yes. A little thing like war did not deter Perlemère. So the good soldier Casson marched off to Alexandre to eat warm potato-and-beef salad and hear about Perlemère's stable of lame horses – ageing ingénues, actors who drank too much, the Rin-Tin-Tin look-alike, Paco, who had already bitten two directors, and an endless list beyond that. A volume business.

Perlemère ordered two dozen Belons, the strongest of the oysters, now at the very end of their season. He rubbed his hands and attacked with relish, making a *thrup* sound as he inhaled each oyster, closing his eyes with pleasure.

then drinking the juice from the shell, a second *thrup*, followed by a brief grunt that meant arguments about the meaning of life were irrelevant once you could afford to eat oysters.

Perlemère was fat, with a small but prominent black moustache – a sort of Jewish Oliver Hardy. *Perlemère, Perlmutter, mother-of-pearl*, Casson thought. Curious names the Jews had. 'I saw Harry Fleischer this morning,' he said. 'Off to MGM.'

'Mm. Time to run, eh?'

'Maybe for the best.'

Perlemère shrugged. 'The Germans hit first. Now we'll settle with them once and for all.'

Casson nodded polite agreement.

'What'd you do last time?' Perlemère demolished an oyster.

'I graduated lycée in 1916, headed for the Normale.' The Ecole Normale Supérieure, the most exclusive college in the Sorbonne, was France's Harvard, Yale, and Princeton all rolled into one. 'My eighteenth birthday, I went down to the recruiters. They asked me a few questions, then sent me off to install cameras on Spads flying reconnaissance over German lines. I changed film, developed it – really the war started me in this business.'

'*Normalien*, eh?' He meant Casson was well-connected; a member, by university affiliation, of the aristocracy.

Casson shrugged. 'I guess it meant something, once upon a time.'

'School of life, over here.' *Thrup*. 'But I haven't done too badly.'

Casson laughed – as though such a thing could be in question!

'I expect this war business will go on for a while,' Perlemère said. 'Your German's stubborn, I'll admit that. He doesn't know when he's beaten. But we'll give them a whipping, just watch.'

Casson took a bite of the potato-and-beef salad, which would have been delicious if he'd had an appetite, and a sip of the *Graves*, which he didn't care for. 'You represent Citrine, Jacques?'

'Not any more. Besides, what do you want with her?'

'Nothing special in mind. I just remembered she used to be with you.'

'Suzy Balcon, Jean-Claude. Remember where you heard that.'

'Oh?'

'I'll send a photo over. She's tall and sophisticated – but she puts your mind in the gutter. Mm. Never mind Citrine.'

Two businessmen manoeuvred down the packed aisle and managed to squeeze themselves around the tiny table next to Casson. 'Two hundred German tanks on fire,' one of them said. 'Just imagine that.'

Back at the office, Gabriella: 'Your wife called, Monsieur Casson. She said to tell you that the dinner has been cancelled, and would you please telephone her when you have a moment. She's at the beauty parlour until three-thirty, home any time after that.'

'Gabriella, do you think you could find me *Le Temps*?' For Casson, a day without a newspaper was agony.

'I can go to the *tabac*.'

'I would really appreciate it.'

'I'll go, then. Oh, Maître Versol asks that you call him.'

'No.'

'Yes, monsieur. I am afraid so.'

Back in his office, Casson retrieved the swollen dossier from the bottom drawer where he'd hidden it from himself. In 1938, someone at Pathé had woken up one morning with a vision: the world could simply not go on without another remake of *Samson and Delilah*. And Jean Casson had to produce. Costume epics were not at all his speciality, but Pathé was huge and powerful and deaf – the only word they could hear was *yes*.

He got a script. Something close to it, anyhow. Signed a Samson who, from medium range in twilight, looked strong, and a reasonable Delilah – overpriced but adequately sultry. Pathé then cancelled the project, paid him based on the escape clauses, and went on to new visions. Casson tied up the project, or thought he did.

One small problem: his production manager had ordered four hundred beards. These were for the extras, and were composed of human hair, prepared by the estimable theatrical makeup house LeBeau et cie. Cost: 5,000 francs. Somewhere just about here the problems began. The beards were, or were not, delivered to a warehouse Productions Casson rented in Levallois. Subsequently, they were returned to LeBeau. Or perhaps they weren't. LeBeau certainly didn't have the beards – or thought he didn't. Casson didn't have them either – as far as he knew. It was all *très difficile*.

Casson made the telephone call, writhing in silent discomfort. LeBeau couldn't actually sue him – the money was too little, the loss of business too great. And Casson couldn't tell LeBeau to take his beards and the rest of it – films could not be made without a theatrical makeup supplier. Still, this was an affair of honour, so Casson had to endure Maître Versol's endless drivel as a weekly punishment. The lawyer didn't attack or threaten him; the world – a murky, obscure entity – was the villain here, see how it took men of exquisite integrity and set them wandering in a forest of lost beards. Where were they? Who had them? What was to be done? *Très difficile*.

When he got off the phone, Gabriella came in with a copy of *Le Temps*. It had a certain puffy quality to it – obviously it had been read, and more than once – but a look in Gabriella's eye told him to be thankful he had a newspaper and not to raise questions about its history.

There wasn't all that much to read: Germany had attacked Belgium and the Netherlands and Luxembourg, the French army had advanced to engage the Wehrmacht on Belgian territory, a stunning assortment of world leaders were infuriated, and:

> The characteristics of the French soldier are well-known, and he can be followed across the ages, from the heroic fighters of the feudal armies to the companies of the *Ancien Régime*, and on to the contemporary era. Are they not the characteristics of the French people? Love of glory, bravery, vivacity?

5:20 p.m.

Headed for the one appointment he'd looked forward to all afternoon – drinks at a sidewalk table at Fouquet – Casson left the office ten minutes before he really had to, and told Gabriella he wouldn't be back.

Marie-Claire had called at four; the dinner was now definitely on for tonight. They had, in a series of telephone calls, talked it out – Yvette Langlade, Françoise, Bruno, and the others – and reached agreement: in her hour of crisis, France must remain France. Here Marie-Claire echoed that season's popular song, Chevalier's *'Paris Reste Paris.'* It was, Casson suspected, the best you could do with a day when your country went to war. Children would be born, bakers would bake bread, lovers would make love, dinner parties would be given, and, in that way, France would go on being France.

And would he, she would be so grateful, stop at Crémerie Boursault on the way home from the office and buy the cheese? 'A good *vacherin*, Jean-Claude. Take a moment to choose – ripe, runny in the middle, French not Swiss. Please don't let her sell you one that isn't perfect.'

'And we're how many?'

18

'Ten, as planned. Of course Françoise and Philippe will not be there, but she telephoned, very firm and composed, and said it was imperative we go ahead. We must. So I called Bibi Lachette and explained and she agreed to come.'

'All right, then, I'll see you at eight-thirty.'

For the best, he thought. He walked down Marbeuf and turned onto the Champs-Elysées. At twilight the city throbbed with life, crowds moving along the avenue, the smells of garlic and frying oil and cologne and Gauloises and the chestnut blossom on the spring breeze all blended together. The cafés glowed with golden light, people at the outdoor tables gazing hypnotized at the passing parade. To Casson, every face – beautiful, ruined, venal, innocent – had to be watched until it disappeared from sight. It was his life, the best part of his life; the night, the street, the crowd. There would always be wars, but the people around him had a strength, an indomitable spirit. *They cannot be conquered*, he thought. His heart swelled. He'd made love all his life – his father had taken him to a brothel at the age of twelve – but this, a Paris evening, the fading light, was his love affair with the world.

He reached in his pocket, made sure he had money. Fouquet wasn't cheap – but, an aperitif or two, not so bad. Then the *vacherin*, but that was all. Marie-Claire's apartment was a ten-minute walk from the rue Chardin, he wouldn't need a taxi.

Money was always the issue. His little house in Deauville was rented. Not that he told the world that, but it was. He did *fairly* well with his gangsters and doomed lovers – they paid his bills – but never *very* well. That was, he told himself, just up ahead, around the next bend in life. For the moment, it was enough to pay the bills. Almost all of them, anyhow, and only a month or two after they were due.

But in Paris that was typical, life had to be lived at a certain pitch. His father used to say, 'The real artists in Paris are the spenders of money.' He'd laugh and go on,

19

'And their palette is – the shops!' Here he would pause and nod his head wisely, in tune with the philosopher-knave side of his nature. But then, suddenly, the real ending: 'And their canvas is life!'

Casson could see the performance in detail – it had been staged often enough – and smiled to himself as he walked down the crowded avenue. Casson wondered why, on the night his country went to war, he was thinking about his father. The father he remembered was old and corrupt, a rogue and a liar, but he'd loved him anyhow.

Casson needed only a moment to search the crowded tables – what he was looking for was easy to find. Amid the elegant patrons of Fouquet, the women with every inch of fabric resting exactly where they wished, the men with each hair exactly where they'd put it that morning, sat a ferocious, Bolshevik spider. Skinny, glaring, with unruly black hair and beard, a worker's blue suit, an open-collar shirt, and bent wire-frame Trotsky eyeglasses. But this one was no artsy intellectual Trotskyite – you could see that. This one was a Stalinist to his bloody toenails and, momentarily, would produce a sharpened scythe and proceed to dismember half the patronage of Fouquet's, while the waiters ran about hysterically, trying to present their bills to a dying clientele.

Ah, Fischfang, Casson thought. *You are my revenge.*

Louis Fischfang was Casson's writer. Every producer had one. Casson told the agents and screenwriters that he spread the work around, and he did – different people were right for different projects. But in the end, when the chips were down, when somebody had to somehow make it all come out right for the people who handed over their hard-earned francs for a seat in a movie theatre, then it was Fischfang and no other.

Though he quivered with political rage, spat and swore like a proletarian, marched and signed and chanted and

20

agitated, none of it mattered, because that fucking Fischfang could write a movie script that would make a banker weep. God-given talent, is what it was. Just the line, just the gesture, just the shot. There could be no Jean Cassons – no Alexander Kordas, no Louis Mayers, no Jean Renoirs or René Clairs – without the Louis Fischfangs of this world.

Fischfang looked up as Casson approached the table. Offered his usual greeting: a few grim nods and a twisted smile. *Yes, here he was*, the devil's first mate on the ship of corruption. Here was money, nice suits, *ties*, and the haughty 16th Arrondissement, all in one *bon bourgeois* package called Casson.

'Did you order?' Casson asked as he sat down.

'Kir.' White wine with blackcurrant liqueur.

'Good idea.'

'Royal.' Not white wine, champagne.

'Even better.'

The waiter arrived with Fischfang's drink and Casson ordered the same. 'It's a strange day to work,' he said, 'but I really don't know what else to do.'

'I can't believe it's come to this,' Fischfang said angrily. 'They' – in Fischfangese this always meant *the government* and *the rich and the powerful* – 'they grew Hitler. Watered him and weeded him and pitchforked manure all around him. They gave him what he wanted in Czechoslovakia and Poland – now he wants the rest, now he wants what *they* have. Hah!'

'So now they'll stop him,' Casson said.

Fischfang gave him a look. There was something knowing and serious about it – *you're naive* – and it made him uncomfortable. They sat for a time in silence, watched the crowd flowing endlessly down the avenue. Then Casson's drink came. '*Santé*,' he said. Fischfang acknowledged the toast with a tilt of the tulip-shaped glass and they drank. Fischfang's grandfather had crawled out of a shtetl in Lithuania and walked to Paris in the 1850s, Casson's roots

21

went back into Burgundy, but as they drank their Kir they were simply Parisians.

'Well,' Casson said acidly, 'if the world's going to burn down we should probably make a movie.'

Fischfang hunted through a scuffed leather briefcase at his feet and brought out a sheet of yellow paper crammed with notes and ink splatters. '*Fort Sahara*,' he said. He took a packet of cheap cigarettes, short, stubby things, from his breast pocket. As the match flared, he screwed up his face, shielding the cigarette with cupped hands as he lit it. 'Lisbon,' he said, shaking out the match. 'The slums. Down by the docks. Women hanging out washing on a line stretched across the narrow street. They're dark, heavy, sweating. All in black. The men are coming home, in twos and threes, carrying their oars and their nets. Kids playing soccer in the street – tin can instead of a ball. Now it's nighttime. Men and women going to the – *cantina*? Wine's being poured from a straw-covered jug. There's a band, people dancing. Here's a young man, Santo. He's tough, handsome, sideburns, rolled-up sleeves . . .'

'Michel Ferré.'

'Yes? That's up to you. For some reason I kept seeing Beneviglia – he speaks French with an Italian accent.'

'Hunh. Not bad. But remember, this is a quota film – life will go smoother if everybody's French.'

To protect the film industry, the government had decreed that a certain portion of a foreign company's French earnings be spent on French films – which meant that major studios, in this case Paramount, had frozen francs that had to be used on what had come to be called 'quota films.'

'Even so, Michel Ferré is perhaps a little old,' Fischfang said. 'Santo is, oh, twenty-five.'

'All right.'

'So he's taking his girl dancing. There's a thwarted suitor, a knife fight in the alley. Suitor dies. We hear whistles blowing, the police are on the way. Cut to the train station – Marseilles. All these tough-guy types, Santo looks like an innocent among them, with his cheap little suitcase. But he survives. Among the thieves and the pimps and the deserters, he somehow makes a place for himself. Maybe he works for a carnival.'

'Good.'

'I see him backlit by those strings of little lights, watching the young couples in love – it should be him and his girl, holding hands. But his friend at the carnival is no good. He plans a robbery – asks Santo to keep a revolver for him. So, he's implicated. They hold up a bank. We see it. The manager runs outside waving his arms, they shoot him –'

'Why not hold up the carnival? The owner's a cheat with a little moustache . . .'

Fischfang nodded and crossed out a line in his notes. 'So they're not gangsters.'

'No. Men on the run from life. The carnival owner knows that, he thinks he can hold back their wages because they can't go to the police.'

'So, once again, Santo has to run. We see him staring through the train window, watching the world of everyday life go by. Then he's someplace, oh, like Béziers. Down to his last sou, he enlists in the Foreign Legion.'

'Then Morocco.' Casson caught the waiter's eye and raised two fingers.

'Well, the desert anyhow. Last outpost at Sidi-ben-something-or-other. The white buildings, the sun beating down, the tough sergeant with the heart of gold.'

'Camels.'

'Camels.'

A woman in a white cape swept past them, waving at someone, silver bracelets jangling on her wrist. Fischfang said, 'Can we do anything about the title, Jean-Claude?'

'It's from Irving Bressler, at Paramount. It says "Foreign

Legion," it says "desert." By the way, who are they fighting?'

Fischfang shrugged. 'Bandits. Or renegades. Not the good Moroccans.'

'Where's the girl, Louis?'

'Well, if the fisherman's daughter goes to Marseilles to be with Santo, she sure as hell can't go to the desert. Which leaves the slave girl, captured by bandits many years ago . . .'

'Kidnapped heiress. She's been rescued and is staying at the fort . . .'

'Native girl. "I'm glad you liked my dancing, monsieur. Actually, I'm only half-Moroccan, my father was a French officer . . ."'

'*Merde.*'

'This is always hard, Jean-Claude.'

They were silent for a moment, thinking through the possibilities. 'Actually,' Casson said, 'we're lucky it's not worse. Somebody in the meeting mumbled something about the hero *singing*, but we all pretended not to hear.'

The waiter arrived with the Kirs. '*Fort Sahara*,' Casson said, and raised his glass in a toast. The sky was darker now, it was almost night. Somewhere down the boulevard a street musician was playing a violin. The crowd at Fouquet's was several drinks along, the conversation was animated and loud, there were bursts of laughter, a muffled shriek, a gasp of disbelief. The waiters were sweating as they ran between the tables and the bar.

'Ending?' Casson said.

Fischfang sighed. 'Well, the big battle. Santo the hero. He lives, he dies . . .'

'Maybe with French financing, he dies. For Paramount, he lives.'

'And he gets the girl.'

'Of course.'

'She's the colonel's wife . . .'

'Daughter.'

24

'Cat.'
'Chicken.'

8:30 p.m.

Casson took the long way on his walk from the rue Chardin to Marie-Claire's apartment on the rue de l'Assomption. A blackout was in effect, and the velvety darkness of the Passy streets was strange but not unpleasant – as though the neighbourhood had gone back a hundred years in time. In some apartments there were candles, but that was typical French confusion at work: a blackout didn't mean you had to cover the light in your windows, it meant you couldn't turn on the electricity. If you did, it would somehow – one never quite understood these things – help the Germans.

The walk to Marie-Claire's took less than fifteen minutes, but Casson saw two moving vans working that night. On the rue des Vignes, three men struggled with a huge painting, something eighteenth century, in a gilded frame. On the next street it was a Vuitton steamer trunk.

Rue de l'Assomption stood high above the Bois de Boulogne, and the views were dramatic. Lovely old trees. Meadows and riding paths. Marie-Claire's horsey friends had their polo club in the Bois, Bruno served in some vaguely official capacity at Le Racing Club de France, there was a season box at the Auteuil racetrack, and a private room could be rented for late supper parties at Pré Catalan, the fin-de-siècle restaurant hidden at the centre of the park.

Casson paused at the entry to the building. This had been his apartment when he'd married, but it belonged to Marie-Claire now. Well, that was the way of the world. The history of ownership of apartments in the 16th Arrondissement, Casson thought, would probably make a more exciting epic of France than the *Chanson de Roland*.

25

The concierge of the building had always loved him:

'Ah, Monsieur *Casson*. It's good to see a friendly face. What a day, eh? What a horror. Oh the vile Boche, why *can't* they leave us alone? I'm getting too old for war, monsieur, even to read it in the papers. Let alone the poor souls who have to go and fight, may God protect them. What's that you have there? A *vacherin*! For the dinner tonight? How Madame *trusts* you, monsieur, if I sent my poor – ah, here's the old elevator; hasn't killed us yet but there's still time. A good evening to you, monsieur, we all would love to see more of you, we all would.'

The elevator opened into the foyer of Marie-Claire's apartment. He had a blurred impression – men in suits, women in bright silk, the aromas of dinner. Marie-Claire hurried to the door and embraced him, *gros bisous*, kisses left and right, left and right, then stepped back so he could see her. Emerald earrings, lime-coloured evening gown, hair a richer blonde than usual, tiny eyes scheming away, clouds of perfume rolling over him like fog at the seaside. 'Jean-Claude,' she said. 'I am glad you're here.' Something to say to a guest, but Casson could hear that she meant it.

And if any doubt lingered, she took him gently by the arm and drew him into the kitchen, where the maid and the woman hired for the evening were fussing with the pots. 'Let's have a look,' she said. Lifted the lid from a stewpot, shoved tiny potatoes and onions aside with an iron ladle and let some of the thick brown sauce flow into it. She blew on it a few times, took a taste, then offered it to Casson. Who made a kind of bear noise, a rumble of pleasure from deep within.

'Ach, you peasant,' she said.

'Navarin of lamb,' Casson said.

Marie-Claire jiggled the top off the *vacherin*'s wooden box, placed her thumb precisely in the imprint made by the woman in the *crémerie*, and pressed down. For his

26

effort, Casson was rewarded with a look that said *well, at least something went right in the world today.*

'Jean-Claude!' It was Bruno, of course, who'd snuck up behind him and brayed in his ear. Casson turned to see the strands of silver hair at the temples, the lemon silk ascot, the Swiss watch, the black onyx ring, the *you-old-fox!* smile, and a glass full of *le scotch whisky.*

Suddenly, the sly smile evaporated. The new look was stern: the hard glare of the warrior. *'Vive la France,'* Bruno said.

They toasted the Langlades with champagne. Twenty years of marriage, of that-which-makes-the-world-go-round. Twenty years of skirmishes and cease-fires, children raised, gifts the wrong size, birthdays and family dinners survived, and all of it somehow paid for without going to jail.

Another glass, really.

With the exception of Bruno, they had all known each other forever, were all from old 16th-Arrondissement families. Marie-Claire's grandfather had carried on a famous, virtually lifelong lawsuit against Yvette Langlade's great-aunt. In their common history all the sins had been sinned, all the alliances broken and eventually mended. Now they were simply old friends. To Casson's left was Marie-Claire's younger sister, Véronique, always his partner at these affairs. She was a buyer of costume jewellery for the Galeries Lafayette, had married and separated very young, was known to be a serious practising Catholic, and kept her private life resolutely sealed from view. She saw the plays and read the books, she loved to laugh, was always a charming dinner companion, and Casson was grateful for her presence. To his right was Bibi Lachette – the Lachettes had been summer friends of the Cassons in Deauville – the last-minute stand-in for Françoise and Philippe Pichard. Her last-minute escort was a cousin (nephew?), in Paris on business from Lyons (Mâcon?), who held a minor position in the postal administration, or perhaps he had to do with bridges. Bibi had been a great beauty in her twenties, a dark and mysterious heartbreaker, like a Spanish dancer. The cousin, however, turned out to be pale and reticent, apparently cultivated on a rather remote branch of the family tree.

With the warm leeks in vinaigrette came a powerful Latour Pomerol – Bruno on the attack. Casson would have preferred something simple with the navarin, which was one of those Parisian dishes that really did have a farmhouse ancestry. But he made the proper appreciative noise when Bruno showed the label around, and for his politeness was rewarded with a covert grin from Bibi, who knew Casson didn't do that sort of thing.

They tried not to let the Germans join them at dinner. They talked about the fine spring, some nonsense to do with a balloon race in Switzerland that had gone wrong in amusing ways. But it was not easy. Somebody had a story about Reynaud's mistress, one of those *what does he see in her* women, ungainly and homely and absurdly powerful. That led back to the government, and that led back to the Germans. 'Perhaps it's just a social problem,' Bernard Langlade said gloomily. 'We never invited them to dinner. Now they're going to insist.'

'They insisted in 1914, and they were sorry they did.' That was Véronique.

'I don't think they've ever been sorry,' said Arnaud, a lawyer for shipping companies. 'They bleed and they die and they sign a paper. Then they start all over again.'

'I have three MGs on the Antwerp docks,' Bruno said. 'Paid for. Then today, no answer on the telephone.'

This stopped the conversation dead while everybody tried to figure out just exactly how much money had been lost. When the silence had gone on too long, Casson said, 'I have a friend in Antwerp, Bruno. He owns movie theatres, and seems to know everybody. With your permission, I'll just give him a call tomorrow morning.'

It helped. Madame Arnaud began a story, Bernard Langlade asked Véronique if he could pour her some more wine. Bibi Lachette leaned towards him and said confidentially, 'You know, Jean-Claude, everybody loves you.'

Casson laughed it off, but the way Bibi moved her breast against his arm clearly suggested that *somebody* loved him.

'Well,' Marie-Claire said, 'one can only hope it doesn't go on too long. The British are here, thank heaven, and the Belgians are giving the Germans a very bad time of it, according to the radio this evening.'

Murmurs of agreement around the table, but they knew their history all too well. Paris was occupied in 1815, after the loss at Waterloo. The Germans had built themselves an encampment in the Tuileries, and when they left it had taken two years to clean up after them. Then they'd occupied a second time, in 1870, after that idiot Napoleon III lost an entire army at Sedan. In 1914 it had been a close thing – you could drive to the battlefields of the Marne from Paris in less than an hour.

'What are the Americans saying?' asked Madame Arnaud. But nobody seemed to know, and Marie-Claire shooed the conversation over into sunnier climes.

They laughed and smoked and drank enough so that, by midnight, they really didn't care what the Germans did. Bibi rested two fingers on Casson's thigh when he filled her glass. The *vacherin* was spooned out onto glass plates – a smelly, runny, delicious success. Made by a natural fermentation process from cow's milk, it killed a few gourmets every year and greatly delighted everyone else. Some sort of a lesson there, Casson thought. At midnight, time for cake and coffee, the maid appeared in consternation and Marie-Claire hurried off to the kitchen.

'Well,' she sighed when she reappeared, 'life apparently *will* go on its own particular way.'

29

A grand production from Ponthieu; feathery light, moist white cake, apricot-and-hazelnut filling, curlicues of pastry cream on top, and the message in blue icing: 'Happy Birthday Little Gérard.'

A moment of shock, then Yvette Langlade started to laugh. Bernard was next, and the couple embraced as everyone else joined in. Madame Arnaud laughed so hard she actually had tears running down her cheeks. 'I can't help thinking of poor "Little Gérard,"' she gasped.

'Having his twentieth wedding anniversary!'

'And so young!'

'Can you imagine the parents?'

'Dreadful!'

'Truly – to call a child that on his very own birthday cake!'

'He'll never recover – scarred for life.'

'My God it's perfect,' Yvette Langlade panted. 'The day of our twentieth anniversary; Germany invades the country and Ponthieu sends the wrong cake.'

Everything was arranged during the taxi ballet in front of the building at 2:30 in the morning. Bibi Lachette's cousin was put in a cab and sent off to an obscure hotel near the Sorbonne. Then Casson took Bibi and Véronique home – Véronique first because she lived down in the 5th Arrondissement. Casson walked her to the door and they said good night. Back in the cab, it was kissing in the backseat and, at Bibi's direction, off to the rue Chardin. 'Mmm,' she said.

'It's been a long time,' Casson said.

Bibi broke away in order to laugh. 'Oh you are terrible, Jean-Claude.'

'What were we, twelve?'

'Yes.'

Tenderly, he pressed his lips against hers, dry and soft. 'God, how I came.'

'You rubbed it.'

'You helped.'

'Mmm. Tell me, are you still a voyeur?'

'Oh yes. Did you mind?'

'*Me?* Jean-Claude, I strutted and danced and did the fucking cancan, how can you ask that?'

'I don't know. I worried later.'

'That I'd tell?'

'Tell the details, yes.'

'I never told. I lay in the dark in the room with my sister and listened to her breathe. And when she was asleep, I put my hand down there and relived every moment of it.'

The cab turned the corner into the rue Chardin, the driver said 'Monsieur?'

'On the right. The fourth house, just after the tree.'

Casson paid, the cab disappeared into the darkness. Casson and Bibi kissed once more, then, wound around each other like vines, they climbed the stairs together.

Suddenly, he was awake.

'Oh God, Bibi, forgive me. That damn Bruno and his damn Pomerol –'

'It was only a minute,' she said. 'One snore.'

She lay on her side at the other end of the bed, her head propped on her hand, her feet by his ear – her toenails were painted red. Once in the apartment, they'd kissed and undressed, kissed and undressed, until they found themselves naked on the bed. Then she'd gone to use the bathroom and that was the last he remembered.

'What are you doing down there?'

She shrugged. Ran a lazy finger up and down his shinbone. 'I don't know. I got up this morning, alone in my big bed, and I thought . . .' Casually, she swung a knee across him, then sat up, straddling his chest, her bottom shining white in the dark bedroom, the rest of her perfectly

31

tanned. She looked over her shoulder at him and bobbed up and down. 'Don't mind a fat girl sitting on you?'

'You're not.' He stroked her skin. 'Where did you find the sun?'

'Havana.' She clasped her hands behind her head and arched her back. 'I always have my bathing suit on, no matter where I go.'

He raised his head, kissed her bottom; one side, the other side, the middle.

'You are a bad boy, Jean-Claude. It's what everyone says.' She wriggled backward until she got comfortable, then bent over him, her head moving slowly up and down. He sighed. She touched him, her hands delicate and warm. *At this rate*, he thought, *nothing's going to last very long*.

Worse yet, their childhood afternoons came tumbling back through his memory; skinny little dirty-minded Bibi, been at the picture books her parents hid on the top shelf. What an idiot he'd been, to believe the boys in the street: *girls don't like it but if you touch them in a certain place they go crazy – but it's hard to find so probably you have to tie them up.*

But then, what an earthquake in his tiny brain. She *wants* you to feel like this, she *likes* it when your thing sticks up in the air and quivers. Well. Life could never be the same after that. 'Thursday we all go to the Lachettes,' his mother would say in Deauville. His father would groan, the Lachettes bored him. It was a big house, on the outskirts of the seaside town, away from the noisy crowds. A Norman house with a view of the sea from an attic window. With a laundry room that reeked of boiled linen. With a wine cellar ruled by a big spider. With a music room where a huge couch stood a foot from the wall and one could play behind it. '*Pom, pom, pom*, I have shot Geronimeau.'

'Ah, Monsieur le Colonel, I am dying. Tell my people – Jean-Claude!'

From the front hall: 'Play nicely, *les enfants*. We are all going to the café for an hour.'

'*Au revoir, Maman.*'

'*Au revoir, Madame Lachette.*'

There were maids in the house, the floors creaked as they went about. Otherwise, a summer afternoon, cicadas whirred in the garden, the distant sea heard only if you held your breath.

'You mustn't put your finger there.'

'Why not?'

'I don't think you're supposed to.'

'Oh.'

A maid approached, the Indian scout put his ear to the waxed parquet. '*Pom, pom!*'

'I die. Aarrghh.'

Aarrghh.

Bibi's head moving up and down, a slow rhythm in the darkness. She was coaxing him – knew he was resisting, was about to prove that she could not be resisted. Only attack, he realized, could save him now. He circled her waist with his arms, worked himself a little further beneath her, put his mouth between her thighs. *Women have taught me kindness, and this.* She made a sound, he could feel it and hear it at once, like the motor in a cat. *Now we'll see*, he thought, triumphant. *Now we'll just see who does what to who*. Her hips began to move, rising, a moment's pause, then down, and harder every time. At the other end of the bed, concentration wavered – he could feel it – then began to wane.

But she was proud, a fighter. Yes, he'd set her in motion, riding up and down on the swell of the wave, but he would not escape, no matter what happened to her. It was happening; she too remembered the afternoons at the house in Deauville, remembered the things that happened, remembered some things that could have happened but didn't. She tensed, twisted, almost broke free, then shuddered, and shuddered again. *Now*, the conqueror thought, let's roll you over, with your red toenails and your white arse and –

No. That wouldn't happen.

The world floated away. She crawled back to meet him by the pillows, they kissed a few times as they fell asleep, warm on a spring night, a little drunk still, intending to do it again, this time in an even better way, then darkness.

A loud knock on the door, the voice of the concierge: 'Monsieur Casson, *s'il vous plaît*.'

Half asleep, he pulled on his trousers and vest. It was just barely dawn, the first grey light touching the curtain. He unbolted the door and opened it. 'Yes?'

Poor Madame Fitou, who worshipped propriety in every corner of the world. Clutching a robe at her throat, hair in a net, her old face baggy and creased with sleep. The man by her side wore a postal uniform. 'A telegram, monsieur,' she said.

The man handed it over.

Who was it for? The address made no sense. CASSON, Corporal Jean C. 3rd Regiment, 45th Division, XI Corps. Ordered to report to his unit at the regimental armoury, Château de Vincennes, by 0600 hours, 11 May, 1940.

'You must sign, monsieur,' said the man from the post office.

A COUNTRY AT WAR

The column came into the village of St-Remy, where the D 34 wandered through ploughed fields of black earth that ran to the horizon, to the fierce blue sky. The mayor waited in front of the boulangerie, his sash of office worn from waist to shoulder over an ancient suit. A serious man with a comic face – walrus moustache, pouchy eyes – he waved a little tricolor flag at the column as it passed. It took two hours, but the mayor never stopped. All along the village street, from the Norman church to the Mairie with geraniums in planter boxes, the people stood and cheered – 'Vive la France!' The war veterans and the old ladies in black and the kids in shorts and the sweet girls.

A unit of the *Section Cinématographique*, attached to the Forty-fifth Division headquarters company, headed north in the column of tanks, petrol trucks, and staff cars. The unit, assigned to take war footage for newsreels, included the producer Jean Casson – now Corporal Casson, in a khaki uniform – a camera operator named Meneval, like Casson recalled to service, and a commander, a career officer called Captain Degrave. They were supposed to have a director, Pierre Pinot, but he had reported to the divisional office at Vincennes, then disappeared; averse to war, the Wehrmacht, or the producer – Casson suspected it was the latter. The unit had a boxy Peugeot 401 painted army green, and an open truck, loaded with 55-gallon drums of petrol, 35-millimetre film stock in cans, and two Contin-Souza cameras, protected from the weather by a canvas top stretched over the truck's wooden framework.

* * *

The village of St-Remy disappeared around a bend, the road ran for a time by the River Ourcq. It was a slow, gentle river, the water held the reflections of clouds and the willows and poplars that lined the banks. To make way for the column a car had been driven off the road and parked under the trees. It was a large, black touring car, polished to a perfect lustre. A chauffeur stood by the open door and watched the tanks rumbling past. Casson could just make out a face in the window by the backseat; pink, with white hair, perhaps rather on in years. The column was long, and probably the touring car had been there for some time, its silver grille pointed south, away from the war.

Casson had hoped, in the taxi on the way to the fortress at Vincennes, that it was all a magnificent farce – the work of the French bureaucracy at the height of its powers. But it wasn't that way at all and in his heart he knew it. At the divisional headquarters, a long line of forty-year-old men. The major in charge had been stern, but not unkind. He'd produced Casson's army dossier, tied in khaki ribbon, his name lettered in capitals across the cover. 'You will leave for the front in the morning, Corporal,' he'd said, 'but you may contact whoever you like and let them know that you've been returned to active duty.'

From a pay phone on the wall of the barracks he'd called Gabriella and told her what had happened. She asked what she could do. Call Marie-Claire, he said, keep the office open as long as possible, explain to the bank. Yes, she said, she understood. There was nothing but composure in her voice, yet Casson somehow knew there were tears on her face. He wondered, for a moment, if she were in love with him. Well, he hoped not. There was nothing to be done about it in any event, the life he'd made was gone. Too bad, but that was the way of the world. Over, and done. Part of him thought *well, good*.

'Perhaps,' she'd said, 'there are certain telephone numbers you should have, monsieur. Or I could call, on your behalf.'

Gabriella, he thought. I never appreciated you until it was too late. 'No,' he said. 'Thank you for thinking of it, but no.'

She wished him luck, voice only just under control, soft at the edges. All during the conversation Meneval, the cameraman, was talking to his wife on the next phone. Trying to calm her, saying that a cat who'd run away would surely return. But, Casson thought, it wasn't really about the cat.

Gabriella had approached the subject of *phone calls* with some delicacy, but she knew exactly what she was talking about. She knew he belonged to a certain level of society, and what that meant. That X would call Y, that Y would have a word with Z – that Casson would suddenly find himself with an office and a secretary and a job with an important title – honour preserved, and no need to die in the mud.

The column left Vincennes at dawn on the twelfth of May, a Sunday. Captain Degrave and Meneval in the Peugeot, Casson assigned to drive the truck – once again, somebody had disappeared.

At first he had all he could handle. The truck was heavy, with five forward gears, the clutch stiff, the gear lever cranky and difficult. You didn't, he learned quickly, shift and go around a corner at once. You shifted – ka, *blam* – then slowly forced the truck around the corner. It was hard work, but once he caught on to that, to approach it as labour, he started to do it reasonably well.

Strange to see Paris through the window of a truck. Grey, empty streets. Sprinkle of rain. Salute from a cop, shaken fist from a street cleaner – *give the bastards one for me*. A toothless old lady, staggering up the embankment after a night's sleep under a bridge, blew him a kiss. *I was pretty, once upon a time, and I fucked soldier boys just like you.* Up ahead, the commander of a tank – its name, *Loulou*, stencilled on the turret – waved a gloved hand from the open hatch.

They moved north, no more than twenty miles an hour because of the tanks, through the eastern districts of Paris. Nobody Casson knew came here – indeed there were people who claimed they lived an entire life and never left the 16th Arrondissement, except to go to the country in August. Here it was poor and shabby, not like Montparnasse; it had no communists or whores or artists, just working people who never got much money for their work. But the real Parisians, like Casson, made the whole city their home. The column crossed the rue Lagny, at boulevard d'Avout. Rue Lagny? My God, he thought, the Veau d'Or! Poor and shabby, yes, but there was always a way to spend a few hundred francs if you knew your way around. The *vin de carafe* was Brouilly, old Brouilly, from some lost barrel, almost black. And the Bresse chicken was hand-fed on the owner's mistress's mother's farm.

Strange how life turns, Casson thought. He suddenly felt the ecstasy of the unbound heart. Going to Belgium, to the war. Well then, he'd go. He'd never used the word *patriot*, but he loved this whore of a France, its narrow lanes, dark and twisted, where you smelled the bread and smelled the piss and bored women leaned on the windowsills – want a ride? The engine of the truck whined, Casson tried a lower gear. But now it grumbled, skipped a heartbeat or two, so he shifted back to the whine.

Rheims

Again the crowds, and everywhere the tricolor. The women hung garlands on the tanks' cannon and handed the crews armloads of flowers, cigarettes, sweets. Casson had a long pull from a bottle of champagne handed through the window and a wet kiss from a girl who jumped on his running board. A priest stood on the steps of Rheims cathedral and held up a crucifix, blessing the tanks as they rumbled past.

A few blocks ahead, the Peugeot was pulled over and Degrave waved at him to stop. 'We'll want this,' he said. Casson and Meneval loaded one of the cameras, set it up on a tripod on the back of the truck. Degrave took over the driving, Casson worked as the director. They circled around through the backstreets, rejoined the column, filmed the women kissing the tank crews and waving the tricolor. Of the priest, a close-up. Casson banged on the roof of the cab and Degrave stopped. A very French priest – rosy skin, fine hair, a certain refinement in the set of the lips. He held the crucifix with passion. They'd shut up in the boulevard movie theatres when they saw this, Casson thought. It was all well and good to screw the boss and hustle the girls, but they'd all made first communion, and they would all send for the priest when the time came. Cut to the faces of the tank commanders as their machines clanked past. Serious, courageous, going to war. Then a fourteen-year-old girl, tears in her eyes as she ran alongside a tank and handed up a branch of white lilac.

The column left the city on the RN 51. By the side of the road, the stone markers said SEDAN—86. Eighty-six kilometres, Casson thought. From here, you could drive to the border in an hour.

The crowd beside the road through Rethel was nothing like the one in Rheims. This crowd was watchful, and silent, and there were no garlands for the tank guns. After that, the villages were empty. There was no mayor, nobody waving, nobody. They had locked their houses and gone away. When Casson turned off the engine, he could hear the distant rumble of artillery.

On the *Route Nationale* there were refugees who had

come south from Belgium. It looked the same, Casson thought, as the newsreels he'd seen of Poland in September of 1939. Exactly the same. To the question *what should be taken?* every family had its own answer – the bed, the painting, the clock. But then, days later, it didn't matter. Exhaustion came, the treasures were too heavy, and into the fields they went.

Rough faces. Flemish, reddened, coarse to French eyes – the thick-handed cousins from the north, pikemen of a hundred armies in wars that lasted a century. The column slowed, then stopped. A nun came to Casson's truck and asked for water. He gave her what he had, she took it away, shared it out among the refugees sitting by the roadside, then brought back the empty bottle. 'God bless you, monsieur,' she said to him.

'Where are you from, sister?'

'The village of Egheze.' Then she leaned closer and whispered, 'They burned the abbey to the ground,' her voice shaking with anger while she held his arm in a steel grip. Then she said, 'Thank you for your kindness,' and walked away, back to the people by the side of the road.

The column stopped at dusk. From the Ardennes forest, up on the Belgian border, the guns thundered and echoed. The tank crews sat on a stone wall, smoked cigarettes, and drank wine from a brown bottle. There was a reservist with them, a man with a double chin and a hopeful smile. For a long time nobody spoke, they just listened to the artillery. 'Well,' the man said, 'it seems the Boche have come a long way south.' The tank crewmen grinned and exchanged glances. 'He's worried we won't win,' one of them said. They all laughed at that. 'Well,' said another, 'one never knows.' That was even funnier. After a moment the first one said, 'Ah, my little *patapouf.*' *Fatty*, he'd called him, but gently, with the tenderness that very hard people sometimes show very soft people. 'You have a day or two left to live,' he said. 'You better take a little more of this.' He handed over the bottle. The man drank, then wiped his lips with the back of his hand and made an appreciative face to show how good the wine was.

A dispatch rider on a motorcycle picked up the day's film. Then Casson followed the Peugeot on a steep, narrow road that wound down to the banks of a river. A series of tight curves – it took Casson four moves to manoeuvre the truck through the final hairpin.

He turned off the ignition, then sat still for a long time. A tiny village, completely deserted, the people fled or sent away. A silent, cobbled street; on one side the river, on the other a few old buildings, crumbling, leaning together, ivy and wild geranium growing up the stone corners and over the tops of the doorways. In the silver moonlight the water and the stone were the same colour. A low hill rose above the tile roofs to a wall masked by shrubbery, then Lombardy poplars rustled in the breeze. Then the stars.

Captain Degrave walked over from the Peugeot and appeared at the window of the truck. 'There's a hotel up the street,' he said. 'The Hotel Panorama. We were supposed to billet there, but the colonial troops have it.'

Casson had seen them on the road earlier that day; Algerian infantry and Vietnamese machine-gun squads. 'I can sleep in the truck,' he said.

'Yes,' Degrave said. 'You might as well.'

Casson lay across the seat, listening to the river – the wash of the water moving along the stone embankment – and the cicadas. He turned on his side and fell asleep.

He had a powerful dream, a dream of lost love found again. His heart swelled with happiness. The woman sat across from him – their knees almost touched – and spoke in whispers, as though people were nearby and could hear them.

'That was love,' she explained. 'We were in love.'

43

He agreed, nodded, their eyes met, they longed to hold each other but it was a public place. 'We can't let it go again,' she said.

'No.'

'We can't.'

He shook his head. If they let it go again it would be gone forever.

He woke up. The guns had stopped, there was just the river and the insects, loud on a summer night.

They worked hard the next day. Degrave started out just as the sun was coming up. They travelled along the river, through a burned village. Casson saw signs in Flemish, so they were actually over the border, in Belgium. They drove for a long time, the roar of the tank engines was deafening, the smell of petrol and scorched oil hung thick in the morning air. At Degrave's signal he pulled to one side. Meneval cranked up the camera until the spring was tight, then they filmed the column – tanks coming over a hill, bouncing on their treads in a cloud of dust. They filmed the Algerians on the march, their faces dark and sweating, and the Vietnamese machine gunners, carrying spare barrels and steel boxes of ammunition. *Moving up to battle, somewhere in Belgium.*

They drove and filmed all day, then stopped in a forest, slept, ate some salted beef and lentils from ration tins. The officers waited for darkness, then ordered the column to move forward. The night was black and very warm. Casson bit his lip as he fought the wheel and shifted gears, dazed from the noise and the heat, close to exhaustion. To his left, on a wooded hillside, a flash lit up a grove of pine trees and the sound of a hollow thump came rolling down the hill, audible above the whine of the engine. What was it? But of course he knew what it was. Fascinated, he stared at the sideview mirror, a small fire flickered at the centre of the dark glass, then the road curved and it was gone. Directly ahead of him, the silhouette of a tank's turret gun traversed back and forth.

A soldier ran in front of him and waved for him to slow down. A group of men, shadows, moved restlessly around something on the ground. Casson saw one white face turned suddenly towards him, the eyes were wide with fright. Then an officer with a swagger stick swept it violently in the direction the column was headed – *move, move* – and Casson stepped on the gas. Another flare on the hillside. Then a flash blinded him. He took a hand from the wheel and pressed his eyes. A loud crack. Followed by a gentle patter as twigs and dirt rained down on the metal roof of the cab. *They're trying to kill you, Jean-Claude.* The idea was an affront, he clenched his teeth and gripped the wheel harder. Two officers stood by a halted tank. After he'd gone past, one of them ran to catch up with him and banged on his door. 'Stop! Is that petrol in the back?'

'Yes, sir.'

'Well then, back the truck up. We need it.'

Casson shifted into reverse, rolled back until he was even with the tank. A commander climbed out of the hatch, then vaulted to the ground. 'That's French fire!' he shouted. 'Idiots! Clowns! What are they doing, shooting up here?'

'I assure you that it is not French fire, Lieutenant.' From his insignia, Casson could see he was a major.

'What, Belgian? English?'

'No.'

Two soldiers wrestled a drum of petrol to the edge of the truck, then Casson helped them to lower it onto its side. One of them attached a hose to the barrel and ran the other end into the tank's fuel pipe. Overhead, the sound of fabric ripping and the top of a tree whipped like a rag in a hurricane. Petrol sloshed on Casson's shoes. The major had a lit cigarette in the corner of his mouth. 'Careful there, you.' An aristocrat, talking to his groom, Casson

45

thought. The major stepped back, his high boots supple and glistening. This was still the cavalry, the hulking tanks were simply machines they were forced to use.

A staff car came speeding through the column and skidded to a stop. A junior officer leaped out, ran up to the major and saluted. 'Major Mollet, sir. The general's compliments. Why are we under fire?'

'It is German artillery.'

'Sir.'

The officer ran back to the car. The petrol drum was empty, Casson started to screw the cap back on the opening as the soldiers coiled the hose. From the car, an angry shout. Then the back door flew open. The junior officer ran around to that side and was joined by the driver. Casson looked down, afraid to stare. At the car, a polite struggle was under way – a muttered curse, a loud whisper. At last they managed to extricate the general from the backseat. He was enormously fat, his breath sighed in and out as he walked over to the major. The major saluted. 'General Lebois, sir.'

'Mollet.' The general touched the brim of his hat with a forefinger. 'What's going on here?'

Two more explosions on the hillside. In the light, Casson could see the general's skin, a web of broken purple veins on his cheeks.

'The Wehrmacht, sir.'

'They can't be this far south.'

'Respectfully, sir, I believe they are.'

'No, it's the damn English. All excited for no reason at all and shooting in the dark.'

'Sir.'

'Send a motorcycle courier over there. Somebody who speaks English.'

'Yes, sir.'

A shell landed on the road, about three hundred yards ahead of them. A truck had been hit. As it started to burn, there were shouts of 'get water,' and 'push it off the road.' Casson could see dark shapes running back and forth. The general growled, deep in his chest, like a dog that doesn't want to move from its place on the rug.

The major said, 'Perhaps it would be faster if we fired back.'

'No,' the general said. 'Save the ammunition. Waste not, want not.'

'Very good, sir,' the major said.

Casson returned to his truck. A glance in the mirror, he could see the two aides, trying to get the general back in his car. Casson moved up the column, working his way around tanks, tapping his horn when people got in the way. It was slow, difficult work, he never stopped shifting gears. He had to wait while one tank attempted to push a second off the road. It had been hit and was on fire, orange flames and boiling black smoke. By the light of the fire Casson could read the name *Loulou* stencilled on its turret.

Dawn. The sky pale, swept with the wisps of white scud that marked the high wind blowing in from the Channel.

The road to the fort on the heights of Sedan worked its way around the edges of the city, then climbed past ploughed fields and old forest. At the gate to the fort, the Peugeot was waved through but Casson was stopped. The sentries were drunk and unshaven. 'What brings you here?' one of them said.

'We're making movies.'

'Movies! You know Hedy Lamarr?'

'Dog dick,' said another. 'Not those kinds of movies. *War* movies.'

'Oh. Then what the hell are you doing up here?'

The second man shook his head, walked over to the truck and offered Casson a bottle through the window. 'Don't let him get to you,' he said. 'Have some of this.'

Casson raised the bottle to his lips and drank. Sharp and

sour. The man laughed as he took the bottle back. 'Come and see us, squire, after this shit's done with.'

The hard Parisian sneer in the voice made Casson smile. 'I will.'

'You can find us up in Belleville, at The Pig's Arse.'

'See you then,' Casson said, shoving the clutch in.

'Red front!' they called after him.

Fortress at Sedan!

Raising and saluting the flag, morning reveille played on a bugle. Domestic life in the barracks – washing clothes, shining boots. Here are the cooks, preparing breakfast for the hungry poilus. A cannon, the famous French 75, is aimed out over the Meuse valley. A vigilant sentry keeps watch with binoculars – no Germans yet, but we're ready for them when they come.

Captain Degrave had an old friend serving with an artillery regiment and the gunners fed them breakfast. Casson ached from the driving, he was filthy with oily soot, and he wanted to shave more than anything else in the world, but the food seemed to bring him back to life. The gunners were countrymen from the Limousin. They'd stewed some hens in a huge iron kettle, added spring onions and wild garlic from the pastures outside the fort, found the last of the winter carrots in an 'abandoned' root cellar, added Tunisian wine, a lump of fat, and a fistful of salt, then served it smoking hot in a metal soup plate. Afterwards he sat back against a stone wall and had a handrolled cigarette stuffed with pipe tobacco. Maybe the world wasn't as bad as it seemed.

It was strange, he thought, to be suddenly pulled from one life and dropped down into another. In Paris it was a May morning, Marie-Claire and Bruno probably making love by the open window that looked out over the Bois de Boulogne. She was, he recalled, at best obliging about it, she really didn't like to do it in the morning; she had to be courted. And then – a little Marie-Claire punishment

– she wouldn't take off her nightgown. She'd pull it up to her chin, then stick her tongue out, saying that if you insisted on making love like a peasant, well then by God you could just make love like a peasant. That was, at least, how she started out. As always with Marie-Claire, things got better later.

Of course it might be different with Bruno, but he doubted it. My God, he thought, it's like another world. Another *planet*. The lawyers, Arnaud and Langlade, would be going off to their offices in an hour or so, smelling like cologne, their ties pulled up just right, flirting with the women they passed in the street.

Casson stood, looked out over the wall at the early sun just lighting up the Meuse, burning off the valley mist. Bibi Lachette would still be asleep, he thought. She seemed like the type who slept late, dead to the world. Would she do it in the morning? Mmm – no, not it – but something. Generous, Bibi. He certainly did like her. Not love exactly, it was more like they were two of a kind, and, he thought, in some parts of the world that might be even better than love.

From the heights the river didn't look like much of a barrier, it was too pretty. Placid blue water that ran in gentle curves, you'd do better to paint it than to try and fight behind it. What had one of the gunners called it? Just a little *pipi du chat* – a cat pee. Christ, he thought, what the hell am I doing in a war?

Sunset. They'd filmed the commanding officer reviewing a company of infantry, backs stiff, thumbs on the seams of their trouser legs. Then Degrave had asked him to take the film over to the regimental headquarters building where the courier from Paris was due at seven to pick it up.

The road was made of cut stone and ran along a parade ground lined with cannon from Napoleon's time. He

49

slowed down when a siren sounded, hoarse and broken, and heard a drone somewhere above him. The last of the orange sun was in his face – he let the truck roll to a stop, shaded his eyes, stared up into the early evening light.

A plane popped out of a cloud, abruptly slid sideways – Casson saw a black Maltese cross as the wing lifted – then dived at a sharp angle. For a moment he was a spectator, fascinated by the theatre of it, clearly it had nothing to do with him. Then the edges of the wings twinkled and the whine of the engine became a scream, rising over the rattle of the plane's machine guns. Casson jumped out of the truck and ran for his life. *Stukas*, he thought. Like the newsreels from Poland.

At the bottom of its dive, the Stuka released a bomb. Casson's ears rang, a puff of warm air touched his cheek, he saw, a moment later, black smoke tumbling upward, lazy and heavy. Just ahead of him, from the roof of the headquarters building, a spray of orange sparks seemed to float into the sky amid the drumming of antiaircraft cannon. Then more Stukas, whine after whine as they dived. Casson reached the building, fought through the shrubbery, then rolled until he got himself wedged between the ground and the base of a brick wall.

He looked up, saw a Stuka turn on its back, then slide into a shallow dive, rotating very slowly as it headed for the earth, a thin line of brown smoke streaming from its engine. Then a second Stuka exploded, a ball of yellow fire, flaming shards spinning through the air. Casson's heart was pounding. Thick smoke stood slow and ponderous above the fort and the wind reeked of petrol. The fuel tanks, he realized, that was what they'd come for, grey domes that stood three storeys high – the smell of burning petroleum was making him dizzy. The drone of the planes faded into the distance, heading north into Belgium.

*　　*　　*

50

They moved to a little village outside the city of Sedan, the vehicles parked in a farmyard. Meneval slept in the car, Degrave and Casson stayed awake, sitting on the running board of the truck. A mile to the west, the fort was still burning, but directly above them the night was starry and clear.

Degrave had a heavy, dark face, dark hair, thinning in front – he was perhaps a little old to be a captain – and there was something melancholy and stubborn in his character.

'We'll film in the blockhouse tomorrow,' he said. 'Down near the river. Then we'll move on somewhere else – the fort can't hold much longer.'

Casson stared, not understanding.

'We've lost the air force,' Degrave explained. 'It's gone – eighty per cent of it destroyed on the first morning of the war.'

After a moment Casson said, 'Then, they'll cross the border.'

Degrave was patient. 'The war is over, Corporal,' he said gently.

Casson shook his head, 'No,' he said, 'I can't accept that.'

Degrave reached inside his coat and produced a crumpled, flattened packet of Gauloises Bleu. Two remained, bent and ragged. Degrave offered the packet, Casson pulled one free with difficulty. Degrave had a special lighter, made from a bullet cartridge, that worked in the wind. After several snaps they got both cigarettes lit.

'We're going to lose?' Casson said.

'Yes.'

'What will happen?'

Degrave stared at him a moment, then shrugged. How could he know that? How could anybody?

The blockhouse was long and narrow, built into the hillside, and very hot and damp. It smelled like wet cement. A squad of gunners lay on the dirt floor and tried to sleep, staring curiously at Casson and the others when they arrived. There were four embrasures, narrow firing slits cut horizontally into the wall. Meneval set up his camera at the far end of the blockhouse, wound the crank and inserted a new roll of film. The sergeant in charge handed Casson a pair of binoculars and said, 'Have a look.'

Casson stared out at the river.

'They tried twice, yesterday. A little way east of here. But they weren't serious. It was just to see what we did.'

A field telephone rang and the sergeant went to answer it. 'Fifteen seventy-two,' he said, a map reference. 'It's quiet. We've got the moviemakers with us.' He listened a moment, then laughed. 'If she shows up here I'll let you know.'

A three-quarter moon. Casson made a slow sweep of the far bank of the Meuse, woods and a meadow in brilliant ashen light. He could hear crickets and frogs, the distant rumble of artillery. Thunder on a summer night, he thought. When it's going to storm but it never does.

Degrave was standing next to him, with his own binoculars. 'Do you know François Chambery?' he asked.

'I don't think so.'

'My cousin. He's also in entertainment – a pianist.'

'He performs in Paris?'

'He tries.'

Casson waited but that was all. 'Where are you from, Captain?'

'The Anjou.'

Casson moved the binoculars across the trees. The leaves rustled, nothing else moved. In the foreground, the river seemed phosphorescent in the moonlight. To the west, the artillery duel intensified. It wasn't thunder anymore, it sounded angry and violent, the detonations sharp amid the echoes rolling off the hillsides. 'They're working now,' somebody said in the darkness.

As Casson swept his binoculars across the forest, something moved. He tightened the focus until he could see tree trunks and leafy branches. Suddenly, a deer leaped from the edge of the woods, followed by another, then several more. They were colourless in the moonlight, bounding down the meadow to the bank of the river, then veering away into a grove of birch trees.

'What is it?' the sergeant said.

'Deer. Something chased them out of the woods.'

4:10 a.m.

The moon fading, the light turning towards dawn shadow. Casson was tired, ran a hand across his face. In the woods, a heavy engine came to life. It sounded like a tractor on a construction site – plenty of fuel fed into it on a chilly morning. Then, others. Behind Casson the soldiers grumbled and got to their feet. There were three Hotchkiss guns aimed out the embrasures. The crews got busy, working bolts, snapping clips into the magazines. Casson could smell the gun oil.

One of the tanks broke cover, just the front end of the deck and the snout of the cannon. 'Leave him alone,' the sergeant said.

The French guns stayed silent. Meneval ran off a few seconds of film – they wouldn't get much, Casson thought, not for another hour. The blockhouse was quiet, Casson could hear the men breathing. The tank reversed, disappeared into the forest. Was it over, Casson wondered. The soldier next to him, gripping the handles of a machine gun, said under his breath, 'And . . . now.'

It was a close guess – only a few seconds off. A whistle blew, the Germans came out of the forest. The German tanks fired – orange flashes in the trees – and French anti-tank cannon fired back from the other blockhouses. The German infantry yelled and cheered, hundreds of them, running down the meadow carrying rubber boats and paddles. Clearly it was something they'd drilled at endlessly – it was synchronized, rehearsed. It reminded Casson of the news footage of gymnastic youth; throwing balls in the air or waving ribbons in time to music. Casson could hear the officers shouting, encouraging the soldiers. Some of the men reached the bank of the river and held the boats so their comrades could climb in.

The Hotchkiss guns opened up, tracer sailing away into the far bank and the troops boarding the rafts. German machine guns answered – fiery red tracer that seemed slow at first, then fast. Some of it came through the slits, fizzing and hissing in the blockhouse with the smell of burnt steel. The French gunners worked hard, slamming the short clips into the guns and ripping them out when they were done. On the far bank of the river, some soldiers bowed, others sat down, rolling on the ground or curling up.

Then it stopped. A few rubber boats turned in the current as they floated away, a few grey shapes floated along with them. The silence seemed strange and heavy. Casson let the binoculars hang on their strap and leaned against the lip of the gunport. Just outside, he heard twigs snapping and pounding footsteps on the dirt path. Two French soldiers ran past, then three more. The sergeant swore and hurried outside. Casson heard his voice. 'Stop,' he called out. 'You cannot do this – go back where you belong.'

The answering voice was cold. 'Get out of the way,' it said.

At dusk, a message on the field telephone: the unit had been ordered out. Degrave's allies in Paris, Casson suspected, knew the battlefield situation for what it was and had determined to save a friend's life. 'We're being sent south,' Degrave explained as they packed up the equipment. 'To the reserve divisions behind the Maginot Line.'

They tried. But in the darkness on the roads leading out of Sedan nobody was going anywhere. Thousands of French troops had deserted, their weapons thrown away. They trudged south, eyes down, among columns of refugees, most of them on foot, some pushing baby carriages piled high with suitcases. Casson saw artillery wagons – the cannon thrown off, soldiers riding in their place – pulled by farm horses; an oxcart carrying a harp, a hearse from Mons, a city bus from Dinant, the fire engine from Namur. Sometimes an army command car forced its way through, packed with senior officers, faces rigid, sitting at attention while the driver pounded on the horn and swore. *Let us through, we're important people, retreating in an important fashion.* Or, as a soldier riding on Casson's running board put it, 'Make way, make way, it's the fucking King.' Then, a little later, as though to himself, he said 'Poor France.'

Casson and the others moved slowly south, at walking speed. Back on the Meuse, the Wehrmacht was attacking again and whatever remained of the Forty-fifth Division was fighting back – floods of orange tracer crisscrossed the night sky above the river.

It was hard work, coaxing the truck forward among the refugees. They slept for an hour, then started up again. In first light, just after dawn, Casson spotted a road marker and realized they'd travelled less than twenty miles from Sedan. And then, prompt to the minute at 7:00 a.m., the Stukas came to work. They were very diligent, thorough and efficient, taking care to visit each military vehicle. Casson ran for the ditch and up went the truck – petrol, cameras, film stock, canned lentils. He sat in the dirt and watched it burn, caught up in a fury that amazed him. It made no sense at all – they'd stopped him from making idiotic newsreels that nobody would ever see – but something inside him didn't like it.

But, whether he liked it or not, that was the end of the *Section Cinématographique* of the Forty-fifth Division, decommissioned in a cow pasture near the village of Bouvellement on a fine May morning in 1940. The Peugeot had also been a victim of the Stukas, though it had not burned dramatically like the truck. A heavy-calibre bullet had punched through the engine, which could do no more than cough and dribble oil when Degrave tried the ignition. 'Well,' he said with a sigh, 'that's that.'

He then gave Meneval and Casson permission to go, filling out official little slips of paper that said they'd been granted emergency leave. For himself, he would make his way to the military airfield at Vouziers, not all that far away, and request reassignment.

Meneval said he would leave immediately for home, just outside Paris. His family needed him, especially his wife, who'd been absolutely certain that he was gone forever.

'You understand,' Degrave said, 'that the fighting is going in that direction.'

'Yes, probably it's not for the best,' Meneval said gloomily. 'But, even so.' He shook hands and said good-bye and headed for the road.

Degrave turned to Casson. 'And you, Corporal?'

'I'm not sure,' Casson said.

'What I would recommend,' Degrave said, 'is that you make your way to Mâcon. There's a small army base north of the city – it's the Tenth Division of the XIV Corps. Ask for Captain Leduc, mention my name, tell him you are an *isolé* – a soldier separated from his unit. They'll give you something to eat and a place to sleep, and you'll be out of the way of, of whatever's going to happen next.'

He paused a moment. 'If the Germans ask, Corporal, it might be better not to mention that you were recalled to service. Or what you did. Other than that, I want to thank you, and to wish you luck.'

Casson saluted. Degrave returned the salute. Then they shook hands. 'We did the best we could,' Degrave said.

'Yes,' Casson said. 'Good luck, Captain.'

Casson headed for Mâcon. Sometimes, in a café, he heard the news on a radio. Nothing, he realized, could save them from losing the war. He left the roads, walked across the springtime fields. He ate bread he found in a bombed bakery in Châlons, tins of sardines a kind woman gave him in Chaumont. He was not always alone. He walked with peasant boys who'd run away from their units. He shared a campfire with an old man with a white beard, a sculptor, he said, from Brittany somewhere, who walked with a stick, and got drunk on some bright yellow stuff he drank from a square bottle, then sang a song about Natalie from Nantes.

As Casson watched, the country died. He saw a granary looted, a farmhouse burned by men in a truck, a crowd of prisoners in grey behind barbed wire. 'We'll all live deep down, now,' the sculptor said, throwing a stick of wood on the fire. 'Twenty ways to prepare a crayfish. Or, you know, chess. Sanskrit poetry. It will hurt like hell, sonny, you'll see.'

The villages were quiet, south of Dijon. The spaniel slept in the midday heat, the men were in the cafés at dusk, the breeze was soft in the faded light that led to evening, and the moon rose as it always had.

THE JADE PAGODA

20 August, 1940

The silence of the empty apartment rang in his ears. The bed had been made – the concierge's sister coming in to clean as she always did – and the only sign of his long absence was a dead fern. Still, he felt like a ghost returning to a former life. And he had to put the fern outside the door so he wouldn't see it.

The heat was almost liquid. He opened the doors to the little balcony but it wasn't all that much better outside. Hot, and wet. And still – as though all the people had gone away. Which they had, he realized. Either fled before the advancing Wehrmacht in June, or fled to the seashore on the first of August. Or both. Practical people on the rue Chardin.

He sat on the edge of the bed, took a deep breath, let it out slowly. The man who had lived here, the producer Jean Casson, Jean-Claude to his friends, little jokes, small favours, a half-smile, *maybe we should make love* – what had become of him? The last attempt at communication was propped against the base of a lamp on the bedside table. A message written in eyebrow pencil on the inside cover of a matchbook from the bar at the Plaza-Athénée. *34 56 08* it said, a phone number. Signed *Bibi*.

He'd spent a long time walking the roads, a long span of empty days in the barracks of a defeated army, and he'd thought, every day, about what had happened up on the Meuse. The machine-gun duels across the river, the French soldiers running away, the refugees on the roads. It seemed strange to him now, remote, an experience that happened to somebody else, in some other country.

He shaved, smelled the lotion he used to wear, then put the cap back on the bottle. Went for a walk. Rue des Vignes. Rue Raffet. Paris as it always was – smelly in the heat, deserted in August. He came to the Seine and rested his elbows on the stone wall and stared down into the river – Parisians cured themselves of all sorts of maladies this way. The water was low, the leaves on the poplars parched and pale. Here came a German officer. A plain, stiff man in his mid-thirties, his Wehrmacht belt buckle said *Gott Mit Uns*, God is with us. Strange God if he is, Casson thought.

The Métro. Five sous. Line One. Châtelet stop, Samaritaine department store, closed and dead on a Sunday. He would survive this, he thought. They all would, the country would. 'Peace with honour,' Pétain had called the surrender. Peace with peace, at any rate, and not to be despised. Just another *débâcle*, the lost war. And French life had plenty of those. There goes the electricity, the Christmas dinner, the love of one's life. *Merde.*

In the back streets of a deserted commercial district he found a little café open and ordered an *express*. The price had doubled, the coffee was thin, and the proprietor raised a cautionary eyebrow as he put the cup down – *this is how things are, I don't want to hear about it*. Casson didn't complain. He was lucky to be alive, paying double for a bad coffee was a privilege.

On the flight south from Sedan he'd been lucky twice. The first time, he was with a company of French infantry, half of them still armed, when they were overtaken by a German column. An officer stood on a tank turret, announced the *Panzerkorps* had no time to deal with prisoners, and directed them to lay their weapons down on the road. When that was done a tank ran over them a few times and the column went on its way. Others had not been so fortunate – they'd heard about whole divisions packed into boxcars and shipped off to camps in Germany.

The second time, Casson was alone. Came around the

curve of a road outside Châlons to find three Wehrmacht officers on horseback. They stared at him as he walked past – a lone, unarmed soldier in a shabby uniform. Then he heard a laugh, glanced up to see a young man with the look of a mischievous elf, or perhaps, if some small thing annoyed him, a murderous elf. 'You halt,' he said. He let Casson stand there a moment, then leaned over, worked his mouth, and spat in his face. His friends found that hilarious. Casson walked away, head down, and waited until he was out of sight before wiping the saliva off.

So what? he told himself. *It didn't mean anything.*

A woman came into the café and caught his eye. She was tall, had a big, soft face, net stockings, short skirt. Casson stood and gestured at an empty chair. 'A coffee?' he said.

'Sure, why not.'

The proprietor brought it over and Casson paid.

'Been out in the country?' she said.

'You can tell?'

She nodded. 'You have the look. Too many healthy Frenchmen around, all of a sudden.' She took a sip of coffee and scowled at the proprietor but he was busy not noticing her. She snapped her handbag open, took out a small mirror, poked at a beauty mark pasted on her cheek. 'Care for a fuck?' she said.

'No, thanks.'

She closed the mirror and put it back in her handbag. 'Something complicated, it'll cost you.'

'What if I just buy you a sandwich?'

She shrugged. 'If you like, but I hate to see this louse have the business.'

Casson nodded agreement.

'Oh, it's going to get real shitty here,' she sighed. 'Before, I was just about managing. Day to day, you know. But now . . .'

Casson took out a packet of cigarettes and they both lit

up. The woman blew a long plume of smoke at the café ceiling. 'Trick is,' she said, 'with these times, is don't let it ruin your life.'

'My mother used to say that.'

'She was right.'

They smoked. A fat little man, commercial traveller from the suitcase he was carrying, looked into the café and cleared his throat. The woman turned around. 'Well hello,' she said.

'Are you, uh . . .'

The woman stood up. 'I have to go,' she said.

'Luck to you.'

'Thanks. And you.'

Monday morning, 7:00 a.m. The concierge knocked on his door. It took him a long time to unwind himself from sleep, dreams, the safety of his very own bed. He staggered to the door.

'Welcome home, Monsieur Casson.'

He stood, swaying slightly, his shirt pulled together in one hand, his trousers held up with the other. 'Madame Fitou,' he mumbled.

She was sweating with anxiety.

'What is it?'

'The car, monsieur.'

'Yes?' He rarely drove it – it mostly stayed in the little garage off the courtyard.

The words came in a rush. 'Well, of course we waited until you returned, and we worried about you so, but of course you know the authorities have made a requisition of all private automobiles, so, ah, it must be turned in. Of course there were posters, while you were away, monsieur. My husband made sure to write down the address, out in Levallois, because we thought, you'd have to be informed, you'd want to be, when you came home . . .' She ran down slowly.

'Oh, yes, of course.'

Now he understood. The poor woman was afraid he'd refuse, that she would be dragged into disobedience, made to suffer for his casual attitude towards authority. 'I'll take care of it this morning, madame,' he said.

She thanked him, he could see the relief in her eyes. She'd lain awake all night, he supposed. In her imagination he had scoffed, jeered at her. Then, disaster. Police.

'I'd better get dressed,' he said brightly, and managed a smile as he closed the door.

Madame Fitou and her sister held the doors open and Casson backed out carefully into the rue Chardin. No point in scratching the body-work, he thought. He let the car idle a moment, then shifted into first gear. He didn't particularly share the national worship of automobiles, but this one had been very hard to get hold of and he was sorry to lose it.

A Simca 302. A model last manufactured in 1934, so those seen around Paris were all of a certain age. A convertible, built low to the ground, always forest green. Walnut dash, soft top, throaty engine. Just the sort of car the producer Jean Casson might be expected to drive. Actually, just the sort of car the producer Jean Casson might be expected to drive – Jensen, Morgan, Riley – the producer Jean Casson couldn't afford.

The 302 was nice enough to look at, but it wasn't at all nice to its owner. It was a sulky, spoiled car that drank fuel, that sputtered and died at traffic lights, that whined if made to go at high speeds, that wanted nothing to do with the weather after October. Still, it was a credible showpiece, and if it misbehaved with an important personage – it knew who was sitting in its passenger seat – Casson would smile and shake his head, helpless. A depraved passion, what could one do.

Of course it drove like an angel on its way to the garage.

65

Out avenue Malakoff on a cloudy August morning, a few sprinkles of rain. Casson worked his way patiently through swarms of bicyclists; clerks and factory workers, young and old, everyone pedalling along together, most of them sour-faced and grim, ringing their bicycle bells when some idiot went too slow or too fast.

The light was red at the intersection of Malakoff and the busy avenue Foch. A black saloon pulled up next to him and Casson and the passenger glanced at each other. German soldiers. Casson turned away. They were junior officers, probably lieutenants. They had the look of young men going to work at a bank or a law office – perhaps the military version, paymaster or judge advocate. Something administrative, he thought, and probably technical.

They were staring at him. He glanced back – *yes?* – but it didn't make them stop. They both wore glasses, one of them had round, tortoiseshell frames, the other silver rims. Their faces were pink, freshly shaved, their hair cut to military length and combed into place with hair tonic, and the way they were staring at him was rude. The light went green. The bicyclists moved off, Casson resisted an urge to speed ahead, hesitated so the saloon could go first.

But it didn't. They were waiting for him. *Conards!* he thought. Jerks. What's your problem? He eased the car into gear and inched forward. I'm not supposed to be driving, he thought. They can see I'm French, and that means I'm supposed to be pedalling a bicycle while they drive a car. His stomach turned over – he didn't want a confrontation, he wasn't sure exactly what that would mean. He let the Simca fade a little, waiting an extra beat between second and third. The saloon's door moved ahead of his, and he saw the two were talking, urgently, then the passenger looked out the window again. Clearly he was concerned, perhaps slightly annoyed.

Porte Maillot. A large, busy traffic circle with avenues radiating like spokes in all directions. A horn blasted behind Casson and he swerved over into the right lane as a Wehrmacht truck tore past him, swaying as it lurched around the circle. Then the saloon was back, the passenger not a bit less irritated. Casson began to feel sick. *What's the problem, Fritz? You think somebody peed in your soup?* He knew the look on the lieutenant's face – righteous indignation, a German religion.

Up ahead, another traffic light at the avenue des Ternes. Now green, but not for long. If they stopped side by side, the Germans were going to get out of their car and make an issue of it. And he wasn't legal, he wasn't supposed to be driving this car. He didn't know exactly what they'd do about it but he didn't want to find out. *You have not behaved correctly, now you must suffer the consequences.* A side street came up on his left, he threw the wheel over and put his foot down.

Rue du Midi. He didn't remember ever being here but he thought he was just at the edge of Neuilly. He stopped in the middle of the block, in front of a villa with an elaborate iron gate in its wall, and lit a cigarette. His hands were shaking. He glanced out the window at the view mirror. There they were. Up the street he could just see the black saloon, out on the avenue, backing up slowly in order to turn into the rue du Midi. They were going to come after him.

The sweat started at his hairline, he jammed the gear shift into first and took off. On his left, a tiny cobbled lane, something dark and lost about it. A place to hide. He turned in, grey plaster walls rose on both sides, there was barely room for a car. He followed a long curve, past an old-fashioned gas lamp, an even narrower alley that opened to his left, a row of shuttered windows. Where was he? It was perpetual twilight in here, the walls so close they amplified the car engine and he could hear every stroke of the pistons.

The street ended at a wall.

Covered with vines and moss, crumbling, twenty feet high. Over the oak and iron doors the chiselled letters on the capstone had been worn almost flat by time – the Abbey of Saint Gervais de Toulouse. Casson turned off the ignition then had to work his way free of the Simca because the walls were so close. He ran to the entry – he thought he could hear the saloon back in the rue du Midi. There was a chain hanging down the portal, he pulled it, heard the clang of an iron bell within the walls. He tried again, then again, glancing back over his shoulder and expecting the Germans at any second.

'Hello!' he called.

From the other side of the door: 'What do you want?'

'Let me in. The Germans are after me.'

Silence. Now he was sure he could hear the saloon – the whine of reverse gear, then the sound of idling where the lane opened to the street. 'Please,' he said. 'Open the door.'

He waited. Finally, a voice: 'Monsieur, you cannot come in here.'

'What?'

The silence seemed to last a long time. 'Please go away, monsieur.'

For a moment, Casson tried to explain it away – it was a Coptic order, or Greek, something exotic. But the man on the other side of the wall was French. 'You should be ashamed of yourself,' Casson said.

Silence.

Casson turned away from the door and ran back down the cobbled lane, in the direction of the rue du Midi, looking for the alley he'd seen. He found it, sprinted into the darkness and right into an iron grille. The shock made him cry out and a trickle of blood ran from his nose. He squatted down, his back against an icy stone wall, and held his hand against his face to stop the blood from getting on his shirt. He was perhaps ten feet down the alley. Out in the lane he heard footsteps, then two shadows moved quickly past the opening where Casson was hidden only by darkness. He forced himself against the wall. One of the soldiers said something, he was short of breath, and his whispered German was excited, perhaps a little frightened. Then the footsteps moved away, and Casson heard a shout as they found the car parked facing the Abbey wall. He could just hear them as they talked it over, then footsteps came back towards the alley, paused, and moved away towards the rue du Midi.

Too French for them in here, Casson thought. It was dark and damp and it smelled of old drains, burnt wood, cat piss, and God knew what else. It was too ancient, too secret. Sitting against the wall and wiping at his bloody nose, Casson felt something like triumph.

He counted to a hundred, then got the Simca backed down the lane and out into the street as quickly as he could. Because if the Germans had lacked the courage to search the alley – and Casson sensed they'd known he was in there – they were certainly brave enough to pick up a telephone once they got to work, and report the Frenchman and his car to the Gestapo, licence plate and all.

As for the feeling of triumph, it didn't last long. In the winding streets of Levallois-Perret – the industrial neighbour of luxurious Neuilly – he stopped the car so a young woman carrying a bread and a bag of leeks could cross the street. A blonde, country-girl-in-Paris, big-boned, with spots of red in her cheeks and heavy legs and hips beneath a thin dress.

Their eyes met. Casson wasn't going to be stupid about it, but his look was open, I *want you*. When her lip curled with contempt and she turned away pointedly it surprised him. Eye contact in Paris was a much-practised art, a great deal of love was made on the streets, some of it even made its way indoors. But she didn't like him. And she was able, her face mobile and expressive, to tell him why. Anybody driving a car since the requisition was a friend of the Occupier, and no friend of hers. Let him seek out his own kind.

A few minutes later he found the garage. It was enormous, packed with row on row of automobiles, all kinds, old and new, banged-up and shiny, cheap little Renaults and Bugatti sports cars. The German sergeant in charge never said anything about *where were you*, he simply took the keys. Casson wondered out loud about a receipt, but the sergeant merely shrugged and nodded his head at the door.

Later that morning he went to his office, but the door was padlocked.

Casson went home and called his lawyer.

Bernard Langlade – whose anniversary he'd celebrated at Marie-Claire's – was a good friend who happened to be a good lawyer. A personal lawyer, he didn't represent CasFilm or Productions Casson. Sent a bill only when he was out of pocket and, often enough, not even then. He looked at papers, listened patiently to Casson's annual tax scheme – taking off his glasses and rubbing his eyes – wrote the occasional letter, made the occasional phone call. In fact Langlade, though trained at the Sorbonne, spent his days running a company that manufactured lightbulbs, which his wife had inherited from her family.

'At least you're home, safe and in one piece,' he said on the phone. 'So let's not worry too much about locked doors. I have a better idea – come and have lunch with me at one-thirty, all right? The Jade Pagoda, upstairs.'

A fashionable restaurant, once upon a time, but no more. It had fallen into a strange, soft gloom, deserted, with dust motes drifting through a bar of sunlight that had managed to work its way between the drapes. The black lacquer was

70

chipped, the gold dragons faded, the waiter sat at a corner table, chin propped on hand, picking horses from the form sheet in the Chinese newspaper.

'Well, Jean-Claude,' Langlade said, 'now we're really in the shit.'

'It's true,' Casson said.

'And I worry about you.'

'Me?'

'Yes. Life under German rule is going to be bad, brutal. And it's going to demand the cold-blooded, practical side of our nature. But you, Jean-Claude, you are a romantic. You sit in a movie theatre somewhere, wide-eyed like a child – it's a street market, in ancient Damascus! A woman takes off her clothes for you – she's a goddess, you're in love!'

Casson sighed. His friend wasn't wrong.

'That must change.'

Langlade took a sip of the rosé he'd ordered with lunch and scowled. He was ten years older than Casson, tall and spare and extremely well-dressed, with iron-coloured hair going white over the ears, large features, dark complexion, and a mouth set in perpetual irony – life was probably not going to turn out all that well, so one had better learn to be amused by it. He raised an eyebrow as he said, 'You have a bicycle?'

'No.'

'We'll get to work on it. Immediately. Before all the world realizes it's the one thing they absolutely must have.'

'Not for me, Bernard.'

'Ah-hah, you see? That's just what I mean.'

Casson poked his fork at a bowl of noodles. It needed sauce, it needed something. 'All right, I'll ride a bicycle, I'll do what I have to do, which is what I've always done. But what worries me is, how am I going to earn a living? What can I do?'

'What's wrong with what you've always done?'

71

'Make films?'

'Yes.'

'What – *The Lost Rhine Maiden? Hitler Goes to Oxford?*'

'Now Jean-Claude . . .'

'I'm not going to collaborate.'

'Why would you? I'm not. I'm making lightbulbs. Your lights will burn out, you'll need replacements. But they won't be Nazi lightbulbs, will they?'

Casson hadn't thought of it quite that way.

'Look,' Langlade said, 'your barber – what's he going to do under the Occupation? He's going to cut hair. Is that collaboration?'

'No.'

'Well, then, what's the difference? The barbers will cut hair, the writers will write, and the producers will make films.'

Casson gave up on the noodles and put his fork down by the plate. 'I won't be able to make what I want,' he said.

'Oh shit, Jean-Claude, when did any of us ever do what we wanted?'

The waiter appeared with two plates of diced vegetables. Langlade rubbed his hands with pleasure. 'Now this is what I come here for.'

Casson stared at it. A carrot, a mushroom, a scallion, something, something else. As Langlade refilled their glasses he said, 'I'll tell you a secret. Whoever can discover a wine that goes with Chinese food will be very rich.'

They ate in silence. The Chinese waiter gave up on the racing form, and his newspaper rattled as he turned the page. 'What was it like here?' Casson said.

'In May and June? Terrible. At first, a great shock. You know, Jean-Claude, the Gallic genius for evasion – we will not think unpleasant thoughts. Well, that's fine, until the bill comes. What they believed here I don't know, perhaps it wouldn't matter if the Germans won. There were women to be made love to, bottles of wine to be opened, questions

72

of life and the universe to be discussed, *important* things. If we lost a war, well, too bad, but what would it matter? The politicians would change the colour of their ties, possibly one would have to learn a new sort of national anthem. After all, the shits that run the country are the shits that run the country – how bad could it be to have a new set?

'Ah but then. We sat here in Paris the second week in May, reading the departmental numbers on the licence plates. It started in the extreme north – one day the streets were full of 10s from the Aube. By midweek we had the 55s from the Meuse and, a day or two later, the 52s from the Haute-Marne. And no matter what the radio said, it began to dawn on us that something was moving south. And so on a Thursday, the first week in June, a great mob – can you guess?'

'Marched on the Elysée Palace.'

'Descended on the luggage department at the Galeries Lafayette.'

Casson shook his head, ate some of the diced vegetables, poured himself some more rosé. By the end of the second glass it wasn't too bad. 'Tell me, Bernard, in your opinion, how long is this going to go on?'

'Years.'

'Two years?'

'More like twenty.'

Casson was stunned. If that were true, life could not be suspended, left in limbo until the Germans went home. It would have to be lived, and one would have to decide how. 'Twenty years?' he said, as much to himself as Langlade.

'Who is going to defeat them? I mean really defeat them – throw them out. The answer hasn't changed since 1917 – the Americans. Look what happened here, a German army of five hundred thousand attacked a nation with armed forces of five and a half million and beat them in five days. Only the Americans can deal with that, Jean-

Claude. But you know, I don't see it happening. Even if Roosevelt decided tomorrow that America had to be involved, even if the senators saw any point in spilling Texas blood for some froggy with a waxed moustache, even *then*, it's years to build the tanks. And get them here – how? Flown by Babar? No, everything has changed, the rules are different. Your life is your country now, my friend. You are a citizen of the nation Jean-Claude, and you will have to learn to live on those terms or you will not survive.'

Langlade had shaken his fork at Casson as he was making his point, now he caught himself doing it and put it down on his plate. Cleared his throat. Took a sip of wine. The waiter turned another page of the newspaper. Casson looked up to see one corner of Langlade's mouth twist up in a sudden smile. '*Hitler Goes to Oxford* indeed!' he said under his breath, laughing to himself.

'And there he meets Laurel and Hardy,' Casson said. 'The college servants.'

It was not the first time he'd had to glue his life back together.

The banks had resumed operations in July, but there had been problems, confusion, and for some reason the cheques to the landlord for the office on the rue Marbeuf had not gone through. The landlord, a fat little creature, shoulders back, tummy sucked in, said 'Such difficult times, Monsieur Casson, how was one to know . . . anything? Perhaps now, life will become, ah, a little more *orderly*.'

He meant: you attempted to take advantage of war and Occupation by not paying your rent promptly, but I'm smarter than that, monsieur!

And he also meant: *Orderly*.

Which was to say, Pétain and everything he believed in – by September Casson had learned to recognize it from

74

the slightest inflection. France, the theory went, *deserved*
to be conquered by Germany because it was such a corrupt,
wicked nation, with a national character so degenerate
it had stormed the Bastille in 1789, a national character
deformed by alcohol, by promiscuity, by loss of the old
moral values.

He's right, Casson thought, one September evening, gently
improving the angle of a pair of legs in silk stockings. The
radio was playing dance music, then Pétain came on, from
Vichy. The usual phrases: 'We, Philippe Pétain,' and
'France, the country of which I am the incarnation.'
   'Ah, the old general,' she said.
   'Mmm,' Casson answered.
   They waited, idling, while Pétain spoke. Waiting was a
style just then – *it will all go away, eventually*.
   'You have warm hands,' she said.
   'Mmm.'
   Lazy and slow, just barely touching each other. Could
there be a better way, Casson wondered, to get through a
speech? When the dance music returned – *French* dance
music, plinky-plinky-plink, none of this depraved 'jazz,'
but upright, honest music, so *Maman* and *Papa* could take
a two-step around the parlour after dinner – he was almost
sorry.

He missed Gabriella. Once the padlock was removed he'd
found the note she'd left for him. It was dated 11 June –
the day after Italy had declared war on an already defeated
France. 'I cannot stay here now,' she'd written. Casson
remembered the barracks where he'd heard the news. The
soldiers were bitter, enraged – what cowardice! The Germans had brutal souls, they did what they did, but the
Italians were a Latin people, like them, and had rushed in
to attack a fallen neighbour.
   'I will miss you, I will miss everything,' Gabriella wrote.

75

She would always remember him, she would pray for his safety. Now she would go back to Milan. The Paris she had longed for, it was gone forever.

Otherwise there was nothing. Mounds of pointless mail, the rooms dusty and silent. Casson sat at his desk, opened files, read papers. What to do next?

Late September it began to rain, he met a girl called Albertine, the daughter of the concierge of a building on the rue Beethoven. On market day, Thursday in Passy, he'd stood at the vegetable cart, staring balefully at a mound of broad yellow beans – there was nothing else. A conversation started, he wondered what one did to prepare these things, she offered to show him.

The affair floated in the broad grey area between commerce and appetite. Albertine was not beautiful, quite the opposite. Some day, perhaps, she would glow with motherhood, but not now. At nineteen she was pinched and red, with hen-strangler's hands and the squint of an angry farmwife. That was, Casson thought, the root of the problem: there was a good deal of Norman peasant blood in the population of Paris and in big Albertine it ran true to type. She came to his apartment, revealed the mystery of the yellow beans – one boiled them, *voilà!* – took off her dress, sat on the edge of the bed, folded her arms, and glared at him.

The time with Albertine was late afternoon, usually Thursday. Then, before she went home, she would make them something to eat. In the old days his dinners had drifted down from heaven, like manna. Life was easy, attractive men were fed. There were dinner parties, or a woman to take to a restaurant, or he'd go to a bistro, Chez Louis or Mère Louise, where they knew him and made a fuss when he came in the door.

That was over. Now the Germans ate the chickens and the cream, and food was rationed for the French. The coupons Casson was issued would buy three and a half ounces of rice a month, seven ounces of margarine, eight ounces of pasta, and a pound of sugar. The sugar he divided – most to Albertine, the remainder for coffee. One had to take the ration stamps to the café in the morning.

So mostly it was vegetables – potatoes, onions, beets, cabbages. No butter, and only a little salt, but one survived. Of course there *was* butter, what the Germans didn't want – one sometimes saw a soldier eating a stick of it, like an ice-cream cone, while walking down the street – could be bought on the black market. He would give Albertine some money and she would return with cheese, or a piece of ham, or a small square of chocolate. He never asked for an accounting and she never offered. What she kept for herself she earned, he felt, by thrift and ingenuity.

The women he usually made love to were sophisticated, adept. Not Albertine. A virgin, she demanded to be taught 'all these things' and other than an occasional *What?!!* turned out to be an exceptionally diligent student. She had rough skin and smelled like laundry soap, but she held nothing back, gasped with pleasure, was irresistibly shame-less, and hugged him savagely so that he wouldn't drift up through the ceiling and out into the night. 'Only in war,' she said, 'does this happen between people like us.'

Casson went to the office but the phone didn't ring.

It didn't ring, and it didn't ring, and it didn't ring. The big studios were gone, there was no money, nobody knew what to do next. Weddings? The director Berthot claimed to have filmed three since July. Rich provincials, he claimed, that was the secret. Watch the engagement announcements in places like Lyons. The couple arrive separately. The nervous papa looks at his watch. The flowers are delivered. The priest, humble and serious, greets the grandmother. Then, the kiss. Then, the res-taurant. A toast!

Casson glued two papers together by licking the edges, then rolled the tobacco into a cigarette. Working carefully, he managed to get it lit with a single match. 'Can you make me one of those?' Berthot asked hungrily.

Casson, that devil-may-care man-about-town, did it. When it took two tries to light the ragged thing, Casson smiled bravely – matches were no problem for him. 'I had an uncle,' Berthot said, 'up in Caen. Wanted to turn me into a shoemaker when I was a kid.' He didn't have to go on, Casson understood, the shoemakers had plenty of work now.

The October rains sluiced down, there was no heat on the rue Marbeuf. He had enough in the bank to last through November's rent, then, that was that. What was what? Christ, he didn't know. Sit behind his desk and hold his breath until someone ran in shaking a fistful of money or he died of failure. He went to the movies in the afternoon, the German newsreels were ghastly. A London street on fire, the German narrator's voice arrogant and cocksure: 'Look at the destruction, the houses going up in flames! This is what happens to those who oppose Germany's might.' Going back out into the grey street in mid-afternoon, the Parisians were morose. The narrator of the newsreel had told the truth.

He answered an advertisement in *Le Matin*. 'Distribute copies of a daily bulletin to newsstands.' It was called *Aujourd'hui à Paris* and listed all the movies and plays and nightclubs and musical performances. The editor was a Russian out in Neuilly who called himself Bob. 'You'll need a bicycle,' he said. Casson said, 'It's not a problem,' remembering his conversation with Langlade. But he never went back – inevitably he would encounter people he knew, they would turn away, pretend they hadn't seen him.

Langlade. Of course that was always the answer, one's friends. He'd heard that Bruno and Marie-Claire were doing very well, that Bruno had in fact received delivery of the MGs left on the Antwerp docks, that he now supplied French and Italian cars to German officers serving in Paris. But something kept him from going to his friends – not least that they were the sort of friends who really wouldn't have any idea how to help him. They'd always looked up to him. They did the most conventional things: manufactured lightbulbs, imported cars, wrote contracts, bought costume jewellery, while he *made movies*. No, that just wouldn't work. They would offer him money – *how much?* they'd wonder. And, after it was gone, what then?

28 October, 1940

He'd brought his copy of *Bel Ami* to the rue Marbeuf as office reading – he'd always wanted to make a film of de Maupassant, everyone did. Then too, he simply had to accept the fact that one didn't find abandoned newspapers in the cafés until after three.

11:35. He could now leave the office, headed for a café he'd discovered back in the Eighth near the St-Augustin Métro, where they had decent coffee and particularly good bread. Where he could pretend – until noon but not a minute later – that he was taking a late *casse-croûte*, mid-morning snack, when in fact it was lunch. And the waiter was an old man who remembered *Night Run* and *The Devil's Bridge*. 'Ah, now those,' he'd say, 'were movies. Perhaps a little more of the bread, Monsieur Casson.'

Casson's hand was on the doorknob when the telephone rang.

He ran to the desk, then forced himself to wait for the end of the second ring before he picked it up and said 'Hello?' Not disturbed, exactly, simply unable to hide the fact that his concentration had been elsewhere, that he'd been busy – perhaps in a meeting, perhaps in mid-sentence as he reached back for the receiver.

'Jean Casson?'

'Yes.'

'Hugo Altmann.' The line hummed for a moment. 'Yes? Hello?'

'Altmann, well, of course.'

'Perhaps you don't – remember me.'

'No, no. I was just . . .'

'Tell me, Casson, can you possibly cancel your lunch today?'

'Well. Yes, I could. It's not anything I can't reschedule.'

'Perfect! You're still on the rue Marbeuf?'

'Yes. Twenty-six, just off the boulevard.'

'Save me parking, will you? And wait for me downstairs?'

'All right.'

'Good. Ten minutes, no more.'

'See you then.'

He ran into the bathroom down the hall and stared into the mirror above the sink. Shit! Well, not much he could do about it now – his shirt was tired, his jacket unpressed. But he'd shaved carefully that morning – he always did – his hair simply looked vaguely arty when he avoided the barber, and his shoes had been good long ago and still were. It was, he thought, his good fortune to be one of those men who couldn't look seedy if he tried.

Altmann he remembered well. He worked for Continental, the largest of the German production companies, with offices out by Paramount in Billancourt. A film executive, typical of the breed. The practical, plodding French of the long-term expatriate – nothing fancy but nothing really wrong. Smooth manners, smooth exterior, but not sly. He was, one felt, constitutionally neat, and courtly by upbringing. Well-dressed, favouring muted tweed suits and very good ties in rich colours. The kind of hair that faded from blonde to no colour at all in the mid-forties, combed back at the age of seven and still in place. Scandinavian complexion, blue eyes – like a frozen lake – and a smile. Always a second drink, always enthusiastic – even about the most godawful trash because you just never knew what people were going to like – always at work. Casson had been at several meetings with him out at Continental, a lunch or two a few years ago, it was all a little hazy.

A last look in the mirror; he ran his fingers through his hair, splashed water on his face, that was the best he could do. Glancing at his watch he hurried out of the bathroom and down the stairs.

Outside, the sun was just fighting its way out of the clouds. Omen? An exquisite Horch 853 swept to the kerb, Altmann waved from behind the wheel. Casson wasn't impressed by cars, but still . . . Silvery-green coachmaker's body, graceful lines, spare tyre – silvery-green metal centre – snugged into the curve of the running board just forward of the driver's door. Casson slid into the leather seat, they shook hands, said hello.

They sped up the rue Marbeuf, then out onto the Champs-Elysées. The Horch had twelve cylinders, five forward gears, and the voice of a sports car, muttering with suspended power every time the clutch was depressed. 'We'll go and eat somewhere in the country,' Altmann said. 'Some days I just can't stand the city, even Paris.'

Out through Neuilly in light traffic; a few military vehicles, a few bicycles, the occasional horse and cart. Next came Courbevoie; empty, winding streets. Then left, following the Seine: Malmaison, Bougival, Louveciennes. The little restaurants facing the water had been for painters and dancers, once upon a time, but the money had always followed the kings, west from Paris and along the river, and eventually the cooks followed the money – the lobsters came and the artists went.

'So,' Altmann said, 'are you doing anything special?'

'Not much. You're still with Continental?'

'Oh yes. Just the same as always. Everything changes, you know, except that it all stays the same.'

Casson laughed. Altmann took a pack of cigarettes out of his pocket, shook it adeptly so that several popped up, and held it across the seat. Casson took one, Altmann lit it, then his own, with a polished lighter.

'We're bigger now,' Altmann continued. 'There's that difference. A good deal bigger, in fact.' A town fell away and they were in the countryside. Corot, Pissarro, they'd all painted up here. Autumn valleys, soft light, white clouds that rolled down from Normandy and lit up the sky. The most beautiful place on earth, perhaps. It struck Casson in the heart, as it always did, and he opened the window to get the glass out of his way. The car drifted to a stop as Altmann prepared to turn. There were yellow leaves on the road, little swirls of them when the wind blew, Casson could hear them scratching along over the rumble of the engine.

They turned right, came back out on the river and headed west. Altmann drew on his cigarette, the exhaled smoke punctuated his words as he talked.

'I hope you're not waiting for me to discuss politics, Casson, because, lately, it's all too complicated for me.' There was a man carrying a basket on a wooden footbridge that crossed the river. He turned to look at the glorious car, shifting the weight of the basket on his shoulder. 'The things I've seen,' Altmann continued, 'in Germany *and* France, the last five years, I really don't know what to say about it.' He paused, then said, 'It didn't even occur to me that my phone call might offend you – but it does now, and if you like I'll turn around and take you back to Paris. It's just that I came back from Berlin and thanked God that Paris was as it always was, that nothing was burned or blown up, that I was going to be able to live here, on some kind of terms anyhow, and to make films. The truth is, you and I are lucky – we can simply get out of the world's way while it destroys itself, we don't have to be crushed by it. Or, maybe, I should turn around. It's up to you, I'll understand one way or the other.'

'It's too nice a day to go back to the city,' Casson said.

'There's bad blood between our countries, it's no good, but it doesn't have to be between us, does it?'

'No, no, not at all.'

Altmann nodded, relieved. On the left a cluster of houses, almost a village. Just on the other side, where the fields began, a restaurant, Le Relais. 'Why not?' Altmann said. The tyres crunched over the gravel by the entry as the Horch rolled to a stop.

Inside it was quiet and it smelled good. A few local people were having lunch, they glanced up as Casson and Altmann came in, then looked away. The *patron* seated them in the bay by the front window, looking out over the flowers in the windowbox. Casson studied the handwritten menu, but there wasn't much choice – basically the *plat* they'd cooked that day and a few substitutes, like an omelette that the kitchen could produce if you just had to have something else. So they ordered what there was – Altmann had a fistful of ration coupons – a platter of warm *langouste*, crayfish, not long out of the river, followed by an *andouille*, the Norman sausage the butchers made from the very bottom of the tub of leftovers, cooked in cider vinegar. All of it so good, in an off-hand way, that it made Casson lightheaded. For wine, what Le Relais offered was the colour of raspberry jam, dry as a bone and sharp as a tack, in litre bottles without label or cork; and when the first was gone a second appeared. All this accompanied by small talk – business was never discussed with food – until the coffee arrived. Then Altmann said, 'Let me lay the situation out for you as it stands today.'

'Good,' Casson said, taking yet another of Altmann's cigarettes.

'The major difference is, they're going to set up a committee called a *Filmprüfstelle*, Film Control Board, that will answer to Goebbels's people in the *Propagandastaffel* up in the Hotel Majestic. Now UFA-Continental is going to have to deal with them, I would not try to tell you otherwise, and they are who they are, enough said. On the other hand, *they* have to deal with *Continental*, and it's not at all clear who's the bigger dog in this yard. Our capitalization has increased to ten million reichsmarks – two hundred million francs. With the cost of making a film in France averaging out to about three and a half million francs, you can see what's going to happen. Certainly there will be quite a lot of waltzing – powdered boobs in ball gowns and all the rest of it, there's always that, but they can't have ten million reichsmarks' worth even if that's what they think they want. We've acquired thirty-nine movie theatres, and we have the laboratories and the processing – once you get to that stage there must be more than Old Vienna, and that's going to come from independent producers and directors. Do you see?'

Casson nodded. He saw. The thirty-nine theatres came in large part from the confiscation of property belonging to Siritsky and Haik, Jewish film exhibitors.

'So when I say,' Altmann continued, 'that the Nazis have to deal with Continental, I mean it. It's felt in Berlin that if French culture is destroyed then we've failed to resolve the difficulties between us. This is *not* Poland, this is one of the greatest cultures the world has ever produced – Hitler himself dares not claim otherwise.' He drank a sip of coffee, then another.

'Now look,' he said, voice lower. 'We're not sure ourselves exactly what they're going to let us do. Obviously a celebration of the French victory in 1918 won't work at the Control Board, but a hymn to Teutonic motherhood won't work at Continental. Between those extremes, if you and I are going to work together, is where we'll work.'

'I won't make Nazi propaganda,' Casson said.

'Don't. See if I care.' Altmann shrugged. 'Casson, you couldn't if you wanted to, all right? Only a certain breed of swine can do that – German swine or French swine. Perhaps you know that a German film, *The Jew Süss*, has broken box-office records for the year in Lyons, Toulouse, and, of course, Vichy.'

'I didn't know that.'

'It's true. But, thank God, Paris isn't Lyons or Toulouse.'

'No.'

'Well?'

'It's a lot to think about,' Casson said.

'You know Leveque?'

'Of course. *The Emissary*.'

'Raoul Mies?'

'Yes.'

'They've both signed to do projects – no details, but we're working on it.'

Casson looked out the window. The Seine was high in its banks, as it always was in autumn, and grey. It was going to rain, the weeds on the river bank bent over in the wind. *Life goes on*, he thought. 'I don't know,' he said quietly.

'Good,' Altmann said. 'An honest answer.' He leaned closer to Casson. 'I have to get up every morning and go to an office, like everybody else. And I don't want to work with every greasy little pimp who wants to be in movies. I want my day to be as good as it can – but I'm flesh and blood, Casson, just like you, and I'll do what I have to do. Just like you.'

Casson nodded. Now they'd both been honest. Altmann started to pour the last of the wine, then put the bottle down and signalled the *patron*. 'What do you have for us – something good.'

The patron thought a moment. 'Cognac de Champagne?'

'Yes,' Altmann said. 'Two, then two more.' He turned back to Casson. 'They'll pay,' he said. 'Believe me they will.'

Casson wasn't sure what he meant. Expensive Cognac? Expensive film? Both, very likely, he thought.

This one cried. Nothing dramatic, shining eyes and 'Perhaps you have a handkerchief.' He got her one, she leaned on an elbow and dabbed at her face. *Bon Dieu,* she said, more or less to herself.

He reached down and pulled the sheet and blanket up over them, it was cold in November with no heat. 'You're all right?'

'Oh yes.'

He rolled a cigarette from a tin where he kept loose tobacco and burnt shreds. They shared it, the red tip glowing in the darkness.

'Why did you cry?'

'I don't know. Stupid things. For a moment it was a long time ago, then it wasn't.'

'Not a girl anymore?'

She laughed. 'And worse.'

'You are lovely, of course.'

'La-la-la.'

'It's true.'

'It was. Maybe ten years ago. Now, well, the old saying goes "nothing's where it used to be."'

From Casson, a certain kind of laugh.

After a moment, she joined in. 'Well, not *that*.'

'You're married?'

'Oh yes.'

'In love?'

'Now and then.'

'Two kids?'

'Three.'

They were quiet for a moment, a siren went by somewhere in the neighbourhood. They waited to make sure it kept going.

'In the café,' she said, 'what did you see?'

'In you?'

'Yes.'

'Truth?'

'Yes.'

'I don't know. I was, attracted.'

'To what?'

'To what. Something, maybe it doesn't have a name. You know what goes on with you – deep eyes, and the nice legs. Right? Try to say more than that and you're chasing desire, and you won't catch it. "Oh, for me it's a big this and a little that, this high and that low, firm, soft, hello, good-bye." All true, only next week you see somebody you have to have and none of it is.'

'That's what attracted you?'

Casson laughed, his face warm. 'You came in to buy cigarettes, you glanced at me. Then you decided to have a coffee. You crossed your legs a certain way. I thought, I'll ask her to have a coffee with me.'

She didn't answer. Put the bottom of her foot on top of his.

'You like this, don't you?' he said softly.

'Yes,' she sighed, bittersweet, 'I do like it. I like it more than anything else in the world – I think about it all day long.'

That autumn the city seemed to right itself. Casson could feel it in the air, as though they had all looked in the mirror and told themselves: you have to go on with your life now. The song on the radio was from Johnny Hess. 'Ça revient,' he sang – it's all coming back. 'La vie recommence, et l'espoir commence à renaître.' Life starts again, and hope begins to be reborn.

Well, maybe that was true. Maybe that had better be

true. Casson went to lunch with an editor from Gallimard, they had a big list that autumn, people couldn't get enough to read. One way to escape, though not the only one. There were long queues at the theatres – for *We Are Not Married* at the Ambassadeurs, or the *Grande Revue* at the Folies-Bergère. The Comédie-Française was full every night, there was racing at Auteuil, gambling at the Casino de Paris, Mozart at Concert Mayol. *The Damnation of Faust* at the Opéra, *Carmen* at the Opéra-Comique.

'What are you looking for?' the Gallimard editor asked. 'Anything in particular?'

Casson talked about *Night Run* and *No Way Out*. What the rules were when the hero was a gangster. The editor nodded and said 'Mm,' around the stem of his pipe. Then his eyes lit up and he said, 'Isn't it you who made *Last Train to Athens*?'

That he loved. Well, Casson thought, at least something. 'Come to think of it,' the editor said, polishing his glasses with the Deux Magots' linen napkin, 'we may have just the right thing for you. Publication not scheduled until winter '42, but you certainly understand that that isn't far off.'

'Too well.'

'*The Stranger*, it's called.'

Casson nodded appreciatively. No problem putting that on a marquee.

'By a writer named Albert Camus, from Algiers. Do you know him?'

'I've heard the name.'

The editor talked about the plot and the setting, then went on to other things. Casson wrote the title on a scrap of paper. It wasn't what he'd made, more like what he'd always wanted to make, maybe would have made if the human-predicament stuff hadn't been thrown overboard during the hunt for money.

'Now I don't know if this is for you,' the editor said, 'but there's a writer named Simone de Beauvoir – she has the cultural programme on Radio Nationale – and she's working on a novel . . .'

Now he had the scent. The next day he spent at the Synops office, where synopses of ideas for films – from novels, short stories, treatments – were kept on file. It was busy; he saw Berthot, hunting eagerly through a stack of folders. 'How's the wedding business?' he asked. Berthot looked sheepish. 'I'm out of it,' he said quietly. 'For the moment.' What the hell, Casson thought. Was he the last one to catch on? The war was over, it was time to go back to business.

'Hello, Casson!' Now there was a voice that caught your attention – foreign, and, by way of compensation, much too hearty. Casson looked up to see Erno Simic, the Hungarian. Or, if you liked your gossip, the 'Hungarian.' A tall man, slightly stooped, a head too large for a pair of narrow shoulders, hooded eyes, a smile, meant to be ingratiating, that wasn't. A French citizen of complex Balkan origins – no matter how many times he told you the story you could never keep it straight. Simic ran a small distribution company called Agna Film, which operated in Hungary and Romania.

'Simic,' he said. 'All going well?'

'Today it is. Tell me please, Jean-Claude, we can eat together sometime soon?'

'Of course. Call me at the office?'

'I will, naturally. There is a Greek place, in the Tenth . . .'

Better every day, his world coming back to life.

Cold at night. None of that your side/my side diplomacy in the bed. Maybe he didn't know her name and maybe the name she told him was a lie and maybe he did the same thing, but three in the morning found them curled and twisted and twined together in the chill air, hugging like long-lost lovers, riding each other's bottoms through the night, arms wrapped around, hanging on to anything they could get hold of.

Cold at night, and cold in the daytime. They had everything rationed now – coal and bread and wine and cigarettes. Only work kept him from thinking about it. Somewhere out in the lawless borderlands of the 19th Arrondissement he found Fischfang, as always at the centre of incredibly complicated domestic arrangements. There were children, there were wives, there were apartments – mistresses, comrades, fugitives. Fischfang was never in one place for very long. Late one afternoon he sat with Casson in a tiny kitchen where a young woman was boiling nappies in a kettle. The coal stove smoked, mildew blackened the walls.

Casson explained that he was back in business, that he was looking for a project, and how the rules had changed.

Fischfang nodded. 'Not too much reality – is that it?'

'Yes. That's how it has to be.'

Fischfang stared out of the window, the sky grey with winter coming. 'Then what you might be able to do,' he said, 'is a Summer Night movie. You know what I mean – the perfect night of summer in the full moon. A certain group of people have gathered in a castle, a country house, a liner on the high seas. A night of love, *the* night of love. Just once, dreams come true. By the end, one couple has parted, but we see that, ah, Paul has always loved Marie, no matter how life has tried to drive them apart. The crickets chirp, the moon rises, the music of the night is sublime. Hurry – life will soon be over, time is short, we have only this night, we must live out our loveliest dream, and it's only a few hours until dawn.'

He wound down. They were both silent. At last Fischfang cleared his throat, lit a cigarette. 'Something like that,' he said. 'It might work.'

*　　*　　*

90

On the way back to his office, Casson saw a girl, maybe sixteen or so, wearing a school uniform, arms wrapped around her books. It was dusk. She looked directly into his eyes, an intimate look, as they moved towards each other on the crowded boulevard. 'Monsieur,' she said. Her voice was urgent, emotional.

He stopped. Yes? What? The usual Jean-Claude, the usual half-smile, whatever you want, I'm here. She thrust a folded paper into his hand, then was off down the street, disappearing into the shadows. He stepped into a doorway, unfolded the paper. It was a broadsheet, a one-page newspaper. *Résistance*, it was called. WE MUST FIGHT BACK, the headline said.

On 17 December, Jean Casson signed with Continental.

HOTEL DORADO

9 December, 1940

Jean Casson sat at his desk at four in the afternoon. He wore an overcoat, a muffler, and gloves. Outside, a winter dusk – thick, grey sky, the lines of the rooftops softened and faded. Looking out his window he could see a corner where the rue Marbeuf met the boulevard. People in dark coats on the stone-coloured pavement, like a black-and-white movie. Once upon a time they'd loved this hour in Paris; gold light spilling out on the cobbled streets, people laughing at nothing, whatever you meant to do in the gathering dark, you'd be doing it soon enough. On these boulevards night had never followed day – in between was *evening*, which began at the first fading of the light and went on as long as it could be made to last. *Sometimes until dawn*, he thought.

He went back to his book, *Neptune's Daughter*, turning the pages awkwardly with his glove, making notes in soft pencil. Work, *work*. The telephone rang, it was Marie-Claire, organizing a dinner. They were trying hard, his little group of friends, he was proud of them. Rolling the holiday boulder up a long and difficult slope – but at least working together. Christmas in France was not the ritual it was in England, but the New Year *réveillon* was important, and you were supposed to eat fine things and feel hopeful.

They talked for a time, the same conversation they'd had for years – they must, he thought, somehow or other like having it. And it ended as it always did, with another telephone call planned – a Marie-Claire crisis could not, by definition, be resolved with a single telephone call.

Neptune's Daughter. Veronica and Perry drinking sidecars in Capri and watching the sun set. 'Where do you suppose we'll be on this day next year?' Veronica asks. 'Will we be happy?' The telephone rang again. Marie-Claire, Casson thought, a forgotten detail. 'Yes?' he said.

'Hello? Is this Jean Casson?' An English voice, accenting the first syllable of Casson. A voice he knew.

'Yes. Who is this, please?'

'James Templeton.'

The investment banker from London. 'It, it's good to hear from you.' Casson's English worked at its own pace.

'How are you getting on, over there?' Templeton asked.

'Not so bad, thank you. The best that we can, you know, with the war . . .'

'Yes, well, we haven't forgotten you.'

Casson's thoughts were flying past. Why was this man calling him? Could it be that some incredibly complicated arrangement was going to allow British banks to invest in French films? There was a rumour that England and Germany continued to trade, despite the war, using middlemen in neutral nations. Or, maybe, a treaty had been signed, and this was a protocol sprung suddenly to life. Maybe, he thought, his heart quickening, the fucking war is over! 'Thank you,' he managed to say. 'What, uh . . .'

'Tell me, do you happen to see much of Erno Simic? The Agna Film man?'

'What? I'm sorry, you said?'

'Simic. Has distribution arrangements in Hungary, I believe. Do you see him, ever?'

'Well, yes. I mean, I have seen him.'

'He can be extremely helpful, you know.'

'Yes?'

'Definitely. Certain business we're doing now, he is somebody we are going to depend on. And since you're a friend of ours in Paris, we thought you might be willing to lend a hand.'

'Pardon?'

'Sorry. To help, I mean.'

'Oh. Yes, I see. All right. I'll do what I can.'

'Good. We *are* grateful. And we'll be in touch. Good-bye, Casson.'

'Good-bye.'

He knew. And he didn't know. He could decide, at that point, that he didn't know. He fretted, waiting until six to walk over to Langlade's office. 'Jean-Claude!' Langlade said. 'Come and have a little something.' From a bottom drawer he produced an old wine bottle refilled with calvados. 'We went to see the Rouen side of the family on Sunday,' Langlade explained. 'So you'll share in the bounty.'

Casson relaxed, sat back in his chair, the calvados was like soothing fire as it went down.

'This is hard-won, I hope you appreciate it,' Langlade continued. 'It took an afternoon of sitting on a couch and listening to a clock tick.'

'Better than what you get in a store,' Casson said.

Langlade refilled the glass. 'My good news,' he said, 'is that suddenly we're busy. Some factory in Berlin ordered these tiny little light-bulbs, custom-made, grosses of them. God only knows what they're for, but, frankly, who cares?' He gave Casson a certain look – it meant he'd been closer to disaster than he'd been willing to let on. 'And you, Jean-Claude? Everything all right?'

'A very strange thing, Bernard. Somebody just telephoned me from London.'

'What?'

'A call, from a banker in London.'

Langlade thought hard for a moment, then shook his head. 'No, no, Jean-Claude. That's not possible.'

'It happened. Just now.'

'They've cut the lines. There isn't any way that some-body could call you from London.'

'You're certain?'

'Yes. Who did you say?'

'An English banker.'

'Not from London, *mon ami*. What did he want?'

'He wasn't direct, but he suggested that I do business with a certain distribution company.'

Langlade stared at the ceiling for a while. When he spoke again, his tone of voice was subtly altered. 'He called from France.' Then, 'What are you going to do?'

'I don't know,' Casson said. 'He's in France, you think?'

'Possibly Spain, or Switzerland, but definitely on the Continent – because the lines under the Channel were cut last June.'

'Well,' Casson said.

'You better think it over,' Langlade said.

Someone knocked discreetly on the office door. Lang-lade, it seemed to Casson, was not sorry to be interrupted.

The apartment was across a courtyard from a dress factory, through a cloudy window Casson could see women work-ing at sewing machines. Fischfang sat at a table in the tiny kitchen, wearing an old sweater, and a blanket around his shoulders. He'd shaved his beard and moustache, the skin looked pale and tender, and his eyes were red, as though he hadn't slept the night before. Outside, a few snowflakes drifted past the window.

'Do you need anything?' Casson asked.

Fischfang shrugged – everything, nothing. The apart-ment belonged to his aunt. When she'd opened the door, Fischfang had taken a moment to make sure it was Casson, then used an index finger to close a drawer in the kitchen table. But not before Casson had caught sight of a revolver.

Casson sat at the table, the aunt served them some

strange drink – not exactly tea – but at least it was hot. Casson held the cup with both hands to keep warm. 'Louis,' he said, 'why do you have a gun? Who's coming through the door?'

Fischfang looked out the window, a muscle in his jaw ticked. Casson had never seen him like this. Angry, of course, but that was nothing new. A communist, he lived on injustice, a vitamin crucial to daily life, and he was always fuming about what X said or Y wrote. But now, something else. This was nothing to do with Marxist fury. Fischfang was scared, and bitter.

'I have been denounced,' he said, as though the words were strange to him.

Casson's face showed sympathy, but in his heart he wasn't surprised. The kind of life Fischfang lived, seething with politics – the Association of Revolutionary Artists and Writers, *left deviation, rotten liberalism*, Stalinists, Trotskyites, Spartacists, and God only knew what else. Denunciation must have been a daily, perhaps hourly, event.

'Maybe you remember,' Fischfang went on, 'that last August the Germans demanded that all Jews register.'

'I remember,' Casson said.

'I didn't.'

Casson nodded once – of course not.

'Someone found that out, I don't know who it was. They turned me in. For money, perhaps. Or some advantage. I don't know.'

The aunt closed a bureau drawer in the other room. From across the courtyard Casson could hear the clatter of sewing machines. The women were hunched over their work, their hands moving quickly. 'Now I understand,' he said. 'You're certain?'

'No, not completely. But things have happened.'

Casson took a breath. 'So then, we'll have to get you away somewhere.'

Fischfang stared at him for a moment. Will you really?

99

When the time comes? Then he looked down, squared a tablet of lined paper on the table in front of him, laughed a little. 'Life goes on,' he said, in a tone that meant he didn't particularly care if it did or not. Then he passed the tablet across to Casson. 'Have a look,' he said.

Spidery writing in blue ink, floating from margin to margin. *Hotel Dorado* it said on top. A sort of miracle, Casson thought, the way these things started from nothing. Just a few words on a piece of paper. For an instant he could smell movie theatre – figures flickering on the screen, the pitch of the voices, the sound of the projector when there was a pause in the dialogue. He pictured the title. On the marquee of the Graumont, just off the place de l'Opéra. He didn't know why there, it was just the theatre he always imagined.

He read on. A little village in the south of France, on the Mediterranean. A fishing village, where a few Parisians come every August to stay at the Hotel Dorado. Autumn, the season over, the hotel deserted. The owners, an old couple, about to retire. The hotel has been sold to a large combine, they're going to tear it down and build a new one, modern and expensive. The couple decides to write to their oldest, most faithful clients. 'The hotel is going out of business, but come and stay with us the last weekend in October, we'll have a glass of wine, a few memories.'

Casson looked up. 'All in one weekend?'

'Yes.'

'That's good.'

'A night when they arrive. A day when we meet them, a long night when everything happens, then a little scene where they get on the train to go back to Paris – except for the ones who are going to run off together and start a new life.'

Casson went back to reading. The characters you'd want – the *Corps Humain*, the human repertory company – were all there. The banker, the confidence man, the actress, the

100

postal clerk and his wife who scrimp and save all year so they can pretend to be upper class for two weeks, the lovers – their spouses left in Paris – the widow, the couple about to separate, giving it one last chance.

'Who's the star, Louis?'

'I thought – one of those ideas that's either a love letter from the gods or a little patch of quicksand meant just for you – it should be a young woman. Lonely, mysterious. Who misses her train and comes there by accident. Not a member of the sentimental company but, finally, its heart. Or, I don't know, maybe that's overdoing it.'

Casson waved him off. 'No, that's what I like about this kind of movie, you can't really overdo it.'

'Who would you want to star?'

Casson watched the falling snow for a time. 'Last May, a hundred years ago if you know what I mean, I had lunch with old Perlemère, who used to represent Citrine, and her name came up in the conversation.'

Fischfang's eyes sparkled. 'That's good. More than one way, if you think about it.'

'Beautiful – not pretty. Mysterious. No virgin. She's been to the wars, she's battle-scarred, but maybe she can try one last time, maybe she can love again, but we don't know until the final scene. It should be – will life let her?'

'A character trying to come back,' Fischfang said. 'Played by an actress trying to come back.'

Casson nodded. 'Something like that.'

They both smiled. Maybe it would work, maybe it wouldn't, like everything else. But they were trying, at least. They could see their breath when they talked in the cold kitchen, outside the snow drifted past. 'I'll get it typed up,' Casson said.

Hugo Altmann tilted his chair back and blew a long, slow, meditative plume of smoke at the ceiling of his office. 'Citrine, Citrine,' he said. 'Do you know, Casson, that she always seemed to me the most elementally *French* actress. The sort of woman, in bed she gives everything. Yet there is something inside her, a bitterness, a knowledge of the world, that spoils it all – you get everything, but it isn't what you wanted.' He paused a moment. 'You've worked with her before?'

'*Night Run.*'

'Ach, of course. And to direct?'

'Don't really know yet.'

'Well, let's find you some development money, and get a screenplay on paper. Who do you have in mind there? Cocteau's working, lots of others.'

'Louis Moreau, perhaps.'

'Who?'

'Moreau.'

'Never heard of him.'

'He's new.'

'Hm. Well, all right, give him a try.' He leaned over towards Casson, his expression shrewd and confidential. 'So, between us, who saves the hotel at the end, eh? I'm betting on the confidence man,' he said with a wink.

It took two weeks to find Citrine. He trudged across the city, office to office, the world of small-time talent agents, booking agents, press agents – everybody knew somebody. Perlemère helped, offering the names of a few friends. In the end, it turned out that she was performing at a cabaret amid the working-class dance halls on the rue de Lappe, out by Bastille. Le Perroquet, the parrot, it was called. Casson pulled his coat tight around him and kept his eyes down – this was not his district, he didn't belong here, and he didn't want a punch in the nose to remind him of it.

Closed, the first time he went. No reason, just closed. The blue neon parrot on a red branch was dark. The next time he tried was on Christmas Eve, and it was open. There was a poster by the door, the name *Loulou* across the bottom. Citrine – though it took him a moment to recognize her – Citrine on a high stool. Top hat, net fabric with rhinestones on top, bare legs crossed down below, spike heels with satin bows, a cabaret smile. *Well, what about you, big boy?*

A Christmas Eve blizzard. The white flakes swirled and hissed and made drifts in the doorways. Now and then a car came sliding down the street, tyres spinning, engine whining as it worked its way around a corner. The blue-painted glass on the street lamps cast Hollywood moonlight on the snow.

Hot inside, steamy, and packed. He tried the stage door, but a doorman dressed like an apache – black sweater and beret and cigarette dangling from the corner of the mouth – ran him off. 'You'll pay. Like the rest of the world, *conard*.'

He paid. To join a hundred German officers jammed together in a small room, reeking of shaving lotion and stale sweat and spilled wine and all the rest of it. There was a master of ceremonies in a dinner jacket, sweating and telling jokes, then zebras, naked girls in zebra masks, bucking and prancing, hoisting their knees up to their foreheads and singing 'Paris smells so sweet.' Saluting British style – whistles from the crowd – then turning around and grabbing their ankles – roars of approval. A fat major next to Casson almost died of pleasure, laughed as tears ran down his cheeks, gave Casson a best-pal whack between the shoulder blades that sent him flying into the crowd.

Then the room went dark, the curtain creaked open, a violet spotlight popped on, and there was Loulou. By then he'd worked his way to a position near the stage where he knew she would be able to see him, and, after the second number, she did. He could tell. At first, *Jesus it's Casson, what's he doing here?* Then the corner of her mouth lifted, not much, but a little: he was there to see her, it was no accident.

But he wasn't going to see her anytime soon. A table of

103

colonels, prominent in the front of the room, demanded the presence of the beautiful Loulou and she was produced, guided to the table by the owner of the Perroquet, an eel in a checked suit. They were merry colonels, they touched her shoulder and told her jokes and tried to speak French and gave her champagne and had quite a time for themselves. Question was, would Hansi be the one to fuck her, or was she going to favour Willi? The battle raged, the competing armies surged back and forth as Casson looked at his watch and realized that the last Métro of the night had left Bastille station.

Finally the owner came around, bowed and scraped and tried to get his *chanteuse* back. Hansi and Willi were in no mood for that, but the owner had a trick up his checked sleeve and sent a phalanx of zebras into action. They arrived neighing and whinnying, sat on the colonels' laps and wiggled about, tickled their chins, stole their eyeglasses and fogged them with their breath.

The colonels roared and turned red. Champagne was poured into glasses and everywhere else – to the colonels it seemed that champagne had found its way to places where champagne had never been before. One ingenious soul filled his mouth until his eyes bulged, then punched his cheeks with his index fingers – *pfoo!* – showering Hansi and Willi, assorted zebras, and Loulou, who wiped her face with her hand as she made her escape and climbed up on the tiny stage.

Most actresses could carry a tune if they had to and Citrine was no different. She simply played the role of a cabaret singer, and she was good at it. The throaty voice, hoarse from cigarettes and drinks in lonely cafés. *I always knew you'd leave me, that I'd be alone.* You could see her man, the little cockerel with a strut. *And there you were, with her, at the table where we used to sit.* Of course there was a kid, in military school somewhere. *Oh well, perhaps once more, for old times' sake.* The eyes, slowly cast down, a few notes from the battered old piano, the spotlight dimming out. Ahh, Paris.

She sent the doorman in the black sweater to get him and they hurried away down an alley, indignant German shouts – 'Loulou! Loulou!' – growing faint as they turned a corner. Which left them in the middle of a blizzard on the wrong end of Paris and no Métro with the curfew hour, one in the morning, long gone.

'We'll walk,' she said with determination. 'It will keep the blood moving. And something will occur.'

'Walk where?'

'Well, Jean-Claude, I stay at a sort of a not-so-good hotel these days – and even not-so-good as it is, they close it down like the Forbidden City after one-thirty. It usually works to sleep on a couch at the club, but not tonight, I think.'

'No.'

'So, we walk.'

'Passy . . .'

She took his arm with both of hers, her shoulder firmly against him, and they walked through the blizzard. He was happy to be held this way, he really didn't care if they froze to death; a set of fine ice statues, one with a smile. *Citrine, Citrine*, he thought. She wore a long black coat and a black beret and a long wool scarf wound around her neck.

'I want you to be in a movie,' he said.

'Tell me about it.'

'You will star.'

'Ah.'

'You'll be in most of the scenes. It's about an old hotel in a little village, somewhere in the Midi. It's been sold, and people come down from Paris one last time, and you wander in from, ah, from the land of the lost strangers.'

'Ah yes, I know this place, I have lived there. We are forever wandering into movies.'

He laughed, she held his arm tight. Somewhere out in the swirling snow, a car, the engine getting louder. They rushed into the first doorway. Lights cut the dark street – police on the prowl. 'Pretend to kiss me,' she said.

They embraced, star-crossed lovers in a doorway. The car – French, German, whoever it was – passed them by. Casson's heart was hammering, it was all he could do not to press his hand against his chest. And nothing to do with the police. *My God, I am fourteen*, he thought. When the car was gone they walked in silence, heads down against the wind.

She'd come to Paris from Marseilles at sixteen – it would have been running away if anybody had wanted her to stay there. Her mother had kept a boardinghouse for merchant seamen, mostly Turks and Greeks, and, the way Citrine put it, 'one of them was probably my father.' Thus her skin was pale, with a shadow beneath it, she had hair the colour of brown olives – worn long – with glints of gold in it, almond-shaped eyes, and to him she'd always smelled like spice – *Byzantine*, whatever that meant. It meant his fantasy side ascendant, he knew, but he thought about her that way anyhow. Across a room she was tall and slim, distant, just the edge of cold. And she was in fact so exotic, striking – a wide, heavy-lipped mouth below sharp cheekbones, like a catwalk model – that she looked lean, and hard. But the first time he'd put his arms around her, he had understood that it wasn't that way; not outside, not inside.

In the course of the love affair she had only once told secrets about her past, about the boardinghouse where she'd grown up. 'How much they loved and respected my mother,' she'd said. 'They waited with me until I was fourteen, and then there were only two of them, and they made sure I enjoyed it.'

'Did they beat you?'

'Beat me? No, not really.'

106

That was all. They were on a train, she turned away and looked out the window. She had said what she wanted to: *yes, I knew too much too young, you'll have to go on from there.*

He had tried – he thought he'd tried, he remembered it that way. She had, too. But they drifted. A day came, and whatever had been there before wasn't there anymore. Another Parisian love affair ended, nobody could really explain it, and nobody tried.

They angled away from the river, into the 7th Arrondissement, towards Passy, hurrying across the Pont de Solférino, where white snow spun over the black river and the wind sang in the arches of the bridge. 'Jean-Claude?' she said, and he stopped.

She looked up at him, there were white crystals of ice in her eyelashes, frozen tears at the corners of her eyes, and she was shivering. 'I think I need to rest for a moment,' she said.

They found a little shelter, in the shallow portal of an ancient building. She burrowed against his chest. 'How can there be nothing?' she said plaintively. She was right, the streets were deserted, no bicycle cabs, no people.

'We're halfway,' he said.

'Only that?'

'A little more, maybe.'

'Jean-Claude, can I ask you a question?'

'Of course.'

'Is there really a movie? Or is it, you know.'

'A movie. *Hotel Dorado*, we're calling it. For Continental, maybe. Of course like always, it's pure air until the great hand from the sky comes down and writes a cheque.'

'I wondered. Sometimes, I think, men want to run their lives backward.'

'Not women?'

'No.'

Not women? Not ever? It was warm where he held her

against him. Slowly he unwound the long scarf, ran it under her chin and around so that her ears were covered.

'Thank you,' she said. 'That's better.'

'Shall we start out again? Sooner we do . . .'

'Listen!' she whispered.

A car? She canted her head, held the scarf away from one ear. He could hear only the hiss of falling snow, but then, faintly, a violin. And then a cello. He looked up the side of the building, then across the street. But the snow made it hard to locate.

'A trio,' she said.

'Yes.'

He looked at his watch. *Oh, France!* 3:25 on the morning of Christmas, in an occupied city, three friends determine to stay up all night and play Beethoven trios – in a cold, dark apartment. She looked up at him, mouth set hard as though she refused to cry.

Rue de Grenelle, rue Vaneau, tempting to take Invalides, but better to swing wide of the Ecole Militaire complex. Military and security offices had been there before and they would still be in operation, with new tenants. Plenty of Gestapo and French police in the neighbourhood. So, find Grenelle again, and take the next small street, less important, in the same direction.

They never heard the car until they were almost on top of it, then they hugged a wall and froze. It was a Citroën Traction Avant, always a Gestapo car because the front-wheel drive worked on nights like these, with chains on the tyres. It was idling – perfectly tuned, it hardly made a sound – the hot exhaust melting the snow behind the rear wheel. Through the back window they could see the silhouette of a man in the passenger seat. The driver had left the car and was standing in front of an apartment building, urinating on the front door.

Casson held his breath. The Germans were only fifty feet

from them. The driver had left the Citroën's door ajar, and the passenger leaned over and called out to him. The driver laughed, said something back. Banter, apparently. Taking a piss in a snowstorm, that was funny. Doing it on some Frenchman's door, that was even funnier. Jokes, back and forth, guttural, thick, incomprehensible. To Casson, it sounded as though somebody was grinding language into broken words that could never be used again. But, he thought, they are in Paris, we are not in Berlin.

The man at the doorway started buttoning up his fly, then, as he hurried towards the car, he said the words 'rue de Vaugirard' – an island of French in the German sentence. So, Casson thought, they were going to the rue de Vaugirard, to arrest somebody on Christmas Eve. Citrine's hand found his, she'd heard it too.

Suddenly the car moved – *backward*. Casson pressed frantically against the wall, Citrine's hand closed like a steel claw. Then the wheels spun, caught, and the car drove off down the street. The Germans hadn't known they were there, they were just making sure they didn't get stuck in the snow.

An hour later, the apartment on the rue Chardin. There was no heat, and Casson preferred not to turn on the lights, often faintly visible at the edges of the blackout curtains. They shed their outer clothes in the bathroom, hanging them over the bar that held the shower curtain so they could drip into the tub as the snow and ice melted.

'Bed is the only place,' he said. He was right, they were both trembling with the cold, and they climbed into bed wearing their underwear.

At first the sheets were as cold as they were, then the body heat began to work. She took a deep breath and sighed, coming gently apart as the night's adventure receded.

'Are you going to sleep?' he said.

'Whether I want to or not.' Her voice was faint, she was barely conscious.

'Oh. All right.'

She smiled. 'Jean-Claude, Jean-Claude.'

'What?'

'Nothing. Go to sleep.'

He couldn't – he ached for her.

She sensed what he was going to do, moved close in a way that made it impossible. 'I can't, Jean-Claude. I can't. Please.'

Why?

As though she'd heard: 'You're going to think a dozen things, but it's that I can't feel that way again, not now. If we were just going to amuse ourselves, well, why not? But it isn't that way with us, you get *inside* me, that's no play on words, I mean to say it. Do you understand?'

'Yes.'

'If it wasn't a war, if I had money. If I just had it in me, the strength to live . . .'

'You're right, I'm sorry. It's just me, Citrine.'

'I know. I know you – you fuck all the girls.' But the way she said it was not unkind.

And even before the sentence ended, she was slipping away. Her breathing changed, and she fell asleep. He watched her for a time. Strange, the way her face worked, she always looked worried when she slept. Sometimes her breathing stopped, for a long moment, then it would start again. *She dies*, he'd thought years ago. *She dies, then she changes her mind.*

They woke up in the middle of Christmas Day. The snow had stopped. She wrote the name of a hotel on a scrap of paper, kissed him on the forehead, said 'Thank you, Jean-Claude,' and went out into the cold.

He left the office at six-thirty. He had a little money now, from Altmann, and a secretary. A cousin of his named Mireille, from the Morvan, his mother's side of the family. She was a dark, unhappy woman with three children and an eternally useless husband. She showed up just about the time the money did, so he hired her – it was simply life's way, he figured, of telling you what you ought to do.

The coldest winter of the century. The price of coal climbed into the sky, the old and the poor got into bed with every scrap of wool they owned and there they found them a week later. German soldiers flooded into Paris, from garrison duty in Warsaw and Prague, and Paris entertained them. Are you tense, poor thing? Have a little of this, and a little of that. England wouldn't give up. The submarine blockade was starving them, but they had never been reasonable, and they apparently weren't going to be now. Well, the French would also survive. More or less.

Out on the street, Casson pulled his coat tight around him and turned towards the Métro station at avenue Marceau. Two stops, Iéna and Trocadéro, and he could walk the rest of the way. The Passy station was closer to the rue Chardin, but that involved a *correspondance*, a change of lines, so if he stayed on the Line 9 train he'd be home in a few minutes. Albertine, tonight. His big, ugly treasure of a farm girl. Something good to eat. Vegetables, cow food – but garlic, salt, a drop of oil, and the cunning way she chopped it all up. Jesus! Was it possible that he'd reached that ghastly moment in life when the belly was more important than the prick? No! Never that! Why, he'd take that Albertine and spread her . . .

'Hey, Casson.'

That voice. He turned, annoyed. Erno Simic, waving his arm and smiling like a well-loathed schoolmate, was trotting to catch up with him. 'Wait for me!'

'Simic, hello.'

'I never called – you're angry?'

'No. Not at all.'

'Well, I been busy. Imagine that. Me. I got phone calls and messages, meetings and telegrams. Hey, now we know the world is upside down. Still it means a few francs, a few *balles*, as they say, eh? So we'll have a drink, on me. I promised a lunch, I'm gonna owe it to you, but now it's a drink. Okay?'

Paris hadn't surprised Casson for twenty years but it did now. Simic took him down the Champs-Elysées to avenue Montaigne, one of the most prestigious streets in the city, then turned right towards the river. They worked their way through a busy crowd in front of the Plaza-Athénée, mostly German officers and their plump wives, then walked another block to a residential building. On the top floor a grand apartment with a view to the river had been converted to a very private bar.

Seated at a white piano, an aristocratic woman wearing a black cocktail dress and a pillbox hat with a veil was playing 'Begin the Beguine.' Simic and Casson were shown to a table by a fat man in a sharkskin suit draped to hide both him and some sort of weapon. The tables on the teak parquet were set far apart, while the walls were covered with naughty oil paintings of naughty, and exceptionally pink, women. The room was crowded; a beautiful woman at the next table drinking tea, on second glance perhaps a prostitute of the most elevated class. By the window, two French colonels of cavalry. Then a table of dark, moustached men, Armenian or Lebanese, Casson thought. There was a famous ballet master – Russian émigré – sitting alone. In the corner, three men who could have been gangsters or black-market butchers, or both. Simic enjoyed Casson's amazement, his big smile broadening from ingratiating to triumphant.

'Hah! It's discreet enough for you, Casson?'

'How long – ?'

Simic spread his hands. 'Summer, as soon as everything settled down. It belongs to Craveur, right?'

Craveur was a famous restaurant owner, his family had been in the business since 1790, when the first restaurants were opened. Simic signalled to a waiter, a plate of petits fours *salés* – herring paste, oysters, or smoked salmon on puff pastry – appeared along with two large whisky-and-sodas.

'It's what I always have,' Simic confided. 'Mm, take all you want,' he said, mouth full.

Casson sipped the whisky-and-soda, lit up one of Simic's Camel cigarettes, and sat back on a little gold chair with a gold cushion.

'Your name came up in a conversation I had,' Simic said. 'With a man called Templeton. You know him, right? Works in a bank?'

'Yes.'

'He vouches for you.'

'He does?'

'Yes. And that's important. Because, Casson, I've still got Agna Film, but now I'm also a British spy.'

'Oh?'

'That's how it is. You're surprised?'

'Maybe a little.' Casson ate an oyster petit four.

'I'm a Hungarian, Casson. Not exactly by birth, you understand, but by nationality at birth. Still, *Mitteleuropa*, central Europe, is the world I understand, just like Adolf – so I see clearly certain things. Some people say that Adolf is a devil, but he's not, he's the head of a central European political party, no more, no less. And what he means to do in France is to destroy you, to ruin your soul, to make you despise yourselves, that's the plan. He wants you to collaborate, he makes it easy for you. He wants you to denounce each other, he makes it easy for you. He wants you to feel that there's no nation, just you, and everybody

113

has to look out for themselves. You think I'm wrong? Look at the Poles. He kills them, because they come from the same part of the world that he does, and they see through his tricks. You understand?'

Casson nodded.

'So we've got to stop that – or else. Right? Myself, I'm betting on the English, and I am going to work with them, and I want you to work with me, to help me do what I have to do.'

'Why me?'

'Why you. You're known to the English – James Templeton has spoken for you, he knows you don't have sympathy with the Germans. It also helps that you're a film producer. You can go anywhere, you can meet anybody, of any class. You handle money, sometimes in large amounts, sometimes in cash. You might take ten people on a train. You might charter a freighter. You might use several telephone numbers, bank accounts – even in other countries. For us, it's a good profession. Do you see?'

'Yes.'

'Want to help?'

Casson thought a moment, he didn't really know what to say. He did want to help. Left to himself he would never have done anything, just gone on trying to live his life as best he could. But he hadn't been left to himself, so, now, he had to decide if he wanted to become involved in something like this.

Yes, he said to himself. But it was what they called *un petit oui* – a little yes. Not that he was afraid of the Germans – he was afraid of them, but that wouldn't stop him – he was afraid of not being any good at it.

'I will help you, if I can,' he said slowly. 'I don't know exactly what it is you want me to do, and I don't know if I'd do it right. Maybe for myself that wouldn't matter, but there would be people depending on me, isn't that true in something like this?'

114

A backhand sweep of the arm, Simic knocked the uncertainty across the room. 'Ach – don't worry! The Germans are idiots. Not in Germany, mind you – there you can't spit on the street, because they got everybody watching their neighbour. But here? What they got is a counter-espionage service, which is lawyers, that's who they hire. But not the Jewish lawyers, they're all gone. And not the top lawyers, they're high up, or they're hiding. Found themselves a little something in this bureau or that office – hiding. So, you don't have to worry. Of course, you can't be *stupid*, but we wouldn't be talking if you were. And, oh yes, you'll make some money in this. We can't have you poor. And you'll get all the ration coupons you need, the British print them in Tottenham.'

'Where?'

'A place in London. But they're very good, never a problem. Suits, food, petrol, whatever you want.'

In a dark corner, the piano player was hard at work: 'Mood Indigo,' 'Body and Soul,' 'Time on My Hands.' Cocktail hour in Paris – heavy drapes drawn over the windows so the world outside didn't exist. The bar filled up, the hum of conversation getting louder as the drinks arrived. The expensive whore at the next table was joined by a well-dressed man, Casson had seen him around Passy for years, who wore the gold seal ring that meant nobility. He was just out of the barber's chair, Casson could smell the talcum powder. The woman was stunning, in a grey Chanel suit.

The waiter brought two more whisky-and-sodas. 'Chin-chin,' Simic said and clinked Casson's glass.

'Tell me what,' Casson said, '*exactly* what, it is that you want me to do.'

Simic looked serious, the big head on the narrow shoulders nodding up and down. 'A proper question, Casson. It's just, I have to be cautious.'

Casson waited.

'Well, to those who know, the place that matters most in this war is Gibraltar. Sits there, controls the entrance to the Mediterranean, means that the British can go into North Africa if they want, then up to Sicily, or Greece. Or Syria. That means Iraqi and Persian oil – you can't fight without that – and the Suez Canal. Can Adolf take Gibraltar? No. Why not? Because he'd have to march across Spain, and for that he needs Franco's permission because Franco is his ally. A neutral ally, but an ally. Don't forget, Adolf helped Franco win his civil war. So, what will Franco do?'

'I don't know,' Casson said.

'You're right! The British don't know either. But what you want, for your peace of mind, is your own man guarding the back door to your big fortress, not the ally of your enemy. Understand?'

'Yes.'

'So, what I'm working on.' Simic lowered his voice, leaned closer to Casson. 'What I'm working on is a nice private Spaniard for the British secret service. A general. An important general, respected. What could he do? What couldn't he do! He could form a guerrilla force to fight against Franco. Or, better, he could assassinate Franco. Then form a military junta and restore the monarchy. Prince Don Juan, pretender to the Spanish throne, who is tonight living in exile in Switzerland, could be returned to Catalonia and proclaimed king. See, Franco took the country back to 1750, but there's plenty of Spaniards who want it to go back to 1250. So the junta would abolish the Falangist party, declare amnesty for the five hundred thousand loyalist fighters in prison in Spain, then declare that Spain's strict neutrality would be maintained for the course of the war. And no German march to Gibraltar.'

Slowly, Casson sorted that out. It had nothing to do with the way he thought about things, and one of the ideas that crossed his mind was a sort of amazement that somewhere there were people who considered the world from this point of view. They had to be on the coldhearted side to think such things, very close to evil – a brand-new war in Spain, fresh piles of corpses, how nice. But, on the other hand, he had been reduced to crawling around like an insect hunting for crumbs in the city of his birth. It was the same sort of people behind that – who else?

The man and the woman at the next table laughed. She began it, he joined in, one of them had said something truly amusing – the laugh was genuine. *You think you know how the world works*, Casson thought, *but you really don't. These people are the ones who know how it works.*

Several times, over the next few days, he put one hand on the telephone while the other held his address book open at the S–T page. *Sartain Frères. Ingrid Solvang. Simic, Erno – Agna Film.* Not a complicated situation, he told himself. Very commonplace. Sometimes we believe we can make a certain commitment but then we find that, after all, we can't. So then, a courteous telephone call: sorry, must decline. *It's just the way things are right now.* Or, maybe, *It's just not something I can do.* Or, *It's just* – in fact, who the hell was Erno Simic that he deserved any kind of explanation at all? So, really, it was Casson explaining to himself.

Out on the boulevard, from the building they'd requisitioned in the first month of the Occupation, the young fascists of the *Garde Française* and the *Jeune Front* goosestepped on the packed snow. Across the street, the optician Lissac displayed a sign that said WE ARE LISSAC, NOT ISAAC. A few doors down, broken windows, where an umbrella-and-glove shop had been forced to advertise itself as an *Entreprise Juive*.

Would murdering Franco stop that?

His heart told him no.

Then do it for France.

Where?

France — was that Pétain? The *Jeune Front*? Those pinched, white, angry little faces, scowling with envy. The patrons of the bar on the avenue Montaigne? The soldiers running away from the battle on the Meuse?

But he didn't dial the telephone. At least, not all the numbers.

And so, inevitably, he arrived at his office one morning to find that a message had been slipped beneath the door. Hocus-pocus, was how he thought about it. An uncomfortable moment, then on with his day. *Hotel Dorado*. That was better medicine than Spanish murder, right?

And so, inevitably, the hocus-pocus itself.

Maybe not the best time for it, an icy night in the dead heart of January. Something that day had reached him, some sad nameless thing, and the antidote, when he found her, was blonde — a shimmering peroxide cap above a lopsided grin. Older up close than she'd first seemed — at a gallery opening — and not properly connected to the daily world. Everything about her off centre, as though she'd once been bent the wrong way and never quite sprung back.

They sat on the couch and nuzzled for a time. 'There is nobody quite like me,' she whispered.

He smiled and said she was right.

She undid a button on his shirt and slid a hand inside. The telephone rang once, then stopped. It bothered her. 'Who is it?' she said, as though he could know that.

But, in fact, he did know. And a minute later, sixty seconds later, it did it again. 'What's going on?' she said. Now she was frightened.

'It's nothing,' he said. Then, to prove it was nothing, 'I have to go out for a while.'

'Why?' she said.

He'd always thought, not all that proud of it, that he was a pretty good liar. But not this time. He'd been caught unprepared, no story made up just in case, so he tried to improvise, while she stared at him with hurt eyes and pulled her sweater back down. In the end, she agreed to wait in the apartment until he returned. 'Look,' he said, 'it's only business. Sometimes, the movie business, you need to take care of something quietly, secretly.'

She nodded, mouth curved down, wanting to believe him, knowing better.

In the street, it was ten degrees. He walked with lowered head and clenched teeth, the wind cutting through his coat and sweater. He swore at it, out loud, mumbling his way along the rue Chardin like a madman hauling his private menagerie to a new location.

At last, half-frozen, he crept down the ice-coated steps of the Ranelagh Métro and installed himself in front of a poster for the Opéra-Comique, a Spanish dancer swirling her skirt. A few minutes later, he heard the rumble of a train approaching through the tunnel. The doors slid open, out came a little man with a briefcase of the type carried under the arm. Casson could have spotted him five miles away, but then, the Germans were 'idiots.' And he, Casson, was so brilliant he'd believed *Erno Simic* when he'd called them that.

The contact was a small man, clearly angry at the world. Peering up and down the station platform he reminded Casson of a character in an English children's story. *The Wind in the Willows*? Waxed moustache, bowler hat, fierce eyebrows, ferocious glare above an old-fashioned collar. Following instructions, Casson turned to the wall and stared at the poster. For a time, nothing happened. The dancer smiled at him haughtily and clicked her castanets in the air.

Finally, the man stood beside him. Cleared his throat. 'An excellent performance, I'm told.'

That was part one of the password. Part two was the countersign: 'Yes. I saw it Thursday,' Casson said.

The contact leaned the briefcase against the wall at his feet and began to button his coat. Then, hands in pockets, he hurried away, his footsteps echoing down the empty platform as he headed into the night. Casson counted to twenty, picked up the briefcase, and went home.

His blonde was bundled in a blanket, snoring gently on the couch. He went into the bedroom and closed the door. Before he put the briefcase on the shelf that ran across the top of his closet – under the bed? behind the refrigerator? – he had a look inside. Three hundred thousand pesetas – about $35,000 in American money – in thirty bundles of hundred-peseta notes, each packet of ten pinned through its upper right-hand corner.

Back in the living room, the blonde opened one eye. 'You don't mind I took a nap,' she said.

'No,' he said.

'Keep me company,' she said, raising the blanket. She'd taken off her skirt and panties.

Casson lay down next to her. It wasn't so bad, in the end. Two cast-aways, adrift in the Paris night, three hundred thousand pesetas in a bedroom closet, air-raid sirens at the southern edge of the city, then a long flight of aircraft, south to north, passing above them. On the radio, the BBC. A quintet, swing guitar, violin – maybe Stephane Grappelli – a female vocalist, voice rough with static. The volume had to be very low: radios were supposed to be turned over to the Germans, and Casson was afraid of Madame Fitou – but he loved the thing, couldn't bear to part with it. It glowed in the dark and played music – he sometimes thought of it as the last small engine of civilization, a magic device, and he was its keeper, the hermit who hid the sacred ring. Some day, in times to come, the barbarians

120

would break camp and trudge away down the dusty roads and then, starting with a single radio, they would somehow put everything back the way it had been.

Very sensitive to the touch, this blonde. Thin, excitable – she sucked in her breath when something felt good. Still, she was quiet about it. That was just common sense. They even pulled the blanket up over their heads, which made everything seem dark and secret and forbidden. Probably he'd laugh at that some day, but just then it wasn't funny, because they really *were* out there, the secret police and their agents, and this was something they probably didn't approve of. It wasn't spelled out – just better to be quiet.

When they were done with one thing, and before they moved on to the next, Casson went to the phone, dialled Simic's number, let it ring once, and hung up. Then he counted to sixty, and did it again. He wondered, as he was counting, if it was a good idea to keep Simic's number in his address book. In fact, where did Simic keep his number?

He crawled back under the blanket, the blonde yawned and stretched, and they began to resettle themselves on the narrow couch. By his ear she said, 'You had better be careful, my friend, doing that sort of thing.'

'Perhaps you prefer I do this sort of thing?'

'I do, yes. Anybody would.' A few minutes later she said, 'Oh, you're sweet, you know. Truly.' Then: 'A pity if you invite them to kill you, *chéri.*'

Lunch, Chez Marcel, *rognons de veau*, a Hermitage from Jaboulet, 1931.

Hugo Altmann held his glass with three fingers at the top of the stem, canted it slightly to one side, poured it half full, then twisted the bottle as he turned it upright. He looked at the wine in his glass, gave it just a hint of a sniff and a swirl before he drank. 'I like the script,' he said. 'Pretty damn smooth for a first draft. Who is this Moreau?'

'Comes out of the provincial theatre, down by Lyons

somewhere. Strange fellow, afraid of his own shadow, keeps to himself pretty much. Has a little cottage out past Orly – lives with his mother, I think. No telephone.'

'Maybe I could meet him, sometime. A very sure hand, Jean-Claude, for the "provincial theatre, down by Lyons."'

Casson shrugged and smiled, accepting the compliment, proud of his ability to unearth a secret talent. He suspected Altmann knew how much he'd depended on Louis Fischfang for his scripts, and he'd intended 'Moreau' as a fiction convenient for both of them. Altmann, however, seemed to think Moreau actually existed.

'Maybe some day,' he said. 'Right now, Hugo, I need him to think about *Hotel Dorado* and nothing else. If he meets you, he might start having *ambitions*.'

'Well, all right.' Altmann chased the last of the brown sauce around his plate with a piece of bread. 'That banker in the first scene – Lapont? Lapère? Don't let anything happen to him. He's magnificent, truly loathsome – I can just see him.'

'I'll tell Moreau he's on the right track. Now, make it *really* good.'

Altmann smiled and took a sip of wine.

'I've been thinking,' Casson said. 'Maybe we should consider a different location.'

'Not the Côte d'Azur?'

'It's commonplace, everybody's been there.'

'That's the point, no?'

'Mmm – I think we have the plot, Hugo. But it's the setting I worry about. The feel of a place that's not the everyday world – come August, you leave your work, you leave the daily life, and you go there. Something special about it. I don't want anybody thinking, "Well, *I* wouldn't sell that hotel – I'd put in a damn fine restaurant and put some paint on the façade."'

'No, I guess not.'

The waiter came to take the plates away. 'There's a *reblochon* today, gentlemen,' he said. 'And pears.'

'Bring it,' Altmann said.

'I've been thinking about Spain,' Casson said.

'Spain?'

'Yes. Down on the Mediterranean. Someplace dark, and very quiet. The *propriétaires* are still French. Expatriates. But the clients are a little more adventurous. They go to Spain for their holidays.'

'Hm.'

'Anyhow, I'd like to go and have a look. Scout locations.'

'All right, it shouldn't be a problem. But, I don't know, it doesn't, somehow – Spain?'

'Could be the key to it all, Hugo.'

Altmann began preparing a cigar, piercing the leaf at the end with a metal pick he took from his pocket. He looked up suddenly, pointed the cigar at Casson. 'You're a liar,' he said. Then he broke out in a wide grin. 'Have to take, uh, somebody down there with you, Jean-Claude? Just in case you need help?' He laughed and shook his head – *you scoundrel, you almost had me there.*

Casson smiled, a little abashed. 'Well,' he said.

Altmann snapped his lighter until it lit, then warmed the cigar above the blue flame. 'Romantic in Spain, Jean-Claude. Guitars and so forth. And one doesn't run into every damn soul in the world one knows. You don't really want to move the story there, do you?'

'No,' Casson said. 'There's a lady involved.'

Altmann nodded to himself in satisfaction, then counted out a sheaf of Occupation reichsmarks on top of the cheque. For a German in an occupied city, everything was virtually free. 'Come take a walk with me, Jean-Claude,' he said. 'I want to pick up some cashmere sweaters for my wife.'

*   *   *

The following afternoon Altmann sent over a letter on Continental stationery and, after a phone call, Casson took it to the Gestapo office in the old Interior Ministry building on the rue des Saussaies. The officer he saw there occupied a private room on the top floor. *SS-Obersturmbannführer* – lieutenant colonel – Guske wore civilian clothes, an expensively tailored grey suit, and had the glossy look of a successful businessman. A big, imposing head with large ears, sparse black hair – carefully combed for maximum coverage – and the tanned scalp of a man who owns a boat or a ski chalet, perhaps both.

His French was extremely good. 'So, we are off to sunny Spain. Not so sunny just now, I suppose.'

'No. Not in January.'

'You've been there before?'

'Several times. Vacations on the beaches below Barcelona, in the early thirties.'

'But not during the civil war.'

'No, sir.'

'Are you a Jew, Casson?'

'No. Catholic by birth. By practise, not much of anything.'

'I regret having to ask you that, but I'm sure you understand. The film business being what it is, unfortunately . . .'

A knock at the door, a secretary entered and handed Guske a dossier. Casson could see his name, lettered across the top of the cardboard folder, and the official stamp of the Paris Préfecture de Police. Guske opened it on his desk and started reading, idly turning pages, at one point going back in the record and searching for something, running an index finger up and down the margin. Ah yes, there it was.

He moved forward again, making the sort of small gestures – rhythmic bobbing of the head, pursing of the lips – that indicated irritation with petty minds that noted too many details, an inner voice saying *yes, yes, then what, come on.*

At last he looked up and smiled pleasantly. 'All in order.' He squared the sheets of paper, closed the dossier, and tied it shut with its ribbon. Then he took Altmann's letter and read it over once more. 'Will your assistant be coming to see us?' he asked.

'No. Change of plans,' Casson said. 'I'm going alone.'

'Very well,' Guske said. He drew a line through a sentence in Altmann's letter and initialled the margin, wrote a comment at the bottom and initialled that as well, then clipped the letter to the dossier and made a signal – Casson did not see how it was done – that brought the secretary back. When she left he said, 'Come by tomorrow, after eleven. Your *Ausweis* will be waiting for you at the downstairs reception.'

'Thank you,' Casson said.

'You're welcome,' Guske said. 'By the way, what did you do during the May campaign? Were you recalled to military service?'

'No,' Casson said. 'I started out to go south, then I gave it up and stayed in Paris. The roads . . .'

'Yes. Too bad, really, this kind of thing has to happen. We're neighbours, after all, I'm sure we can do better than this.' He stood, offered a hand, he had a warm, powerful grip. 'Forgive me, Herr Casson, I must tell you – we do expect you to return, so, please, no *wanderlust*. Some people here are not so understanding as I am, and they'll haul you back by your ears.'

He winked at Casson, gave him a reassuring pat on the shoulder as he ushered him out of the office.

Casson couldn't reach Citrine by telephone. A clerk answered at the hotel desk, told him that guests at that establishment did not receive phone calls – maybe he should try the Ritz, and banged the receiver down. So Casson took the Métro, out past the Père-Lachaise cemetery, walked for what seemed like miles through a neighbourhood of deserted factories, finally found the place, then read a newspaper in the dark lobby until Citrine came sweeping through the door.

When he suggested they go to his apartment she gave him a look. 'It's work,' he said. 'I'm going to Spain tomorrow, and you know what an office is like at night.'

They took a bicycle taxi up to the Passy shopping district, by the La Muette Métro and the Ranelagh gardens. It was just getting dark. 'We'll want something to eat, later on,' he explained.

Her eyes opened wide with feigned innocence. 'And look! A bottle of wine. Someone must have left it here.'

'Work and supper, my love. Home before curfew.'

Truce. She walked with him in the way he'd always liked, hand curled around his arm, pressed tight to his side, yet gliding along the street like a dancer. That was good, but not best. Best was how she used to slip her hand in his coat pocket as they walked together. That would make him so happy he would forget to talk, and she would say, innocent as dawn, 'Yes? And?'

For a winter evening La Muette wasn't so bad. The little merry-go-round wouldn't be back until the spring, but there was an organ-grinder, a blind man who smiled up at the sky as he turned the handle. Casson gave him all his change. The snow drifted down, a flake at a time, through the blue lamplight.

He'd stored up a hoard of ration coupons, even buying some on the black-market bourse that now functioned at a local café. So, for a half-hour, he could once again be the casual man-about-town. 'The smoked salmon looks good, doesn't it.' They decided on a galantine of vegetables. 'A little more, please,' he said as the clerk rested her knife on the loaf and raised an eyebrow. For dessert, two beautiful oranges, chosen after long deliberation and a frank exchange between Citrine and the fruit man. Also, a very small, very expensive piece of chocolate.

There was a long queue in front of the boulangerie. The smell of the fresh bread hung in the cold air, people stamped their feet to keep the circulation going. This queue was always the slowest – portions had to be weighed, ration coupons cut out with scissors – and sometimes a discussion started up. 'Has anybody heard about North Africa?' Casson looked around to see who was speaking. A small, attractive woman wearing a coat with a Persian-lamb collar. 'They say,' she continued, 'an important city has been captured by the English.' She sounded hopeful – there'd been no good news for a long time. 'Perhaps it's just a rumour.'

It was not a rumour. Casson had heard the report on the French service of the BBC. The city was Tobruk, in Libya. Twenty-five thousand Italian troops taken prisoner, eighty-seven tanks captured by Australian and British soldiers. He started to answer, Citrine gave him a sharp tug on the arm and hissed in his ear, *'Tais-toi!'* Shut up.

Nobody in the queue spoke, they waited, in their own worlds. On the way home to the rue Chardin, Citrine said, 'You must be born yesterday. Don't you know there are informers in the food queues? They get money for each radio the Germans find, they have only to persuade some fool to say he heard the news on the BBC. Jean-Claude, please, come down from the clouds.'

'I didn't realize,' he said.

He had almost spoken, he had actually started to speak when Citrine stopped him. They would have searched the apartment. Looked in the closet.

'You must be careful,' she said gently.

On the rue Chardin, a gleaming black Mercedes was idling at the kerb. The radio! *No*, he told himself. Then the door opened and out came the baroness, smothered in furs, who lived in the apartment below him. 'Oh, monsieur, good evening,' she said, startled into courtesy.

The man who'd held the door for her, a German naval

officer, stepped to her side and made a certain motion, a
slight stiffening of the posture, a barely perceptible inclination of the head; a bow due the very tiniest of the petit
bourgeois. He was pale and featureless, one of those aristo-
crats, Casson thought, so refined by ages of breeding they
are invisible in front of a white wall. There was an awkward moment – introduction was both unavoidable and
unthinkable. The baroness solved the problem with a
small, meaningless sound, the officer with a second stiffening, then both rushed towards the Mercedes.

'What was that?' Citrine asked, once they were in the
apartment.

'The baroness. She lives down below.'

'Well, well. She's rather pretty. Do you –?'

'Are you crazy?'

They took off their coats. Citrine walked around the
small living room, moved the drape aside and stared out
over the rooftops. The Eiffel Tower was a dim shape in the
darkness on the other side of the river. 'It's all the same,'
she said. 'Except for the lights.'

'Oh look,' he said. 'A bottle of wine. Someone must
have left it here.'

For the occasion, a pack of Gauloises. They smoked, drank
wine, played the radio at its lowest volume. Citrine paged
through the script, following the trail of SYLVIE as it wound
from scene to scene. Casson watched her face carefully –
this was Fischfang's first real test. Altmann could be fooled,
not Citrine. She scowled, sighed, flipped pages when she
grew impatient. 'How old is this Sylvie, do you think?'

'Young, but experienced. In the important moments,
much older than her years. She wants very much to be
frivolous – her life carried her past those times too quickly –
but she can't forget what she's seen, and what she knows.'

Citrine concentrated on a certain passage, then closed
the script, keeping the place with her index finger. She

met Casson's eyes, became another person. '"My dreams? No, I don't remember them. Oh, sometimes I'm running. But we all run away at night, don't we."'

Casson opened his copy. 'Where are you?'

'Page fifty-five, in the attic. With Paul, we're . . .' She hunted for a moment. 'We're . . . we've opened a trunk full of old costumes.'

'For the carnival, at Lent.'

'Oh.' She turned to the wall, crossed her arms. '"My dreams."' She shook her head. '"No. I don't remember them."' *I don't want to remember them.* And somehow she bent the word *dreams* back towards its other meaning. She relaxed, dropped out of character. 'Too much?'

'I wish Louis were here. He'd like it that way.'

'You?'

'Maybe.'

'You want to direct this, don't you.'

'I always want to, Citrine. But I know not to.'

8:30. A second bottle of wine. Scarlatti from the BBC. The room smelled like smoke, wine, and perfume. 'Did you know,' she said, 'I made a movie in Finland?'

'In Finnish?'

'No. They dubbed it later. I just went ba-ba-ba with whatever feeling they told me to have and the other actors spoke Finnish.'

'That doesn't work,' Casson said. 'We did a German version that way, for *The Devil's Bridge.*'

Citrine's eyes filled with soft passion, she leaned forward on the couch, her voice a whisper. 'Ba, ba-ba. Ba-ba-ba?'

Casson extended the wine bottle, holding it over Citrine's glass. 'Ba ba?'

'Don't,' she said, laughing.

He smiled at her, poured the wine. Happiness rolled over him, he felt suddenly warm. Perhaps, he thought, paradise goes by in an instant. When you're not looking.

'I'm almost asleep,' she said.

Warmth rolled over him, he felt suddenly happy. He went to the radiator and put a hand on it. 'A miracle,' he said. The apartment hadn't been like this for months. From somewhere, coal, apparently abundant coal, had appeared, and Madame Fitou had decided, against all precedent, to use a great deal of it. This was, he realized, a rather complicated miracle.

'Suddenly,' he said, 'there's heat.'

Citrine spread her hands, meaning obvious conclusion. 'Don't you see?'

'No.'

'A beautiful baroness, a dashing German officer, coal is delivered.'

It felt good in the apartment, they were in no hurry to leave. The Occupation authority, grateful for a compliant population, had given Paris a Christmas present: extension of curfew to 3:00 a.m. Casson and Citrine talked – *Hotel Dorado*, life and times, the way of the world. They'd never disagreed about big things, it had gone wrong between them somewhere else. They liked eccentricity, they liked kindness, coincidence, people who lost themselves in the study of planets or bugs. They liked people with big hearts. They wanted to hear that in the end it all turned out for the best.

Just after midnight she wandered into the kitchen, dabbed her finger in some galantine gelatin left on a plate and licked it off. A moment later Casson came in to see what she was doing, found her standing by the pipe that ran, mysteriously, through the corners of all the kitchens in the building. She was listening to something, hand pressed over her mouth, like a schoolgirl, to keep from giggling.

'What –?' he said.

She touched a finger to her lips, then pointed to the

pipe. He listened, heard faint sounds from below. It made no sense at first.

'Your baroness?' she whispered.

'Yes?'

'Is getting a red bottom.'

Sharp reports – slow and deliberate, demure little cries. There was only one thing in the world that sounded like that.

'*Tiens*,' Casson said, amazed. 'And in the kitchen.'

Citrine listened for a time. 'Well,' she said, 'I predict you'll have a warm winter.'

Later he walked her to the Métro – she wouldn't let him take her back to the hotel. 'Good night,' he said.

She kissed him on the lips, very quickly and lightly, it was over before he realized it was happening. 'Jean-Claude,' she said. 'I had a good time tonight. Thank you.'

'I'll call you,' he said.

She nodded, waved at him, turned and went down the stairs of the Métro. *She's gone*, he thought.

A CITIZEN OF
THE EVENING

Night train to Madrid.

The air was ice, the heavens swept with winter stars, white and still in a black sky. Jean Casson had done what he'd done, there was no going back. The train pulled slowly from the Gare de Lyon, clattered through the railyards south of the city, then out into the night.

A first-class compartment; burgundy velveteen drapes, gleaming brass doorknobs. Casson pressed his forehead against the cold window and stared out into the dark countryside. Looking out train windows was good for lovers. *Citrine, Citrine.* They'd made love in a train once; lying on their sides in a narrow berth, looking out at the backyards of some town, sheets hanging on washing lines, cats on windowsills, smoke from chimneys on tile roofs. It was a long autumn that year and nobody thought about war.

Staring out of train windows good for lovers, not so bad for secret agents. *We are all adrift in the world, we do what we have to do.* Casson turned out the lamps so he could see better. Outside, the Beauce. Old, deep France – *France profonde*, it was said. A flat plain where they grew wheat and barley, sometimes a forest where long ago they'd hunted bear with Beauceron dogs. A knock at the door, his heart hammered. 'Monsieur?' Only a steward in a white jacket, peering at a list.

'Monsieur Dubreuil?'

'No, Casson.'

'Monsieur Casson, yes. Would you wish the first or second seating?'

135

'Second.'

'Very good, sir.'

He closed the door, the rattle of the train subsided. A man with eyes shadowed by the brim of a fedora came down the corridor, glanced into Casson's compartment. *Calm down*, Casson told himself. But he couldn't. The tanned, smiling Colonel Guske kept forcing himself to the front of Casson's attention. He wasn't a smart lawyer – Simic had been right there, Casson thought – but he was the sort of man who got things done. Worked hard, full of vigour and stupefying optimism about life. *Must get that spinnaker rigged! Must keep the racquet straight on my backhand! Must get to the bottom of that Casson business!*

He closed his eyes for a moment, took a deep breath. Forced himself to take comfort from the dark countryside beyond the window. The French had fought and marched across these plains for centuries. They'd fought the Moslems in the south, the Germans in the east, the British in the west. The Dutch in the north? He didn't know. But they must have, some time or other. The War of the Spanish Succession? The Thirty Years War? Napoleon?

Calm down. Or they'd find him dead of fear, staring wide-eyed at the scenery. Then it would be their turn to worry about the three hundred thousand pesetas. Of course, he thought, they wouldn't worry very long. Or, perhaps, it would just stay where it was – God only knew what would be lost forever in this war. The train slowed, and stopped. Outside, nothing special, a frozen field.

Compartment doors opening and closing, the sound of a slow train rumbling past. Something to do, anyhow. He got up and joined the other passengers, standing at the windows in the corridor. A freight train, flat cars loaded with tanks and artillery pieces under canvas tarpaulins, gun barrels pointing at the sky. He counted thirty, forty, fifty, then stopped, the train seemed to go on forever. His heart fell – what could he, what could any of them do against these people? Lately it was fashionable in Paris to avert one's eyes when seated across from Germans in the Métro. Yes, he thought, that would do it – the French won't look at us, we're going home.

His fellow passengers felt it too. Not the German aviators at the end of the car, probably not their French girlfriends, drunk and giggling. But the man who looked like a butcher in a Sunday suit, and Madame Butcher, they had the same expression on their faces as he did: faintly introspective, not very interested, vague. Strange, he thought, how people choose the same mask. Tall man, head of an ostrich, spectacles. A professor of Greek? A young man and his older friend – theatre people, Casson would have bet on it. The woman who stood next to him was an aristocrat of some sort. Late forties, red-and-brown tweed suit for travelling, cost a fortune years ago, maintained by maids ever since.

She felt his eyes, turned to look at him. Dry, weather-beaten face, pale hair cut short and plain, eight strokes of a brush would put it in place. Skin never touched by makeup. Faded green eyes with laugh wrinkles at the corners her only feature. But more than sufficient. She met his glance; gave a single shake of the head, mouth tight for an instant. *How sad this is*, she meant. And I don't know that we can ever do anything about it.

He acknowledged the look, then by mutual agreement they turned back towards the windows. Tanks on flat cars crept past, canvas stiffened by white frost, at that speed the rhythm of the wheels on the rails a measured drum-beat. Then it was over, a single red lantern on the last car fading away into the distance. Casson and his neighbour exchanged a second look – *life goes on* – and returned to their compartments.

The train got under way slowly, dark hills on the horizon just visible by starlight. The woman reminded him of some-one, after a moment he remembered. A brief fling, years ago, one of his wife's equestrienne pals – whipcord breeches and riding crops. A long time since he'd thought of her. Bold and funny, full of prerogatives, afraid of neither man nor beast, rich as Croesus, cold as ice, victor in a thousand love affairs. She had a white body shaped by twenty years of bobbing up and down in a saddle, hard and angular, and in bed she was all business, no sentimental nonsense allowed. She did, on the other hand, have delicious, fruit-flavoured breath, particularly noticeable when she had him make love to her in the missionary position.

He'd wondered about her – connections with diplomats, months spent abroad, nights in exotic clubs one heard about from friends – wondered if she wasn't, perhaps, involved with the secret services. Just as he'd wondered what sort of hobbies she pursued with the riding crop. But he never asked, and she never offered. Her life belonged only to her; no matter if she spied, whipped, made millions, she didn't talk about it.

Now, stupidly, he felt better – *just being near a woman*. But it was true. He dozed, woke up at Auxerre station. The blackout made the station ghostly, the waiting passengers shapes in the darkness. The doors opened, just enough time for people to get on the train, then closed. The locomotive vented white steam that hung still in the freezing air. He waited for the coach to jerk forward as the engine got under way.

Instead: the door at the end of the corridor was thrown open and a voice called out '*Kontrolle*.' Casson sat up so suddenly it hurt his back. In the corridor, German voices, shouting instructions. What? This couldn't happen. *Once the train leaves Paris, nobody bothers you, the Germans can't be everywhere*. In panic, he twisted to look out on the platform: pacing shadows, silhouettes of slung rifles just visible in the darkness. *The darkness*. He tested the window, no give. Of course, windows in a railway coach, you had to be strong. *Strong enough.* A door slammed in the passageway, another opened. *Jump out the window, crawl under the train.* Across the track. Running full speed. Out into the street. Auxerre. Who did he know? Where did they live? Someone, there was always someone, someone would always help you. The door to his compartment opened. *'Kontrolle.'*

He stood up.

Something in German, a wave of the hand. *Sit down.* He sat. There were two of them, SS officers, leather coats open to black uniforms with lightning insignia, steel-handled Lugers in high-riding leather holsters. They hadn't been in the train very long – he could feel the cold air on them.

'Papiere.'

A gloved hand extended. Casson fumbled for his identification in the inside pocket of his jacket. His fingers had gone numb. The passport, the *Ausweis*, the envelope. He took them out. *No, not the envelope.* Clumsy, maladroit. His arm had no feeling in it, the hand thick and slow. *Take back the envelope.* He swallowed, there was something caught in the centre of his chest.

'Was ist los?'

No, not this, this doesn't concern you. He placed passport and travel permit on the glove, started to put the envelope back in his pocket. His hand wouldn't work at all. He folded the envelope in half and stuffed it in, spreading his lips in what he hoped looked like a smile. Sorry to be so stupid, sorry to be trouble, sorry sir, regret, excuse.

Didn't work.

Something interesting here. The officer now looked closely at him for the first time. Not very old, Casson thought, in his thirties, perhaps. A fleshy face – fat later on – small eyes, cunning. This job was the most important thing that had ever happened to him. *Not* in a shop. *Not* in a garage. Casson looked down. The man hooked a gloved index finger under his chin and raised his head to where he could see Casson's eyes. What are you? What are you to *me*? Just one more pale Frenchman? Or a fatal error?

Lazily, the German inclined his head towards the luggage rack. '*Valise,*' he said softly.

Casson's hands were shaking so badly he had a hard time getting his suitcase down from the luggage rack. The Germans waited, the heavy-faced one taking a second look at his papers and making a casual remark to his colleague. Casson recognized only one word – *Guske.* As in, *It's Guske who signed the travel permit, the dossier must be handled in his office.* The response was brief, neutral – and something more. Respectful? As in, *Well, sometimes you come across these things.*

The officer turned on the lamps in the compartment. Whatever was caught in Casson's chest now swelled, and made it hard to breathe. He fumbled with the lock, finally laying the suitcase open on the seat. It looked harmless enough; two shirts, side by side, one of them fresh from the *blanchisserie*, the other worn, then folded for packing. There was a nice leather case that held razor and shaving soap. Socks, shorts. The copy of *Bel Ami* that he'd meant to read on the train.

The heavy-faced officer picked up the book. Held it by the spine and shook it, a slip of paper used as a bookmark fell out and drifted to the floor. Next he felt the front and back covers, riffled the pages, worked a finger down between the spine and the binding and ripped it off, holding it up to the light, checking one side, then the other, then tossing it and the book onto the seat. He reached over, lifted one corner of a shirt, saw nothing very interesting beneath it – a newspaper, perhaps – and dropped it back into place.

They handed Casson back his identity papers and left. He heard them – opening the next door in the passageway, shouting orders – as though they were men in a dream.

Very slowly, he slid the papers back into the inside pocket of his jacket. Next to the envelope. His fingers rested on the envelope for a moment. *What they would have done to me.*

In the dining car, the second seating, 10:30. The only light, flickering candles on the white tablecloths. The woman in the tweed suit was shown to his table. 'Monsieur, I hope you don't mind.' No, not at all, he was glad for the company. The waiter brought a bottle of wine, cold vegetable salad with an oily mayonnaise, nameless fish in railroad sauce – to Casson it barely mattered.

'I am called Marie-Noëlle,' she said. 'Meeting on a train, you see, we don't have to wait ten years for first names.'

He smiled, introduced himself. He would be happy to call her Marie-Noëlle, but he did wonder what the rest might be.

She sighed – it always came to this. There was, she confessed, 'a thoroughly disreputable person sometimes addressed as Lady Marensohn,' but it wasn't really her. The title was by marriage – a husband who had died long ago, something in the small nobility of Sweden, a diplomat of minor status. 'Terribly concerned with jute,' she said grimly. 'Morning and night.' She herself had been born into a family called de Vlaq, from the Dutch-Belgian border, 'even smaller nobility, if that's possible,' and grown up on family estates in Luxembourg – 'they called it wine, but, you know, really . . .'

She smoked passionately – Gitane followed Gitane, lit with strong fingers stained yellow by nicotine – and laughed constantly, a laugh that usually ended in a cough. 'To hell with everything,' she said, 'that's what it says on my family crest. Citizen of the evening, resident of Paris since time began, and the only nobility I acknowledge is in good works for friends.'

A German officer covered with medals moved down the

141

aisle between tables, his girlfriend followed along behind, vividly rouged and lipsticked, wearing a tight cap of glossy black feathers. When they'd gone by, Marie-Noëlle made a face.

'Don't care for them?' Casson said.

'Not much.'

'But you can leave, can't you?'

She shrugged. 'Yes. Maybe I will, but, where to go?'

'Sweden?'

'Brr.'

'Switzerland, then.'

'Switzerland, Switzerland. Yes, there's always that. Geneva, grey but possible. On the other hand, the visa. I mean, you have to know . . . God. *Well*. Not just to nod to. Last September, a friend of mine went through it. She tried the embassies, the Americans, the Portuguese, and the Swiss. Spent hours in queues but in the end all she could get was a Venezuelan resident card, which cost her a fortune, and, worse yet, the only place she could go with it was Venezuela.'

She stubbed out a Gitane, lit another. 'Well, she tries. She does try. She's positive, she's cheerful. She's all the things you're supposed to be. "So different," she writes. "The Latin culture – sunny one minute, stormy the next. And Caracas – intrigue!" Of course it's ghastly, and she's miserable. It isn't Paris, it's a kind of horrid not-Paris. She sees the other émigrés, most of them grateful to be alive, but all they can talk about is when will it end, when can we go back, when can life be what it always was.'

The train slowed, they peered out the window, trying to see past the reflection of the candle flame in the black glass. They were at the edge of a small city, passing the cottages that lined the track. Then came the dark cathedral with tall towers, winding streets, the railway station brasserie, and finally the platform. BOURGES, the sign said. Now a port of entry for the unoccupied part of France governed by Vichy.

The French border police were waiting on the platform, holding their capes tight around them and stomping their feet to keep warm. 'More police,' Marie-Noëlle said acidly.

'French, this time.'

'Yes, there's that to be said for it.' She exhaled smoke through her nose and mouth when she talked. 'Tell me,' she said, leaning over the table, her voice lowered, 'they didn't give you too bad of a time, did they? The SS? I was listening, next door, but I couldn't hear much.'

'Not too bad,' he said.

The train jerked to a stop with a hiss of steam. The gendarmes came down the aisle, asking politely for papers. They knew they were in the first-class dining car, rolled the *Madames* and *Monsieurs* off their tongues, had a desultory glance at each passport, then left with a two-fingered salute to the visor of the cap. *Only a formality, of course you understand.*

'Remarkable,' Marie-Noëlle said, when the police had gone to the next table. 'You are perhaps the only person I know who's ever had a decent photograph in a passport.'

Casson held it up and said, 'What, this? I wouldn't let him in my country.'

'Yes, but look here – is this not the aunt kept locked up in the attic?'

He smiled, it was even worse than that.

'Now, monsieur,' she said, a mock-serious note in her voice, 'how am I going to persuade you to allow me to buy us a brandy?'

He would not allow it. He insisted on paying for the brandies, and for those that followed. Meanwhile they smoked and talked and made the dinner last as long as they could. Very late at night, after the stop at Lyons, the train started the long run down the Rhône valley, the sky cleared and the moon ran beside them, a yellow disc on the still river.

She grew tired, and reflective, not so sure about the world. 'What do you think,' she asked, 'in your heart. Must I leave this country?'

'Perhaps,' he said. *Peut-être*, could be. In diplomacy it meant yes – yes with regret. 'Of course,' he went on, 'it's not something I can do, so maybe I shouldn't be giving advice.'

'Not something you can do?'

'No.'

'What stops you?'

He looked puzzled.

'In a few hours,' she said, 'you'll be in Spain. Sunny Spain, *neutral* Spain. From there, ships leave daily, to every port in the world. But why wait for a booking on a ship? There is a ferry, in Algeciras, it goes across to Ceuta. One simply pays and walks on. Then, it takes less than an hour, you are in Spanish Morocco. Once there, well . . .'

It was true. Why hadn't it occurred to him? He had three hundred thousand pesetas in a suitcase, a travel permit for Spain. A thousand stories began this way – an opportunity, a sudden decision, then freedom, a new life. It took courage, that was all. He saw himself doing it: walking off the ferry with raincoat tossed over one shoulder, hat brim turned down, valise in hand, turning to look back one last time at the dark mass of Europe. Why not? What would he be giving up – a movie that would never be made? A woman who was never going to love him again? A city that would never be the same?

But then, from somewhere deep inside, the sigh of common sense. The man with the raincoat and the hat brim turned down wasn't him. 'Perhaps,' he said, 'you will join me for a drink, Madame Marie-Noëlle. At Fouquet's, one of the tables on the boulevard.'

A corner of her mouth turned up in a grin, she flirted with him a little. 'Chilly for the outdoor tables, monsieur. No?'

'I meant, in the spring.'

'Ah.' She considered it. 'Probably, I will meet you there,' she said, then shook her head slowly, in gentle despair for both of them. 'Charming. The last romantic.'

He sat back in the chair; it was very late at night. 'It is the only trick I know,' he said. Then, after a moment, 'You're one too.'

'No, no,' she said. 'I'm something else.'

Port Bou, the Spanish frontier, 4:40 p.m.

Here the passengers had to leave the train and wait in queues; customs, border formalities. Casson had been through it before, years earlier, and when he'd thought about the crossing it had seemed to him the second most likely place he might be arrested. The passengers stood quietly, nobody made jokes. Cold, thin air in the Pyrenees, jagged ridges, white mist, snowfields fading in the last light. The *Guardia* sentries pacing up and down the lines were like ghosts from Napoleon's wars; leather tricorn hats, greatcoats, long, thin rifles that looked like muskets. He searched everywhere for Marie-Noëlle, but she had disappeared. Left the train, apparently. Where – Narbonne? Perpignan? Would she have said? No, probably not. But it was a loss. He'd planned on going through the frontier with her, somebody to talk to, easier to pretend that you weren't scared.

The queue marked *Entrada*. Two uniformed officers and a civilian sat at a plank table in a shed heated by a smoky wood stove. The line of passengers was kept back twelve feet from the table – a distance where the tension of the examination could be felt but the questions, and the follow-ups, could not be heard. The final line, *Entrada*. From here the passengers drifted away, in twos and threes, to a coach on the south-bound local, idling at the far end of the station, that ran on the Spanish-gauge track. They walked briskly – really, how had they allowed themselves to worry like that – and made a point of not looking back. There was one couple, elderly, well-dressed, being returned to the French train, and a young woman, being led away by two men in overcoats, but that was all. The young woman looked at Casson, trying to tell him something with her eyes. The men at her side followed the glance – an accomplice, perhaps? – and Casson had to look away. He hoped she'd had time to see that he understood, that he would remember what had happened to her.

Casson got through. They studied his papers, running an index finger under the important phrases. The civilian wore a coat with a fur collar and a pince-nez. 'The reason for your visit, señor?'

'For a film, to look at possible locations.'

'What kind of film?'

'A romantic comedy.'

The man passed his papers to one of the *Guardia*, who stamped *Entrada-27 Enero 1941* in his passport and initialled it.

The Spanish train was old and dirty, cold air flowed up through the floorboards. All the way to Barcelona he stared out the window, seeing nothing. His mouth was dry, he swallowed but it did not seem to help. The compartment was crowded; two Luftwaffe officers, two women who might have been sisters, a fat, unshaven man who slept for most of the journey. Casson told himself that nothing would happen. He simply had to believe in himself – the world would always respect a self-confident man, and nothing would happen. He was sweating, he could feel it under his arms, even in the chilly compartment, and he tried to be surreptitious about wiping it away from his hairline.

The outskirts of Barcelona. There had been fighting here in 1937. The track was elevated and he could see into apartments; rooms with black flash marks on the walls, charred beams, dressers with drawers pulled out, a bed standing on end. The passengers stared in silence as the train crawled past. Then the fat man woke up and abruptly pulled the curtains closed. Why did he do that? Casson wondered. Was he Spanish? French? Republican? Falangist? Casson swallowed. The man stared at him, daring him to say something. Casson looked at his feet, his fingers touched the envelope in his pocket.

Barcelona station, 8:10 p.m.

The train to the southern coast wasn't due to leave until 10:20. Casson went to the station buffet, took a dry bun with a crust of pink icing and a tiny cup of black coffee, and found a table by the back wall. Of course he was watched.

For their eyes, he played the traveller. Dug into his valise, retrieved his copy of *Le Matin* and spread it out on the table – JAPANESE FOREIGN MINISTER WARNS USA NOT TO INTERFERE IN ASIAN AFFAIRS. Took traveller's inventory, checking his railway ticket and passport, putting French francs in this pocket, pesetas in that pocket. In fact, he needed to change money, and reminded himself to keep the receipt from the *cambio*. The border police had recorded the amount of French francs he'd brought into the country and they'd want a piece of paper when he went back out.

And he was going back out.

He'd studied what he intended to do, walked through it in his mind, hour by hour, step by step. So that, if it suddenly felt wrong, he could walk away. A patriot, he reminded himself, not a fool. There would be hell to pay if he abandoned the money. But then, he was a film producer, there'd been hell to pay before in his life, and he'd paid it.

Better now, he calmed down. This was something he could do. *Go out of the door, if you like,* he told himself. He liked hearing that, he could answer by saying *no, not yet, nothing's gone wrong.*

He refolded the newspaper and returned it to his valise, next to the torn copy of *Bel Ami.* Made sure, one last time, of passport, money, and all the rest of it, and, oh yes, a certain envelope in the inside pocket of his jacket. He tore it open, took out a receipt with *Thos. Cook Agency* printed across the top, and a first-class railway ticket, Paris/Barcelona.

The watchers were probably watching – after all, that's how they made their living – but there wasn't very much for them to watch at Casson's table. Just another traveller, nervous as the rest, fussing with his papers before resuming his journey. He stood, drained the last little sip of coffee, and picked up his valise. On the way out of the buffet he balled up the envelope and tossed it in the trash.

The baggage room was off by itself, at the end of a long corridor with burned-out lamps and NO PASARÁN daubed on the walls with red paint. Casson stood at the counter and waited for thirty seconds, then tapped the little bell. For a moment, nothing happened. Then he heard the deliberate, uneven rhythm of somebody walking with a pronounced limp. It went on for a long time, the office was at the other end of the room and the clerk walked slowly, with great difficulty. A short, dark man with a pencil-thin moustache, an angry face, and an eight-inch heel on a built-up shoe. On the breast pocket of his smock was a lapel pin, bright silver, a signal of membership in something, and Casson sensed that this job came from the same place the pin did, it was a reward, given in return for faith and service. To a political party, perhaps, or a government bureau.

Be normal. Casson handed over the receipt. 'Baggage for Dubreuil.'

The clerk peered at the number, then said it aloud, slowly. Standing on the other side of the counter, Casson could smell clothes worn for too many days. The clerk nodded to himself; yes, he knew this one, and limped off, disappearing among the rows of wooden shelves piled to the ceiling with trunks and suitcases. Casson could hear him as he searched, up one aisle, down the next, walking, then stopping, walking, then stopping. Somewhere in the back, a radio played faintly, an opera.

It was going to work. He could feel it, and permitted himself just a bare edge of relief. It was going to work because it wasn't complicated. He had simply gone to his customary travel agent at the Thomas Cook office on the rue de Bassano, told him an associate named Dubreuil was accompanying him to Spain, and purchased two first-class, round-trip tickets, checking Dubreuil's suitcase through to Barcelona. The standard procedure would have been for the agent at Cook's to demand Dubreuil's passport, but Casson had done a great deal of business there over seven or eight years and the travel agent wasn't going to get fussy over details with a valued customer.

Prevailing opinion in Paris had it that checked baggage, stacked high in icy freight cars, was not searched very seriously at the Spanish frontier. If the worst happened, however, and a Spanish customs guard discovered a suitcase full of pesetas and turned it in instead of stealing it, they could look for Dubreuil all they wanted; they'd never find him because he didn't exist. There was, for Casson, a brief moment of exposure, when he had to pretend to be Dubreuil in order to claim the suitcase, but that was going to be over in a few seconds and he would be on his way.

The clerk returned to the counter, his face bland and

satisfied. He handed Casson a slip of paper, and said 'Not here,' in Spanish. Casson looked at his hand, he was holding the baggage receipt.

'Pardon?' He hadn't understood, he'd thought –

'Not here, señor.'

Casson stared at him. 'Where is it?'

A shrug. 'Who can say?'

Casson heard train whistles in the distance, the clash of couplings, the opera on the clerk's radio. They would kill him for this.

'I don't understand,' he said.

The clerk stepped back a pace. His next move, Casson realized, would be to roll down the metal shutter. The man's face was closed: a suitcase didn't matter, a passenger didn't matter, what mattered was the little silver pin on his blue smock. Against that magic, this insistent Señor Dubreuil was powerless.

'The train from Port Bou . . .' Casson said.

The hand started to reach for the shutter, then decided that the moment had not quite arrived and contented itself with sliding casually into a pocket. 'Good evening, señor,' the clerk said.

Casson turned away quickly. He didn't know where to go or what to do but he felt he had to put distance between himself and the baggage room. He trotted back up the corridor, the valise bouncing in his hand, footsteps echoing off the cement walls. Breathing hard, he made himself slow down, then walked through the station buffet and found the platform where the Port Bou train had come in. The track was empty.

'Missed your train?'

English. A huge man with a huge grey beard, sitting on a baggage cart surrounded by two battered wooden boxes, an old carpetbag, and a collapsed easel tied with a cord. 'Have you missed your train, monsieur?' Phrasebook French this time, plodding but correct.

Casson shook his head. 'Lost baggage.' *Perdu*. Meant lost, all right, much more so, somehow, than in any other language. That which was *perdu* joined lost time, lost love, lost opportunity and lost souls in a faraway land where nothing was ever seen again.

'Damn the luck.'

Casson nodded.

'Speak English?'

'Yes.'

'Just come in from the border?'

'Yes.'

'Hm.' The man looked at his watch. 'Only left thirty seconds ago. Did you leave it on the train?'

'No. It was checked baggage.'

'Ah-hah! Then there's hope.'

'There is?'

'Oh yes. Sometimes they don't take it off. They forget, or they just don't. They're Spanish, you see. Life's so bloody, *conditional.*'

'It's true,' Casson said gloomily.

'You might catch it, you know, if you don't dawdle. It stops at a village station just south of Barcelona, that train. The 408 local.' The man glowered with conviction and took a much-thumbed little booklet from his coat. Among the English, Casson knew, were people who suffered from a madness of trains. Perhaps this was one of them.

'Yes,' the man said. 'I'm right. Here it is, Puydal. A Catalonian name. Arrival, 9:21.' The man looked up. 'Well,' he said, 'for God's sake hurry!'

Casson moved quickly. This didn't happen only in Spain. In France too, your baggage popped up here, disappeared there, sometimes reappeared, sometimes was never heard from again. At the corner of the station, a long line of taxis. He jumped in the first one and said 'Puydal station. Please hurry.'

The driver turned the key in the ignition. And again.

Finally, the engine caught, he gave it a few seconds, then swung slowly out into the street, and accelerated cautiously. Casson glanced at his watch. 9:04. At this rate they would never get there in time.

'Please,' Casson said. *Por favor.*

'Mmmm –' said the driver: yes, yes, a philosopher's sigh. Vast forces of destiny, stars and planets, the run of time itself. A candle flickered, the course of life drifted one point south. ' – Puydal, Puydal.' Clearly, this was not his first trip to Puydal railroad station.

In the event, the sigh was accurate.

Puydal was where you went when all was lost, Puydal was where fate got a chance to mend its ways and the stationmaster's spaniel bitch was sitting on the Dubreuil suitcase. Casson had gone to the Galeries Lafayette to buy one, then discovered an Arab in business on a side street selling the homely classic – pebbled tan surface with a dull green and red stripe that half the world seemed to own.

'Ah, so this is yours?' said the stationmaster. 'May I just, Señor Dubreuil, have the briefest glance at your passport?'

They don't ask for the passport, they ask for the ticket.

Casson handed over his passport. 'I am Señor Casson,' he said. 'The friend of Señor Dubreuil. He is sick, *enfermo*, I am to collect his baggage.' He dug into his pocket, took out a handful of francs, pesetas, coins of many lands. 'He told me, "a gratuity," in appreciation, he is sick, it's cold . . .'

The stationmaster nodded gravely and took the money, shooed his dog off and saluted. '*Mil gracias.*' Casson grabbed the suitcase and trotted out the door to find the same taxi. 'Barcelona station,' he said to the driver, looking at his watch. The express to the southern coast was due to leave in seventeen minutes, they would never make it. 'Please hurry,' he said to the driver.

There were no other cars, the taxi bumped along the

152

cracked surface of the old macadam road, one headlight aimed up in the pine trees, the other a faint glow in the darkness. The engine missed, the gears whined, the driver sang to himself under his breath. Casson hoisted the suitcase onto his lap and opened it a crack. Yes, still in there. Thank God. Folded up in threadbare shirts and pants he'd bought at a used-clothes cart out in Clignancourt. He leaned back, closed his eyes, felt clammy and uncomfortable as the sweat dried on his shirt in the cold night air. It was time to admit to himself he had no idea what he was doing – he'd read Eric Ambler, he had a general idea of how it was all supposed to work, but this wasn't it.

28 January, 1941. The Alhambra Hotel, Málaga

A Spanish casino in winter. Cold grey sea, storms that blew rain against the window and sang in the stucco minarets. In the dining room, a string orchestra, a thé dansant, the songs Viennese, the violins flat. Still, the guests danced, staring into the private distance, the women wearing jewels and glass and Gypsy beads, the men in suits steamed over the green-stained bathtubs. Refugees, fugitives, émigrés, immigrants, stateless persons, wanted by this regime or that, rich or shrewd or lucky enough to get this far but no farther, washed up at the end of Europe, talking all night – in Bessarabian Yiddish or Alsatian French – stealing rolls from breakfast trays in the halls, trying to tip the barman with Bulgarian lev.

In the courtyard, a Moorish garden; rusty fountain, archway hung with dead ivy that rustled in the wind. Casson walked there, or by the thundering sea, ruining his shoes in the grey sand. But, anything not to be in the room. He'd placed an advertisement in ABC, the Monarchist daily, in the *Noticias* section. SWISS GENTLEMAN, COMMERCIAL TRAVELLER, SEEKS ROOM IN PRIVATE HOME FOR MONTH OF

FEBRUARY. Then, he waited. Three days, four days, a week. Nothing happened. Perhaps the operation had been cancelled, and they'd just left him there. On his walks he composed long letters to Citrine, things he would never be able to write down – very beautiful things, he thought. In the casino he gambled listlessly, betting red and black at the roulette table, sticking at seventeen in blackjack, breaking even and walking away. A woman slipped a note in his pocket – *Would you like to visit to me? I am in the Room 34*. Maybe he would have liked to, but now he didn't know who anybody was or what they were after.

He was shaving when the telephone rang, two long notes. He ran into the bedroom. 'Yes?'

'Are you the gentleman who advertised in the newspaper?'

The number given in the newspaper had not been for the Alhambra.

'Yes,' he said.

'I wonder, perhaps we could meet.'

French, spoken well by a Spaniard.

'All right.'

'In an hour? Would that be convenient?'

'It would.'

'The hotel has a bar . . .'

'Yes.'

'It's three-twenty. Should we say, four-thirty?'

'Good.'

'I'll see you then.'

'Good-bye.'

Casson took a table in the corner, ordered a dry sherry. Beyond the curtained window the rain drummed down. At the next table a couple in their thirties was having a conspirators' argument. *He* should make the approach, say *this*, and tomorrow evening was the very last moment they could wait to do it. She was afraid, there was only this one

154

chance, what if they tried and failed. Maybe it would be better not to give themselves away, not just yet.

A bellboy in hotel uniform, silver tray with an envelope on it. 'A message for you, sir.'

Casson tipped him, opened the envelope. Expensive notepaper, elegant handwriting. 'Please forgive the inconvenience, but the meeting has been moved. To the yacht *Estancia*, last slip, C dock, in the harbour. Looking forward to meeting you.' Signed with initials.

'May I send a message back?' Casson asked the boy.

'The gentleman has left, sir.'

So be it. They had looked him over in the bar, checked to see if he was alone, and now they were going to do business. He folded the note and put it in his pocket, paid for the sherry, and walked out the front door of the hotel. The rain was running brown in the cobbled street. Well, he'd get wet. No, that wouldn't work. He'd have to go back upstairs and get a raincoat.

He'd learned to be sensitive to sudden changes of direction – he'd come back to the room unexpectedly one night and heard, thought he heard, some commotion on the balcony just as he got the door unlocked and open. There was nothing to see, the balcony door was locked when he tried it. But somebody had been in the room, then left when they heard him at the door. How did he know? He didn't know how, he just did. And, more, it was somebody he didn't want to catch, because he wasn't exactly sure where that might lead.

He got out of the elevator, then paused at the door. Put the key in, turned it, entered. Silent. The damp, still air undisturbed.

Outside it was dusk, low clouds scudding east, patches of yellow sky over the water out towards the African coast. The palm trees lining the *Paseo* were whipping in the gale, loose fronds blown up against the sea-wall. Casson put his head down, held on to his hat, and hurried towards the harbour. Two women in black shawls ran past, laughing, and a man in a cloth cap rode by on a bicycle, a straw basket hung on one arm.

The harbour, C dock; in the last slip, the *Estancia*. A small, compact motor yacht, elegant in the 1920s, then used hard over the years and now beginning to age – varnish worn off the teak in places, brasswork showing the first bloom of verdigris. The portholes were shuttered, the boat seemed deserted, bobbing up and down on the harbour swell amid the orange peels and tarred wood. Casson stood for a moment, rain dripping off the brim of his hat. Somewhere in his heart he turned and went back to Paris, a man who'd lived, for a moment, the wrong life. A wave broke over the end of the dock, white spray blown sideways by the wind. He took a deep breath, crossed the gangplank, rapped sharply on the door to the stateroom.

The door swung open immediately, he stepped inside and it closed behind him. The room was dark, and silent, except for creaking planks as the *Estancia* strained against its moorage. The man who had opened the door watched him carefully, his fingers resting on a table by a large revolver. Apparently this was Carabal – described to Casson as a Spanish army officer, a colonel. But no braid or epaulets. Pale grey suit and spectacles; sparse, carefully combed hair, and the bland face of a diplomat, reddened by excitement and winter weather. In his forties, Casson thought.

'I'm to say to you that we met, at the Prado, last April,' Casson said.

Carabal nodded, acknowledging the password. 'It was July' – countersign – 'in Lisbon.'

There was someone else on the boat – he changed position, and Casson could feel the shift of weight in the floorboards. Casson reached into the pocket of his raincoat, took out a key, handed it to Carabal. 'It's on the sixth floor,' he said. 'Room forty-two. The suitcase is in the closet.'

Carabal took the key. 'Three hundred thousand?'

'Yes.'

'Good. General Arado will contact your principals.'

'How will that happen?'

'By letter. Hand-delivered in Paris on the fifteenth of February.'

'All right.'

'We will go forward.'

'Yes.'

'Good luck to all of us,' Carabal said, opening the door.

Casson turned and left. On the dock, he raised his face to the wind-blown rain. *Thank God that's over.*

The walk back along the *Paseo* was glorious. Shattered cloud over the sea, puddles like miniature lakes – surface water ruffled by the gusting wind, a priest on a mule, the street lamps coming on in first darkness. Golden light, fluttering palm trees. '*Buenas noches*,' said the priest.

Back in the Alhambra, he felt the weight lift. Thank God it was over, now he could go back to his own life. After the war, a good story. *A revolver!* He took his wet shoes off, jacket and trousers and shirt and socks, crawled into bed in his underwear. The pillow felt cool and smooth against the skin of his face. What was it, seven in the evening? So what. He didn't care. He would order from room service if he felt like eating.

An omelette. They could manage that. He had captured, by means of lavish tips, the allegiance of the room-service waiter, a man not without influence in the kitchen. That meant the omelette did not have to swim in oil and garlic and tomato sauce, it could be dry, with salt and parsley. He needed something like that now.

Oatmeal! He'd discovered it during a trip to Scotland.

157

Steel-cut, they'd say, meaning the best, with yellow cream from an earthenware pitcher. He'd ordered it every morning; dense, gooey stuff – delicious, soothing. Of course down here they would never have such a thing.

Who had put the little slip of paper in his pocket? The redhead, he was almost sure of it. Pearl earrings, dancer's legs. Haughty, the chin tilted up towards heaven. Passionate, he thought, that kind of a sneer could turn into a very different expression, an *O* – surprised by pleasure. Or playful indignation. How dare you. He liked that, an excellent trick. Jesus, women. They thought up all these things, a man had no chance at all. And then, like Citrine, they turned away from you. How long could he mourn? It wasn't good not to make love. Unhealthy, there were all sorts of theories.

Tired. It scared him, what this little enterprise had taken from him in strength and spirit. Oh Lord, he was so tired. No redhead for him, not tonight. She wouldn't do it anyhow, not now, not after he'd ignored the note. *What? Monsieur! How dare you presume*. Ah, but, even better, the redhead says yes, they go to his room. She likes to kiss, that hard mouth softens against his. White skin, blue veins, taut nipples. Then later he admits the note excited him. 'Note?' she says.

For a moment he was gone, then he came back. A strange little dream – a hallway in a house. Somebody he'd known, something had happened. It meant nothing, and he could not stay awake any longer. He took a deep breath and let it out very slowly to tell himself that the world was slipping back into place.

Oatmeal.

The phone. Those two sustained notes, again and again. He clawed at it, knocked the receiver off the cradle, groped around the night table until he found it, finally mumbled, 'What? Hello?'

'Jean-Claude! Hey it's me. I'm here. I owe you a drink, right? So now I got to pay up. Hello?'

Simic.

'Jean-Claude? What goes on there? Not *asleep*. Hey, shit, it's nine-thirty. Wait a minute, now I see, you're getting a little, right?'

'No, I'm alone.'

'Oh. So, well, then, we'll have a drink. Say, in twenty minutes.'

Casson's mind wasn't working at all. All he could say was yes.

'In the bar downstairs. Champagne cocktail – what about it?'

'All right.'

'*A bientôt!*' Triumphant, Simic very nearly sang the words.

Don't be a rat, Casson told himself. He's happy, you be happy too. Not everything needs to fit in with your mood about it.

He staggered into the bathroom. What was Simic doing in Málaga? If he'd been intending to come, why hadn't he brought the money himself? Well, there was, no doubt, a reason, he would know it soon enough. He stood in the tub, pulled the linen curtain closed, inhaled the damp-drain odour of Spanish beach hotels. Five showerheads poked from the green tile – maybe in summer you'd be splendidly doused from every side. Not now. Five tepid drizzles and the smell of sulphur. *Putain de merde*. He threw handfuls of water on himself, then rubbed his face with a towel.

He got dressed, tied his tie, brushed his hair. Simic wasn't going to make a night of it, please God. Whorehouses and champagne and somebody with a bloody nose bribing a cop at dawn.

Down the hall, checked his watch, he was right on time. Pressed the bell for the elevator. It started up, humming and grinding, then stopped with a squeak. *Maybe if they left some oil out of the food and put it on the elevator.* All right, victory for the Alhambra, he would walk downstairs. No, here it came, slow and noisy. The door slid open, the elevator boy, about fifteen, in hotel uniform, mumbled good evening. Strange, he was pale, absolutely white. He slid the door closed. Everything smelled in this hotel, that included the elevator. Stopped on three. Bulky man in a dinner jacket, who stood back against the wall and cleared his throat. Finally, the lobby.

The bar dark and very active, Spaniards having a drink before their eleven o'clock dinner hour. Fifteen minutes, then a table came open, next to a rubber plant. Casson tipped the waiter, sat down. Now, what could he order that would not do battle with the gruesome champagne cocktail he was going to be forced to drink? A dry sherry, and a coffee. A dish of salted almonds arrived as well. There was a string trio in the lobby, three elderly Hungarians who played their version of Spanish music. 10:10. Simic, where are you?

He sent the waiter to the bar for cigarettes. A brand called Estrella. Very good, he thought. Strong, but not too dry. He smoked, drank some sherry, ate an almond, took a sip of coffee. Why, he wondered, did he have to be the one to fight Hitler? Langlade was making light-bulbs, Bruno was selling cars. He ran down a list of friends and acquaintances, most of them, as far as he knew, were doing what they'd always done. Certainly it was harder now, and the money wasn't so good, and you had to go to the *petits fonctionnaires* all the time for this permission and that paper, but life went on. His father used to say to him – Jean-Claude, why do you always have to be the one? 10:20.

Simic hadn't meant tomorrow night, had he? Was he in the hotel when he called? It had sounded that way, but as long as the call was local you couldn't really tell. By now, Casson had decided that maybe a celebration was a good idea. After all, they'd done it, hadn't they. Run money over the border, bribed a Spanish general. Despite the Gestapo and the vagaries of Spanish railroads. Strange – what was an English artist doing at Barcelona station?

10:22. Casson stood up, peered around at the other tables. That had happened to him once at Fouquet – his lunch appointment waiting at one table, he at another, both of them very irritated by the time they'd discovered what they'd done.

Well then, all right. A few minutes more and he was going back upstairs. The war was over for the night. Let the Germans rule the French for a thousand years, if they could stand it that long, he was going back to the room. Now, of course, he was hungry, but he wasn't going to sit alone in the dining room. He ate another almond. 10:28. He watched the second hand crawl around the face of his watch, then he stood up. Just as somebody was coming towards him, weaving among the tables. Well, finally. But, not Simic. Marie-Noëlle – of all people.

What a coincidence.

She sat across from him, ordered a double brandy with soda, got a Gitane going.

'I do have somebody joining me,' he said apologetically. 'A man I know from Paris.'

'No,' she said, 'he isn't coming.'

'Who isn't?'

'Your friend. Simic.' She wasn't joking. He tried to make sense of that but couldn't.

She stared at him; worried, angry, tapped her index finger against the table, looked at her watch. 'I'm leaving tonight,' she said. 'But, before I go, it's my job to decide about you, monsieur. As to whether you are a knave, or just a fool.'

He stared at her.

'So,' she said.

161

He didn't know what to say. His first instinct was to defend himself, to say something reasonably witty and fairly sharp. But he didn't. She wasn't joking, to her the choice was precisely described, insulting, but not meant as an insult. And, he somehow knew, it mattered. At last he said quietly, 'I am not a knave, Marie-Noëlle.'

'A fool, then.'

He shrugged. Who in this life hasn't been a fool?

She canted her head to one side. Was this something she could believe? She searched his face. 'Used?' she said.

'Could be.'

'Used?'

'By Simic.'

'How?'

'To steal from us.'

'Who is "us"?'

'My employers. The British Secret Intelligence Service. In London.'

This was a lot to take in but, somehow, not completely a shock. At some level he had understood that she wasn't just somebody met on a train. 'Well,' he said. 'You mean, the people in the business of bribing Spanish generals.'

'They thought they were, but it was a fraud. A confidence scheme – seven hundred thousand pesetas before your delivery, another million to come after that.'

Casson lit a cigarette, shook his head as if to clear it.

'Simic was an opportunist,' Marie-Noëlle said. 'Apparently he'd dabbled with intelligence services before. In Hungary? Romania? France, perhaps. Who knows. He had a good, instinctive sense of how the game is played, of how money changes hands, of what kinds of things people like to hear. When the Germans took over he saw his chance – he could get rich if he came up with an operation that felt really authentic.'

'And Carabal? Is he a colonel in the Spanish army?'

'Yes. Also a thief, one of Simic's partners.'

'General Arado?'

'A monster, but not a traitor. Credible – for Simic's purpose. A history of support for the Bourbon monarchy. But, no inclination to overthrow the Falange. No inclination for politics at all.'

Casson scowled, stared down at the table. He had assumed he was smarter than Simic, but maybe it was simply that he was above him, socially, professionally. He'd been worse than a fool, he realized. 'And me?' he said.

'You. We are treating that as an open question. You'd been mentioned by a former business associate, and when Simic asked for a name we gave him yours. But then, after that, who knows. Under occupation, people do what they feel they have to do.'

'You think I took your money.'

'Did you take it?'

'No.'

'Somebody did. Not what you brought down, we have that back, but there was an earlier payment, and some of that is missing.'

'What happens to Carabal?'

'Can't touch him. There's an office theory that General Arado found the whole business amusing, and that Carabal's career will not suffer at all.'

'And Simic?'

She spread her hands, palms up. *What do you think?*

'We went and had a drink,' Casson said. 'He explained to me the importance of Gibraltar, it was very persuasive.'

'It is important.'

'But they won't attack it.'

'No,' she said. 'Because of the wind.'

Casson didn't understand.

'It blows hard there, changes direction – it's tricky. You've seen those Greek amphoras in hotel lobbies, they plant geraniums in them. Sometimes they wash up on the beach, from the ocean floor. Well, think how they

163

happened to be down there in the first place – obviously somebody got it wrong. A wind like that, the Germans can't do what they did with the Belgian forts, they can't use paratroops, or gliders. As for an attack over land, the peninsula is narrow, and heavily mined from one side to the other. The roads are terrible, and the Spanish-gauge railway track is different, which means the Wehrmacht can't run trains through France – they'd have to change over, and we'd know about it right away. That leaves an attack from the sea, which would have to be staged from Spanish Morocco, and the cranes at the port of Ceuta aren't big enough to lift heavy tanks and artillery onto ships.'

'So then, why pay Spanish generals to overthrow Franco?'

'You have to understand the nature of the business. It has, like everything else, fashion, what the hemline is to the prêt-à-porter. So once an idea is, ah, born – memos written, meetings held – it takes on a life of its own. For a time, it's the local religion, and nobody wants to be the local atheist. Erno Simic understood that, understood how vulnerable we were to big, nasty schemes, and he decided to make his fortune. He would have played us along; the general is thinking, the general is nervous, the general has decided to go ahead, send a sniper rifle and a box of exploding sweets. And on, and on. But, you know, somebody found a way to see if General Arado was actually in on it, and he wasn't.'

'So everything I did . . .'

'Meant nothing. Yes, that's right. On the other hand, if the Seguridad or the Gestapo had caught you with the money . . .'

Casson sat back in the chair, the life in the bar was growing brighter and louder. The Spanish brandy wasn't very expensive, after a while it inspired a certain optimism. 'Tell me something,' he said. 'Are you really Lady Marensohn?'

164

'Yes. I am pretty much who I said I was. There's just this one little extra dimension. Of course, I'd *prefer* you not to talk about it. As in, not ever.'

'No, I won't.' He thought a moment. 'I hope you understand – Simic was what he was, but I believed in the scheme, I really thought it would damage Germany.'

Marie-Noëlle nodded. 'Yes, probably you did. It was my job, on the train, to find out who you were. As far as I can tell, you were drawn in, used. The people I work for, on the other hand . . .'

She paused a moment, she wanted to be accurate. 'The people I work for,' she said. 'You have to understand, Britain is living on the edge of a cliff – and these people were never very nice people in the first place. Now the issue is survival, national survival. So they are, even more – difficult. Cold. Not interested in motive – words don't matter, what matters is what's done. So, perhaps, they feel it isn't over between you and them. Because if you sat down and joined, knowingly, with Simic, what, frankly would be different in your explanation? You'd say exactly what you've said.'

Casson thought about it for a time, to see how that wasn't actually the case, but it was. 'What can I do?' he said.

'Go back home, Monsieur Casson. Live your life. Hope for British success in 1941, and German failure. If that happens, there is every possibility that, for you, life will simply go back to being what it always was.'

NEW FRIENDS

FRIDAY NIGHT, 6 MARCH, WE'RE HAVING A COCKTAIL
AMÉRICAIN, 5 to 8. PLEASE COME, JEAN-CLAUDE, IT'S
BEEN FOREVER SINCE WE'VE SEEN YOU.

Casson stood in Marie-Claire's living room, talking to
Charles Arnaud, the lawyer. Everyone in the room was
standing – one didn't sit down at a *cocktail Américain*.
Casson sipped at his drink. 'A cuba libre, they called it. It
has rum in it.'

Arnaud rapped a knuckle twice against his temple and
made a knocking noise with his tongue. It meant strong
drink, and a headache in the morning. Casson offered a
sour smile in agreement. 'Always the latest thing, with
Bruno,' he said.

'Have I seen you since I came back from Belgrade?'
Arnaud said.

'No. How was it?'

Arnaud grinned. He had the face, and the white teeth,
of a matinee idol, and when he smiled he looked like a
crocodile in a cartoon.

'Bizarre,' he said. 'A visit for a week, a month of stories.
At least. I went down there for a client, to buy a boatload
of sponges, impounded in Dubrovnik harbour under a
Yugoslav tax lien. Actually, at that point, I'd become a part
owner.' Arnaud was even less a conventional lawyer than
Langlade – had for years been retained by shipping companies, but had a knack for becoming a principal, briefly,
in crisis situations where a lot of money moved very
quickly.

169

'I always stay at the Srbski Kralj. You know it?' Arnaud said.

'I don't.'

'King of Serbia, it means. Best hotel in town, wonderful food, if you can eat red peppers, and they'll send girls up all night. The bartender is a pimp, also a marriage broker – something interesting there if you think about it. Anyhow, what I have to do down there is clear, I have to hand over a certain number of dinar, about half the bill, directly to the tax collector, then they'll let the ship go, the sponges belong to us, and we know some people who buy sponges. Takes all kinds, right? So, I'm waiting around in the bar one night – these things take the most incredible amount of time to arrange – and I start talking to this fellow. You *have* to put this in a movie, Jean-Claude – he's, mmm, enormous, heaven only knows what he weighs, shaved head, moustache like a Turkish wrestler. A munitions dealer, won't say exactly where he's from, only that he's a citizen of Canada, in legal terms, and would love to go there some day.'

Casson smiled, things happened to Arnaud.

'But, what really struck me about this man was, he was wearing an extraordinary suit. Some kind of Balkan home-spun material, a shimmering green, the colour of a lime. Vast, even on him, a tent. On his feet? Bright yellow shoes – also enormous. He could barely walk. "Pity me," he says, "looking like I do. An hour ago I met with Prince Paul, the leader of Yugoslavia, on the most urgent matters."

'And then he explains. A day earlier he'd been in Istanbul, closing a deal for Oerlikons, Swiss antiaircraft cannon, with the Turkish navy. Now he's done with that, and he has to get to Belgrade, but the choice of airlines isn't very appetizing, so he books a compartment on the Orient Express, Istanbul to Belgrade, should arrive just in time for his meeting. That night he goes to the dining car, sits across the table from a Hungarian actress – she says. A

170

stunner, flaming red hair, eyes like fire. They drink, they talk, she invites him to come to her compartment. So, about ten o'clock our merchant, wearing red pyjamas and bathrobe, goes to the next sleeping car and knocks on the lady's door. Well, he says, it's even better than advertised, and they make a night of it. He gets up at six the next morning, kisses her hand, and heads back to his room. Opens the door at the end of the car, and what do you think he sees?'

'I don't know. His, ah, his wife's mother.'

'Oh no. He sees *track*. The train had been divided into two sections at the Turkish border, and now his wallet, his money, his passport, and his suitcase are heading for Germany – where he does not want them to go – and he's off to see Prince Paul in red pyjamas. Well, the next stop is in Bulgaria, Sofia, and he gets off. In the station he manages to borrow a coin, and telephones his Bulgarian representative. "Buy me a suit!" he says. "The biggest suit in Sofia! And get down to the railroad station in a hurry!" Also a shirt, and a pair of shoes. Pretty soon the agent shows up and there's the boss, all three hundred pounds of him, sitting on a bench, surrounded by a crowd of curious Bulgarians. The fellow puts on the suit, drives to the Canadian legation, demands they call the next station, have the baggage taken off the train before it reaches Germany, and have it put on the next train to Belgrade.

'And they did it.'

'He said they did. But he had his meeting in the big suit.'

'The Balkans,' Casson said. 'Somehow it's always – did you ever meet the man who ate the Sunday paper?'

'Savovic! Yes. He ate also a Latin grammar, and a fez.'

Véronique, Marie-Claire's sister who bought costume jewellery for the Galeries Lafayette, came over with a German officer on her arm. 'You two are having a good time,' she said. 'I would like to present *Oberleutnant* Hempel.'

'*Enchanté*,' Hempel said.

171

'*Oberleutnant* Hempel is in transport.'

Hempel laughed. He seemed a good-natured man, quite heavy, with thick glasses. 'My friend Bruno and me, we are in the automobile business.' His French was ghastly and slow, a comma after every word. 'Every kind of automobile, we got garages full of them, out in Levallois.'

Casson smiled politely. Was he going to be offered an opportunity to buy his own car back from Bruno and the Germans? Bruno already had the apartment and the wife – not that Casson begrudged him the latter – but having the car as well seemed excessive.

Arnaud never stopped smiling. One had a few friends, but mostly people were meant to be used, one way or another, and if you weren't born knowing that you had better learn it somewhere along the way. He nodded encouragement as Hempel spoke, *yes, that's right*, even said a few words in return, the Horch, the Audi, Bavarian Motor Works. Now he had a lifelong friend. '*Ja! Ja!*' the officer said. He was sweating with gratitude. Véronique chose that moment to escape, smiling and backing away. Arnaud caught Casson's eye – glanced up at the ceiling. *Quel cul.*

Casson drank some more of the cuba libre. He'd be taking off his clothes and dancing on the table in no time at all. *Olé!* This was his third concoction and it was getting him good and drunk, perhaps that was acceptable at a real American cocktail party, but not in Passy. Still, maybe it didn't matter. Hempel laughed at something Arnaud said. Casson looked closer. Had he actually understood the joke? No – a German stage laugh. Very hearty. And this idiot had his car.

A hand took his elbow in a hard grip. 'Come with me,' Marie-Claire hissed in his ear. He smiled and shrugged as he was towed away. They wound their way through the chattering crowd in the smoky living room, around the corner, into the bedroom – a kidding *tiens!* from Casson, Marie-Claire whispering 'I have to talk to you.' She hauled him into the bathroom and shut the door firmly behind them. He peered around drunkenly. This had once been his, he'd shaved here every morning.

'Jean-Claude,' she said, still whispering, 'what am I going to do about this?'

'What?'

'What. This *boche*, this *schleuh*. He brings them home, now.'

'I don't know,' he said. 'Maybe it's the wise thing to do.'

'You don't believe that!' A fierce whisper. Then she moved closer to him, an aura of whisky and perfume hung around her. Suddenly she looked worried. 'Do you?'

'No.' After a moment he said, 'But,' then sighed like a man who was going to have to tell more of the truth than he wanted to, 'I'm afraid that it will turn out that way.'

She looked grim – bad news, but maybe he was right. Someone laughed in the living room. 'After all,' he said, 'what matters to Bruno is that he *does well*. Right?'

She nodded.

'Well, that's how it is with him. If you take that away – what's left?'

She was going to cry. He set his glass carefully on the rim of the sink and put his arms around her. She shuddered once and leaned into him. 'Come on,' he said softly. 'It's just the life we live now.'

'I know.'

'So, the hell with it.'

'I'm scared,' she said. 'I can't do it – I'm going to make a mistake.' A tear started at the corner of her eye. 'Oh no,' she said, stopping it with her finger.

'We're all scared,' he said.

'Not you.'

'Yes, me.' He reached over her shoulder, took a facecloth off a peg and, hand behind his back, let cold water run on it. He squeezed it out and gave it to her, saying 'Here,' and she held it on her eye.

She looked up at him, shook her head. 'What a circus,' she said. She put her free hand on his chest, gave him a wry smile, then kissed him on the mouth, a moment, a little more, and warm. Casson felt something like an electric shock.

A discreet knock on the door. Véronique: 'There are people here, Marie-Claire.'

'Thank you.'

In the living room, taking her coat off by the door, Bibi Lachette. 'Jean-Claude!' she called out, eyes bright, mouth red and sexy. 'This is Albert.'

Fair-haired, pink-cheeked from the cold, a perfectly groomed moustache and goatee. 'Ah yes,' he said, unwinding himself from a complicated, capelike overcoat. 'The film man.'

10 March, 11 March, 12 March

Please be spring. If nothing else, that. The trees at the entrances to the Métro, where warm air vented from down below, always bloomed first. Yes, said the newspapers, it had been the coldest winter in a hundred years. Privately, more than one person in Paris – and in Prague and in Warsaw and in Copenhagen – thought that God had punished Europe for setting itself on fire, for murdering the innocent, for evil. But then too there was, particularly in that scheme of things, redemption. And *now* would be a good time for it. The wind still blew, getting out of bed in the morning still hurt, the skin stayed rough and cracked, but the winter was breaking apart, collapsing, exhausted by its valiant effort to kill every last one of them.

Fischfang had barely survived; no coal, too many women and children, never enough to eat. He stared at himself in a mirror hung on a bare wall, his face thin and angry. 'Look what they have done to me,' he said to Casson.

174

'They ate all the food while we starved. Sometimes I see one, plump and happy, strutting like a little pigeon. This is the one, I tell myself. This one goes in an alley and he doesn't come out. I've been close, once or twice. I think if I don't do something my head will explode.'

Casson nodded that he understood, taking wheat flour and milled oats and a can of lard from a sack and setting it on the table. All he could manage but, he thought, probably not enough. He wondered how much more Fischfang could take.

Yet, a mystery. *Hotel Dorado* was luminous. Not in the plot – somewhere in deepest Fischfang-land there was no real belief in plots. Life wasn't this, and therefore that, and so, of course, the other. It didn't work that way. Life was this, and then something, and then something else, and then a kick in the arse from nowhere. In *Hotel Dorado* anyhow, the theory worked. A miracle. How on earth had Fischfang thought it up? The characters floated about, puzzled ghosts in the corridors of a dream hotel, a little good, a little bad, the usual tenants of life. They shared, all of them, a certain gentle despair. Even the teenager, Hélène, had seen the world for what it was – and love might help, might not. There were six tables in the dining room, the old waiter moved among them, you could hear the hum of conversation, the bump of the door to the kitchen, the clatter of pots and pans as the proprietor cooked dinner. Thank heaven it wasn't Cocteau! The Game of Life as a provincial hotel – Madame Avarice, Baron Glutton, and Death as the old porter. Fischfang's little hotel was a little hotel, life was a weekend.

Suddenly he realized that they would applaud in the theatres. He almost shivered at the idea, but they would. They'd sit in the darkness and, despite the fact that nobody who'd worked on the film could hear, they would clap at the end, just to celebrate what it made them feel.

*   *   *

175

It wasn't finished, of course – there were fixes that would have to be made – but it was there. Hugo Altmann called him the morning after he'd sent over a copy, demanded to meet the reclusive screenwriter, discovered his lunch appointment that afternoon had cancelled.

'Who would you like to direct?' he asked over coffee.

'I've thought about it.'

'And?'

Casson hesitated, chose not to open the bidding.

'Well,' Altmann said. 'Suppose you could have anybody in the world?'

'Really?'

'Yes. I mean, let's start there, anyhow.'

Casson nodded. 'René Guillot, perhaps, for this.'

'Yes,' Altmann said. His ears reddened. 'That might work very well.'

Altmann was looking at him a certain way: here was Jean Casson, CasFilm, *No Way Out* and *Night Run* and all that sort of thing. Nothing wrong with it. It put people in the seats. Everybody made a little money – if they were careful. He was easy to work with, not a prima donna. On time, pretty much, on budget, pretty much. Not unsuccessful. But now, *Hotel Dorado*. This was different.

20 March, 21 March, 22 March

Maybe, this morning, the window could be opened. Not too much, just a little. After all, this wasn't exactly a wind, more like a breeze. Somehow, against all odds, spring was coming. One could get used to the rationing, to the Germans, to the way things were, and then one simply did what had to be done. And, if you managed to avoid a trap or two, and kept your wits about you, there were rewards: a draft of *Hotel Dorado* went into Altmann's office, money came out. That allowed Casson to eat in black-market restaurants twice a week. His apartment felt comfortable – the warming of the season replacing the heating of the baroness. In general, life seemed to be working better. For example his telephone line had been repaired – Madame Fitou told him the crew had been there – even before he realized it was out of order.

At night, he slept alone.

His friends had always claimed that Parisian women knew when a man was in love. Which meant? He wasn't sure, but something had changed. He didn't want the women in the cafés, and, when he decided he did, they didn't want him. He stared at himself in the mirror, but he looked the same as he had for a long time. So, he thought, it must be happening on the subconscious level – mysterious biology. He was, for the moment, the wrong ant on the wrong leaf.

He didn't dream about Citrine – he didn't dream. But he thought about her before he went to sleep. How she looked, certain angles, certain poses, his own private selection. Accidental moments, often – she would as likely be putting on a stocking as taking it off. She ran past a doorway because there was no towel in the bathroom. Or she made a certain request and there was a tremor in her voice. For him, those nights in early spring, she would do some of the things she'd done when they'd been together, then some things he had always imagined her doing, then some things she'd probably never done and never would. He wondered what she would have felt had she seen the movies he made of her. Of course, she made her own movies, so it wouldn't be a great shock. Would he like to see those? Yes. He would like to.

Thought about her. And talked to her. Shared the tour of daily existence. She actually missed quite a bit here – maybe she would have been excited by Casson's images of lovemaking, maybe, but she certainly would have laughed at the comedies he found for her.

177

At last, in the middle of February, he'd given in and written a love letter. Based on the ones he'd composed in Spain – on the beach and in the railway cars. Wrote it down and put it in an envelope. *Citrine, I love you.* It wasn't very long, but it was very honest. Even then, there was a lot he didn't say – who wants a blue movie in their love letter? Still, the idea came across. He read it over, it was the best he could do. Somewhere between walks-on-the-beach and sixty-nine, a few sentences about life being short, a few more on mystery, mostly just Jean-Claude, wide open, on paper.

Casson went out to Billancourt studios, where René Guillot was directing a pirate film.

> *Seize hommes sur*
> *le coffre d'un mort,*
> *yo ho ho*
> *la bouteille de rhum!*

> *Boisson et diable*
> *ont tué les autres,*
> *yo ho ho*
> *buvons le rhum!*

'Michel?'

'Yes, Monsieur Guillot?'

'Could you move up the mast a little higher?'

'Yes, sir.'

'And, everybody, we need it deeper, more baritone, stronger. Yo ho ho! Let's run through it once, like that, and Etienne? Hold the bottle of rum up so we can see it – maybe give it a shake, like this. Yes. All right, "*Seize hommes sur . . .*"'

Casson stood near Guillot's canvas chair – Guillot smiled and beckoned him over.

Casson spoke in an undertone. 'Jean Lafitte?'

'Blackbeard.'

'Mmm.'

Casson recognized the wooden boat, supported beneath the keel by scaffolding. It had been featured in scores of pirate and adventure films; a Spanish galleon, a British frigate, a seventy-four-gun ship-of-the-line in the Napoleonic navy. It was manned, that afternoon, by singing pirates. Some clung to the mast, there were several at the helmsman's wheel, one straddling the bowsprit and a score of others, in eyepatch and cutlass, headscarf and earring and striped jersey. Only luck, Casson felt, had so far saved him from working in the genre. Guillot, he'd been told, was there as a favour, to finish a job left undone by a journeyman director who had disappeared.

Later they sat in the canteen, amid electricians and carpenters, and ate sausage sandwiches washed down with thin beer. 'It's a very good screenplay,' Guillot said. 'What's this nonsense about a recluse in the countryside?'

'It's Louis Fischfang.'

'Oh. Of course. He's still here?'

'Yes.'

Guillot's expression said *not good*. He smoothed back his fine white hair. He'd been famously handsome when he was young. He remained famously arrogant – egotistical, selfish, brilliant. An *homme de la gauche* consumed with leftist causes, he'd made a passionate speech at the World Congress Against War in Amsterdam in 1933, then denounced Soviet communism after the Hitler-Stalin pact of 1939.

'You think Altmann's a Nazi?' he said quietly.

Casson shrugged.

Guillot thought about it for a moment, then he said, 'I should've left.'

'Why didn't you?'

'I'm French. Where the hell am I going to go?'

179

They drank some beer. Guillot spooned mustard onto his sausage. 'I wonder about the title,' he said. '*Hotel Dorado*. What about something like *Nights of Autumn*? That's not it, but I'm feeling for loss, a little melancholy, something bittersweet. You know me, I like to go right at things. Then also, it struck me, why is the stranger a woman? Better a man, no?'

'We talked about it,' Casson said. 'We like the idea of a woman. Travelling alone, vulnerable, a small part saint but she doesn't know it. The way the Americans use an angel – always clumsy, or absent-minded. The idea is that *strong* and *good* are two different things.'

Guillot stopped chewing – jowls and pouchy eyes immobile – and stared at him for a moment. Then nodded once, *all right – I accept that*, and went back to his food.

'You know,' Guillot said, 'the last time I heard your name was from Raoul Mies. You'd just signed with Continental, in October I think, and Mies decided that maybe he would too.'

'You're serious?'

Guillot spread his hands, meaning *of course*.

'Altmann told me that Mies and, ah, Jean Leveque had signed. So, I decided it would be all right for me.'

The electricians at the next table laughed at something. Guillot gave Casson a sour smile. 'An old trick,' he said.

Casson pushed his food aside and lit a cigarette.

'I don't blame you,' Guillot said. 'But there's nothing you can do about it now.'

'I should've known better.'

Guillot sighed. 'The war,' he said. It explained everything. 'It's fucked us,' he added. 'And the bill isn't even in.'

Casson nodded.

'As for this project,' Guillot said, 'one thing we can do is take it south. It's not heaven, it's Vichy. Instead of Goebbels's people at the Hotel Majestic there's the COIC, the

Comité d'Organisation de L'Industrie Cinématographique. It's not all that different – they won't give membership cards to Jews – but there are two reasons to consider it. One is that it's still French, whatever else it is, they don't mean what they say and as long as you stand there they keep talking, and two, you can get out of the country down there a lot easier than you can here.' He lowered his voice. 'That I do know, because I had somebody *find out*. And maybe that's what, uhh, your writer ought to hear about.'

'He will,' Casson said.

They sat in silence for a time. Finished the beer. The electricians looked at their watches, stood up and left. 'Well,' Guillot said – it meant time to go back to work. 'You can stay, of course, if you like.'

'I have a meeting back in Paris,' Casson said.

He met Guillot's eyes, was reassured. They weren't children, they'd spent their lives in the film business, were not strangers to betrayal and back-stabbing. And they were French, which meant they knew how to evade, to improvise, to *reculer pour mieux sauter* – to back up in order to get a better jump. 'Tell me one thing,' Casson said, 'just for curiosity's sake. Why, of all things, Blackbeard?'

'I think it's the godchild of some office that Altmann talks to. I mean, it's just something for the kids on Saturday afternoons, and to play in the countryside, where they'll watch anything that moves. You see, Blackbeard is *English*. A pirate, a brute. In this movie, he walks the plank.'

Casson shook his head, in awe at such nonsense. '*Mon Dieu*,' he said sorrowfully.

Guillot smiled, leaned towards Casson, spoke in a conspirator's undertone. 'Yo ho ho,' he said.

That night when he got home Casson discovered that his letter to Citrine had been returned. He held it in his hands. Somebody had obviously read it, possibly the censors, but, more likely, those bastards at the hotel. He had put the letter in the envelope as he'd been taught in lycée, so that the greeting was the first thing the reader saw when the letter was unfolded. Somebody had put it back in the wrong way. Written across the front of the envelope *Gone Away. Left No Address.*

He didn't read it.

He sat on the couch, still wearing his raincoat, the apartment dark and lifeless. Forty-one-year-old producers. Twenty-nine-year-old actresses with a certain smoky look. What, pray tell, had he thought would happen? He leaned his head back against the cushion. She had left, all right. And one reason was to make certain he was locked out of her life. She knew herself, she knew him, she knew better.

Once again he'd been stupid: had decided that what he wanted to be true, was. And it wasn't. Thus Altmann had deceived him, then Simic, then with Citrine, he'd deceived himself. This couldn't go on. He heard his father saying 'Jean-Claude, Jean-Claude.'

By force of will, he turned himself back towards commerce. *Survival*, he thought, that's what matters now. It wasn't a time for love affairs – maybe that was what Citrine understood better than he ever could, survival was more important than anything. The city had no difficulty with that, at the end of winter it discovered it was somehow still alive, then went back to business with a vengeance. It wasn't very appealing, some of it, but then it never had been. You work in a whorehouse, Balzac told them. Don't let anybody see how much you enjoy it and get your money up front.

Casson, that first week in April, had a new friend. An admirer. Perhaps, even, an investor. A certain Monsieur Gilles de Groux. Nobility, the real thing, in fact de Groux de Musigny, Casson checked the listing in *Bottin Mondain* and the *Annuaire des Châteaux*. He had a huge, draughty house out in the forest of St-Germain-en-Laye, just outside

Paris, where his family had moved in 1688 in order to commiserate with the Catholic pretender James II, who'd slipped into France earlier that year. William of Orange got the English throne, as it happened, but the de Groux family remained, walking on the miles-long Grande Terrasse that looked out over the city of Paris, breeding Vendéean basset hounds, reading books in leather covers.

It was Arnaud who had suggested his name to de Groux. Casson called him after their first meeting. 'He wants to make films, he says.'

'Yes,' Arnaud said. 'That's what he told me.'

'Where did you say you met?'

'Renaissance Club.'

'How rich is he?'

Arnaud had to take a moment to think about this. All around them, in the 16th Arrondissement, were the world's great masters of the art of pretending to be rich. 'The money, I believe, is from Limoges. China. Since the eighteen-hundreds. Does he live well?'

'Big house in St-Germain. Creaky floors. Gothic maids.'

'Sounds right.'

'You think he really wants to make films?'

'Perhaps. I can't say. Maybe he wants to meet film stars. He certainly wanted to meet you. Hello? Jean-Claude?'

'Yes, I'm still on.'

'You ought to get that repaired.'

'Are you going to the Pichards on Friday?'

'I'd planned to.'

'See you there.'

'Yes. Keep me posted on what happens, will you?'

'I will.'

There were film producers who made a living by knowing how to meet rich people and what to say to them, but for Casson it somehow never worked out. Some stubborn dignity always asserted itself, they sensed that, the grand schemes came to nothing. But de Groux was, in Casson's experience, something completely new. A tall, thin, shambling fellow, no family close by, a shaggy white moustache stained by tobacco, hair that needed cutting, old wool sweaters that smelled like dogs, and a yellow corduroy jacket with buttoned pockets, a survival of the artists-and-models Montparnasse of 1910. No less an aristocrat, of course, for a little eccentricity. A certain drape hung between him and the world; installed at birth, removed with death, never to be shifted in between.

He was, however, very intent on making a film. And it was the apparatus of the business that seemed to fascinate him. He wanted to visit the office on the rue Marbeuf, he insisted they have lunch at the Alsatian brasserie on the corner – assuming that Casson often ate there. He wanted to have a drink at Fouquet – or Rudi's, or Ubu Roi – wanted to go out to Billancourt, wanted to visit the nightclubs around Bastille. In the process they would talk about very nearly everything before returning, rather dutifully it seemed to Casson, to the business at hand.

'I always come back to *The Devil's Bridge*,' he would say. 'That same kind of, feeling, the mood of, what would you say?'

'I don't know. Escape?'

'Yes, well, perhaps. But maybe more. We should be ambitious, I think. That's what's wrong with people, these days.'

They talked a great deal, and over time it crossed Casson's mind that this man had never actually seen a film.

'Tell me, Gilles,' he would say. 'What's your favourite?'

'Oh, I can never keep the titles straight.'

Vague, perhaps, but very accommodating. Any time or place was good for him, and he never missed an appointment. He travelled in a chauffeured Citroën, seemed to have all the petrol he needed, had lots of money and ration stamps, and an insatiable curiosity. What did Casson think about the Catholic church? What about Pétain? De Gaulle? The Popular Front? England, Churchill, the French Communist Party.

Good talk, intelligent and cultured. De Groux had spent half a century reading and conversing – born to a rich and idle life, your job was to discover the meaning of existence, then to let your friends know what it was. The discussion of the new film was carried on all over Paris, Casson was even invited to a supper party at de Groux's hunting lodge in the Sologne. *Oh Citrine, I wish you could be here to see this. That's a real oryx head over the fireplace, that's a real duke by the fire, he's carrying a stick with a real ivory horse's head, and he's wearing a real leather slipper with the little toe cut away to ease his gout.*

A cast of characters well beyond Jean Renoir. Adèle, the niece from Amboise. Real nobility – look at those awful teeth. Washed-out blue eyes gazed into his, a tiny pulse beat sparrowlike at the pale temple. Wasn't her uncle the dearest man – insisting that poor old Pierrot be stabled in his horse barns? This proud beast, now retired, who had pounded so faithfully down the paths of the Bois de Fontainebleau after the fleeing hart – would Monsieur care to visit him? *Citrine, I confess I wanted to.* Go to the stable and wrestle in the straw, hoist the silk evening dress and pull down the noble linen. For the son of a *grand-bourgeois* crook from the 16th, a once-in-a-lifetime opportunity. One *never* met such people, they were rumoured to exist, mostly they appeared in plays. There really was game for dinner, dark and strong – perhaps the fabled bear paw, Casson couldn't bring himself to ask – with black-blood gravy. And real watery vegetables. 'Film!' said a cousin from Burgundy. 'No. Not really.' Casson assured him it was true. And the man drew back his lips and actually brayed.

There they were, and I among them. Sad it couldn't last – de Groux was a spy, really, what else could he be? It scared

185

Casson because somebody was going to a lot of trouble, and Casson didn't think he was worth it. Or, worse, he was worth it but he just didn't realize why.

Back at the rue Chardin, a visit to the cellar with a flashlight. Ancient stone walls, a child's sled, a forgotten steamer trunk, a bicycle frame with no wheels. On one wall, black metal boxes and telephone lines. What was he looking for? He didn't know. Whatever made that hissing sound. He peered at the wires, seeking a device he could neither name nor describe. But there was nothing there. Or nothing he could see. Or, maybe, nothing at all, it was all in his mind. French phones made noise – why not this noise?

'Tell me,' de Groux said, 'a man in your position. You must have influence somewhere – a sympathetic politician, perhaps. It's hard to get the permissions, all the *fiches* one must have to do your job. I tell you I'm worried, my friend. All the money we're going to spend. It's not that I don't have it, I have pots of it. It's these musty old lawyers, and the family. They see an old man having a fling, and they worry I'll actually open my fist and a sou will fly out. So you see, I don't want all this to founder on the whim of some little *petit fonctionnaire*. I want to assure myself that when the great battle of the clerks is fought, we are the ones left standing when the smoke clears.'

Va te faire foutre, I tell him in my heart, Citrine. Go fuck thyself. But, in the real world: 'Well, Gilles, frankly I have stood in the queues myself. I have filled in my share of forms. Sometimes an assistant has been there to help but it's so difficult, you see, crucial, that one must involve oneself. It's that kind of commitment you must have. In the film business.'

'No. Really? Well.'

A blind reptile, he thought. But it knows there's a nest, and young, and it senses warmth.

*   *   *

186

And then, it happened again – it seemed everybody wanted to be his friend that spring. This time he was at the office. Four o'clock on a long, wet, grey afternoon, the street outside shiny with rain. His secretary knocked, then opened the door. 'A Madame *Duval* to see you,' she said, her voice disapproved of the name – who does she think she is, using an alias?

His heart sank. He'd been happily lost in his work, a thousand miles from reality. 'Well, send her in,' he said.

She sat across from him, wearing a dark suit and a hat with a veil, knees primly together and canted slightly to one side. One of those fortyish Frenchwomen with a sour face and beautiful legs. 'I am,' she said, 'the owner of the Hotel Bretagne. Where your friend, the actress called Citrine, was living.' Her voice was tense – this was not an easy visit.

'Yes?'

'Yes. Last Friday, the night clerk happened to tell me that you had written her a letter. By the time it reached the hotel she had left, so he marked it *Gone Away* and returned it.' She paused a moment, then said, 'He was – was not unpleased at this. A film actress, a producer, star-crossed, an unhappy ending. He was delighted, really, he's a man who takes pleasure in the misfortunes of others, and has reached an age where he's not shy about letting the world know it. It's sad, really.'

'I believe he opened the letter and read it,' Casson said angrily. 'Shared it with his friends, perhaps, and they all had a good laugh.'

The woman thought for a moment. 'Opened it? No, not him, he doesn't begin to be that bold, he simply marked the envelope and returned it. And, in the normal course of things, that would be that.'

There was more, Casson waited for it.

'However,' she said, taking a breath, 'I had, *we* had, a certain experience. I knew who she was, although she was

187

using another name – I had seen her in the movies, and nobody else looks like that. Now, I do not live at the hotel, of course, but I happened to be there, late one night, and I went to the second-floor bath to wash out a glass. It was very quiet just then, about two in the morning, and, without thinking, I simply walked in. Well, she was taking a bath. Naturally I excused myself, immediately closed the door. But –'

She hesitated.

'What happened?'

'Nothing actually happened. It took me a minute to realize what I'd seen. There were tears in her eyes, and on her face. And there was a razor blade resting on the soap dish. That's all I saw, monsieur, yet you could not be mistaken, there was no question about what was going to happen in that room. I said through the door, "Madame, is everything all right?" After a moment she said "Yes." That was the end of it, but it's possible that the intrusion saved a life – not for any reason, you understand, reason wasn't involved.'

'When was this?'

'Sometime in February. Maybe. Really, I don't remember. About two weeks later we spoke very briefly. I was working on the book-keeping, she'd come in from doing an errand and asked for her key at the desk. We talked for a minute or two, she never referred to what had happened. She told me she would be leaving at the end of the week, had found something to do in Lyons, in the *Zone Non-Occupée*, and she mentioned the name of a hotel.'

'Was she unhappy?'

'No. Thoughtful, perhaps. But, mostly, determined.'

'She is that.'

'Then, after I talked to the clerk, I decided I ought to come and see you, to tell you where she is. For a time I wasn't sure, I didn't know what to do. I argued back and forth with myself. In the end, I'm doing this not because

I insinuate myself in the lives of strangers' – the idea was so unappealing she grimaced – 'but because I believe, after thinking about it, that she meant for me to do it.'

They were quiet for a moment. Casson was conscious of the sound of tyres on the rainy street below his window.

'The way she spoke to me,' the woman said slowly, 'it was as though her emotions, her feelings about life, were uncertain. She didn't know exactly what to do, so she left matters in the hands of fate. It didn't mean all that much to me at the time – I have the hotelkeeper's view of the world, disorder, chaos, stolen towels. I remembered later only because she was who she was, but I did remember. A letter had come, the clerk noticed the return address – he recalled who you were, certainly, and once I was told about it I had to do something. Probably the letter concerns only a forgotten handkerchief.'

'No. More than that.'

She nodded to herself, confirming what she'd believed. Opened her purse, took out a hotel envelope, reached over and placed it on the corner of his desk. Then stood up. 'I hope this is the right thing to do,' she said.

Casson stood quickly. 'Thank you,' he said. 'Madame, thank you. I should have offered you something, forgive me, I, perhaps a coffee, or . . .'

A gleam of amusement in her eye. 'Another time, perhaps.' He was clearly disconcerted – she enjoyed that, particularly in men like Casson. She extended a gloved hand, he took it briefly. Then she was gone.

He tore open the envelope, found the name and telephone number of a hotel in Lyons written on a slip of paper. At the end of the day he met Bernard Langlade for a drink. 'Is it hard to find out who owns a hotel?' he said.

'Shouldn't be.'

Casson told him the name and location. Langlade called him in the morning. 'I take it back,' he said. 'The Hotel

189

Bretagne, on the Faubourg Saint-Antoine, is owned by a *Société Anonyme*, in Switzerland.'

'Is that unusual?'

'No. It's done, sometimes. For tax purposes, or divorce. And, with time and money, you could probably find a name. Of course, even then –'

'No, thank you for looking, Bernard, but probably best just to let it go.'

Langlade made a sound that meant *much the wiser choice*. 'Especially these days,' he said.

Especially these days. There was no calling Citrine from his infected telephone. Every call a new name on somebody's list. He could still see Lady Marensohn across the table in the bar of the Alhambra Hotel. Perhaps it was over, perhaps they believed him, perhaps not.

He'd taken the Métro home from work that night, a man got off behind him. Made the first turn with him, then the second. Casson paused at the window of a boulangerie. The man looked at him curiously and walked by. *Well, how am I supposed to know?* he thought. You're not, came the answering voice, you're not.

Merde alors. After all, it wasn't as though clandestine instincts were unknown in this city. All right, maybe it wasn't the British Secret Intelligence Service one had to elude. But it was husbands or lovers, wives or landlords or lawyers. Casson let it get to be 7:30 in the evening, then left the apartment. By now, when he went out in the street, everyone he saw was an operative – an anonymous little man in an Eric Ambler novel who lived in a rented room and spied on Jean Casson. So, he thought, is it you – in your dinner jacket? Or you, a clerk on the way home? Or you, the lovers embracing on the bridge? He hurried along, head down, through the rainy streets, through the fog that pooled at the base of the park railings. He trotted down the Métro stairs, left at the other end of the platform,

190

reversed direction, doubled back, at last sensed he was unobserved and headed towards the river.

Chez Clément – the little sign gold on green, faded pastel and flaked by time and weather. At the end of a tiny street where nobody went, steamed glass window, the hum of conversation and the clatter of dinnerware faintly heard. Inside the door, the smell of potatoes fried in butter every night since 1890. Clément came out of the kitchen, wiping his hands on a towel. Face scarlet, moustache immense, apron tied at one shoulder. 'Monsieur Casson.' It was like being hugged by a wine-drenched onion. How infernally clever, Clément told him, to stop by this evening, all day long they'd been working, at the stove, in the pots, what luck they'd had, one never saw this any more, perhaps the last –

No, alas, not tonight, he couldn't. Casson inclined his head towards the cloakroom and said delicately, *'Le téléphone?'*

Not *a* telephone, *the* telephone. The one Clément made available to his most cherished customers. Clément smiled, *of course*. The heart had reasons of its own, they had to be honoured, sometimes not at home.

He reached the hotel in Lyons. Madame was out.

Was there a message?

No.

12 April. 11:20 a.m.

The rain continued, soft cloudy days, nobody minded. Casson walked down the Champs-Elysées, turned right on avenue Montaigne, a few minutes later leaned on the parapet of the Pont de l'Alma, looking down into the Seine. A blonde woman walked by; lovely, wearing a yellow raincoat. On the banks, rain beaded along the branches of the chestnut trees and dripped onto the cobblestones. The river had risen to spring tide, lead-coloured water curling around the piers of the bridges, crosscurrents black on grey, shoals catching the light, rain dappling the surface, going to Normandy, then to sea. *Just a boat*, he thought. How hard would it be? Magic, a child's dream. Carried away to safety on a secret barge.

Casson looked at his watch, lit a cigarette, leaned his weight on the parapet. He could see, at one end of the bridge, a newspaper kiosk – an important day, the headlines thick and black. German planes had set Belgrade on fire, armoured columns had entered Zagreb, Skopje had been taken, soon the rest of Macedonia, and the *Panzerkorps* was driving hard on Salonika.

He crossed to the Left Bank, entered the post office on the avenue Bosquet. It was crowded, people in damp coats, impatient and irritated, smoking and grinding out their cigarettes on the wet tile floor. He waited for a long time, finally reached the counter, gave the clerk a telephone number, went to the *cabine* and waited for the short ring.

'Hotel du Parc.' The voice sounded very far away. 'Hello? Are you there?'

Casson gave the name.

'Stay on the line.' The sound of the receiver being set down on a wooden countertop.

He waited. In the next *cabine* a woman was shouting at some relative somewhere in France. Where was the money, they were supposed to send it, it should have come days ago, no she didn't want to hear about the problem.

The clerk picked the receiver up. 'She's coming now.'

Then: 'Hello?'

'Hello.'

A pause. 'It's you.'

'Yes.'

'I had to leave.'

'Yes, I know. How is Lyons?'

'Not so bad. I'm in a play.'

'Really?'

'Yes. A small part.'

'What sort of play?'

'A little comedy. Nothing much.'

'You sound good.'

'Do I?'

'Yes.'

The line hummed softly.

'Citrine, I wrote you a letter.'

'Where is it?'

'It went to the other hotel, but it came back. The woman there told me where you were.'

'What does it say?'

'It's a love letter.'

'Ah.'

'No, really.'

'I wonder if I might read it, then.'

'Yes, of course. I'll send it along – I just wanted to hear your voice.'

'The mail isn't very good, these days.'

'No, that's true.'

'Perhaps it would be better if you were to bring it.'

'Yes. You're right. Citrine?'

'Yes?'

'I love you.'

'When can you come here?'

'As soon as I can.'

'I'll wait for you.'

'I'll let you know when.'

'I'll wait.'

'I have to say good-bye.'

'Yes. Until then.'

'Until then.'

16 April, 1941

Now the trees had little leaves and clouds of soft air rolled down the boulevards at dusk and people swore they could smell the fields in the countryside north of the city. Casson bought a train ticket, and made an appointment at the rue des Saussaies to get an *Ausweis* to leave the occupied zone and cross over to the area controlled by Vichy.

A warm day, the girls were out. Nothing better than Frenchwomen, he thought. Even with rationing, they insisted on spring – new scarves, cut from last year's whatever, a little hat, made from a piece of felt somebody had left in a closet, something, at least *something*, to say that love was your reward for agreeing to live another day and walk around in the world.

On the top floor of the old Interior Ministry building, even *SS-Obersturmbannführer* Guske knew it was spring. He came around the desk to shake hands, as tanned and well-oiled as ever, every one of his forty hairs in its proper place, a big leathery smile. Then, with a sigh, he got down to business. Made himself comfortable in his chair and studied the dossier before him, a sort of *now where were we* feeling in the air. 'Ah yes,' he said. 'You went last to Spain to see about locations for a film. So, how did it go for you?'

'Very well. One or two villages were, I can say, perfect. Extremely Spanish. The church and the tile roofs, and the little whitewashed houses.'

'Indeed! You're making me want to go.'

'It's a change, certainly. Very different from France.'

'Yes, here it is, Málaga. My wife and I used to go to Lloret-de-Mar every summer, until they started fighting. Find a *pension* in a little fishing village. What dinners! *Besugo, espadon*, delicious. If you can persuade them to hold back a little on the garlic, excellent!' He laughed, showing big white teeth. Looked back down at the dossier. Read for a moment, then a slight discomfort appeared on his face. 'Hmm. Here's a memorandum I'd forgotten all about.'

He read carefully, perhaps for three or four minutes. Shook his head in pique at something small and irritating. 'I know you are famous for petty bureaucrats in France, but I tell you, Herr Casson, we Germans don't do so badly. Look at this nonsense.'

'Sir?'

'I don't have the faintest recollection of anything, you understand, I see people from dawn to dusk, of course, and I only remember the, well, the bad ones, if you know what I mean.' He raised his eyebrows to see if Casson had understood.

'What's happened is,' he continued, 'you told me, or, I thought you told me, that your army service was back in the 1914 war, but here it says that you – well, the people down at the Vincennes military base sent on to us a record that says you were transferred to a unit that was reactivated in May of 1940. Could that be right?'

'Yes. I was.'

'Well, I apparently got it wrong the last time we talked because now somebody's gone and written a memorandum in your file saying that you, well, that you didn't actually tell the truth.'

'I don't really know what I . . .' Casson felt something flutter in his stomach.

'Ach,' Guske said, quite annoyed now. He stood up, walked towards the door. 'I'm going to go down the hall and have this put right. I'll be back in a minute.' He opened the door and gestured towards a chair in the hall. 'Please,' he said. 'I'll have to ask you to wait in the corridor.'

Guske marched off down the hall. Casson wanted to get up and run out of the building, but he knew he'd never make it, and when they caught him he wouldn't be able to explain. He wasn't being threatened, exactly. It was something else – he didn't know what it was, but he could feel it reaching for him.

Hold on, he told himself.

He very nearly couldn't. He closed his eyes, heard type-writers, muted conversations, doors opening and closing, telephones. It was just an office.

Forty minutes later, Guske came back down the hall shaking his head. In a bad humour, he waved Casson into his office. 'This is extraordinarily irritating, Herr Casson, but this man at the other end of the hall is acting in a very unreasonable fashion. I mean, here we've had a simple misunderstanding, you gave me some information and it didn't happen to hold with some piece of paper that some-body sent here, and now he's going to be difficult about it.'

Casson started to speak, Guske held up his hand for silence.

'Please, there's nothing you can say that will help. I am certainly going to take care of this problem – you can have every confidence in me – but it's going to take a day or two, maybe even a little more. Your trip to Lyons, is it so very urgent?'

'No.'

'Good. Then I'm relieved. And you'll appreciate I have to work with this fellow, I can't be getting around him every five minutes. But he's going to have to learn to separate these things – here is something that must con-cern us, over there is just a nuisance, a little pebble in the shoe. Eh?'

Guske stood and offered his hand. 'Why don't you call me back a week from today? Yes? I'm sure I'll be able to give you the answer you want. These telephone numbers in your file, for home and office, they're correct?'

'Yes.'

'Very good. Then I'll see you in a week or so. Good day, Herr Casson. Please don't think too badly of us, it will all be made right in the end.'

*   *   *

Two days later, a Friday afternoon, a commotion in the *réception* of his office. Casson threw open his door, then stared with astonishment. It was a man called Bouffo – a comic actor, he used only that name. A huge man, gloriously fat, with three chins and merry little eyes – 'France's beloved Bouffo,' the publicity people said. Casson's secretary, Mireille, was standing at her desk, vaguely horrified, uncertain what to do. Bouffo, as always in a white, tentlike suit and a grey fedora, was leaning against the wall, fanning himself with a newspaper, his face the colour of chalk. 'Please, my friends,' he said. 'I beg you. Something to drink.'

'Will you take a glass of water, monsieur?' Mireille asked.

'God no.'

'Mireille,' Casson said. 'Please go down to the brasserie and bring back a carafe of wine, tell them it's an emergency.' He handed her some money.

'Now Bouffo,' he said, 'let's get you sat down.' Casson was terrified the man was going to die in his office.

'Forgive me Casson – I've had the most terrible experience.'

Casson took his arm – he was trembling – and helped him onto the couch. Up close, the smell of lilac-scented talcum powder and sweat. 'Please,' Casson said, 'try to calm yourself.'

'What a horror,' Bouffo said.

'What happened?'

'Well. You know Perlemère?'

'Yes. The agent?'

'Yes. Well, some time ago he represented me, and he owed me a little money, and I thought I'd just kind of drop in on him, unannounced, and see if I could collect some of it, you know how things are, lately. So, I went over to his office, which is just the other side of the boulevard. I was in that little lobby there, waiting for the elevator, when

197

there was a commotion on the staircase. It's Perlemère, and there are three men with him, a short one, very well-dressed, and two tough types. Detectives, is what they were.'

'You're sure?'

'Yes. One knows.'

'German?'

'French.'

'And?'

'They're arresting Perlemère.'

'*What?*'

'He's telling them he knows this one and that one and there'll be hell to pay once his important friends find out how he's being treated and all this kind of thing. But, clearly, they don't care. Perlemère tries to stop on the staircase and says "Now see here, this has gone far enough" and they hit him. I mean, they really hit him, it's not like the movies. And he cried out.'

Bouffo stopped a moment and caught his breath. 'I'll be all right,' he said. 'Then, one of them called him a Jew this and a Jew that, and they hit him again. It was sickening. The sound of it. There were tears on Perlemère's face. Then, they saw me. And one of them says, "Hey look, it's Bouffo!"'

'What did you do?'

'Casson, I was terrified. I gave a sort of nervous laugh, and I tipped my hat. Then they brushed by me. Perlemère looked in my eyes, he was pleading with me. There was blood on his mouth. I held the door open a crack after they went out – they threw him in a car, then they drove away. I didn't know what to do. I started to go home, then I remembered your office was over here and I thought I better find a place where I could sit down for a moment.'

Mireille returned, carrying a carafe of wine. Casson poured some in a water glass and gave it to Bouffo. 'No good, Casson.' He wasn't talking about the wine. Shook his head, tried to take deep breaths. 'No good. I mean, who do you go to?'

Sunday night, late – one-thirty in the morning when he looked at his watch. He was reading, wearing an old shirt and slacks. Restless, not ready to sleep. Blackout curtains drawn, light of a single lamp, a very battered Maigret novel, *The Nightclub*, he'd bought at a stall on the Seine. The buzzer by his door startled him. Now what? He laid the book face down on the chair, turned off the lamp, went out onto the terrace. Down below, a dark shape waited at the door. Then a white face turned up towards him, and a stage whisper: 'Jean-Claude, let me in.' Gabriella, with a small suitcase.

He hurried down the stairs, the marble steps cold on his feet because he was wearing only socks. He unlocked the door and pushed it open. He heard a stirring from the concierge apartment, called out, 'It's just a friend, Madame Fitou.'

Back in the apartment he poured a glass of red wine and set out some bread and blackcurrant jam. Gabriella was exhausted and pale, a smudge on the elbow of her coat. 'It happened on one of the trains,' she told him. 'Really I can't remember which one it was. I had a first-class compartment, Milan to Turin, then I took the night train to Geneva, eventually the Dijon/Paris express. Then I just barely managed to catch the last Métro from the Gare de Lyon.'

'Gabriella, why?'

'I told my husband I was coming up here to see an old girlfriend – as far as anybody knows I arrive tomorrow morning, eight-thirty, on the train from Milan. Do you see what I did?'

'Yes.'

'Jean-Claude, could I have a cigarette?'

199

He lit it for·her. She took a deep breath and sat back in the chair. 'I had to see you,' she said.

This was not the same Gabriella. She'd changed the way she looked – had her hair cut short, then set. She wore three rings: a diamond, a wide gold wedding band with filigree, and an antique, a dull green stone in a worn silver setting, ancient, a family treasure. Clearly she had a new life.

Their eyes met, a look only possible between people who've made love, then she looked away. No, he thought, it isn't that. They'd had one night together, it had been intimate, very intimate. He had wanted her – long legs, pure face – for months, but she turned out not to be someone who lost herself, or maybe just not his to excite. As for her, he'd realized later that she'd been in love with him, the real thing. So, in the end, neither one got what they wanted.

She sighed, met his eyes again, ran a hand through her hair. 'I'm married now,' she said softly.

'Gabriella, are you in trouble?'

She shook her head. 'No,' she said, 'it's you.'

'Me?'

'Yes. One morning last week, after my husband left for work, two men came to the house. One was from the security service, in Rome, and the other was German. Educated, soft-spoken, reasonably good Italian. The German asked the questions – first about my time in Paris, then about you. "Please, do not worry yourself, signora, this is simply routine, just a few things we need to know." He asked about your politics, how did you vote, did you belong to a political party. It was very thorough, carefully done. They knew a great deal about your business, about the films you'd made, about Marie-Claire and your friends. He asked what sorts of foreigners did you know. Did you travel abroad? Often? Where to?

'I made a great show of trying to be helpful, but I tried

200

to persuade them that most of my work was typing letters and filing and answering the telephone. I just didn't know much about your personal life. They seemed to accept that. "And signora, please, if it's all the same to you, we'd rather he didn't know we'd been around asking questions." That was a threat. The Italian looked at me a certain way. Not brutal, but it could not be misunderstood.'

'But you came here anyhow.'

She shrugged. 'Well, that was the only way. You can't say anything on the phone, they read your mail. We've had Mussolini and the *fascisti* since 1922, so we do what we have to do.'

'Not everybody,' he said.

'Well, no, there are always – you learn who they are.'

They talked for a long time, closer than they'd ever been. Trains and borders, special permits, passports. It wasn't about resistance, it was about secret police and day-to-day life. What had it been, he thought, since the May night they'd spent together – ten months? Back then, this gossip would have been about books, or vacations. 'At the queue for the railway controls,' she said, 'they always have somebody watching to see who decides to turn back.'

She yawned, he took her by the hand into the bedroom. She washed, changed into silk pyjamas, slid under the blankets. 'Talk to me a minute more,' she said. He turned the lights off, sat on the floor and leaned back against the bed. They kept their voices low in the darkness. 'It is very strange at home now,' she told him. 'The Milanese don't believe they live in Italy. You mention Mussolini and they look to heaven – yet one more of life's afflictions that has to be tolerated. If you say "what if we are bombed?" they become indignant. What, *here*, in Milan? Are you crazy?'

It felt good to talk to a friend, he thought, never better than when your enemies are gathering. It felt good to conspire. 'It's hard to imagine –' he said, then stopped. Above him, a gentle snore. *Good night, Gabriella*. Ration coupons – did he have enough to take her for coffee in the morning? Yes, he would have a demitasse, it would just work out.

Really, he thought, who was this Guske to tell him what to do with his life? How did it happen that some German sat in an office and told Jean Casson whether or not he could have a love affair with a woman who lived in Lyons?

THE NIGHT VISITOR

24 April, 1941

4:20 a.m., the wind sighing across the fields, the river white where it shoaled over the gravel islands. Jean Casson lay on his stomach at the top of a low hill, wrapped up in overcoat and muffler, dark hat worn at an angle, a small valise by his side. The damp from the wet earth chilled him to the bone but there was nothing he could do about it. At the foot of the hill, standing at the edge of the river, two border guards, the last of the waning moonlight a pale glow on their helmets, rifles slung over their shoulders. They were sharing a cigarette and talking in low voices, the rough German sounds, the *sch* and *kuh*, drifting up the hillside.

The boy lying next to him, called André, was fifteen, and it was his job to guide Casson across a branch of the River Allier into the *Zone Non-Occupée*. André stared intensely, angrily, at the *sales Boches* below him. These were *his* hills, this was *his* stream, these teenagers below him – nineteen or so – were intruders, and he would, in time, settle with them. By his side, his brown-and-white Tervueren shepherd waited patiently – Tempête he called her, Storm – her breath steaming as she panted in the icy morning air.

These were in fact his hills – or would be. They belonged to his family, the de Malincourts, resident since the fifteenth century in a rundown château just outside the village of Lancy. He raised his hand a few inches, a signal to Casson: be patient, I know these two, they chatter like market ladies but they will, eventually, resume their rounds. Casson gritted his teeth as the wet grass crushed

205

beneath him slowly soaked his clothing. Had they left the château as planned, at two in the morning, this would not have happened.

But it was the same old story. He was scheduled to go across with another man, a cattle-dealer from Nevers who couldn't or wouldn't get a permit to enter the Vichy zone. The cattle-dealer arrived forty minutes late, carrying a bottle of cognac that he insisted on opening and sharing with various de Malincourts who had chosen to remain awake in honour of the evening crossing – the father, an aunt, a cousin and the local doctor, if Casson remembered correctly. Everybody had some cognac, the fire burned low, then, at 3:20, a telephone call. It was the cattle-dealer's wife, he'd received a message at his house in Nevers and he didn't have to go across the line after all. That left Casson and André to make the crossing later than they should have, almost dawn, and that invited tragedy.

The sentries had themselves a final laugh, then parted, heading east and west along the stream. The dog made a faint sound, deep in her throat – *sentries leaving*. No, Casson told himself, it wasn't possible. But then, he thought, dogs understand war, its memory lived in them, and this one's traditional business was herding stock to safety. A small cold wind, just enough to lift the soft hair on the dog's neck, made Casson shiver. He'd been offered an oilskin, hanging amid shotguns and fishing baskets and rubber boots in the gunroom of the château, but he had declined. Well, next time he'd know better.

André, in short trousers and sweater, seemed not to notice. 'Please, sir,' he whispered, 'we will go down the hill now. We will stay low to the ground, and we will run. Now I count one, and two, and three.'

He rose and scrambled down the hill in the classic infantry crouch, the Tervueren in a fast trot just behind his left heel – dogs were always trained left, thus the right side, the gun side, remained unhampered. Casson did the best he could, shocked at how stiff he'd become just lying on the damp earth for thirty minutes.

At the foot of the hill, André took his shoes off, tied them at the laces, hung them around his neck, then stuffed his socks in his pockets. Casson followed his example, turning up his trousers as far as the knee. André stepped into the stream, Casson was right behind him. The water was so close to ice that it was barely liquid. 'My God,' he said. André shushed him. Casson couldn't move, the water washed over his shins. André grabbed his elbow with a bony hand and shoved him forward. The dog turned to make sure of him, soft eyes anxious – did this recalcitrant beast require a nip to get it moving? No, there it went, swearing beneath its breath with every step. Relieved, the Tervueren followed, close by André. For Casson, the sharp gravel of the midstream island was a relief for a few yards, then the water was even deeper and the dog had to swim, her brown ruff floating on the surface. At last, the far bank. The Tervueren shook off a great cloud of icy spray – just in case some part of Casson's clothing had accidentally remained dry. 'Ah, Tempête,' André said in mock disappointment, and the dog smiled at the compliment.

André sat in the grass to put his shoes and socks back on, Casson did the same. Then they ran up the side of a low hill until they reached a grove of poplar trees on the skyline. André stopped to catch his breath. 'Ça va, monsieur?'

'Ça va, André.'

He was a wiry kid with black hair that fell over his forehead, the latest in a long line of pages and squires that had been going off on one mission or another since the crusades. This was, after all, not really knight's business, conduction of a fugitive. The knight, red-faced, ham-fisted de Malincourt, was back at the château, where he'd settled in to wait for his son with a night-long discussion on the advantages of Charolais over Limousin steers, the price of

207

rye seed, and the national disposition of Americans, who would, he thought, take their time before they got around to deciding they needed to come back over the sea and kill some more Germans.

Casson stayed quiet for a moment, hands on knees. Then a whip cracked the air in the poplar grove. Instinctively, André and Casson flinched. Then two more cracks, close together, this time a spring twig clipped from a branch. The dog – fear had been bred out of her many generations earlier – gave them an inquiring look: *Is this something you'd like me to see about?* André raised the bottom of his sweater, revealing the cross-hatched wooden grip of a huge, ancient revolver, but it was Casson's turn to take somebody by the elbow and before this particular war could get fairly underway they were galloping down the reverse slope of the hillside. They took cover for a moment, then headed south, towards a little road that would, eventually, take Casson to Lyons. At the next hilltop there was a view back to the river, a dull silver in the first light of dawn, and very beautiful.

He had a fantasy about how it would be in Lyons – the lover as night visitor. Long ago, when he'd been sixteen and in his next-to-last year at lycée, he'd had his first real love affair. In a world run by parents and teachers and maids it wasn't easy to find privacy, but the girl, Jeanette – eyes and hair a caramel shade of gold, dusting of pale freckles across the bridge of the nose – was patient and cunning and one day saw an opportunity for them to be alone. It could happen, thanks to a complicated fugue of family arrangements, very early one Sunday morning at the apartment of her grandmère in the 7th Arrondissement. Casson found the door open at dawn, went to a room where a slim shape lay buried beneath heavy quilts. Perhaps asleep, or just pretending – on this point he'd never been certain. He undressed quietly, stealthily, and slid in next to her. Then, just at that moment, she woke up, her smooth body warm and naked next to his, and breathed *'mon amour'* as she took him in her arms.

So he calculated his arrival at the Hotel du Parc for just after midnight. But no sleeping maiden awaited his caress. The hotel, high on the bank of the promontory formed by the Saône and the Rhône, was a Victorian horror of chocolate-coloured brick, turrets and gables, off by itself in a small park behind a fence of rusted iron palings, with a view over a dark bridge and a dark church. Brooding, sombre, just the place for consumptive poets or retired generals. Just the place for the night visitor.

However.

When Casson climbed the stone stairway that went from the street to the little park, he discovered every light in the hotel ablaze and the evening air heavy with the scent of roasting chickens. A trio – bass, drums, accordion – was pounding away at the Latin rhythm of the dance called the Java. There were shouts of encouragement, and shrieks of laughter – in short, the noisy symphony that can be performed only on the instrument of a hundred drunken wedding guests.

In the middle of it, Sleeping Beauty. She was barefoot, wearing a sash improvised from a tablecloth and shaking a tambourine liberated from the drum kit. She also had – a moment before he could believe his eyes – a rose clenched firmly between her teeth. 'Hey!' she cried out. 'Hey, hey!' She was leading a long line of dancers, first the groom – in his late thirties with a daring set of muttonchop whiskers, next his bride – some few years older, black hair pinned up, a dark mole on her cheek, bright red mouth, and eyes like burning coals.

The line – little kids and grandparents, friends of the groom, the bride's sisters, assorted hotel guests, at least one waiter – snaked from the dining room through the lobby, around an island of maroon velvet sofas, past the desk and the night manager wearing a wizard hat with a rubber band under his chin, and back to the dining room, hung with yards of pink crêpe paper. Casson stood by the door, taking it all in. A fireman performed on the French horn. A man beckoned a woman to sit on his lap and they roared with pleasure as the spindly chair collapsed beneath them. Four feet protruded from the drape of a tablecloth, the people under the table either dead asleep or locked in some static, perhaps oriental, version of coition – it would have been hard to say and nobody cared.

The line reappeared in the lobby, Citrine in the lead, cheeks flushed, long hair flying, a particular expression on her face as she capered – the 'savage dancer' of every Gypsy movie MGM had ever made. Then she saw him – 'Jean-Claude!' – and ran to hug him. Her small breasts were squashed against his chest, she smelled like wine and chicken and perfume. She pulled back a little, her eyes shone, she was drunk and happy and in love.

Much later, they went up the stairs to her room on the top floor. Very slowly, they went up. On a table in the dining room he had discovered a bowl of red-wine punch, a single lemon slice floating on top, a glass ladle hung on the rim. Therefore, one took this step, then this. Many of these old hotels had been built with a tilting device that operated after midnight, so one had to go upstairs very, very deliberately. It helped to laugh.

The room was small, but very safe – the door secured by what appeared to be a simple lock that took a primitive iron key. But this turned out to be a deeply complicated system, to be used only by cellists or magicians – people with clever fingers. Probably Casson and Citrine could have opened the door themselves, at some future date, but a Good Samaritan happened to walk down the hall in a bathrobe and insisted on coming to their aid.

A small room, dark patterns on the wallpaper and the rug and the bedspread and the chair. Cold; rain a steady patter on the roof, and damp. Casson managed to get his tie off – over his head – threw his shirt and trousers at a chair, turned to find Citrine looking sultry, wearing one stocking and an earring. They met somewhere on the bed; stupid, clumsy and hot, bawdy and shameless and prone to laugh. So drunk they weren't very good at anything, hands and mouths working away, too dizzy with getting what they wanted to be graceful or adept. But, maybe better that way: nothing went right, nothing went wrong, and they were too excited to care.

It was like being a kid again, he wanted her too much to be seductive. Her fault, he thought – the way she was, so many shadows and creases, angles and dark alleys; inside, outside, in between. She crawled around, as hot as he was, knees spread or one foot pointing at the ceiling. They didn't stay in one place very long, would find some position that made them breathe hard and fast but then, something else, something even better.

On and on it went. He didn't dare to finish, just fell back now and then to a condition of lazy heat. Not her; from time to time she gasped, shuddered, would stop for a moment and hang on to to him. Just the way, he thought, women were. They could do that. So, she came for both of them. Until, very late at night, she insisted – whispering to him, coaxing – and then he saw stars.

Of course he forgot to give her the letter. Nearly dawn when he remembered; watching her while she slept, in the grey light he could see the colour of her hair and her skin, rested a hand on her hip, she woke up and they smoked a cigarette. Out the window, the Lyonnais moon a white quarter-slice from a children's book – it looked like a cat ought to be sitting on it. He rolled off the bed, dug around in his valise, gave her the letter and lit a candle so she could read it. She kissed him, touched his face, and yawned. Well, he thought, when you've been fucking all night it's not really the best time for a love letter.

Five days, they had.

After that there would be too much moonlight for crossing the line back into occupied France. They walked by the grey river, swollen in the spring flood. Late in the afternoon they had a fire in the little fire-place in Citrine's room and drank wine and made love. At night she had to go to the theatre. Casson came along, sat in the wings on a folding chair. He liked backstage life, the dusty flats, paint smells, stagehands intent on their business – plays weren't about life, plays were about curtains going up and down – actresses in their underwear, the director making everybody nervous. Casson enjoyed being the outsider.

It was a romantic comedy, a small sweet French thing. The cousin from the country, the case of mistaken identity, the secret message sent to the wrong person, well, actually the right person but not until the third act. Citrine played the ingénue's best friend. The ingénue wasn't bad, a local girl with carefully done-up hair and a rich father and good diction. But, next to Citrine, very plain. That didn't matter so much – it only made the boyfriend come off a little more of an idiot than the playwright really intended.

The audience was happy enough. Despite rationing they'd eaten fairly well, a version of traditional Lyonnais cooking, rich and heavy, not unlike the audience. They settled comfortably into the seats of the little theatre and dozed like contented angels through the boring parts.

Five days.

Dark, cool, spring days, sometimes it rained – it was always just about to. The skies stayed heavy; big, slow clouds moving south. Casson and Citrine sat on a bench by the river. 'I could come to Paris,' she said.

'Yes,' he said. 'But the life I live now is going bad.'

212

She didn't understand.

'My phone's no good. I'm followed, sometimes.'

'If the Germans are after you, you better go.'

He shrugged. 'I know,' he said. 'But I had to come here.'

They stared at the river, a long row of barges moving south, the beat of the tugboat's engine reaching them over the water. Going to places far away.

She recited in terrible English: 'The owl and the pussycat, it went to the sea, in the beautiful pea-green boat.'

He laughed, rested the tips of two fingers against her lips.

The tugboat sounded its horn, it echoed off the hillsides above the river, a fisherman in a rowing boat struggled against the current to get out of the way.

Citrine looked at her watch and sighed. 'We better go back,' she said.

They walked along the quay, people looked at them – at her. Almond eyes, wide, wide mouth, olive-brown hair with gold tints, worn loose, falling over her shoulders. Long brown leather coat with a belt tied at the waist, cream-coloured scarf, brown beret. Casson had his hands shoved deep in the pockets of a black overcoat, no tie, no hat, hair ruffled by the wind. He seemed, as always, a little beat-up by life – knowing eyes, half-smile that said it didn't matter what you knew.

They walked like lovers, shoulders touching, talking only now and then. Sometimes she put her hand in the pocket of his coat. They wore their collars up, looked theatrical, sure of themselves. Some people didn't care for that, glanced at them a certain way as they passed by.

They turned into a narrow street that wound up the hill towards the hotel. Casson put his arm around her waist, she leaned against him as they walked. They stopped to look in the window of a boulangerie. Between the panniers of baguettes were a few red jam tarts in flaky crust. He

213

went in and bought two of them, in squares of stiff bakery paper, and they ate them as they climbed the hill.

'How did you find the *passeur*?' she asked. It meant someone who helped you cross borders.

'Like anything else,' he said. 'Like looking for a travel agent or a doctor, you ask friends.'

'Did it take a long time?'

She had crumbs in her hair, he brushed them out. 'Yes,' he said. 'I was surprised. But then, it turned out my sister-in-law knew somebody. Who knew somebody.'

'Perhaps it's dangerous now, to ask friends.'

'Yes, it could be,' he said. 'But you do what you have to.'

Their last night together he couldn't sleep.

He lay in the darkness and listened to her breathing. The hotel was quiet, sometimes a cough, now and then footsteps in the hall as somebody walked past their door. Sometimes he could hear a small bird in the park below the window. He smoked a cigarette, went from one part of his life to another, none of it worked, all of it scared him. Careful not to wake her, he got out of bed, went to the window, and stared out into the night. The city was silent and empty, lost in the stars.

He wanted to get dressed and go out, go for a long walk until he got tired. But it wasn't wise to do that any more, the police would demand to see your papers, would ask too many questions. When he got tired of standing, he sat in a big chair. It was three in the morning before he slid back under the covers. Citrine woke up, made a little noise of surprise, then flowed across the bed and pressed tight against him. At last, he thought, the night visitor.

'I don't want you to go away,' she said by his ear.

He smoothed her hair. 'I have to,' he said.

'Because, if you do, I will never see you again.'

'No. It isn't true.'

'Yes it is. I knew this would happen. Years ago. Like a fortune-teller knows things – in dreams.'

After a time he said, 'Citrine, please.'

'I'm sorry,' she said. She took his hand and put it between her legs. 'Until we go to sleep,' she said.

29 April, 1941

She insisted on going to the train with him. A small station to the north of Lyons, they took a cab there. He had to ride local trains all day, to Chassieu and Loyettes and Pont-de-Chéruy, old Roman villages along the Rhône. Then, at dusk, he would join the secret route that ran to a village near the River Allier, where one of the de Malincourts would meet him.

The small engine and four coaches waited on the track. 'You have your sandwiches?' she said.

'Yes.'

She looked at her watch. 'It's going to be late.'

'I think it's usual,' he said.

Passengers waited for the doors to open. Country people – seamed faces, weatherbeaten, closed. The men wore old scarves stuffed down the fronts of buttoned suit jackets, baggy trousers, scuffed boots. The women wore shawls over their heads, carried baskets covered with cloths. Casson stood out – he didn't belong here, and he wasn't the only one. He could pick out three others, two men and a woman. They didn't live in Chassieu either. Taking the little trains was a good idea – until four or five of you tried it at the same time. Well, too bad, he thought, there's nothing to be done about it now.

'What if you came down here,' she said quietly.

'To live, you mean.'

'Yes.'

He paused a moment. 'It isn't easy,' he said. Clearly he had worked on the idea.

'Maybe you don't want to,' she said.

'No. I'm going to try.'

She took his arm, there was not much they could say, now. The engine vented steam, a door opened in one of the coaches and a conductor tossed his cigarette away and stationed himself at the bottom of the steps. The people on the platform began to board the train.

'Remember what we talked about last night,' he said, leaning close so she could hear him. 'If you have to move, a postcard to Langlade's office.'

She nodded.

'You're not to call me, Citrine.'

The conductor climbed to the bottom step and shouted 'All aboard for Chassieu.'

He took her in his arms and she held on to him, her head on his chest. 'How long?' she said.

'I don't know. As soon as I can manage it.'

'I don't want to lose you,' she said.

He kissed her hair. The conductor leaned out of the coach and raised a little red flag that the driver could see. 'All aboard,' he said.

'I love you,' Casson said. 'Remember.'

He started to work himself free of her arms, then she let him go. He ran for the train, climbed aboard, looked out the cloudy window. He could see she was searching for him. He rapped on the glass. Then she saw him. She wasn't crying, her hands were deep in her pockets. She nodded at him, smiled a certain way – *I meant everything I said, everything I did*. Then she waved. He waved back. A man in a raincoat standing nearby lowered his newspaper to look at her. The train started to pull out, moving very slowly. She couldn't see the man, he was behind her. She waved again, walked a few paces along with the train. Her face was radiant, strong, she wanted him to know he did

216

not have to worry about her, together they would do what had to be done. The man behind Citrine looked towards the end of the station, Casson followed his eyes and saw another man, with slicked-down hair, who took a pipe out of his mouth, then put it back in.

All day long he rode slow trains that rattled through the countryside and stopped at little stations. Sometimes it rained, droplets running sideways across the window, sometimes a shaft of sunlight broke through a cloud and lit up a hillside, sometimes the cloud blew away and he could see the hard blue spring sky. In the fields the April ploughing was over, crumbled black earth ran to the trees in the border groves, oaks and elms, with early leaves that trembled in the wind.

Casson stood in the alcove at the end of the car, staring out the open door, hypnotized by the rhythm of the wheels over the rail points. His mind was already back in Paris, holding imaginary conversations with Hugo Altmann, trying to win him over to some version of René Guillot's strategy. The objective: move *Hotel Dorado* to the unoccupied zone, under the auspices of the committee in Vichy rather than the German film board. It would have to be done officially, it would take Guske, or somebody like him, to stamp the papers. But, with Altmann's help, it might be possible.

On the other hand, Altmann liked the film, really liked it, probably he'd want to keep it in Paris. Was there a way to ruin it for him? Not completely – could they just knock off a corner, maybe, so it wasn't quite so appealing? No, they'd never get away with it. Then too, what about Fischfang? As a Jew, nobody was going to give him the papers to do anything. But that, at least, could be overcome – he'd have to enter the *Zone Non-Occupée*, the ZNO, just as Casson had, then slip into a false identity, down in Marseilles perhaps.

217

No, that wouldn't work. Fischfang couldn't just abandon his assorted women and children to the mercies of the Paris Gestapo, they'd have to come along. But not across the river, it probably couldn't be done that way. *New papers.* That might work – start the false identity on the German side of the line. How to manage that? Not so difficult – Fischfang was a communist, he must be in contact with Comintern operatives, people experienced in clandestine operations – forging identity papers an everyday affair for them.

Or, the hell with *Hotel Dorado.* He'd let Altmann have it, in effect would trade it for Citrine. Of course he'd have to find some way to live, to earn a living in the ZNO, but that wouldn't be impossible. He could, could, do any number of things.

The train slowed, a long curve in the track, then clattered over a road crossing. An old farmer waited on a horse cart, the reins held loosely in his hand, watching the train go past. The tiny road wound off behind him, to nowhere, losing itself in the woods and fields. In some part of Casson's mind the French countryside went on forever, from little village to little village, as long as you stayed on the train.

Back in Paris, he telephoned Altmann.

'Casson! Where the hell have you been? Everybody's been looking for you.'

'I just went off to the seashore, to Normandy, for a couple of days.'

'Your secretary didn't know where you were.'

'That's impossible! I *told* her – if Altmann calls, give him the number of my hotel.'

'Well, she didn't.'

'Hugo, I'm sorry, you'll have to forgive me. You know what it's like, these days – she does the best she can.'

'Well . . .'

'Anyhow, here I am.'

'Casson, there are people who want to meet you. Important people.'

'Oh?'

'Yes. I have organized a dinner for us. Friday night.'

'All right.'

'Do you know the Brasserie Heininger?'

'In the Seventh?'

'Yes.'

'I know it.'

'Eight-thirty, then. Casson?'

'Yes?'

'Important people.'

'I understand. That's this Friday, the fourth of May.'

'Yes. Any problem, let me know immediately.'

'I'll be there,' Casson said.

He hung up, wrote down the time and place in his appointment book.

The Brasserie Heininger – of all places! What had got into Altmann? He knew better than that. The Heininger was a garish nightmare of gold mirrors and red plush – packed with Americans and nouveaux riches of every description before the war, now much frequented by German officers and their French 'friends.' Long ago, when he was twelve, his aunt – his father's charmingly demented sister – would take him to the Heininger, confiding in a whisper that one came 'only for the crème anglaise, my precious, please remember that.' Then, in the late thirties, there'd been some sort of wretched murder there, a Balkan folly that spread itself across the newspapers for a day or two. His one visit in adult life had been a disaster – a dinner for an RKO executive, his wife, her mother, and Marie-Claire. A platter of Heininger's best oysters, the evil Belons, had proved too much for the Americans, and it was downhill from there.

Well, he supposed it didn't matter. Likely it was the

219

'important people' who had chosen the restaurant. Whoever they were. Altmann hadn't been his usual self on the telephone. Upset about Casson's absence – and something else. Casson drummed his fingers on the desk, stared out the window at the rue Marbeuf. What?

Frightened, he thought.

A bad week.

Spring in the river valleys – tumbled skies and painters' clouds – seemed like a dream to him now. In Paris, the *grisaille*, grey light, had descended over the city and it was dusk from morning till night.

He went out to the Montrouge district, beyond the porte de Châtillon and the old cemetery, to the little factory streets around the rue Gabriel, where Bernard Langlade had the workshop that made lightbulbs. The nineteenth century; tiny cobbled streets shadowed by brick factory walls, huge rusted stacks with towers of brown smoke curling slowly into a dead sky.

He trudged past foundries that seemed to go on for miles; the thudding of machines that hammered metal – he could feel each stroke in his heart – the smell, no, he thought, the *taste*, of nitric acid on brass, showers of orange sparks seen through wire mesh, a man with a mask of soot around his eyes, hauling on a long wrench, sensing Casson's stare and giving it back to him. Casson looked away. His films had danced on the edges of this world but it was a real place and nobody made movies about these lives.

He got lost in a maze of smoked brick and burnt iron and asked directions of two workmen who answered in a Slavic language he couldn't understand. He walked for a long time, more than an hour, where oil slicks floated on a canal, then, at last, a narrow opening in a stone wall and a small street sign, raised letters chiselled into the wall in the old Paris style, IMPASSE SAVIER. At the end of the alley, a green metal door – Compagnie Luminex.

Inside it was a beehive, workers sitting at long assembly tables, the line served by a young boy in a cap who, using every ounce of his weight, threw himself against the handle of an industrial cart piled high with metal fittings of various shapes and sizes. In one corner, a milling machine in operation, its motor whining from overuse. It was hot in the workroom – the roar of a kiln on the floor below explained why – and there were huge noisy blowers that vibrated in their mounts.

'Jean-Claude!'

It was Langlade, standing at the door of a factory office and beckoning to him. He wore a grey smock, which made him look like a workshop foreman. In the office, three women clerks, keeping books and typing letters. They were heavily built and dark, wearing old cardigans against the damp factory air, and had cigarettes burning in ashtrays made from clamshells. Langlade closed the half-glass door to the workshop floor, which reduced the flywheel and grinding noises to whispered versions of themselves. They shook hands, Langlade showed him into a small, private office and closed the door.

'Jean-Claude,' he said fondly, opening the bottom drawer of his desk, taking out a bottle of brandy. 'I can only imagine what would get you all the way out here.' He gave Casson a conspiratorial smile – clearly an affair of the heart was to be discussed. 'Business?' he said innocently.

'A little talk, Bernard.'

'Ahh, I thought – maybe you just happened to be in the neighbourhood.' They both laughed at this. Langlade began working on the cork.

'Well, in fact I called your office, three or four times, and they told me, Monsieur is out at Montrouge, so I figured out this is where I'd have to come. But, Bernard, *look* at all this.'

Langlade smiled triumphantly, a man who particularly

wanted to be admired by his friends. 'What did you think?'

'Well, I didn't know. What I imagined – three or four workmen, maybe. To me, a lightbulb. I never would have guessed it took so much to make a thing like that. But, really, Bernard, the sad fact is I'm an idiot.'

'No, Jean-Claude. You're just like everybody else – me included. When Yvette's *Papa* died, and she told me we had this odd little business, I hadn't the faintest idea what to do about it. Sell it, I supposed. And we tried, but the country had nothing but labour trouble and inflation that year, and nobody in France would buy any kind of industrial anything. So, we ran it. We made Christmas-tree lights and we had small contracts with Citroën and Renault for the miniature bulbs that light up petrol gauges and so forth on dashboards. Actually, Jean-Claude, to make a lightbulb, you have to be able to do all sorts of things. It's like a simple kitchen match, you never think about it but it takes a lot of different processes, all of them technical, to produce some stupid little nothing.' He grunted, twisted the cork, managed to get it free of the bottle.

'Bernard,' Casson said, gesturing towards the work area, 'Christmas-tree lights? *Joyeux Noël!*'

Langlade laughed. He searched the bottom drawer, found two good crystal glasses. He held one up to the light and scowled. 'Fussy?'

'No.'

'When I'm alone, I clean them with my tie.'

'Fine for me, Bernard.'

Langlade poured each of them a generous portion, swirled his glass and inhaled the fumes. Casson did the same. 'Well, well,' he said.

Langlade shrugged, meaning, if you can afford it, why not? 'When the Germans got here,' he said, 'they began to make big orders, for trucks, and those armoured what-nots they drive around in. We did that for five months, then they asked, could you buy some more elaborate equipment, possibly in Switzerland? Well, yes, we could. There wasn't much point in saying no, the job would just go across the street to somebody else. So, we bought the new machinery, and began to make optical instruments. Like periscopes for submarines, and for field use also, a type of thing where a soldier in a trench can look out over the battlefield without getting his head blown off. We don't make the really delicate stuff – binoculars, for instance. What we make has to accept hard use, and survive.'

'Is there that much of it?'

Langlade leaned over his desk. 'Jean-Claude, I was like you. A civilian, what did I know. I went about my business, got into bed with a woman now and then, saw friends, made a little money, had a family. I never could have imagined the extent of anything like this. These people, army and navy, they think in thousands. As in, thousands and thousands.' Langlade gave him a certain very eloquent and Gallic look – it meant he was making money, and it meant he must never be asked how much, or anything like that, because he was making so much that to say it out loud would be to curse the enterprise – the jealous gods would overhear and throw down some bad-luck lightning bolts from the top of commercial Olympus. Where the tax people also kept an office.

Casson nodded that he understood, then smiled, honestly happy for a friend's success.

'Now,' Langlade said, 'what can I do for you?'

'Citrine,' Casson said.

A certain smile from Langlade. 'The actress.'

'Yes.'

'All right.'

'We have become lovers, Bernard. It's the second time – we had a *petite affaire* ten years ago, but this is different.'

Langlade made a sympathetic face; yes, he knew how it was. 'She's certainly beautiful, Jean-Claude. For myself, I couldn't stop looking at her long enough to go to bed.'

Casson smiled. 'We just spent a week together, in Lyons – that's between you and me by the way. Now, I've had some kind of problem in the Gestapo office on the rue des Saussaies. Bernard, it's so stupid – I went up there to get an *Ausweis* to go to Spain, and they asked me about military service and something told me not to mention that I'd been reactivated in May and gone up to the Meuse. You know, there are thousands of French soldiers still in Germany, in prison camps. I decided it would be safer not to admit anything. So, I didn't. Well, time went by, somebody sent a paper to somebody else, and they caught me in a lie.'

Langlade shook his head and made a sour face. The Germans were finicky about paper in a way the Latin French found amusing – until the problem settled on their own doorstep.

'The next thing was, they started reading my mail and listening to my phone. So, when I was with Citrine down in Lyons, I told her that if she wanted to get in touch with me she could send a postcard to your office, your law office in the 8th is the address I gave her.'

He waited for Langlade to smile and say it was all right, but he didn't. Instead, his expression darkened into a certain kind of discomfort.

'Look, Jean-Claude,' he said. 'We've known each other for twenty years, I'm not going to beat around the bush with you. If Citrine sends me a postcard, well, I'll see that you get it. On the other hand, next time you have a chance to talk to her, would it be too much to ask for you to find some other way of doing this?'

Casson wasn't going to show what he felt. 'No problem at all, Bernard. In fact, I can take care of it right away.'

'You can understand, can't you? This work I'm doing matters to them, Jean-Claude. It isn't like they're actually watching me, but, you know, I see these military people all the time, from the procurement offices, and all it would take would be for my secretary over in the other office to decide she wasn't getting enough money, or, or whatever it might be. Look, I have an idea, what about Arnaud? You know, he's always doing this and that and the other, and it's just the sort of thing that would appeal to him.'

'You're right,' Casson said. 'A much better idea.'

'So now, here's what we'll do. Let's go back to Paris – I can call a driver and car – and treat ourselves to a hell of a lunch, hey? Jean-Claude, how about it?'

Friday, 4 May. 4:20 p.m.

End of the week, a slow day in the office, Casson kept looking at his watch. Seven hours – and the dinner at Brasserie Heininger would be over. Of course, he lied to himself, he didn't have to go, the world wouldn't come to an end. No, he thought, don't do that. 'Mireille?' he called out. 'Could you come in for a minute?'

'Monsieur?'

'Why don't you go home early, Mireille – it won't be so crowded on the train.'

'Thank you, Monsieur Casson.'

'Could you mail this for me, on the way?'

Of course.

A postcard – the people who watched the mail supposedly didn't bother with postcards – telling Citrine to write him care of a café where they knew him. He had to assume Mireille wasn't followed, that she could mail a postcard without somebody retrieving it. It meant he could save an anonymous telephone he'd discovered, in an office at one of the soundstages out at Billancourt, for a call he might want to make later on.

Mireille called out good night and left, Casson returned to the folder on his desk. Best to prepare for an important meeting. The folder held various pencil budgets for *Hotel*

Dorado, a list of possible changes to the story line, names of actors and actresses and scenic designers – they were just now reaching the stage where certain individuals were, almost mystically, *exactly right* for the film. Also in the folder, a list of new projects Altmann had mentioned over the last few months; you never knew when one of these 'ideas' was going to leap out of its coffin and start dancing around the crypt.

Casson read down the page and sighed out loud. Ah yes, the Boer War. The whole industry was planning movies about the noble Boers that spring, somebody in Berlin – Goebbels? – had decided to make them fashionable. A group of farmers, not exactly German but at least Dutch, thus Nordic and sincere, had carried out guerrilla actions and given the British army fits in South Africa. A war, according to German thinking, that made England look bad: imperialist, power-hungry, and cruel. One German company, Casson had heard, was about to go into production on something called *President Kruger*, a Boer War spectacle employing 40,000 extras.

The phone.

Now what?

Maybe he shouldn't answer. No, it might be Altmann, some change of plans, or even, gift from heaven, dinner cancelled. 'Hello?'

'Monsieur Casson?'

'Yes?'

'Maître Versol here.'

What? Who? Oh Jesus! The lawyer for the LeBeau company!

Versol cleared his throat, then continued. 'I thought I would telephone to see if any progress has been made on locating our missing inventory. You will recall, monsieur, some four hundred beards, fashioned from human hair and of a superior quality, provided for your use in the film *Samson and Delilah*.'

'Yes, Maître Versol, I do remember.'

'We feel we have been very patient, monsieur.'

'Yes,' Casson said. 'That is true.'

He let Versol go on for a time, as he always did, until the lawyer felt honour had been satisfied and he could hang up.

Casson looked at his watch again. Almost five. He lifted the top from a fancy yellow box, unfolded the tissue paper, studied the tie he'd bought on the boulevard earlier that day. Navy blue with a beige stripe, very austere and conservative. Just the thing, he hoped, for the 'important people' who had inspired that strange little note in Altmann's voice. Probably it wouldn't matter at all, it would simply mean he had done the best he could.

On the way home, between the La Muette Métro and the rue Chardin, he stopped at the busy café where they saw him every morning. He leaned on the copper-covered bar and drank a coffee. 'I may get a postcard here,' he confided to the proprietor. 'It's from *somebody* – you understand. I'd rather my wife didn't see it.'

The proprietor smiled, rubbing a glass with a bar towel. 'I understand, monsieur. You may depend on me.'

8:40 p.m.

The Brasserie Heininger, throbbing with Parisian life on a Friday night. Once past the blackout curtains: polished wood, golden light, waiters in fancy whiskers and green aprons. Very fin-de-siècle, Casson thought. Fin-de-something, anyhow.

Papa Heininger, the fabled proprietor, greeted him at the door, then passed him along to the mâitre d'. The man said good evening with a certain subtle approval, more to do with what he wasn't than what he was – he wasn't

227

Romanian, wasn't wearing a bright-blue suit, wasn't a coal merchant or a black-market dealer or a pimp.

'Monsieur Altmann's table, please.'

A polite nod. *A German, true, but a German executive.* Not so bad, for that spring. Party of four, all men, thus ashes on the tablecloth but at least a vigorous attack on the wine list. 'That will be table fourteen, monsieur. This way, please.'

Not the best table but certainly the most requested: a small hole in the mirror where an assassin had fired a submachine gun the night the Bulgarian headwaiter was murdered in the ladies' WC. The table where an aristocratic Englishwoman had once recruited Russian spies. The table where, only a few nights earlier, the companion of a German naval officer had been shooting peas at other diners, using a rolled-up *carte des vins* as a blowpipe.

The three men at the table rose, Altmann made the introductions. Clearly they'd been there for a while, most of the way through a bottle of champagne. Herr Schepper – something like that – gestured to the waiter for another to be brought. He had fine white hair and a fine face, a pink shave and shining eyes. One of a class of men, Casson thought, who are given money all their lives because people don't really know what else to do with them. This one was, if Casson understood Altmann correctly, a very senior something at UFA, the Continental Film parent company in Berlin.

The other man waited his turn, then smiled as he was introduced. They shook hands, shared a brief *reniflement* – the term came from the world of dogs, where it meant a mutual sniff on first meeting – then settled back down at the table. *Herr Franz Millau.* Something in the way Altmann articulated the name enabled Casson to hear it perfectly.

He was – nobody exactly said. Perhaps he was 'our friend' or 'my associate' or one of those. Not a particularly impressive exterior. High domed forehead; sandy hair. An old thirty-five or a young forty-five. Eyeglasses in thin silver frames, lawyer eyeglasses, worn in a way that suggested he only took them off before he went to sleep. And a small, predatory mouth, prominent against a fair complexion that made his lips seem brightly coloured. He was not unpleasant in any way Casson could put a name to, so, what was wrong with him? Perhaps, Casson thought, it was a certain gap, between an unremarkable presence, and, just below, a glittering and pungent arrogance that radiated from him like the noonday sun. Herr Millau was powerful, and believed it was in the natural order of things that he should be.

Herr Schepper did not speak French. That kept them busy, with Altmann as translator, discovering that he loved Paris, had attended the opera, was fond of Monet, liked pâté de foie gras. A fresh bottle of Veuve Clicquot arrived, and, a moment later, an astonishing seafood platter. Everyone said ah. A masterpiece on a huge silver tray: every kind of clam and oyster, cockle and mussel, whelk and crayfish – Judgement Day on the ocean floor. *'Bon appétit!'* the waiter cried out.

One small complication.

Altmann and Schepper had to go on to a certain club in a distant arrondissement, where they were to have a late supper with a banker. Schepper said something in German. 'He says,' Altmann translated, ' "you must take good care of the people with the money." ' Schepper nodded to help make the point.

'That's certainly true,' Casson said.

'Well then,' Millau said, 'you two should be going. Perhaps Monsieur Casson will be kind enough to keep me company while I eat my supper.'

Merde. But everybody else seemed to agree that this was

the perfect solution, and Casson was effectively trapped. A glass of champagne, a few creatures from the sea, some additional travelogue from Herr Schepper, then everybody stood up to shake hands and begin the complicated business of departure.

At which moment, from the corner of his eye, Casson spotted Bruno. A party of six or seven swept past like ships in the night, Casson had only a blurred impression. Some German uniforms, a cloud of perfume, a woman laughing at something that wasn't funny, and, in the middle of it – Bruno in a silk tie and blinding white shirt, a young woman – blonde, green-eyed – on his arm. Their eyes met, Bruno winked. *Good to see you getting about with the right people, at last – glad you've seen the light.* Then they went around the corner of a wall of banquettes and disappeared.

Altmann and Schepper left.

'Friend of yours?' Millau said.

'Acquaintance.'

'Some more champagne?'

'Thank you. How do you come to speak French like that, if you don't mind my asking?'

'No, I don't mind. As a youngster I lived in Alsace – you know, *un, deux, trois, vier, fünf.*'

Casson laughed politely.

'That's the way to learn a language, as a child,' Millau said.

'That's what they say.'

'What about you, *Sprechen Sie Deutsch?*'

'No, not at all.'

'Maybe some English, then?'

'A little. I can get along in a commercial situation if everybody slows down.'

Millau took a heavy black cigar from his pocket, stripped off the band and the cellophane. 'Perhaps you'd care to join me.'

'No, thank you.'

Millau took his time lighting up, made the match flame jump up and down, at last blew out a stream of smoke, strong, but not unpleasant. He shook his head. 'I like these things too much.'

Casson lit a Gauloise.

Millau leaned on the table, spoke in a confidential tone. 'Let me begin by telling you that I'm an intelligence officer,' he said. 'Reasonably senior, here in Paris.'

'I see,' Casson said.

'Yes. I work for the *Sicherheitsdienst*, the SD, in the counterespionage office up on the avenue Foch. We started out as the SS foreign service, and in a sense we still are that, though success has brought us some broader responsibility.'

Millau paused, Casson indicated he understood what had been said.

'We've been getting to know you for a few months, Monsieur Casson, keeping an eye on you, and so forth, to see who we were dealing with.'

Casson laughed nervously.

'Ach, the way people are! I assure you, we can't be surprised or offended by all these little sins, the same thing, over and over. We're like priests, or doctors.'

He stopped for a moment to inhale on the cigar, making the tip glow red, to see if it was still lit. 'We got on to you down in Spain – the British were interested in you, and that was of interest to us. We were . . . nearby, when you met with a woman who calls herself Marie-Noëlle, Lady Marensohn, a representative of the British Secret Intelligence Service who we believe attempted to recruit you for clandestine operations. She is, by the way, residing with us at the moment.'

Casson felt the blood leave his face. Millau waited to see if he might want to comment, but he said nothing.

'Our view, Monsieur Casson, is that you did not accept recruitment.'

Casson waited a beat but there was nowhere he could hide. 'No,' he said, 'I didn't.'

Millau nodded, confirming a position held in some earlier discussion. 'And why not?'

There wasn't any time to think. 'I don't know.'

'No?'

Casson shrugged. 'I'm French – not British, not German. I simply want to live my life, and be left in peace.'

From Millau's reaction Casson could tell he'd given the right answer. 'And who would blame you for that, eh?' Millau said with feeling. 'What got us into this situation in the first place was all these people meddling in politics. All we ever wanted in Germany was to be left alone, to get on with our lives. But, sadly, that was not to be, and you see what happened next. And, more to come.'

Casson's expression was sympathetic. He realized that Millau possessed a very dangerous quality: he was likeable.

'We have no business fighting with England, I'll tell you that,' Millau said. 'Every week – I'm sure I'm not saying something you find surprising – there's some kind of initiative; diplomatic, private, what have you. At the Vatican or in Stockholm. It's just a matter of time and we'll settle things between us. Our real business is in the east, with the Bolsheviks, and so is Britain's business, and we're just sorry that certain individuals in London are doing everything they can to keep us apart.'

'Hmm,' Casson said.

'So, that's where you come in. My section, that is, *AMT* IV, is particularly concerned with terrorist operations, sabotage, bombing, assassination. We fear that elements within the British government plan to initiate such acts in France, a carefully organized campaign – and if a number of people die it is of no particular concern to them, they tend to be very liberal with French life.'

Millau made sure this had sunk in, then he said, 'This isn't a fantasy. We know it's going to happen, and we

232

believe they will contact you again. This time, we want you to accept. Do what they ask of you. And let us know about it.'

The brasserie was noisy, people talking and laughing, somebody was singing. The air was thick with cigarette smoke and the aroma of grilled beef. Casson took his time, stubbing out the Gauloise in an ashtray. 'Well,' he said.

'How about it?'

'Well, I don't think they'll actually approach me again,' Casson said. If Marie-Noëlle talked to them, he realized, he was finished. Would she? Considering what they did to people, would she? 'I made it clear to them it wasn't something I was going to do.'

'Yes,' Millau said softly, meaning that he understood. 'But I'll tell you what.' He smiled, conspiratorial and knowing. 'I'll bet you anything you care to name that they come back to you.'

3:20 a.m.

The music on his radio faded in and out – if he held the aerial he could hear it. *Adagio for Strings*, Samuel Barber. Coming in from far away. Outside it rained on and off, distant thunder muttering up in Normandy somewhere. The worst of the storm had come through earlier – on the way home from the Brasserie Heininger he'd had to take shelter in the Métro to avoid getting soaked, standing next to a woman in a sweater and skirt. 'Just made it,' he'd said as the rain poured down.

'A little luck anyhow,' she'd agreed. 'I have to go see somebody about a job tomorrow and this is what I have to wear.'

Oh, what kind of job – but he didn't.

They stood quietly, side by side, then the rain stopped and she left, swinging her hips as she climbed the staircase just so he would know what he'd missed. He knew. He lay on top of the covers in the darkness and listened to the violin. It would have been nice to have her with him; big, pale body rising and falling. But Citrine, I didn't.

Good times they'd had in the Hotel du Parc. He'd been leaning against a wall, a cigarette in the corner of his mouth. She told him he looked like a place Pigalle tough guy and he'd given her back the classic line, *'Tiens, montrez-moi ton cul.'* Show me your arse. In lycée, they used to wonder if M. Lepic, the Latin teacher, said that to Mme. Lepic on Saturday night.

Casson peered at his watch on the table beside the bed. A few minutes after three. What if he went out somewhere and called the hotel in Lyons – let it ring and ring until an infuriated manager answered. *This is the police. I want to speak with the woman in Room 28. Now!*

Sirens. Air-raid sirens. Now what? Antiaircraft fire – to the north of the city, he thought. Like a drum, in deliberate time. Then he heard aeroplanes. He swung his legs off the bed, made certain the apartment was dark, went out on the terrace.

Searchlights, north of him, across the river. The AA guns working away, four or five beats to the measure, little yellow lights climbing to heaven. And, then, planes overhead, a lot of them, flying low, the drone hammering off the walls in the narrow rue Chardin. Across the street and down a little way, a couple in nightshirts out on their balcony, the woman with a fur stole thrown around her shoulders, gazing up at the sky. Then he saw others, the whole neighbourhood was out.

To the north, bombs, close enough to hear the articulated explosions. Orange light stuttered against the sky – he could see clearly the dark undersides of rain clouds, like frozen smoke, lit by fires. The British are at work, he thought. Among the factories on the outskirts of the city. When the bombing faded to a rumble, fire sirens joined the air-raid sirens. Then the all-clear sounded, and the fire engines were joined by ambulances.

Casson got tired of standing on the terrace, sat against the wall just inside his living room. First edge of false dawn in the spring, the sky not so dark as it was, a few birds singing on the rooftops. The sirens had stopped. now there remained only a certain smell on the morning air. The smell of burning. He was falling asleep. Now that it was dawn, he could sleep, since whatever might come in the night would have to wait another day.

Then, Monday morning, when he got to the office at ten, Mireille had a message for him. 'A woman telephoned, a Madame Detweiler.'

'Who?'

'The secretary of an officer called Guske. From the rue des Saussaies.'

'And?'

'She said to tell you that your *Ausweis* to go to the Vichy zone is under consideration, it doesn't look like there's going to be a problem, and they will have a determination for you by May fifteenth. If you have any questions, you are encouraged to call *Obersturmbannführer* Guske.'

'Thank you, Mireille,' he said, and went into his office.

Was that good news, he wondered, or bad? After a moment he realized it wasn't good or bad, it wasn't anything. It was simply their way of talking to him. It was simply their way of telling him that they owned him.

THE SECRET AGENT

Casson stood on the balcony, just after midnight, and stared out over the jagged line of rooftops. The city was ghostly in blue lamplight, and very quiet. He could hear distant footsteps, and night birds singing in the parks. The preparation of an escape, he thought, whatever else it did, showed you your life from an angle of profound reality. Where to go. How to get there. Friends and money must be counted up, but then, *which* friends – who will really help? How much money? And, if you can't get that, how much? And then, most of all, when? Because *these* doors, once you went through them, closed behind you.

There's no question when, he told himself, the time is now. If it isn't already too late.

A few things had to be settled before he left. He started Tuesday morning, getting in touch with Fischfang. This lately was not easy – messages left with shopkeepers, calls returned from public telephones – but by the end of the week they met at a vacant apartment out in the 19th, that looked out on the railyards.

The apartment was for rent, the landlord's agent a plump little gentleman wearing an alpine hat with a brush. 'Look around all you like, boys,' he said as he opened the door. 'And as to the rent, they say I'm a reasonable man.' He winked, then trotted off down the staircase.

Fischfang was tense, shadows like bruises beneath his eyes, but very calm. Different. It was, Casson thought, the revolver. No longer kept in a drawer, perhaps worn under the arm, or in the belt – it had a certain logic of its own and changed the person who carried it.

And Fischfang hadn't come alone, he had a friend – a helper or a bodyguard, something like that. Not French, from somewhere east of the Oder, somewhere out in Comintern land. Ivanic, he called himself. In his twenties, he was dark-eyed and pale, with two days' growth of beard, wore a cap tilted down over sleepy eyes. He waited in the kitchen while Casson and Fischfang talked, hands clasped behind his head as he sat against a wall.

Casson gave Fischfang a lot of money, all he could. But, he thought, maybe it didn't matter any more. Now that it was time to meet in vacant apartments, now that Ivanic had showed up, maybe the days of worrying about something as simple as money were over. Fischfang put the packet of francs away, reached inside his jacket, handed Casson a school notebook with a soft cover.

'New draft,' Fischfang said. 'Though I somehow get the feeling,' he added ruefully, 'that our little movie is slipping away into its own fog.'

Casson paged through the notebook. The scenes had been written in cafés, on park benches, or at kitchen tables late at night – spidery script densely packed on the lined paper, coffee-stained, blotted, and, Casson sensed, finely made. He could feel it as he skimmed the lines. It was autumn, a train pulled into a little station, the guests got off, their Paris clothes out of place in the seaside village. They went to the hotel, to their rooms, did what people did, said what they said – Casson looked up at Fischfang. 'Pretty good?'

Fischfang thought a moment. 'Maybe it is. I didn't have too much time to think about it.'

'Not always the worst thing.'

'No, that's true.'

Casson paced around the room. The apartment was filthy – it smelled like train soot, the floor was littered with old newspaper. On the wall by the door somebody had written in pencil, *E. We've gone to Montreuil.* In the railyard

240

below the window, the switching engines were hard at work, couplings crashed as boxcars were shunted from track to track, then made up into long trains. Casson peered through the cloudy glass. Fischfang came and stood by his side. One freight train seemed just about ready to go, Casson counted a hundred and twenty cars, with tanks and artillery pieces under canvas, cattle wagons for the horses, and three locomotives. 'Looks like somebody's in for it,' he said.

'Russia, maybe. That's the local wisdom. But, wherever it's going, they won't like it.'

'No.' Directly below them, a switching engine vented white steam with a loud hiss. 'Who's your friend?' Casson said quietly.

'Ivanic? I think he comes from the NKVD. He's just waiting for the fighting to start, then he can go to work.'

'And you?'

'I'm his helper.'

Casson stared out at the railyard, clouds of grey smoke, the railwaymen in faded blue jackets and trousers.

'We all thought,' Fischfang said slowly, his voice almost a whisper, 'that life would go on. But it won't. Tell me, so much money, what does it mean, Jean-Claude?'

'I have to go away.'

Fischfang nodded slowly, he understood. 'It's best.'

'They're after me,' Casson said.

Fischfang turned and stared at him for a moment. 'After you?'

'Yes.'

'Did you do something?'

'Yes,' Casson said, after a moment. 'Nothing much – and it didn't work.'

Fischfang smiled. 'Well then, good luck.'

They shook hands. 'And to you.'

There was nothing else to say, Casson left the apartment, Ivanic watched him go.

*　　*　　*

That afternoon he went up to the Galeries Lafayette, the huge department store just north of Opéra. He found the buyers' offices on the top floor and knocked on Véronique's door. 'Jean-Claude!' she said, pleased to see him. A tiny space, costume jewellery everywhere; spread across a desk, crowded on shelves that rose to the ceiling – wooden bracelets painted lustrous gold, shimmering glass diamonds in rings and earrings, ropes of glowing pearls. 'The sultan's treasure,' she said.

For herself she had great honesty of style – wore a black shirt with a green scarf tied at the neck. Short hair, clear eyes, a great deal of intelligence and a little bit of expensive perfume. 'Let's take a walk around the store,' she said.

They walked from room to room, past bridal gowns and evening gowns, floral housedresses and pink bath-robes. 'Have you heard about Arnaud and his wife?' she said.

'No. What's happened?'

'I had lunch with Marie-Claire yesterday, she told me they weren't living together. He moved out.'

'Why is that? They always seemed to have, a good arrangement.'

Véronique shrugged. 'Who knows,' she said gloomily. 'I think it's the Occupation. Lately the smallest thing, and everything comes apart.'

It was busy in the luggage department – fine leather and brass fittings from the ancient saddlery ateliers of Paris. A crowd of German soldiers, businessmen with their wives, a few Japanese naval officers.

'Véronique,' he said. 'I need to go south again.'

'Right now the moon is full, Jean-Claude.'

'So it would be, what, fourteen days?'

'Well, yes, at least. Then there are people who have to be talked to, and, all the various complications.'

A woman in traditional Breton costume – black dress,

242

white hat with wings – was demonstrating a waffle iron, pouring yellow batter from a cup into the iron, then heating it over a small gas burner.

'All right,' he said. 'There's a chance I'll get an *Ausweis*. In a few weeks. Maybe.'

'Can you wait?'

'I'm not sure. Things, things are going on.'

'What things, Jean-Claude? It's important to tell me.'

'I'm under pressure to work for them. I mean, really work for them.'

'Can you refuse?'

'Perhaps, I'm not sure. I've been over it and over it, probably the best thing for me is to slip quietly into the ZNO, pick up Citrine, then go out – to Spain or Portugal. Once we're there, we'll find some country that will take us. I can remember May of last year – then it mattered where you went. Now it doesn't.'

They stood together at a railing, looking out from the dress department over the centre of the store. Two floors below, the crowds shifted slowly through a maze of counters packed with gloves, belts, and handbags. Silk scarves were draped on racks, and women's hats, with veils and bows and clusters of cherries or grapes, were hung on the branches of wooden trees. 'If you leave before the *Ausweis* comes,' Véronique said, 'and there's some way you can arrange to have it sent over to your office, it would be very important for us to have it. For somebody, it could mean everything.'

'I will try,' he said.

'About the other, situation, I'll be in touch with you. Soon as I can.'

They kissed each other good-bye, one cheek then the other, and Casson walked away. Looking back over his shoulder he saw her smile, then she waved to him and mouthed the little phrase that meant *have courage*.

*   *   *

243

It rained. Thirty-three Wehrmacht divisions advanced in Yugoslavia. Others crossed the border into Greece. Stuka bombers destroyed the city of Belgrade. An interzonal card from Lyons arrived at a Paris café, addressed to J. Casson. 'Waiting, waiting and thinking about you. Please come soon.' Signed with the initial X. A dinner party at the house of Philippe and Françoise Pichard. His brother, wounded a year earlier in the fighting in Belgium, had never returned home, but they had word of him, a prisoner of war, doing forced labour in an underground armaments factory in Aachen. Bruno was trying to pull strings in order to get him out.

It cleared. Fine days; windy, cool, sunny. Zagreb taken. The RAF blew up the Berlin opera house. Bulgarian and Italian troops joined the attack on Yugoslavia. Casson had lunch with Hugo Altmann at a black-market restaurant called Chez Nini, in an alley behind a butcher's shop out in Auteuil. Fillets of lamb with baby turnips, then a Saint-Marcellin. Now that he was in contact with SD officers, Altmann was afraid of him – that meant money, replacing what he'd given Fischfang, and a meaningful contribution to the escape fund. Altmann gave his tenth hearty laugh of the afternoon. 'My secretary will have a cheque for you tomorrow, it's no problem, no problem at all. We *believe* in this picture, that's what matters.'

It rained. Dripped slowly from the branches of the trees on the boulevards. Casson went to see Marcel Carné's *Le Jour Se Lève* at the Madeleine theatre, script by Jacques Prévert, Jean Gabin playing the lead. The Occupation authority announced the opening of the Institute of Jewish Studies. The inaugural exhibition, to be presented by a well-known curator, would show how Jews dominated the world through control of newspapers, films, and financial markets. Marie-Claire telephoned, Bruno was impossible, she didn't know what to do. 'Some afternoon you could come for tea,' she said. 'It rains like this and I am so sad.

I walk around the apartment in my underwear and look at myself in the mirrors.' Fighting around Mount Olympus in Greece. Bulgarian troops in Macedonia. On a small errand he went out to the Trinité quarter, a street of fortune-tellers and dusty antique shops. He walked head down through the rain, dodging the puddles, staying under awnings when he could. A black Citroën swung sharply to the kerb, Franz Millau climbed out of the passenger side and opened the back door. 'Come for a ride,' he said with a smile. 'It's no good walking today, too wet.'

They drove to a small villa in the back streets of one of the drearier suburbs, Vernouillet, squat brick houses with little gardens. The driver was introduced as Albert Singer, a blunt-headed, fair-haired man so heavy in the neck and shoulders his shirt collar was pulled out of shape around the button. At the villa, Millau asked him to make a fire. He tried, using wooden crates broken into kindling, newspapers, and two wet birch logs that were never going to burn anything. Stubborn, he squatted in front of the fireplace, lighting match after match to the corner of a damp section of the *Deutsche Allgemeine Zeitung*. For a time, Millau watched him with disbelief. Finally he said, 'Singer, isn't there any dry paper?'

'I'll look,' Singer said, struggling to his feet.

'What can you do?' said Millau, resigned. 'He does what I tell him, so I have to keep him around.'

Casson nodded sympathetically. The room smelled of disuse, of mildew and old rugs; something about it made his heart beat faster. 'Do you mind if I smoke?'

'No. In fact I will join you.' Millau got out a cigar and went to work on it. With the lights off and shutters closed, the parlour was in shadow. 'Did you see the papers this morning?' Millau said.

'Yes.'

'Awful, no?'

'What?'

'The bombing. Out at the Citroën plant. Three hundred dead – and to no particular purpose. The assembly line was up and running again by ten in the morning. Casson, no matter your politics, no matter what you think of us, you have a moral obligation to stop such things if it is in your power to do so.'

Casson made a gesture – the world did what it did, it didn't ask him first.

'I'll let you in on one secret – we have a special envoy in London now, trying to work out, at least a cease-fire. At least let the horror stop for a moment, so we can think it over, so we can maybe just talk for a time. You can't find *that* wrong, can you?'

'No.'

'I mean, we must be honest with each other. We're fellow human beings, maybe even fellow Europeans – certainly it's something we could discuss, but I won't insist on that.'

'Europeans, of course.'

'Now look, Casson, we need your help or this whole thing is going to blow up in our faces. The people I work for in Berlin have taken it into their heads that you're willing to cooperate with us and they've stuck me with the job of making that cooperation a reality. So, I don't really have a choice.'

Singer returned with some newspaper, crumpled up a few pages and wedged them under the grate. He lit the paper, the room immediately smelled like smoke.

'Flue open?'

'*Ja.*'

Millau made a face. Reached into an inside pocket, took out an identity card, handed it over. Casson swallowed. It was his passport photograph. Underneath, the name Georges Bourdon. 'Now this gentleman was to be used by the English, and I mean *used*, to assist a terrorist action that is planned to take place in the Paris region. The bombing last night killed three hundred Frenchmen – what these people want to do, and we aren't sure exactly what that is, will no doubt kill a few hundred more. What we need from you is to play the part of this Bourdon person for a single night, then we're quits. You will spend a few hours in a field, is all that is required, then I can report back to Berlin that all went well, that you tried but didn't do much of a job, and in future we're going to work with somebody else.

'I'm an honourable man, Monsieur Casson, I don't care if you want to sit out this war and make movies – after all, I go to the movies – as long as you don't do anything to hurt us. Meanwhile, if things turn out as I believe they will, Europe is going to be a certain way for the foreseeable future, and those people who have helped us out when we asked for their help are going to be able to ask for a favour some day if they need to. We have long memories, and we appreciate civilized behaviour. Now, I've said everything I can say –'

There was a wisp of white smoke floating along the ceiling. Singer gazed upward from where he was squatting in front of the fire.

'You stupid ass,' Millau said.

'I'm sorry,' Singer said, standing and rubbing his hands. 'It's too wet to burn, sir.'

Millau put a hand against the side of his head as though he were getting a headache. 'Now look,' he said to Casson. 'In a few days we'll be in contact with you, we'll tell you where and when and all the rest of it. Keep the card, you'll need it. Somebody will ask you if you're Georges Bourdon, and you'll say that you are, and show them your identity card. So, now, you know most of what I can tell you. Don't say yes, don't say no, just go home and think it over. What's best for you, what's best for the French people. But I would not be wholly honest if I didn't tell you that we need a French person, somebody approximately of your age and circumstance, to be at a certain place on a certain date in the very near future.'

He paused a moment, trying to decide exactly how to say what came next. 'You have us in a somewhat difficult position, Monsieur Casson, I hope you understand that.'

He took a train back to Paris, got off at the Gare St-Lazare at twenty minutes after six. For a time he was not clear about what to do next, in fact stood on the platform between tracks as the crowds flowed around him. Finally there was a man's voice – Casson never saw him – saying quietly, 'Don't stand here like this, they'll run you in. Understand?'

Casson moved off. To a rank of telephone booths by the entry to the station. Outside, people were hurrying through the rain in the gathering dusk. Casson stepped into a phone booth, put the receiver to his ear and listened to the thin whine of the dial tone. Then he began to thumb through the Paris telephone book on a shelf below the telephone. Turned to the *B* section. *Bois. Bonneval. Bosquet. Botine. Boulanger. Bourdon.*

Albert, André, Bernard, Claudine, Daniel – Médecin, Georges. 18, rue Malher. *42 30 89.*

Seeing it in the little black letters and numbers, Casson felt a chill inside him. As though hypnotized, he put a *jeton* in the slot and dialled the number. It rang. And again. A third time. Once more. Five. Six. Seven. Eight. Casson put the receiver back on its hook. Outside, a woman in a green hat tapped on the door of the booth with a coin. 'Monsieur?' she said when he looked at her.

He left. Walked east on the rue de Rome. The street was crowded, people shopping, or going home from work, faces closed and private, eyes on the pavement, trying to get through one more day. Casson came to a decision, turned abruptly, hurried back to the telephones at the Gare St-

Lazare. *Véronique*. He didn't remember exactly where she lived – he'd dropped her off the night of Marie-Claire's dinner party a year ago – but it was in the Fifth somewhere, the student quarter. He remembered Marie-Claire telling him, eyes cast to heaven in gentle despair at the curious life her little sister had chosen to live. *Yes, well,* Casson thought.

It took more than the polite number of rings for Véronique to answer.

'Yes?'

'It's Jean-Claude.'

Guarded. 'How nice to hear from you.'

'I need to talk to you.'

'Very well.'

'Where should we meet?'

'There's a café at the Maubert market. Le Relais. In a half-hour, say.'

'See you then.'

'Good-bye.'

She wore a trenchcoat and a beret, a tiny gold cross on a chain at the base of her throat. She was cold in the rain, sat hunched over the edge of a table at the rear of the workers' café. Casson told her what had happened, starting with Altmann's dinner at the Heininger. He handed her the Georges Bourdon identity card.

She studied it a moment. 'Rue Malher,' she said.

'Just another street. He could be rich, poor, in between.'

'Yes. And for profession, *salesman*. Also, anything.'

Véronique handed the card back.

'What do you think Millau meant when he said I'd put them in a difficult position?'

She thought a moment. 'Perhaps – you have to remember these people work for organizations, and these places have a life of their own. Department stores, symphony orchestras, spy services – at heart the same. So, perhaps,

249

this man told a little fib. Claimed he had somebody who could be used a certain way. Thinking, maybe, that such a situation could be developed, in the future, so he'd just take credit for it a little early. On a certain day, perhaps, when he needed a success. Then, suddenly, they're yelling *produce the goods!* Well, now what?'

Casson stubbed out a cigarette. The café smelled like sour wine and wet dogs, a quiet place, people spoke in low voices. '*Merde*,' he said.

'Yes.'

'I think, Véronique, I had better talk to somebody. Can you help?'

'Yes. Do you know what you're asking?'

'Yes, I know.'

She looked in his eyes, reached out and squeezed his forearm. She was strong, he realized. She got up from the table and went to the bar. A telephone was produced from beneath the counter. She made a call – ten seconds – then hung up. She stood at the bar and talked to the proprietor. Laughed at a joke, kidded with him about something that made him shake his head and tighten his mouth – what could you do, any more, the way things were, a pretty damn sad state of affairs is what it was. The phone on the bar rang, Véronique answered it, said a word or two, hung up, and returned to the table.

'It's tomorrow,' she said. 'Go to the church of Saint-Étienne-du-Mont, that's just up the hill here. You know it?'

'Across from the school.'

'That's it. You go to the five o'clock mass. Take a seat near the crypt of Sainte Geneviève, one seat in from the centre aisle. Carry a raincoat over your left arm, a copy of *Le Temps* in your right hand. You will be approached. The man – he uses the name Mathieu – will be holding his hat in his left hand. He will ask you if he might have a look at your newspaper if you're done reading it. You will tell him politely no, your wife hasn't read it yet.' She paused a moment. 'Do you have it?'

'Yes.'

She leaned over the table, coming closer to him. 'For the best, Jean-Claude,' she said. Then, 'Really, it's time. Not just for you. For all of us.'

They said good-bye. He left first, walked to the Maubert-Mutualité Métro. There was a Gestapo control after 8:00 p.m. at the La Motte-Picquet *correspondance*, where he normally would have changed trains for his own station, so he got out two stops early and walked to a station on Line Six.

'Excuse me, may I see the paper if you're done with it?'

He was quite ordinary, a plain suit over a green sweater, raincoat, hat – held in left hand, as promised. But there was something about him, the skin of his face rough and weathered a certain way, hair a deep reddish brown, moustache a little ragged – that made it immediately apparent that he was British. Thus something of a shock when he spoke. He opened his mouth and perfect native French came out. Later he would explain: mother from Limoges, father from Edinburgh, he'd grown up in the Dordogne, where his family owned a hotel.

They left the church, walked down the hill, crossed boulevard St-Michel and entered the Luxembourg Gardens. Handed over a few sous to the old lady in black who guarded the park chairs, and sat on a terrace. It was crowded, couples holding hands, old men with newspapers, just below them boys launching sailboats in the fountain, keeping them on course with long sticks.

They were silent for a moment, Casson got a sense of the man sitting beside him. He was scared, but bolted down tight. He'd done what he'd done, signed up for clandestine service in time of war. Hadn't understood what that meant until he got to Paris, saw the Germans in operation, at last realized how easy it was going to be to make the wrong mistake – only a matter of time. After that, he woke up scared in the morning and went to bed scared at night. But, he wasn't going to let it finish him. Something else would, not that.

'Well,' he said. 'Perhaps you'll tell me what happened.'

Casson had taken the time to think it through and had the answer rehearsed. Simic. The money taken to Spain. The period of surveillance. Finally, the two contacts with Millau. Mathieu listened attentively, did not react until Casson repeated what he'd been told about Marie-Noëlle being in German custody.

'And you didn't tell anybody,' Mathieu said.

'No.'

For a moment there was nothing to be said, only the sound of the park, the birds in late afternoon, the boys by the fountain shouting to one another.

'I'm sorry,' Casson said. 'It didn't occur to me to tell someone about it – I really don't know anything about how this works.'

'Was that all – they had her in custody?'

'Yes.'

'Well, at least we know now.'

'You'd met her?'

'No. I suspect she was with the other service, not mine. They're the intelligence people, we're operational. We blow things up. So, what we do isn't exactly secret. Rather the opposite.'

'You're in the army, then.'

'No, not really. I was a university teacher. Latin drama – Plautus and Terence, mostly. Seneca, sometimes. But I heard they were looking for people who spoke native French, and I was the right age – old enough to know when to run, young enough to run fast when the time came. So, I applied. And then, a stroke of luck, I got the job.'

252

Casson smiled. 'When was that?'

'The autumn after the invasion here.'

'Eight months.'

'Yes, about that.'

'Not very long.'

Mathieu took off his hat, smoothed his hair back. 'Well, they did have training, especially the technical part. But for the rest of it, they taught us the classic procedures but they also let us know, in so many words, that people who have done well at this sort of thing tend to make it up as they go along.'

Mathieu stared at something over Casson's shoulder, Casson turned around to see what he was looking at. Down a long *allée* of lime trees, a pair of French policemen were conducting a snap search – a darkhaired couple handing over various passes and identity cards.

'Let's take a little walk,' Mathieu said. They moved off casually, away from the search.

'I'm going to have to ask London what they want to do with you,' Mathieu said. 'It will take a few days – say, next Thursday. Now, in a minute I'm going to give you a telephone number. Memorize it. It's a bookstore, over in the Marais. You call them up – use a public phone, of course – and ask them some question with an Italian flavour. Such as, do you have two copies of Dante's *Vita Nuova*? Leave a number. If a call doesn't come back in twenty minutes, walk away. You may be contacted at home, or at your office, or en route. If nothing happens, return to that phone at the same time the following day, also for twenty minutes. Then once again, on the third day.'

'And then, if there's still no response?'

'Hmm, they say Lisbon is pleasant, this time of year.'

28 May, 1941. 4:20 p.m.

'Hello?'

   'Good afternoon. Do you have a tourist guide for Naples?'

   'I'll take a look. Can I call you back?'

   'Yes. I'm at *41 11 56.*'

   'Very good. We'll be in touch.'

   'Good-bye.'

29 May, 1941. 4:38 p.m.

'Hello?'

   'Did you call about a guidebook for Naples?'

   'Yes.'

   'All right, I have an answer for you. I spoke with my managing director, he wants you to go ahead with the project.'

   'What?'

   'Do what they ask.'

   'Agree to what they want – is that what you mean?'

   'Yes.'

   'Are you sure about this?'

   'Yes.'

   'Can we get together and talk about it?'

   'Later, perhaps. What we will want to know is what they ask you to do. That's important. Do you understand?'

   'Yes. I'm on their side.'

   'That's correct – but don't overdo it.'

   'I won't.'

   'Are you going to be able to do this?'

   A pause. 'Yes.'

   'You will have to be very careful.'

   'I understand.'

   'Good-bye.'

   'Good-bye.'

'Monsieur Casson?'

'Yes.'

'Franz Millau. Have you thought over our discussion?'

'Yes.'

'How do you feel about it now?'

'If there's a way I can help – it's best.'

'Will you be at your office for an hour or so?'

'Yes.'

'An envelope will be delivered. Monsieur Casson?'

'Yes?'

'I will ask you one time only. Did you mention, or allude to, the discussion we had, to anybody, in any way whatsoever? Think for a moment before you answer me.'

'The answer is no.'

'Can you tell me please, why is that?'

'Why. It might take a long time to explain. Briefly, I was raised in a family that understood that your first allegiance is to yourself.'

'Very well. Expect the envelope, and we'll be in touch with you soon. Good-bye.'

'Good-bye, Herr Millau.'

'And good luck.'

'Yes, always that. Good-bye.'

'Good-bye.'

9 June, 3:20 p.m.

On his way to the Gare de Lyon to catch the 4:33 to Chartres, he stopped at the café where he had his morning coffee. The proprietor went back to his office and returned with a postcard. *Greetings from Lyons – View of the Fountain, place des Terreaux*. 'All is well, monsieur?'

'Yes. Thank you, Marcel. For keeping the card for me.'

'It's my pleasure. Not easy, these times.'

'No.'

'It's not only you, monsieur.'

Casson met his glance and found honest sympathy: liaisons with lovers or with the underground, for Marcel what mattered were liaisons, and he could be counted on. Casson reached across the copper-covered bar and shook his hand. 'Thank you again, my friend,' he said.

'*De rien*.' It's nothing.

'I'm off to the train.'

'*Bon voyage*, monsieur.'

He read it on the train, sweaty and breathing hard from having jumped on the last coach as it was moving out of the station. A control on the Métro, a long queue, French police inspectors peering at everyone's identity cards as the minutes marched past and Casson clenched his teeth in rage.

The writing on the card was careful, like a student in lycée. It touched his heart to look at it.

> My love, it's 3:40 in the morning, and it feels and sounds the way it does late at night in these places. My chaos of a life is right here by my side – it likes to stay up late when I do, and it won't go to bed. You would say not to care, so, maybe, I don't. I write to say that spring is going by, that nothing changes in this city, and I wonder where you are. I am very alone without you – please try to come. I know you are trying, but please try. I do love you. X

He looked up to find green countryside, late afternoon in spring among the meadows and little aimless roads. *Citrine*. For just a moment he was nineteen again – to go to Lyons you took the Lyons train. Or you went to a town along the ZNO line and found somebody to take you across. Then

256

you found your lover and together you ran to a place where they would never find you. *No*. That didn't work. Life wasn't like that. And it didn't matter how much you wanted it to be.

The sun low in the sky, long shadows in a village street, a young woman in a scarf helping an old woman down the steps of a church, Café de la Poste, an ancient cemetery – stone walls and cypress trees, then the town ended and the fields began again.

As it turned out, he could have let the express to Chartres leave without him. A long delay, waiting for the 6:28 local that would eventually find its way to Alençon. He used the time to buy paper and an envelope at a stationer's shop across from the terminal, then wrote, sitting on a bench on the platform as the sun went down behind the spires of the cathedral.

He loved her, he was coming, life in Paris was complicated, he had to extricate himself.

He stopped there, thought for a time, then wrote that if there had to be a line drawn it would be a month from then, no more. Say, July 1. A voice inside him told him not to write that but he didn't listen to it. He couldn't just go on and on about *soon*. She needed more than that, he did the best he could.

The train was two hours late, only three passengers got off at Alençon; a mother and her little boy, and Casson, feeling very much the dark-haired Parisian, lighting a cigarette as he descended to the platform, cupping his hands to shield the match flare from the evening wind.

'You must be Bourdon.' He'd been leaning against a baggage cart, watching to see who got off the train. He was barely thirty, Casson thought. Leather coat, longish – artfully combed hair, the expectantly handsome face of an office lothario.

257

'That's right.'

'I'm Eddie Juin.'

They walked into a maze of little lanes, three feet wide, washing hanging out above their heads. Turned left, right, right, left, down a stairway, through a tunnel, then up a long street of stairs to a garage. It was dark inside, fumes of petrol and oil heavy in the air, cut by the sharp smell of scorched metal. 'I wonder if you could let me have a look at your identity card,' Juin said.

'Not a problem.'

Casson handed over the Bourdon card, Juin clicked on a flashlight and had a look. 'A salesman?'

'Yes.'

'What is it you sell, if I can ask?'

'Scientific equipment – to laboratories. Test tubes, flasks, Bunsen burners, all that sort of thing.'

'How do you do, with that?'

'Not too badly. It's up, it's down – you know how it is.'

Juin handed the card back, went to a stained and battered desk with a telephone on it, dialled a number. 'Seems all right,' he said. 'We're leaving now.'

He hung up, opened a drawer, took out several flashlights, put them in a canvas sack and handed it to Casson.

'Is this your place?' Casson asked.

'Mine? No. Belongs to a friend's father – he lets us use it.' He ran the beam of the flashlight over the steel tracks above the pit used to work under cars, then a stack of old tyres, then showed Casson what he meant him to see. 'Better button up your jacket,' he said, voice very proud.

It *was* beautiful. A big motorcycle, front and rear fenders stripped, the paint worn away to a colour that was no colour at all. 'What year?' Casson said.

'1925. It's English – a Norton.'

Juin climbed on, jiggled the fuel feed on the right handlebar, then rose in the air and drove his weight down hard on the kick starter. The engine grumbled once and

258

died. Juin rose again. Nothing on the second try, or the third. It went on, Juin undaunted. At last, a sputtering roar, a volley of small-arms fire and a cloud of smoke from the trembling exhaust pipe. Casson hauled up the metal shutter, then closed it again after Juin was out, and climbed on the flat seat meant for the passenger. 'Don't try to lean on the curves,' Juin shouted over the engine noise.

They flew through the streets, bouncing over the cobbles, bumping down a stairway, the explosive engine thundering off the ancient walls, announcing to every Frenchman and German in the lower Normandy region that that idiot Eddie Juin was out for a ride.

They sped over a bridge that spanned the Sarthe, then they were out in the countryside, Casson imagining that he could actually smell the fragrant night air through the reek of burned oil that travelled with the machine. They left the Route Nationale for a *route départementale*, then turned onto a packed dirt road that didn't have a number but probably had a local name, then to a cowpath, five miles an hour over rocks and roots, across a long hillside on a strip of beaten-down weed and scrub, over the hill to a valley spread out in the moonlight. Juin cut the engine and they rolled silently for a long time, coming to a stop at last on the edge of a flat grassy field.

It seemed very quiet, just a few crickets, once the engine was off. Casson climbed off the motorcycle, half frozen, blowing on his hands. 'Where are we?' he asked.

Eddie Juin smiled. 'Nowhere,' he said triumphantly. 'Absolutely nowhere.'

1:30 a.m. Three-quarter moon. They sat by the motorcycle, smoking, waiting, watching the edge of the woods at the other end of the field.

'Alençon doesn't seem so bad,' Casson said.

'No, not too bad, and I'm an expert. I grew up in at least six different places, one of those families that never stopped

259

moving. Saves money, my dad said – some bills would never quite catch up with us – and, he'd say, it's an education for life!' Juin laughed as he remembered. 'It's Lebec who's from Alençon, and his uncle, who's called Tonton Jules. Then there's Angier, and that's it. Tonton Jules farms over in Mortagne, the rest of us met up in Paris.'

'At the office.'

'Yes, that's it. We all worked for the Merchant Marine Ministry, first in Paris, then over on the coast, in Lorient. We didn't have it too bad – snuck out early on Friday afternoons, chased the girls, caught our share. But when the Germans came they tossed us out, of course, because they put their submarine pens in over there, for the blockade on the English. So that left us, Athos, Porthos, and Aramis from the fourth floor, with time on our hands. Well, what better than to find a way to fuck life up for the *schleu*? Return the favour, right? And as for Tonton Jules, they captured him on the Marne in 1915, sent him to Germany in a cattle car. Apparently he didn't care for it.'

He paused for a moment and they both listened for engines but it was very quiet. 'So,' he said, 'how is it in Paris these days?'

'You miss it?'

'Who wouldn't.'

'People are fed up,' Casson said. 'Hungry, tired, can't get tobacco, there's no coffee. In the beginning they thought they could live with it. Then they thought they could ignore it. Now they want it to go away.'

'Wait a minute.' Juin stood up. Casson heard the faint throb of a machine in the distance. Juin reached inside his coat and took out a snub-nosed automatic.

A farm tractor towing a haywagon materialized at the end of the field, Casson and Eddie Juin went to meet it. Tonton Jules swayed in the driver's seat. He was a fat man with one arm, and he was drunk. His nephew Lebec was

260

dark and clever, could have been Eddie Juin's brother.
Angier had an appealing rat face, Casson guessed he would
go anywhere, do anything. Easy to imagine him as a kid
jumping off railway bridges for a dare. '*Salut*, Eddie,' he
said. 'Are we on time?'

Juin just laughed.

They heard the plane at 3:12 a.m., headed south of east.
They each took a flashlight and stood in a line with Juin
to one side to make the letter *L*. This showed wind direction
when, as the plane came closer, they turned on the lights.
Juin then blinked the Morse letter *J* – a recognition signal
for that night only, which meant *we're not a bunch of Germans trying to get you to land in this field*. The plane did not
respond, flew straight ahead, vanished. Then, a minute
later, they heard him coming back. Juin tried again, and
this time the pilot confirmed the signal, using the plane's
landing lights to flash back a Morse countersign.

The plane touched down at the other end of the field,
then taxied towards them, bouncing over the uneven
ground. No savoir-faire now, they ran to meet it, Tonton
Jules wheezing as he tried to keep up. It wasn't much to
look at, a single propeller, fixed landing wheels in over-
sized hubs, and wings propped on struts. On the fuselage,
next to a freshly painted RAF roundel, was a black flash
mark and a peppering of tiny holes. With difficulty the
pilot forced back the Perspex window panel, then tore the
leather flying cap from his head. He allowed himself a
single deep breath, then called out over the noise of the
engine. 'Can somebody help? Ahh, *peut-être*, can you –
aidez-mah?'

'You are hurted?' Lebec said.

'No. Not me.'

He was very young, Casson thought, not much more
than nineteen. And he certainly didn't look the hero – tall
and gangly, unruly hair, big ears, freckles. The man sitting

261

behind him grabbed the edge of the cockpit with his left hand and clumsily struggled to his feet. Clearly his right arm had been damaged. He appeared to be cursing under his breath. Angier used the tail fin to scramble up on the back of the plane, then slid himself forward to a point where he could help the man get down to the ground.

The pilot looked at his watch. 'We should move along,' he said to Casson. 'I'm to leave here in three minutes.'

'All right.'

'You'll have to help me get the tail swung round. And, don't forget, *n'oublah* thing, the two, uh – *deux caisses, deux valises*.' The last burst forth with the fluency of the determinedly memorized.

Lebec climbed onto the wing, then helped the pilot work two suitcases and two small wooden crates free of the cockpit. 'Damned amazing, what you can get in here,' the pilot said. Lebec smiled – no idea what the pilot was saying but an ally was an ally.

They handed down the cargo – carried off to Tonton Jules's wagon – then Lebec jumped to the ground and saluted the pilot, who returned the salute with a smile, then tossed his flying cap back on and tried a parting wave, devil-may-care, as he revved the engine. 'Best of luck, then,' he shouted. *'Bonne shan!'*

He reached up, pulled the housing shut. Eddie Juin took hold of the tail assembly and started to turn the plane into the wind, everybody else ran to help him. The plane accelerated suddenly, there was a blast of hot exhaust as it pulled away, then a roar of fuel fed to the engine as it struggled into the air. It flopped back down, bounced off the field, touched one wheel a second time, then caught the wind and climbed into the darkness. The people on the ground listened for a time, peering into the dark sky, then lost the whine of the receding engine among the night sounds of the countryside.

*   *   *

262

Verneuil, Brézolles, Laons – Casson drove east towards Paris in the spring dawn.

The end of the operation had been complicated. *Système D*, Casson thought, always *Système D*, make do, use your ingenuity, improvise – it was simply the way life was lived. They'd left the field headed for a small village nearby, where a man who drove a milk truck to Paris twice a week was supposed to pick up the supplies delivered from England, leaving Casson and the operative free to take the train into the city. But the truck never appeared, so Eddie Juin had to come up with an alternative. Off they went to another village, where a barn on the outskirts hid a Renault – a four-year-old Juvequatre model, slow, steady, inexpensive, a family car.

Casson drove through first light, staying on the 839. The two crates and two valises were in the boot. Next to him, the man he had come to think of as the sergeant – though he used the name Jerome – bled slowly into the pale-grey upholstery.

'It's not so bad,' he said. 'You could hardly call it shrapnel. More like, specks. But, iron specks, so I'll have to see a doctor, sooner or later. Still, not bad enough for me to go back to England – no point at all to that.'

'What happened?'

'Well, at first everything went perfectly. We came in at eight thousand feet over the coast at St-Malo – no problem. Picked up the railway line to Alençon a minute later – we spotted the firebox on a locomotive going east and we just flew along with him. Next we had yellow signal lights, for ten miles or so, coming out of the big freight junction in Fougères. After that, the track was between us and the moon and we just followed the glow on the rails. But somebody heard us, because ten minutes later a searchlight came on and they started shooting. Nothing very serious, a few ack-ack rounds, and Charley thought maybe a machine gun. Then it was over, but my arm had gone numb and I realized we'd been hit.'

Casson slowed down for a hairpin turn at the centre of a sleeping village, then they were back among the fields.

He saw now how they worked it. First came Mathieu, the university man, getting the system organized. Next came the sergeant – almost certainly a technician. Why else bring him in? Short and muscular, working-class face, speaking French in a way that would fool nobody. Not his fault, Casson thought. Likely something he'd taken up years ago in hopes it would advance him in the military. So he'd put in his time in classrooms, dutifully rolled his *r*'s and nasalized his *n*'s, but finally to very little purpose – he might as well have worn a bowler hat with a Union Jack stuck in the band and whistled 'God Save the King' for all the good it was going to do him.

Casson slowed for a one-lane bridge, the stream below running full in spring flood, water dark blue in the early light. The sergeant had winced when he tapped the brake. 'Sorry,' Casson said.

'Oh, it's nothing. Twenty minutes with a doctor and I'll be fine.'

'It won't be a problem,' Casson said.

Well, he didn't think it would be. What doctor? He only knew one doctor, his doctor. Old Dr Genoux. What were his politics? Casson had no idea. He was brusque, forever vaguely irritated by something or other, and smelled eternally of eucalyptus. He'd been Casson's doctor for twenty years, since university. One day Casson had noticed his hair was white. Good heavens! He couldn't be a Vichyite or a Fascist, could he? Well, if not him, who else? The dentist? The professor at the Sorbonne faculty of medicine who lived across the street? Arnaud had once had a girl-friend who was a nurse. No, that wasn't going to work, old Genoux would just have to do the job.

*   *   *

He worked his way through the medieval town of Dreux, intending to pick up the 932 that wound aimlessly into the Chevreuse valley. But then he somehow made a mistake and, a little way beyond the town, found himself instead on the N 12, with a sprinkling of early traffic headed for Paris. Well, all the roads went to the capital, the N 12 was as good as any other.

Going over a rail crossing, the springs plunged and the cargo gave a loud thump as it shifted in the boot. The sergeant opened his eyes and laughed. 'Don't worry about *that*,' he said confidently.

An explosion, is what he meant. The shipment from England included radio crystals, which would allow clandestine wireless-telegraph sets to change frequencies, 200,000 francs, 20,000 dollars, four Sten carbines with 4,000 rounds of ammunition, time pencil detonators, and eighty pounds of the explosive cyclonite, chemically enhanced to make it malleable – *plastique*.

'The trick,' he added, 'is actually getting it to go off.'

The town of Houdan. A place Casson had always liked, he'd come here with Marie-Claire for picnics in the forest – *long ago and far away*. They'd owned a set of chairs and a table that could be folded up and carried in the boot of the car. She always brought a cloth for the table, he would pick up a pair of langoustes with green mayonnaise from Fauchon, and they'd sit by a field for hours and watch the day.

The road turned north, the sun was up now, light glistening on the wet fields, the last of the ground mist gathered over the streams. The sky had turned a delicate, morning blue, with a rose blush on the horizon. Something world-weary about these dawns in the country around Paris, he'd always felt that – *well, all right, one more day if you think it's going to do you any good*. The next village on the road seemed closed up tight, the shutters still pulled down over the front of the café. Casson spotted a road

265

marker and decided to take the 839. The town ended, there was a bridge, then a sharp left-hand curve through a wood, which straightened out to reveal some cars and trucks and guards with machine pistols.

Control.

They had a moment, no more. Casson hit the brake, rolled past five or six policemen who waved him on, down a lane formed by portable barriers – crossbraced *x*'s of sawn logs strung with barbed wire. Coming up on the control, Casson and the sergeant had turned to each other, exchanged a look: *well, too bad*. That was all. Then Casson said, 'Close your eyes. You're injured, unconscious, almost gone.'

A young officer – *Leutnant* – in Wehrmacht grey appeared at the window. '*Raus mit uns*.' He was impatient, holster unsnapped, hand resting on his sidearm.

Casson got out and stood by the half-open door, nodded towards the passenger side of the car. 'There's a man hurt,' he said.

The *Leutnant* walked around to have a look, bent over and peered into the car. The sergeant's eyes were closed, mouth open, head back. A bloody rag around his arm, a dark stain on the upholstery. The *Leutnant* hesitated, looked in Casson's direction. Casson saw a possibility. 'I don't really know exactly how he got himself in this condition but it's important that he see a doctor as soon as he can.' He said it quickly.

The *Leutnant* froze, then squared his shoulders and walked away.

The road lay in shadow – six in the morning, shafts of sunlight in the pine forest. Five cars had been stopped, as well as two rickety old trucks taking pigs to market. Amid the smell and the squealing, a German officer was trying to make sense of the drivers' papers while they stood to one side looking sinister and apprehensive. By the car ahead of

266

Casson, four men, dark, unshaven, possibly Gypsies, were trying to communicate with a man in a raincoat, perhaps a German security officer. Suddenly angry he yanked the door open, and a very pregnant, very frightened woman struggled out with hands held high in the air.

The young *Leutnant* came striding back to Casson's car, a policeman in tow – an officer of the *Gendarmerie Nationale*, French military police with a reputation for brutality. The gendarme was angry at being asked to intervene. 'All right,' he said to Casson, 'what's going on?'

'This man is injured.'

'How did it happen?'

'I'm taking him to a doctor.'

The gendarme gave him a very cold look. 'I asked how.'

'An accident.'

'Where?'

'Working, I believe. In a garage. I wasn't there.'

The gendarme's eyes were like steel. *Salaud* – you bastard – trying to play games with me? In front of a German? I'll take you behind a tree and break your fucking head. 'Open the boot,' he said.

Casson fumbled with the latch, then got it open. The intense odour of almonds, characteristic of plastic explosive, came rolling out at them. The *Leutnant* said 'Ach,' and stepped back. 'What is it?' the gendarme said.

'Almonds.'

The two valises were in plain sight, packed with francs, dollars, radio crystals, and explosive. Tonton Jules, just before they left, had tossed an old blanket over the two crates holding the sten guns and ammunition. Casson, at that moment, had thought it a particularly pointless gesture.

'Almonds,' the gendarme said. He didn't know it meant explosive. He did know that Casson had been caught in the middle of something. Parisians of a certain class had no business on country roads at dawn, and people didn't injure their upper arms in garage accidents. This was resistance of some kind, that much he did know, thus his patriotism, his honour, had been called into question and now he, a man with wife and family, had to compromise himself. He stared at Casson with pure hatred.

'You had better be going,' he said. 'Your friend ought to see a doctor.' For the benefit of the *Leutnant* he made a Gallic gesture – eyes shut, shoulders up, hands in the air: *Who knows what these people are doing, but it's clearly nothing that would interest men of our stature.*

He waved Casson on, down the road towards Paris. *Salaud.* Don't come back here.

10 June, 1941

'Hello?'

'Good morning. I was wondering if you might have a life of Verdi, something nice, for a gift.'

'The composer?'

'Yes.'

'I'm not sure, we may very well have something. Can we call you back?'

'Yes. I'm at *63 26 08.*'

'All right. We'll be in touch.'

'Good-bye.'

'Good-bye.'

This time they met in the church of Notre-Dame de Secours, then walked in the Père-Lachaise cemetery. At the gate, Mathieu bought a bouquet of anemones from an old woman.

They walked up the hill to the older districts, past the crumbling tombs of vanished nobility, past the Polish exiles, past the artists. They left the path at the Twenty-fourth Division and stood before the grave of Corot.

'Are you sure of the doctor?' Mathieu asked.

'No. Not really.'

'But the patient, can return to work?'

'Yes.'

'We'll want him to work on the twenty-third.'

'It won't be a problem.'

'His arrangements?'

'He's up in Belleville, in the Arab district. Above a Moroccan restaurant – Star of the East on rue Pelleport. If he can stand the couscous, from dawn to midnight, he'll be fine. I suggested to the owner that the wound was received in an affair of *family honour*, in the *south*, somewhere below *Marseilles*.'

'Corsica.'

'Yes.'

Mathieu gave a brief, dry laugh. 'Corsica, yes. That's very good. The owner is someone you know?'

'No. A newspaper advertisement, *room for rent*. I put on a pair of dark glasses, paid three months in advance.'

Mathieu laughed again. 'And for the rest?'

'Hidden. Deep and dark, where it will never be found.'

'I'll take your word for it. When are you going to make contact?'

'Today.'

'That sounds right. Difficult things – the sooner the better.'

'Difficult –' Casson said. It was a lot worse than *difficult*.

Mathieu smiled a certain way, he meant it was no easier for him, that he was just as scared as Casson was.

Making sure that nobody was looking at them, Mathieu took a folded square of paper from his pocket and slipped it among the stems of the anemones. Then he leaned over, placed the flowers on the tomb.

'Corot,' Casson said.

'Yes,' Mathieu said. 'He's off by himself, over here.'

They walked back down the hill together, then shook

hands at the boulevard corner and said good-bye. 'They'll make you go over it, you know. Again and again. From a number of angles,' Mathieu said.

Casson nodded that he knew that, then turned and walked to the Métro.

It was Singer who picked him up in a black Traction Avant Citroën on the evening of 15 June and drove him out to the brick villa in Vernouillet. The parlour, even as the weather warmed up, still felt dark and damp and unused. Millau had a technician with him, a man who wore earphones and operated a wire recorder to take down what Casson said.

Millau had just shaved – a tiny nick freshly made on the line of the jaw. He worked in shirtsleeves, his jacket hung in a closet, but despite the suggestion of informality the shirt was freshly pressed and laundered a sparkling white. He was, evidently, going to meet someone important later that evening. Only after they'd greeted each other and made small talk did Casson realize he'd been wrong about that. *Jean Casson* was the someone important – the shave and the white shirt were for, well, not so much him as an important moment in Millau's life.

Mathieu had been right. He was made to go over the story again and again. He was comfortable with plots and characters, had spent much of his professional life in meetings where people said things like *what if Duval doesn't return until the following evening?* That gave him a slight advantage but not all that much, and the mistakes were always there, waiting for him. Perhaps they wouldn't be noticed. He'd changed the Alençon names to code names – fish. *Merlan* drove the car, *Rouget* the truck, *Anguille* sat beside him, the shotgun on his lap.

It ran, he hoped, seamlessly into the truth: the single-engine Lysander a single-engine Lysander, the pilot young and gangling and rather awkward, and the navigation guides were as they'd been: signal lights along the track, locomotive fireboxes, and the glow of moonlight on the steel rails. They had come in at 8,000 feet over St-Malo, were later hit by an antiaircraft burst – Millau nodded at that. The copilot was slightly wounded. The shipment included radio crystals and money, Sten guns and *plastique*.

'And where is it now?' Millau asked.

'In the store room of an empty shop, down among the old furniture workshops in the Faubourg St-Antoine. I bought the *droit de bail* – the lease – from an old couple who retired to Canada just at the beginning of the war. It was for a long time a *crémerie* – you can still smell the cheese. The address is eighty-eight, rue des Citeaux, just off the avenue St-Antoine, about a minute's walk from the hospital. In the back of the shop is a storage locker, lead lined, no doubt for cold storage using blocks of ice. The shipment is in there, I've padlocked the door, here are the keys.'

'You bought it direct? From Canada?'

'From a broker in Paris. LaMontaine.'

'Who is expected to come there?'

'They haven't told me that. Only that it must be kept safe and secure.'

'Who said that, exactly?'

'Merlan.'

'Beard and spectacles.'

'No, the tall one who drove the car.'

'When did he say it?'

'The last thing, before I left. I would be contacted, he said.'

'How?'

'At home.'

'The Bourdon address?'

'Yes.'

'Good. That simplifies things for us. It will be of great interest, of course, to see who collects the explosive and spends the money, who uses the radio crystals – to send what information. It's like a complicated web, that reaches here and there, and grows constantly. It may be a long time before we do anything. In these operations you must be thorough, you have to get it all. You'll see – before it's done it will involve husbands and wives, lovers and childhood friends, brothers and sisters, and the local florist. Love finds a way, you see. And we find out.'

'Clearly, you are experienced.'

Millau permitted himself a brief, tight smile of pleasure in his achievement. 'Practice makes perfect,' he said. 'We've been taking these networks apart since 1933, in Germany. Now in France, we've had one or two – we'll have more. No offence meant, my friend, but the French, compared to the German communist cells, well, what can one say.'

He would remember the evening as a certain moment, almost a freeze-frame; three men looking up at him from a table on the crowded *terrasse* of a restaurant, Fouquet as it happened, on a warm evening. All around them, a sea of faces, the world at night – desire and cunning, love and greed, the usual. A Brueghel of Paris in the second spring of the war.

Casson had been driven back to the city by Singer, asked by Millau to join him 'and some friends' for a drink. As he approached, the men at the table – Millau with his fine eyeglasses and cigar, and two pale bulky northern men, Herr *X* and Herr *Y*, looked up and smiled. *Ah, here he is!* Superbly faked smiles – *how much we admire you*.

They chatted for a time, nothing all that important, a conversation among men of the world, no fools, long past idealism. Poor Europe, decadent and weak, very nearly gobbled up by the Bolshevik monster. *But for them*. Not said, but clearly understood.

The champagne arrived, brought by a waiter who had

served him many times in the past. 'Good evening, Monsieur Casson.' Three menus in German, one in French.

Herr X wore a small pin, a black-and-gold swastika, in his lapel. 'One thing we wonder,' he said, leaning forward, speaking confidentially. 'We were talking to Millau here before you arrived and you told him that there was a copilot on the flight. We hear it a little differently, that the Lysander brought in an agent. Can you see any reason why somebody would say that?'

'No,' Casson said. 'That's not what happened.'

Millau raised his glass. 'Enough work!' he said.

For a time it was true. Herr Y was from East Prussia, the Masurian lakes, where stag was still hunted from horseback every autumn. 'And then, what a feast!' Herr X worked over in Strasbourg. 'Some problems,' he said reflectively, 'but it is at heart a reasonable part of the world.' Then, a fine idea: 'I'll tell you what, I'll get in touch with you through Millau and you'll come over there for a day or two. Be a change of pace from Paris, right?'

It was after midnight when Casson got home. He tore his jacket off and threw it on the bed. He'd sweated through his shirt, it was wringing wet. He took it off, then went into the bathroom and looked at himself in the mirror. God. It was black under his eyes. A dark, clever, exhausted man.

THE ESCAPE

18 June, 1941

He met Mathieu at dusk, in the waiting room of the Gare d'Austerlitz. They walked in the Jardin des Plantes.

'They know what happened,' Casson said. 'That an agent was brought in.'

Mathieu walked in silence for a moment. 'Who is it?' he said at last.

Eddie Juin? Lebec? Angier? 'I don't know.'

'It will have to be shut down.' Mathieu was very angry.

'Yes. Perhaps it's only – you know, the French talk too much. Somebody told somebody, they told somebody else. Each time, "now, don't tell anybody." Or, just maybe, it could have happened in London. People in offices, people who work at airfields.'

'Yes, it could have,' Mathieu admitted. Too many people, too many possibilities. 'At least we found out. They would have taken over the network and run it.'

The gravel path was bordered by spring beds, tulip and daffodil, poet's narcissus, the air heavy with manure and perfume.

'They want me to go to Strasbourg,' Casson said.

'Did they say why?'

'No.'

'Will you go?'

'I have to think about it, probably I will.'

They walked in silence for a minute or two, then Casson said, 'Mathieu, how long does this go on?'

'I can't say.'

'There's a record being built – a wire recording they

made in Vernouillet, I've been seen with them. What if the war ends?'

'We'll vouch for you.'

They reached the end of the path, a wire fence. Beyond were rakes and shovels and wheelbarrows. Mathieu took his hat off, ran a thumb around the lining to secure it, then put it back on, pulling the brim down with thumb and forefinger. 'Don't do anything until the twenty-third, then we'll talk again. That's the night – all hell's going to break loose and we're using that to get our job done. Meanwhile, you should go on as usual.'

They came to the gate, shook hands. 'Be careful,' Mathieu said.

Casson couldn't sleep the night of the twenty-third. He went to an after-curfew bar and drank wine. The bar was in a cellar off an alley, it had a packed-earth floor and stone walls. A long time ago, some madman had managed to coax an upright piano down the narrow staircase – perhaps he'd taken it apart. Clearly it was never going anywhere again, and that gave somebody the idea for a nightclub. The piano's sounding board was muffled with a blanket, and an old woman in a gown played love songs and sang in a whispery voice. The cigarette smoke was thick, the only light from a single candle. Casson paused at the bottom of the stairs, then a woman took him in her arms and danced with him.

She smelled of cleaning bleach and brilliantine, had stiff hair that scratched against his cheek. They never spoke. She didn't press herself into him as they danced, just brushed against him, touched him enough so he could feel everything about her. When the sirens started up, she froze. A man nearby called out in a hushed voice, 'No, please. One must continue,' as though that were a rule of the house.

The rumbling went on for a long time, sharply felt in

278

the cellar because stone foundations built in the Middle Ages carried the vibrations of the bombs and the gunnery beneath the city. A plane went down that night on the rue St-Honoré, a Wellington bomber made a fiery cartwheel along the street, sliced through a jeweller's and a millinery shop, then came to rest in the workroom of a dress designer.

Walking home after curfew, Casson stayed alert for patrols, kept to the walls of the buildings. The streets rang with sirens and ambulance bells, searchlights swept the sky, there was a second wave of bombers, then a third. The southern horizon flickered orange just as he slipped into the rue Chardin, and he felt the concussions in the marble stairs as he climbed to his apartment.

Later the telephone rang. He'd fallen asleep on top of the covers, still dressed. 'Yes?' he said, looking at his watch. It was twenty minutes past five.

'Jean-Claude?'

'Yes?'

'It's me.' It was Marie-Claire, she was crying. He waited, finally she was able to speak. 'Bernard Langlade is dead, Jean-Claude.'

He went to the Langlades' apartment at seven, the smell of burning was heavy in the air. At the newspaper stands, thick headlines: VILMA AND KAUNAS TAKEN, WEHRMACHT ADVANCES IN RUSSIA. Then, just below, PARIS BOMBED, REPAIRS TO FACTORIES ALREADY BEGUN.

He was the last to arrive. Arnaud opened the door, Casson could see the Pichards, Véronique, a few friends and relatives talking in quiet voices. The Langlades' two grown children were said to be en route to Paris but the bombing had caused havoc on the railroads and they weren't expected until nightfall. When Casson entered the living room, Marie-Claire hugged him tight. Bruno was in the kitchen, he shook his head in sorrow. 'This is a rotten thing, Jean-Claude,' he said. 'Believe me, there will be something important done in his memory, a subscription. I'll be calling you.'

Yvette Langlade sat on the end of the couch. She was white, a handkerchief gripped tight in her fist, but very self-possessed. Casson pulled a chair up next to her and took her hand, 'Jean-Claude,' she said.

'I'm sorry.'

'I'm glad you could be here, Jean-Claude.'

'What happened?'

'He went out to Montrouge, to the factory.'

'In the middle of the night?'

'Something went wrong earlier in the evening – a door left open, or maybe an alarm went off. I'm not sure. A detective called, demanded that Bernard come out to Montrouge and make sure everything was secure. Because of the defence work, the police are very sensitive about things like that. So, he went –'

She stopped for a moment, looked away. The friends who'd arrived first were busy, had claimed the small jobs for themselves: Marie-Claire and her sister making coffee, Françoise Pichard straightening up the living room, her husband answering the telephone.

'He had to do what they told him,' Yvette said. 'So he changed his clothes and went back out to Montrouge. Then, then they called. This morning. And they told me, that he was gone.' She waited a moment, looked away. 'They asked a lot of questions.' She shook her head, unable to believe what had happened. 'Did Bernard store explosives in the factory, they wanted to know. I didn't know what to say.' She took a deep breath, pressed her lips together, squeezed Casson's hand. 'It's *madness*,' she said. 'A man like Bernard. To die in a war.'

Véronique brought him a cup of coffee – real coffee, courtesy of Bruno – and they exchanged a private look. He didn't know exactly what part she played in the British operation, but she could have known that sabotage was planned under cover of an air raid. Now, he thought, her look suggested that she did know. He read sympathy in her eyes, and sorrow. But, also, determination. 'Careful with this,' she said, handing him a cup and saucer. 'It's very hot.' She turned to Yvette. 'Now,' she said, 'I'm going to bring you some.'

'No, dear. Please, I can't.'

'Yes, you can. I'm going to go and get it. And Charles Arnaud has just gone out for fresh bread.'

After a moment of resistance, Yvette nodded, accepting, giving in to the inevitable. Véronique went off to get the coffee.

My fault, Casson thought. His heart ached for a lost friend. Not that he would survive him very long. They would meet in heaven, Langlade would explain what was what, the best way to deal with it all. Casson wiped his eyes. *Merde*, he thought. They'll kill us all, with their stupid fucking wars.

24 June, 9:10 a.m.

'Good morning.'

'Good morning. I'm looking for a copy of the *Decameron*, by Boccaccio.'

'Any particular edition?'

'No. Whatever you have.'

'I'll take a look, I'm sure we have something.'

'I'm at 43 09 19.'

He was in a café on the boulevard St-Germain, noisy and crowded and anonymous. The phone rang a moment later.

'Yes?' It was Mathieu on the line.

'I've decided to go to Strasbourg. Right away, because I need to be in Lyons on the first of July.'

'Please understand, about Strasbourg, that we really don't know what's going on there.'

'Perhaps I can find out.'

'It will help us, if you can.'

'I'll call Millau this morning, let him know I'm ready to go.'

'All right.' There was a pause, a moment's hesitation. 'You have to walk very lightly, just now. Do you understand?'

'Yes. I know.'

All day he felt numb and lifeless. He went to the office, though it seemed to him now a dead place, abandoned, without purpose. He looked in the bottom drawer of his desk, found the notebook with the last version of *Hotel Dorado* and began to read around in it. A few days earlier he'd tried to locate Fischfang, but now he really had disappeared. Perhaps gone underground, or fled to Portugal. Maybe arrested, or dead. Perhaps, Casson thought, he would never know what happened.

He began to clean up his files – this actually made him feel better, so he made some meaningless telephone calls to settle meaningless problems. Soon it was time for lunch; he went to the bank for cash, then returned and took Mireille to the Alsatian brasserie on the corner, slipping black-market ration stamps to the waiter, ordering the grandest *choucroute* on the menu. *Bernard*, he thought, *you used to eat this with me even though you hated it*. Warm sauerkraut, garlic sausage, it made him feel better, and he silently apologized to Langlade because it did.

He flirted with Mireille all through lunch. How it used to be when they were young. Going out dancing in the open pavilions in the early days of spring, falling in love, secret affairs, stolen hours. The bones in the backs of her hands sharply evident, Mireille worked vigorously with knife and fork, delicately removing the rind from a thick slice of bacon as she talked about growing up in a provincial city. 'Of course in those days,' she said, 'men didn't leave their wives.'

It was still light when he got home. Trudged up the stairs, put the key in the lock, and opened the door. Standing at the threshold, he smelled cigarette smoke and froze. *It is now*, he thought. Inside, a board creaked, somebody moving towards the door.

'Well, come in.' Citrine.

He put his hand on his heart. 'My God, you scared me.' He closed the door, put his arms around her, and hung on tight, inhaling her deeply, like a dog making sure of somebody from a long time ago. Gauloises and a long train ride on her breath, along with the liquorice drop she'd eaten to hide it, very good soap, her skin that always smelled as though she'd been in the sun, some kind of clove and vanilla perfume she'd discovered – the cheaper the better, the way Citrine saw it.

'It's all right I came?' she said. She could feel his head nod yes. 'I thought, oh, he's alone long enough. I'll just go up there and throw the schoolgirls out – probably he's tired of them by now.'

He walked her down the hall and back into the living room. They sat close together on the couch. 'How did you get in?'

'Your concierge. She will not stand in the way of true love. Especially when it's movie actresses. Also, she knew me from before. Also, I bribed her.'

'That's all it took?'

She laughed. 'Yes.'

He kissed her, just a little. She was wearing a tight brown sweater, chocolate, with her yellow scarf tied to one side. A pair of very expensive nylon stockings caught the early evening light.

'I don't care if you're mad,' she said.

'I'm not mad.'

She studied him a moment. 'Tired,' she said. 'What is it?'

He shrugged. 'I don't even look in the mirror.'

'A long time by the sea, I think.'

'Yes.'

'Under the palm trees.'

'Yes. With you.'

She lay on her side on the couch and he did the same – there was just room. 'Do you want to make love right away?' she said.

'No. I want to lie here. Later, we can.'

The evening came, birds sang on the roof across the street, the sky darkening to the deep Parisian blue. She took the stockings off and put them carefully aside. He could just see her in the living-room dusk as she put one foot at a time on a chair and rolled each stocking down.

She headed back to the couch, he held up his hand.

'Yes?'

'Why stop?'

'What?'

He smiled.

'You can't mean –' Her 'puzzled' look was very good; heavy lips apart, head canted a little to one side. 'Well,' she said. She understood now, but was it the right thing? She reached around behind her for the button on the waistband of her skirt. 'This?'

'Yes.'

The telephone rang. It startled him – nobody called at night. It rang again.

'They'll go away,' she said.

'Yes,' he said, but he sat upright on the couch. *Answer the phone*. On the third ring he stood up.

She didn't like it.

'I have to,' he said.

He walked into his bedroom and picked up the receiver. *'Casson!'* Mathieu screamed. *'Get out! Get out!'* The connection was broken.

'Citrine.'

She ran into the bedroom.

'We have to leave.'

She disappeared into the living room, swept up coat, valise, handbag. Stockings in hand, she forced her feet into her shoes. Casson went to the balcony, opened the doors, looked out. Two black Citroëns were just turning into the rue Chardin. He slammed the doors, ran back into the living room. 'Right now,' he said.

They ran out the door, then down the stairs, sliding on the marble steps. Citrine slipped, cried out, almost fell as they flew around the mid-floor landing, but Casson managed to pull her upright. *What were they doing?* They had no chance, none at all, of beating the Citroëns to the street door. They reached the fourth floor, he pulled Citrine after him, down to the end of the hallway, a pair of massive doors. There was a buzzer in a little brass plate, but Casson swung his arm back and pounded his fist against the wood. Eight, nine, ten times. The door was thrown open, the baroness stood there, wide-eyed with fright, hand pressed between her breasts. 'Monsieur!' she said.

Casson was out of breath. 'Please,' he said. 'Will you hide her?'

The baroness stared at him, then at Citrine. Slowly, the surprise and shock on her face turned to indignation. 'Yes,' she said, her elegant voice cold with anger. 'Yes, of course. How could you think I would not?' She took Citrine by the hand and gently drew her into the apartment.

As the door swung closed, Citrine stepped towards him, their eyes met. She had time to say 'Jean-Claude?' That was all.

Casson did try, tried as hard as he could. Raced down four flights of stairs, footsteps echoing off the walls. When

285

he reached the street, the men in raincoats were just climbing out of their cars. They shouted as he started to run, were on him almost immediately. The first one grabbed the back of his shirt, which ripped as he fought to pull free. He punched the man in the forehead and hurt his hand. Then somebody leaped on top of him and, with a yell of triumph, barred a thick forearm across his throat. Casson started to choke. Then, a cautionary bark in harsh German, and the arm relaxed. The man who seemed to be in charge was apparently irritated by public brawling. A word from him, they let Casson go. He stood there, rubbing his throat, trying to swallow. The man in charge never took his hands out of the pockets of his belted raincoat. A sudden kick swept Casson's feet from under him and he fell on his back in the street. From there, he could see people looking out their windows.

24 June, midnight

Midnight, more or less – they'd taken his watch. But from the cell in the basement of the rue des Saussaies he could hear the trains in the Métro, and he knew the last one ran around one in the morning.

He was in the basement of the old Interior Ministry – he'd had no idea they had cells down here, but this one had been in use for a long time. It was hard to read the graffiti on the walls, the only light came from a bulb in a wire cage on the ceiling of the corridor, but much of it was carved or scratched into the plaster, and by tracing with his finger he could read it – the earliest entry *16 octobre, 1902, Tassot.* And who was Tassot, and what had he done, in the autumn of 1902? Well, who was Casson, and what had he done, in the spring of 1941?

The wall was covered with it. Phrases in cyrillic Russian, in Polish, what might have been Armenian. There was

Annamese, and Arabic. Faces front and profile. Crosses. Hearts – with initials and arrows. Cocks and cunts, with curly hairs. Somebody loved Marguerite – in 1921, somebody else Martine. This one wrote *Au revoir, Maman*. And that one – a tall one, Casson had to stand on his toes – was going to die in the morning for freedom.

When he heard a deep rumbling sound, he thought for a moment that the RAF was attacking the factory districts at the edge of the city. *And under cover of the bombing, said Wing Commander Smith-Wilson, our commando team will attack the Gestapo office on the rue des Saussaies and rescue our valiant agent from his basement prison.* But it wasn't bombing, it was thunder. Rain pattering down in a courtyard above him somewhere. A spring rainstorm, nothing more.

'One thing I will tell you.' A deep voice, from a cell some way up the corridor. Good, educated French, the melancholy tone of the intellectual. Not exactly a whisper, but the voice low and private, confidential. 'Can you hear me?'

'Yes.'

'Are you injured?'

'No.'

'Then I will tell you one thing: sooner or later, everyone talks. And it's easier on you if it's sooner.'

He waited, heart pounding, but that was all.

There was no bed, he sat on the stone floor, back against the damp wall. The last Métro train faded away, the hours passed. Perhaps he could have hidden with the baroness, but then, not finding him, they would have searched the building. They had, no doubt, searched his apartment, but there was nothing for them to find there. Now, what remained was a final scene, he'd manage it as well as he could. The post in the courtyard, the blindfold. Farewell, my love.

What worried him came before that – 'sooner or later

everyone talks.' *I don't want to tell them*, he thought. But he had no choice, and he knew it.

They came for him an hour later.

A functionary, and his helper, an SS corporal in a black uniform. The functionary was a small man in his twenties, wearing a mole-coloured suit with broad lapels. Hair parted in the middle; weak, sulky mouth. He said to the corporal, 'Unlock this door.' Disdainful, chin in the air – *you see, I run things around here*. Casson stood, they walked on either side of him, down the corridor, then up long flights of stairs.

Somebody's son, Casson thought. A high official in the Nazi party – what shall we do with poor *X*? Well, this is what they'd done with him. They reached the top floor, Casson had been here before, for his meetings with Guske. All around him, office life: people talking and laughing and rushing about with papers in their hands. Typewriters racketing, telephones ringing. Of course, he thought, the Gestapo worked a night shift just like the police. A clock on the wall said 3:20. They took him to Guske's office, made him stand against a wall at attention. 'Could I have some water?' he said. He had a terrible, burning thirst – was that something they were doing to him on purpose?

'Nothing for you,' said the functionary. He picked up the phone, dialled two digits. A moment later: 'We have him ready for you now, Herr *Obersturmbannführer*.'

Guske arrived a few minutes later, all business and very angry. He gave Casson a savage glare – very much the honest fellow betrayed by his own good nature. Well, they'd see about *that*. He was dressed for an important evening; dark suit and tie, cologne, sparse hair carefully arranged for maximum effect. On his pocket, a decoration – swastika and ribbon. To Casson's guards he said 'Get out,' in a voice only just under control. Then paced the office until a heavy woman in SS uniform rushed in with a file. Guske took it from her and slammed it on his desk, and she ran out of the office.

Guske walked slowly over to him and stood there. Casson looked away. Guske drew his hand back and slapped him in the face as hard as he could, the sound was a crack like a pistol shot. Casson's face was hot, and tears stood in the corners of his eyes.

'It's nothing,' Guske said. 'Just so we understand each other.' He went back to his desk and settled in, still breathing hard. He thumbed through the file for a moment but he really didn't have his concentration back. He looked up at Casson. '*I'm* the stupid one. I gave you my hand in friendship, and you turned around and gave me the *Dolchstoss* – the stab in the back. So, good, now it's clear between us and we'll go on from there. And, when I'm finished with you, Millau gets what's left.' He sniffed, turned one page, then another. 'The trouble is, we have not come to a true understanding of this country. The Mediterranean type is unfamiliar to us – it does not hesitate to lie, because, the way it sees the world, honour means nothing. But then, when it thinks nobody is looking, it runs out of its burrow, where it hides, and gives somebody a vicious little bite.'

Guske read a note pinned to the inside cover of the dossier. 'What is HERON? Code for what?'

'I don't know.'

Guske's face was mottled with anger. 'And who is Laurent?'

Casson shook his head.

Guske stared at him. Casson heard the typewriters and the telephones, voices and footsteps. The rain outside the window. It seemed very normal. 'I need,' Casson said, 'to use the bathroom.'

Guske thought about it for a moment, then opened the door and called out, 'Werner, come and take him down the hall.'

The functionary came on the run. Took him past offices, a long way it seemed. Around a corner. Then to an unmarked door, which he opened, saying 'Be quick about it.' He closed the door. Casson stood in front of a urinal.

On the wall above the sink, a window. Grey, frosted glass. Probably barred, but not so Casson could see. But then, he thought, why would they have bars? This is the Interior Ministry. The top floor. For the French, the most important people would be housed on the second floor. In former times, the top floor would have served the Ministry's minor bureaucrats – what would they want with bars in a bathroom? Casson walked to the sink and turned the tap on, drank some water, put his hand on the glass of the window. Top floor, he thought, six storeys down to a courtyard.

You'll die.

But then, what did that matter? Better now, he thought, before they go to work on me.

'Just a minute.'

He put his index fingers under the two handles and very gently pushed up. Nothing. Locked. He could back up to the door, take a run, and jump through it, smashing the glass, tumbling six storeys to the courtyard below. He pushed harder, the window moved. Opened an inch. The night air rushed in, it was black outside, and pouring rain.

Lower the window. Go back to Guske's office. Explain everything to him. Try to talk your way out of it – crawl, do whatever you have to do.

He listened, held his breath. Against the background hum of office business he could just make out Werner's voice. It spoke German, but Casson could easily understand the tone of it. He was explaining something – he was being important. Casson raised the window, perhaps a foot. A damp, sweet wind blew in on him and he could hear distant thunder, a storm up the Seine somewhere, the sound rolling down across the wheatfields into Paris.

He put one knee on the edge of the sink, pulled himself through the window, then froze, terrified, unable to move. The night swirled around him, the courtyard a thousand feet below, the wet cobblestone gleaming in the faint spill of light from blacked-out windows. He forced himself to look around: the window was set out a little from the slanted plane of the roof, slate tile angled sharply up to the peak – copper sheathing turned green with age. To the left: a cascade of white, foamy water. He followed it, found an ancient lead gutter, eaten through by time and corrosion, water pouring through the hole, spilling off the edge of the roof and splashing into the courtyard below.

If he stood on the window ledge . . .

He had to force his body to move – he was trembling with fear. He got himself turned around, feet dangling into space, pulled himself to his knees by using the inside handles of the window, then stood up, back to the courtyard. The rain was cold on his face, he took a deep breath. The gutter ran to a second roof, at right angles to the one he faced. He could inch over – feet on the gutter, body pressed flat against the slate – and climb the angle. He would then be – he would then be somewhere else.

He heard the bathroom door open, heard Werner cry out. He let go of the window handles, lifted his right foot from the ledge and placed it on the gutter. Werner ran towards the window, Casson left the ledge and let his weight shift to the gutter. It rolled over, dumping its water, then dropped three inches. Casson bit down against a scream and clawed at the wet slate for traction.

Werner's head appeared through the window. He was pale with terror, his carefully combed hair hanging lank from its centre parting. Suddenly he leaned out, took a swipe at Casson's ankle. Casson crabbed sideways along the gutter.

From Werner, a taut little laugh – just kidding. 'Tell me, what on earth do you think you're doing out there?'

Casson didn't answer.

'Mm?'

Silence.

'Perhaps you will end it all, eh?' His voice was low, and edged with panic. It was, at the same time, hopeful. To allow an escape was unthinkable, but suicide – maybe they wouldn't be quite so angry with him.

Casson couldn't speak. He closed his eyes, felt the rain on his hair and skin, heard the storm in the distance. From the darkness, from the very root of his soul, he said slowly, 'Leave me alone.'

A minute passed, frozen time. Then Werner gave an order, his voice a shrill whisper. 'You come back in here!' Casson could hear a life in the words – all the failures, all the excuses.

Casson moved another step, the gutter sagged. He stretched his arms as high as they would go, discovered a mossy crack between the slate tiles. He tried it – it was possible, just barely and not for long.

Now Werner saw everything he'd worked for about to fall apart. 'One more step,' he said, 'and I call the guards.'

Casson counted to twenty. 'All right,' he said. 'I'm coming back.' But he didn't move. He could imagine Guske in his office, looking at his watch.

'Well?'

'I can't.'

'You must try!'

'My feet won't move.'

'Ach.'

Teeth clenched with fury, Werner wriggled through the window then stood on the ledge. 'Just stay still,' he said. 'I'll help you.'

Casson drove the tips of his fingers through the moss, into the shallow crack. Werner stepped daintily off the ledge, made sure of his balance, then, leaning his weight on the roof, began to move slowly sideways. Casson shifted his weight to his hands, lifted his right leg as high as it would go and rammed it back down against the gutter.

Nothing happened.

Until Werner's next step – then he mewed with fear as the gutter came away. Then he vanished. For part of a second he thought it over, at last allowed himself a loud whine of indignation that ended, briefly, in a scream. The lead gutter hit the cobbles with a dull clatter.

Thirty seconds, Casson thought, no more. The crack between the tiles deepened, and he moved along it quickly. Reached the corner where the two wings of the building met, shinned up the angle to the peak, lay flat on the copper sheathing and tried to catch his breath. As he looked over the other side he saw a row of windows – the same type he'd just crawled out of. The only difference was a narrow spillway, wedged between the slanted roof and a stone parapet.

Now they discovered Werner.

He heard shouts from the courtyard, somebody blew a police whistle, flashlight beams swept everywhere, across the façades of the building and the roof. He rolled off the peak and let himself slide down to the spillway. There he stayed on his knees, looked over the parapet, saw a sheer drop to a narrow street. He had no idea what it might be, the city was a maze – secret courtyards, blind alleyways, sense of direction meant nothing.

He ran along the the spillway, looked in the first window. Blackout curtain. At the next, the curtain was slightly askew. He could see an office in low light, a cleaner in a grey smock was polishing the waxed parquet with a square of sheepskin tied to a broom. Casson tapped on the window.

The man looked up. Casson tapped again. The man walked slowly to the window and tried to see out. *The Lost King*, Casson thought. An old man with snow-white hair and thin lips and rosy skin. He moved the blackout curtain aside and cranked the casement window open a few inches. 'What are you doing out there?' he asked.

'I escaped. Over the roof.'

'Escaped? From the Gestapo?'

'Yes.'

'*Bon Dieu*.' He ran a hand through his hair, smoothing it back, thinking. 'Well, over here we're the National Meteorological office, but, we have our Germans too, of course.' He stopped, the shouts from the courtyard on the other side of the building could just be heard. 'Well, then, monsieur, I expect you may want to climb in here, and permit us to hide you.'

25 June, 1941

'Good morning.'

'Good morning. I was wondering if you have, a certain book.'

'Yes? What would that be?'

'An atlas.'

'Yes? Of what country?'

'France.'

'Perhaps, we could call you back?'

'No. I'll be in later.'

'But sir . . .'

He hung up.

Not the same person, and, he thought, not French. German.

25 June, 1941

The baroness answered the phone in a cool, distant voice. 'Hello?'

'Hello. This is your neighbour, from upstairs.'

'Oh. Yes, I see. Are things going well? For you?'

'Not too badly. My friend?'

'Your friend. Has returned to Lyons. I believe, without difficulties.'

'I'm glad to hear it.'

'You are, you know, very fortunate to have such a friendship.'

'Yes, I do know that.'

'In that case, I hope you are careful.'

'I am. In fact, I ought to be going.'

'Good-bye, then. Perhaps we'll meet again, some day.'

'Perhaps we will. And, madame, thank you.'

'You're welcome, monsieur.'

25 June, 1941

'Galeries Lafayette.'

'Good morning. I'm calling for Véronique, in the buyers' office.'

'One moment, please.'

'Hello?'

'Hello, may I speak with Véronique, please.'

'I'm sorry, she hasn't come in today, perhaps she'll be in tomorrow. Would you care to leave a message?'

'No, no message. I'll call back tomorrow.'

'Very well. Good-bye.'

'Good-bye.'

A café in the Tenth, busy and crowded. Casson went back to his table. Took a sip of his chicory-laced coffee. The Lost King and his colleagues had been very generous, had given him a shirt, a cap, an old jacket, and a few francs. They had even hit upon a scheme to persuade the Gestapo that their intensive search of the building was likely to prove fruitless – one of the men who took care of the furnace

295

had sneaked upstairs to the street floor of the Interior Ministry and, simply enough, left a door open.

Still, kind as they'd been, Casson was in some difficulty. Everything was gone: apartment, office, business, friends, bank accounts, passport. He was down to fourteen francs and Citrine – who would be safe, he thought, as long as she stayed in Lyons and didn't call attention to herself.

So then, he asked himself, *what next?* He imagined Fischfang, sitting across the table, ordering the most expensive drink on the menu. Now that the hero has given his pursuers the slip, what becomes of him? *His uncle dies, he inherits*. Casson looked at his watch, but there was nothing on his wrist.

He drank up his coffee, left a tip, and went out to the street. A clock in the window of a jewellery store said 10:10, Casson started walking. A long walk, from the 10th Arrondissement all the way across the river to the Fifth. He had no identity papers, so the Métro, with its snap searches, was dangerous. Besides, he thought, he really couldn't afford the five sous it cost for a ticket.

A warm day, the city out in its streets. Casson hadn't shaved, he pulled the worker's cap down over one eye, walked with hands in pockets. Good camouflage, he thought. Women going off to the shops gave him the once-over – a little worn, this one, could he be refurbished? He took the rue Pavée in the Jewish district, past a chicken store with feathers floating in the air. He saw a tailor at work through an open shop door, the man felt his eyes, looked up from a jacket turned back over its lining, and returned Casson's wry smile.

He crossed the Seine on the Pont d'Austerlitz, stopped for a time, as he always did, to stare down at the river. Still swollen and mud-coloured from the spring rains, it rubbed against the stone piers of the bridge, mysterious in the rolls and swirls of its currents, opaque and dirty and lovely – the soul of its city and everybody who lived there knew it.

He worked his way around the rough edges of the Fifth, avoiding the eyes of Wehrmacht tourists, taking the side streets. The place Maubert was hard on him – the smell of roasting chicken and sour wine was heavy on the air, and Casson was hungry.

The café where he'd met Véronique earlier that spring was deserted, the proprietor rubbing a dry glass with a towel and staring hypnotized into the street. Casson stood at the bar and ordered a coffee. The owner jiggled the handle on the nickel-plated machine, produced a loud hiss and a column of steam, the smell of burnt chicory, and a trickle of dark liquid.

'Seen Véronique today?' Casson asked.

In return, an eyebrow lifted in the who-wants-to-know look. 'Not today.'

'Think she might be in later?'

'She might.'

'Mind if I wait?'

'Fine with me.'

He waited all day. He took his coffee to the last table in the back, kept the cup in front of him, pored over yesterday's newspaper, and, at last, broke down and spent three francs in a *tabac* for a packet of Bulgarian cigarettes.

A workers' café, Véronique had called it. Yellow walls dyed amber with smoke, slow, steady stream of customers – a red wine, a beer, a coffee, a *marc*, a *fine*, elbows on the bar. At six, some students came down the hill and stood in a crowd by the door, imitating one of their professors and having a good loud laugh. Casson looked a second time, and there was Véronique, in the middle of it, getting an envelope from the owner.

She was startled when he appeared next to her. Then she nodded her head towards the square. 'Let's go for a walk, Jean-Claude.'

297

They walked from cart to cart in the Maubert market, pretending to shop, staring at baskets of eels and mounds of leeks. Casson told her what had happened to him, Véronique said he'd been lucky. As for her, she'd been warned in person, at the office. 'I'm leaving tonight, Jean-Claude. I just stopped at the café for a final message.'

'Leaving for where?'

'South. Over the mountains.'

They were standing in front of a mound of spring potatoes, red ones, the smell of wet earth still on them.

'Jean-Claude,' she said. 'I want you to go to number seven, in the rue Taine. Immediately. The man there will take care of you. You know where it is?'

'No.'

'Bercy. Near the wine warehouses.'

'All right.'

An old man in an ancient, chalk-striped suit strolled over to the potato cart and stood near them, just close enough to overhear what they might be saying. Casson wanted to bark at him, Véronique took his arm and walked him away. 'Oh this city,' she said in a low voice.

They stood in front of a barrow filled with dusty beets, the little girl minding the store was no more than eleven. 'Ten sous, *'sieur et 'dame*,' she said hopefully.

Véronique took a breath and let it out slowly. Casson could tell she sensed danger. 'So now,' she said quietly, 'we've done this shopping, and, old friends that we are, it's time to part. We'll kiss each other farewell, and then we'll go.'

Casson turned to her and they kissed left and right. He saw that her eyes were shining. 'Good-bye, my friend,' she said.

'*Au revoir*, Véronique.'

The last he saw of her, she was walking quickly through the crowd in a narrow lane between market stalls. Just as she turned the corner, she gave him a sudden smile and a little wave, then she vanished.

It was the sharp edge of the war on the rue Taine – an apartment of little rooms, all the blinds drawn, above a dark courtyard. There was a .45 automatic on the kitchen table, and a Sten gun in the parlour, candlelight a dull sheen on its oiled barrel. The operative was British, but nothing like Mathieu – this man was born to the vocation, and 1941 was the year of his life.

'You're going to England,' he said. 'We're closing down the network, saving what we can, but you can't stay here.'

It was the right, probably the only, thing to do, but Casson felt something tear inside him.

'You'll like England,' the operative said. 'We'll see you don't starve, and you'll be alive. Not everybody is, tonight.'

Casson nodded. 'A telephone call?'

'Impossible. Sorry.'

'Perhaps a letter. There's somebody, in Lyons.'

It was the wrong thing to say. 'Help us win the war,' the operative said. 'Then you'll go home. Everything will be wonderful.'

An hour later they brought in a wounded British airman, face the colour of chalk. Casson sat with him on a battered sofa and the man showed him a photograph of his dog.

At midnight, two French railwaymen came for the airman.

At 1:30, Casson was escorted to another apartment in the building. His photograph was taken, then, at 2:10, he was handed a new identity – passport with photo, *Ausweis*, work permit – a thousand francs and a book of ration stamps.

Back at the first apartment, he dozed for a time. The operative never slept, worked over coded transmissions –

there was a clandestine radio in another building in the neighbourhood, Casson guessed – and listened to the BBC at low volume. Sometimes he made a note of the time – the *Messages Personnels* were long over for the night, but Casson thought he was being signalled by what songs were played, and the order they were played in.

Casson left at dawn. The woman who took him out was in her fifties, with dark red hair and the hard accents of northeast France. A Pole, perhaps, but she didn't say. He sat silent in the passenger seat as she drove. The car was a battered old Fiat 1500, but it was fast, and the woman made good time on the empty roads. She swung due east from Bercy, and was out of Paris in under a minute. They stopped for a German control at the porte de Charenton, and a French police roadblock in Montreuil. Both times the driver was addressed – as the passports were handed back by the officers – as 'Doctor.'

After that, they virtually disappeared, curved slowly north and west around the city on the back streets of small towns and secondary roads. By eight in the morning they were winding their way towards Rouen on the east – much less travelled – bank of the Seine. Outside a small village the driver worked her way down a hillside of packed dirt streets to the edge of the river, just across from the town of Mantes. The car rolled to a stop at the edge of a clearing, two black-and-white spaniels ran barking up to the driver and she rumpled their ears and called them sweethearts.

Beyond a marsh of tall reeds, Casson could see a house-boat – bleached grey wood with a crooked piece of pipe for the stove – tied up to a pole dock. A young man appeared a moment later, asked the driver if she wanted coffee. 'No,' she sighed. 'I can't stop.' She had to be somewhere in an hour, was already going to be late. To Casson she said, 'You'll remain here for thirty hours, then we'll move you

north to Honfleur. These people are responsible for you –
please do what they ask.'

'Thank you,' Casson said.

'Good luck,' the driver said. 'It won't be long now.'

A family lived on the houseboat, a young man and his
wife and their three little girls. Casson was taken to a
bedroom with heavy drapes on the windows. The woman
brought him a bowl of lentils with mustard and a piece of
bread. 'It's better if you stay inside when it's daylight,' she
said. He spent the day dozing and thumbing through a
stack of old magazines. At dusk, they said he could take
the air for a half-hour. He was happy for that, sat on the
sagging dock and watched birds flying over the river. There
was a mackerel sky just before dark, the last red of the
sun lighting the clouds, then a dark, starless evening, and
a breeze that rustled in the leaves of the willow trees that
grew on the river bank.

His heart ached – he could only unwind the past, looking
for another road that might have led to a better place, but
he could not find it. He tried to tell himself that Citrine
would understand, would sense somehow that he'd
escaped from the Germans and would come back to her
in time.

He really did try.

He went back out again at dawn. Cruel of this countryside,
he thought, to be so beautiful when it was being taken
from him. The Vexin – above Paris along the river – was
fighting country, rather bloodsoaked if you knew the history. But then, people fought over beautiful things, a side
of human nature that didn't quite have a name. The oldest
of the little girls, seven perhaps, came out to the dock and
said '*Maman* says the sun is coming up now, and will the
monsieur please take coffee with us.'

As good a moment as any to say good-bye, he thought,

the little girl standing close to him on the dock. Just a bend in a river, and dawn was always good to a place like this, grey light afloat on the water, a bird calling in the marsh.

Later that day they took him up to the port of Honfleur in a truck. The driver was in charge of the final stage of the escape line and briefed Casson as they drove. 'You'll go out on a fishing boat. We leave at dawn, sail to the mouth of the river with the rest of the fleet and stand to for German inspection. You will be hidden below decks – your chances of passing through the inspection are good, the Germans search one boat in four, and use dogs only now and then. After the inspection the fleet will be fishing – for conger eel – in a group. A German plane flies over periodically, and we are permitted only enough fuel for thirty-five miles of cruising. Sometime during the afternoon, you will be transferred to a trawler allowed to work farther out at sea, a trawler with an overnight permit. These boats are sometimes searched by German mine-sweepers. At the midpoint of the Channel, between French and British waters, you'll be taken on a British navy motor launch, and put ashore at Bournemouth.'

He stayed that night in another bedroom with heavy curtains – this time in a house on the outskirts of a coastal village. Then, at 4:30 a.m. on the morning of 28 June, he was taken to a small fishing boat in the port of Honfleur, and led to a secret compartment built behind the below-decks cabin – entered by removing a section of wall from the back of a storage locker.

He was joined first by a young woman, exhausted but calm, clearly at the end of a long and difficult assignment. They were never to speak, but did exchange a smile – bittersweet, a little hopeless – that said virtually everything there was to say. What sort of world was it, where they, where people like them, did the things they had done?

Moments later, the arrival of an important personage; a

302

tall, distinguished man, his wife, his teenaged sons, and three suitcases. Casson guessed this was a diplomat or senior civil servant, being brought to London at de Gaulle's request. The man looked around the tiny space with a certain muted displeasure – he'd clearly not been informed that he was going to have to *share* a hiding place, and it was not at all to his taste.

The compartment was sealed up and they got under way almost immediately, the throb of the engine loud in the small space. Casson, his back resting against the curved wood of the hull, could feel the water sliding past. There was no light, it was very hot, he could hear the others breathing. The boat slowed, then stopped for inspection, and as the engine idled the smell of petrol grew stronger and stronger in the compartment. Above them, boots stamping on the deck. The Germans were talking, laughing with each other – they felt really good today, they'd had a triumph of some kind. Time crawled, the boat rising and falling on the heavy swell in the harbour. Casson felt sweat gather at his hairline and run down his face.

Then it ended. The German patrol boat started up with a roar, their own engine accelerated, and the boat moved forward; somebody on the other side of the wall said, 'All right, that's over. We'll let you out as soon as we clear the harbour.'

On deck, Casson breathed the salt air, gripped the railing, and watched the land fall away as the boat moved out to sea. It was the end of the night, hills dark against the sky, faded moon, white combers rolling in to shore.

Good-bye.

Forever – he knew that. This was what life cost you, you lost what you loved. He closed his eyes and saw her, felt her breath on his face, felt her skin against him. Then he was in the sea.

Cold. The shock of it made him gasp, then swim for his

life. Behind him, great volleys of angry threats and curses. Ahead of him, now he could see it, the beach.

Citrine.

HOTEL DE MER (**1944**) Brilliantly written and directed by René Guillot, the last weekend of a small seaside hotel in the south of France. Danielle Aubin (Citrine) is ravishing as a mysterious stranger.

Red Gold

Alan Furst

Reluctant spy Jean Casson returns to Occupied Paris under a new identity. Wanted by the Gestapo, he must stay away from the civilized circles he knew as a film producer, and must somehow struggle to survive among the shadowy backstreets and cheap hotels of Pigalle – with no job, no home and no friends or family. His first experience of espionage had almost cost him his life, yet as the war drags on and he witnesses the sacrifices of his fellow citizens, Casson drifts back into the dangerous, unpredictable world of resistance and sabotage . . .

'Just when it looked as if Robert Harris had cornered the market in historical thrillers, along comes Alan Furst with a book that Harris could not better if he lived to be 100. *Red Gold* not only out-Harrises Harris with its immaculate period setting, but displays a warmth and subtlety that have eluded the other man. Wartime Paris, with its moral complexities, is beautifully evoked.'
Sunday Telegraph

'Alan Furst's sequence of spy novels deserves to be as fêted as Patrick O'Brian's sea stories. His sense of visual detail is gloriously cinematic. These are the kind of novels in which a swirl of snow falls onto shining black cobbles, and the lights of a passing tram illuminate the profile of the lovers as they kiss in a doorway: film noir for a noir world.' *Evening Standard*

'Cracking entertainment. Furst recreates the atmosphere of wartime Paris with all the cinematic flair of *Casablanca*. A book that brings an era to life with a feeling of authenticity that can only be described as breathtaking and wholly addictive.' *The Times*

'Hard to resist . . . much to enjoy. Atmospheric, always convincingly authentic . . . I can recommend it to anyone who enjoys a good spy thriller.' *Mail on Sunday*

ISBN 0 00 649903 1

The Polish Officer

Alan Furst

'Excellent . . . beautifully written, intensely atmospheric and dramatically convincing. *The Polish Officer* is a work of quiet subtlety that will niggle in the memory far longer than most novels of espionage.'   *Sunday Times*

In 1939, as the German army ravages his country, Captain Alexander de Milja enlists in the newly formed Polish underground and undertakes the first of many daring acts of defiance and disruption: transporting Poland's gold reserves to safety hidden on board a refugee train. As the war continues duty takes him, under a series of false identities, from Warsaw to Paris and the frozen Ukraine – enduring a life of dark shadows and perpetual deception, always on the run, always just one step ahead of death.

'A page-turner, yes, but also one of the most evocative works of history I have come across. Read and learn.'
Observer

'Wonderfully written . . . Furst is the laureate of the vast, mysterious tracts of Eastern Europe. An extraordinarily fine novel.'   *Glasgow Herald*

ISBN 0 00 649356 4

Dark Star

Alan Furst

In the back alleys and glittering salons of night-time Europe, war is already underway as Soviet intelligence and the Nazi Gestapo confront each other in an intricate duel of espionage. On the front line is André Szara, a born survivor – of the Polish pogroms, the Stalinist purges and the Russian civil wars. His only goal is to keep going in a world where betrayal can come at any time. But slowly, inextricably, he is drawn into the dark intrigues of pre-war Europe where life is a grey uncertainty of cheap hotel rooms, love affairs that cannot last and friends who have ceased to exist . . .

'Outclasses any spy novel I have ever read.'
RICHARD CONDON, author of *The Manchurian Candidate*

'Imagine discovering an unscreened espionage thriller from the late 1930s, a classic black-and-white movie that captures the murky allegiances and moral ambiguity of Europe on the brink of war . . . Nothing can be like watching *Casablanca* for the first time, but Furst comes closer than anyone has in years.' *Time*

'To call *Dark Star* a classic spy story – which it is – is to do less than justice to Alan Furst's gifts. He writes with restraint, yet brings to life better than most historians the world of fear in which so many human beings felt trapped.'
ALAN BULLOCK, author of *Hitler and Stalin*

'Alan Furst creates moods, nuances and subtleties with the skill of Eric Ambler and John le Carré.' NELSON DEMILLE

'A jewel – a gripping thriller which is also a novel of quality and a fascinating history lesson.' *Daily Mail*

'Espionage oozing from every shadow – writing of a high calibre.'
Sunday Expr

ISBN 0 00 651131 7

Night Soldiers
Alan Furst

In Bulgaria in 1934 nineteen-year-old Khristo Stoianev sees his brother kicked to death by a gang of strutting thugs. Realising the growing menace of Fascism, he takes a risk on the promise of Communism and flees to Moscow, where he is trained as an agent of the NKVD, precursor of the KGB, and forms a close bond with a group of fellow students. His first mission is to Catalonia, where he is soon caught up in the bloody horrors of the Spanish Civil War. Then he learns that he is about to become the victim of one of Stalin's purges, and is forced to flee once again, this time to Paris . . .

'Furst's intelligent, ambitious, absorbing novel charges along from the rise of Fascism in Bulgaria, to Spain during the Civil War, to France and back to Eastern Europe as World War II draws to an end. The history is deftly incorporated; the viewpoint civilized; the characters and the settings picturesque; the adventures exciting; the writing pungent.'   *New York Times*

'Captures with exceptional fidelity and remarkable descriptive powers the shifting political and national loyalties that marked European life in the decade leading up to and including World War II. The idea of portraying the beginnings of the Cold War in the rubble of 1945 Eastern Europe is ingenious. Best of all is the chilling trail of treachery and betrayal, as the Russian Revolution – in the guise of the NKVD – devours its adherents.'   *Washington Post*

'*Night Soldiers* has everything the best thrillers offer – excitement, intrigue, romance – plus grown-up writing, characters that matter, a crisp, carefully researched portrait of the period in which our postwar world was shaped.'   *USA Today*

nd absorbing . . . an unusual viewpoint, solid research ely elegant writing make this pure pleasure to read.'
                                                        Kirkus Reviews

130 9